Haven of Rest Trilogy

The Storm
Book 1

The Anchor
Book 2

The Haven
Book 3

By

Ronna M. Bacon

The Storm

Franklin (Frankie) Brennan is a beat-up street cop, tired and ready to quit. His boss and good friend, Chief Caleb Logan, instead suggests he help at the local youth centre. There he meets Deirdre Johnson McNabb, niece of fellow officer Ben Johnson. Finding herself in the middle of search for information by men brought in from overseas, it is up to Frankie to help keep her one step ahead of them and alive. While all this is going on, Deirdre challenges Frankie to find his way back to the peace and calm he can only find through trusting God. Her words to him are that if Christ calmed the Sea of Galilee, there is not a storm in his life Christ can't calm.

The Anchor

Rachel Andrews has returned to her home town after fleeing years earlier, afraid for her life. Targeted by an unknown assailant, she is reluctant to accept help. Timothy Johnson, an old friend, refuses to let her push away, determined to help find the ones responsible. Through the trouble that follows her, Rachel learns she does have an anchor for her life as she is drawn back to her faith in God.

The Haven

Rebecca Brogan has had a stalker for years, one she fears was responsible for her husband's death. Gideon Andrews has returned to Riverville to be near his sister and to put to rest the remnants of his life as a foster child. Together they are on the run, trying to stay one step ahead of the stalkers and stay alive. Through it all, Rebecca comes to her haven of rest in God.

Verses

Psalm 34:17-20

17 The righteous cry out, and the LORD hears them; he delivers them from all their troubles. 18 The LORD is close to the brokenhearted and saves those who are crushed in spirit. 19 The righteous person may have many troubles, but the LORD delivers him from them all; 20 he protects all his bones, not one of them will be broken.

Dedication

To whoever is facing a storm, needing to find an anchor, and then to come home to His haven.

The Storm

Haven of Rest Trilogy

Book 1

by

Ronna Bacon

Dedication

This book is dedicated to all those who have been
through a storm, who have felt the power of God
work in a quiet way or a mighty way to calm the
storm without or within.

Matthew 11:28
Come to Me, all *you* who labor and are heavy laden,

and I will give you rest.

Mark 5:39, 40

Then He arose and rebuked the wind, and said to the
sea, "Peace, be still!" And the wind ceased and there
was a great calm.
But He said to them, "Why are you so fearful?
How *is it* that you have no faith?"

Table of Contents

Prologue

He watched from the sidelines as she handed over her boarding pass and then walked onto the plane. He followed and found his seat two rows back and on the other side. It would be a long flight, he knew, but she was going nowhere he couldn't see her.

It was a long twelve hours later that their flight landed. He was tired and ready to go home but first he had to follow her and find out where the information was he had to retrieve. He had been given word from the streets she had it in her possession.

He watched once again as she retrieved her luggage and then headed for a taxi. His friend was waiting for him and they quickly followed. But it was strange. She was not headed for her home town. Instead, she was heading to the next terminal that local flights flew from. This changed everything. He had to scramble to get in line behind her to find out where she was going. By the time he had reached the counter, the flight was full and he was turned away. He cursed to himself. This was not going the way it should. Reluctantly he booked a seat on the next flight, that left in the morning. She would already be on the ground there for twenty-four hours by the time he arrived. He shared a look with his companion. This was not good. The one who had hired him and sent him overseas to that worn-torn country to follow her and retrieve that information was not going to be pleased. He really didn't want to be the one to tell that person.

He watched as the small plane took off into the night sky. Soon the lights had disappeared. He hoped it was not a sign that's what would happen to him if he failed.

Chapter 1

Frankie Brennan was tired and worn out. The years of being a street cop and undercover for many of them had taken their toll on his body, mind and spirit. He had tried to resign, but Caleb Logan, the town Police Chief, had refused to accept it. Instead, he had suggested Frankie take some vacation time and sort things through.

Frankie looked around the church entry and wondered why he was there. Ben Johnson, a fellow police officer, had looked at him one day during the past week and told him to be here this morning. Frankie had taken a look at him, hesitated and then agreed. He knew he needed something to change but he wasn't sure how he was ever going to find his way back to what he had been. That man was gone, he was sure.

He turned as he felt a little girl race by him, gold ringlets flying. He thought she was maybe three, but she went by so quick he wasn't sure. He listened to what she was saying.

"Miss Dee, Miss Dee. You're here. You're really here."

A young woman who had been standing near him turned at the sound of the child's voice. A smile broke out and she bent to gather the little one into her arms. The little girl ended up nose to nose with her as she hugged her.

"I am?" she asked. "I am really, really, really here?"

The little one's head bobbed up and down quickly. "You are, you are. And you have to sit with me."

"No, really, I do?" At the vigorous head nod, she smiled again. "Okay, I guess I do. Let's go find your Mom."

Frankie watched as she walked away, the child in her arms. A touch on his shoulder and he turned. Ben was standing there watching him, a look in his eye that Frankie had trouble reading.

"Come on, Frankie. Let's go find Marg. She said she would save a seat for us at the back."

Frankie was uncomfortable waiting for the service to start. It had been too long and things seemed too different now. Marg reached over and patted his hand.

"Relax," she said. "They won't ask you to take part in anything this week."

He shot her a wide-eyed look.

"They'll wait until next week." She looked at him, face straight but a twinkle in her eye.

He narrowed his eyes at her, then responded, "Do you think they would wait another week?"

She laughed softly. "Frankie, you'll be fine."

As the service was starting, the young woman he had seen in the entry passed the end of their row of chairs. She lightly touched Ben on the shoulder who looked up and smiled. He went to stand to let her in and she shook her head and pointed to another row. He sat back down and watched her.

The hair on Frankie's neck bristled. Something was happening. He knew that feeling from the streets. There was evil in the building. He shot a quick look around but couldn't pinpoint anyone in particular. He would have to have a talk with Ben when church was over.

But he never got a chance to speak with Ben. With a muttered word to Marg, Ben had left before the end of the service. Marg mentioned to Frankie that sometimes people in the church needed help at the end of service and Ben was one of the men who always volunteered.

Frankie looked around once again. He still had that feeling, he knew it only too well. Who was it?

Ben met Frankie the next morning for coffee. At this point, Frankie was convinced that he may have imagined the feeling and didn't pursue it.

"Caleb mentioned that he had suggested you look into working at the youth centre." Ben watched his young friend, trying to gauge his reaction and thoughts.

Frankie hesitated before speaking. "He did, Ben. I'm not sure though that's what I want to do." Frankie stared at his coffee cup. "I'm not sure what I really want."

Ben nodded. He figured that was how Frankie was feeling. "Why don't we head over there and you can get a feel for how it runs and what would be expected. They really need a man who can work with the young men and be a mentor to them."

Frankie snorted. "Like I can do that?"

Ben stopped him from continuing. "You're beat up right now, down in spirit and heart. You have no idea what you want to do, whether you want to continue as an officer or go into something different. Your faith has taken a real beating in the last few months, if not years." Ben hesitated, not sure how his next words would be accepted. "You hide it well, Frankie. I know you were in love with Ashling." Frankie's eyes shot to his. "Not too many people know that. I know you well. That's how I knew."

Frankie stared out the window at the parking lot. "I was. But Liam is the one she needs." He stopped, swallowed, and then continued, "I don't know if I will ever find that one for me."

"God knows, Frankie, God knows exactly who you need. Have patience." Ben pulled out some money for their coffee and stood. "Come with me. We'll head for the youth centre. It's not that far, you can come back for your truck."

As they entered the youth centre, they could hear voices from the gym. Ben took a look at Frankie, then headed that way. They stopped just inside the door.

The young woman Frankie had observed in the church stood there, in jeans, soft jade sweater, sneakers and with her shoulder length brown hair swinging loose. In front of her stood a youth of about 14, switchblade in hand.

Frankie made a move to go forward, but a hand on his arm stopped. Ben shook his head and motioned for him to wait.

"Peter, you know the rules. No weapons in the centre and that is a weapon." Her voice was soft and calm, her stance relaxed.

The youth looked at the knife and then at her. He shook his head and clicked the knife open and shut. "No one takes my knife, Miss D. No one."

She tilted her head and looked at him. "Well, here we do." The fingers on her extended hand wiggled. "Now, let's have it. You know we have certain rules for everyone, and weapons are one of them.”

He shook his head but was starting to look uncertain.

She looked at the ceiling, sighed and then looked back at him. “Peter, I have had some real tough guys hassle me. I have been threatened with kitchen knives, machetes, switchblades, revolvers, rifles, semi and automatic weapons. I have had bombs explode not far from me. I have been targeted in ways you will never know and by men and boys tougher than you. Now, the knife.”

Peter sneered. “Yeah, right. You’re just saying that. When would someone like you ever have been threatened like that?”

She sighed again, then spoke, her voice too low for the men to catch her words. Peter’s eyes began to grow round, his mouth dropped open, and then his hand slackened on the knife. She reached for it and took it gently from him.

“Next time, Peter, leave these at home. You don’t want the problems that will come if you don’t.”

Peter’s mouth opened and closed a few times as he stared at her. Then he turned and ran past the men. Frankie turned to watch him.

Ben walked up to the young woman and then stood by her side, watching as she flicked the knife open and closed. Frankie approached them slowly, not sure what to expect. So far, it had been an interesting introduction to the youth centre.

Ben finally sighed, held out his hand, and she dropped the knife into it. He stared at the ceiling. “Still bullying the boys are you, Deirdre? At least this time, you didn't drop him in his tracks and disarm him that way."

She shoved him with her shoulder, Frankie watching in amazement as she did so. "Behave, Benny, or I'll tell Marg you're being bad again."

Ben laughed, then asked, "So, who taught you again?"

She shook her head as she turned to look at him. "You know well who. My uncle." She patted his cheek. "Right, Uncle Benny?"

Ben threw his head back and laughed at her nonsense, then hugged her. "So glad you're home safe from overseas. But then I see this and think maybe you might be safer over there."

She stood back, hands on his arms, and studied him. "Funny you should say that. I've had that feeling again in the last few days."

Ben sobered. "And you didn't say anything?"

"Ben, stop. A feeling isn't enough to go on." She looked over at Frankie. "Are you going to introduce me to your friend, or does he have to listen to you berate me?"

Ben just shook his head. "You know your family wants you to be safe. Being here is a concession to that."

She grimaced. "I know and I hate that."

She turned to Frankie and held out her hand. "Ben's being too bossy to introduce us. I'm Deirdre McNabb. Ben's a relative in case you missed that."

Frankie shook her hand. "Frankie Brennan."

He watched as she tilted her head and studied him through hazel eyes. She shook her head. "No, what's your full name? Frankie doesn't suit."

His eyes widening in shock, he looked past her at Ben, who was trying hard not to laugh. He stammered, "It's Franklin, but no one calls me that but my Mom."

She thought about that, then shook her head. "Nope, that won't work. The kids here will eat you alive with that name.   We'll come up with something."

She turned and walked out the door, Ben trailing behind her. He turned and looked back at Frankie, who was just standing there, staring.

"Come along, Franklin."   Ben's smile widened. "It will be interesting to see what name she comes up with."

"You didn't warn me, Ben. You should have."

"What would be the fun in that?" Ben started to laugh again. "By the way, she's the one who runs the centre." Ben laughed harder as Frankie stopped, mouth dropping open, and stared at him.

Chapter 2

Frankie had been at the centre for a week. He was still trying to wrap his head around the scene he had seen when Ben had walked him into the building. Deirdre was loved by all the youths and seemed to be everywhere. He was still waiting for her to come up with a name for him and it would be interesting when she did.

He stood late that Friday afternoon near the front desk, waiting for Deirdre or Miss D as the youth called her to come from her office. They had agreed to a dinner meeting to discuss his tasks. He watched as an older well dressed gentleman came in and looked around. He stopped at the desk and while Frankie couldn't hear his words, he watched the young woman he was talking to. Something just didn't seem right, and he approached them.

"Can I help you with something?"

The man turned, his eyes narrowed as he looked Frankie up and down, shook his head and walked out.

"What was that about?" Frankie asked the girl, Amy he thought.

"I don't know. It was really strange. He wanted to know about Miss D and whether she was around and when she was or wasn't." She looked at Frankie. "I didn't tell."

"I know you didn't. If you ever had anyone like that again, excuse yourself and come find me. I'll deal with them."

Amy continued to watch him, then said, "I'm glad you're here. That's not the first time someone has come in like that asking about Miss D. In fact, there was one the other day…" Her voice died away.

"The one the other day had an accent. I don't know what though."

Frankie nodded. "Just find me."

He turned as Deirdre came up behind him.

She studied him for a minute, then looked at the door. "All set?" she asked.

"I am if you are." Frankie held the door for her.

"What was that all about?" she asked as they walked towards the down town area.

Frankie shook his head. "I'm really not sure. Amy said someone was questioning her about your hours. I told her to call me next time."

Deirdre shook her head. "You're not around all the time."

"I know, but when I am, that will be part of my job."

Deirdre looked frustrated but waited to speak until they had been seated in the town's Italian restaurant. "Frankie, you mean well, but in case you missed it, I have been all over the world and in many war-torn areas and trouble spots. That's what I do. It's who I am. I can take care of myself. And I can't do that if I am smothered."

Frankie sat back and thought about what she had said. "I apologize. I should have talked to you first. I realize you have been all over but please understand, protecting people is who I am."

She laid her hand on his folded hands. "I understand. Part of why I really didn't want to move here is because Ben can smother. He doesn't mean to but he can. My parents have finally realized I can take care of myself but Ben still sees the little girl I was.   My experiences have changed me to some extent, I think, just like yours have changed you."

Frankie went to speak but stopped when she glanced around the restaurant, with an almost frightened look on her face.

"What's wrong?"

"I don't know but for the last ten days or so since I came back I have felt like I was being followed.   I haven't been able to pinpoint anyone though.   I never had this feeling overseas, just once I was on the plane coming back."

Frankie looked around, noting faces.   "I have had the same feeling when I am around you.   I felt it at your church the first Sunday I was there."

She shivered as she listened to him.   "That's getting a little too close for comfort.   Don't tell Ben, he'll smother me more than he already does."

He started to shake his head, then watched her face.   Against his better judgement, he nodded.

As they walked back towards their vehicles in the dusk, Frankie kept an eye on their surroundings. Something was off and he couldn't figure out just what.   Movement to their right caught his attention, and he pulled Deirdre over and behind him.   A blow to his head sent him to his knees.   He heard angry words as he tried to stay on his knees and break through the blackness that threatened to engulf him.

He felt hands on his arms and a voice calling to him. He shook his head and then wondered why he did such a stupid thing.

He was finally able to focus enough to see Deirdre before him, concern on her face.

"What happened?" he muttered.

"Strangest thing. That thug walloped you, asked me where something was, and then just took off."

"Help me up." Frankie staggered a bit as he came to his feet. "Did you get a look at him?"

"Tall, thin, jeans, hoodie, dress shoes - what thug wears dress shoes anyway - couldn't see hair or eyes, but I have his voice imprinted on my memory."

Frankie studied her. No, it didn't make sense. What had he wanted and why did he think she had it?

"Do you have any idea of what he was after?"

She shook her head. "Not a one. And do not tell Ben. He won't let me walk alone even in the daylight if you do."

Frankie grinned at her. "I wouldn't want to meet you in a dark alley. You're scary."

She shoved him, and then grabbed his arm to help him balance. "Shh. No one's supposed to know that."

They turned once more to walk to their vehicles, Frankie catching her hand in his. To his surprise, she made no effort to remove it.

"It is strange. We'll figure it out."

"Right," she said, "somehow, some place, somewhere. I just don't like the feeling I'm being watched. It's very unnerving."

Frankie stopped by her car and turned to watch her. She was calm and peaceful in her stance but he caught the uncertainty and a bit of fear in her eyes. She turned her eyes to him and caught him staring at her.

"Be careful, Franklin, I can put you down before you could even blink."

He laughed. "I understand that you can, Ben's been talking." He sobered. "I just don't want you to get hurt. And not on my watch. I don't want to answer to Ben or even Marg." He shuddered dramatically.

"Well, then, I guess we won't tell them." She turned to lean against her car. "Can I ask you something, Frankie?" At his nod, she continued, "What are you planning to do now that you're not sure you want to continue as a police officer?"

He leaned his hip against the car and once again studied her face. He sighed. "Deirdre, I really don't know. Working the streets and especially the last bit with Ashling and Liam, it really took a toll on me. My heart needs to be refreshed. I need to find my way back to God and my faith certainly needs strengthening. Right now, I feel like I am in a huge storm that has no end."

She nodded. "I can understand that. I have had some others say that to me but it hasn't been as strong as what you say." She stopped, and tilting her head, watched him. "I do know that Jesus calmed that storm on Galilee. If He can calm a storm like that, how He must be able to calm the storms in our souls. What are you willing to give or do to find that peace and comfort in your life?"

Frankie thought about that. "You ask hard questions, Miss D. That gives me a lot of think about."

"First Frankie, humble yourself, get down on your knees, and just open your heart. Just listen. Listening is hard. As humans, we want to be the ones talking. With God, we need to listen first. The path He asks you to walk through the storm to the peace on the other side may be a lot harder than anything you have ever done before."

Frankie hesitated, then spoke, "That sounds like personal experience."

She turned to unlock her car. "It is. One day, I'll tell you about it. It's not real pretty."

Frankie held her door for her and before he shut it, he spoke. "Thanks for taking time for dinner. I enjoyed tonight, well except for that little bit near the alley. And thank you for being bold with your words. You may just have reached through the storm to me."

He thought he saw tears glinting in her eyes but her voice was steady. "I have been praying for you. Go home, Frankie, spend time on your knees."

He nodded, then watched her drive away. As he climbed into his truck, he saw headlights pull away from the curb and follow her. That's not right, he thought, and pulled his truck up behind the vehicle. He followed it and then it suddenly veered away. He didn't like that one bit. He followed Deirdre to make sure she was home safe and then parked his truck at the curb. He had time to watch and wait.

A tap at his window awakened him. He stretched then looked over at the passenger window. Deirdre stood there, hands on hips, frown on her face.

He turned the ignition on enough so he could lower the window on her side. "Morning," he said, voice gruff.

"What are you doing here?" She demanded. She was not pleased with him, he could tell. "Go home, Frankie. I don't need you playing babysitter."

He turned off the truck and scrambled out to go after her as she set off down the sidewalk.

"Deirdre, wait." She stopped as he came up behind her. "You were followed last night when you left work. The car broke off when I came up behind it, but it was definitely after you."

Her posture was stiff and straight. She didn't answer him.

He came around to stand in front of her. She had a closed, shuttered look on her face. "Did you hear what I said?"

Her hazel eyes raised to him and he caught a glint of something he couldn't read. "Go home, Frankie. As I said, I don't need a babysitter." She brushed by him and continued down the street.

Hand on his head, he stared after her. Really? He told her she was followed and then she brushed it and him off? He ran to catch up with her.

"Go away, Frankie."

He pulled her to a stop. "No, I won't, Deirdre. Someone is following you. I won't let anything happen to you."

She spun and stared at him and then just shook her head. "No, don't try. I don't need a rescuer. It won't work, you know." He stared at her, puzzlement on his face. "I won't be a replacement." She poked him in the chest. "You need to figure out what you want and where you're going, and that you have to do on your own. I won't be part of it."

She strode away, leaving him standing staring after her. Did he just totally blow it with her, he wondered? He turned to do as she ask, but his instincts was telling him differently and he turned back.

As he turned back, he saw a car pull up beside her and a man step out. Deirdre had stopped and then stepped back from him. Frankie saw the man reach for her arm to pull her towards the car. He wasn't close enough, he thought, as he ran towards them.

Deirdre was not happy with Frankie and her mind was on the confrontation she had just had with him. She wasn't paying as particular attention to her surroundings as she normally did. The car stopping and the man exiting startled her and she stepped back. When he reached for her arm, she stepped back further. She shook her head and when he persisted, she stepped back further. She could hear running footsteps coming up. That had to be Frankie, she thought. He's too far away yet.

She reached for the man's wrist and with a little flurry of moves that would have made her friends from the streets overseas proud, she had him on the ground. Frankie slid to a stop beside her.

"Yep, I really wouldn't want to meet you in a dark alley." He reached down and hauled the man to his feet.

"Okay, mister. What's your problem? Why are you bothering this lady?"

The man, clothes dusty from the streets, brushed himself off. "I was just asking for directions and she attacked me."

"Sorry, buddy. That's not what happened. You would have had her in your vehicle if she hadn't made those moves, and by the way, I really want to learn those moves. So how about it? Tell us the truth and exactly why you tried to abduct her."

The man, in his late 30s Frankie figured, stared at him, then with a sudden movement, shoved him towards Deirdre and then was gone. Frankie watched in disgust as the man's car sped off.

"I didn't even get the plate number," he muttered.

A voice beside him quoted it. He spun and looked at her. She shrugged and then repeated it.

"How do you do that?" he demanded. "You would have made a good officer."

She shrugged. "I always have had a good memory."

He turned her around towards her home. "Come on, let's go get some breakfast. And if I see Eddie or Caleb, I'll pass on that number. No, I won't go to Ben. I promise."

"Thank you, Frankie. I appreciate that." She sighed and looked up at the brilliant blue sky. "I'm thinking I will have to tell you my story before long. I just can't shake you, can I?"

He smiled and shook his head. "No, I don't think you can. You're my friend and I don't let friends go." To himself, he added, and you are one of those friends I want in my life forever.

He seated her in a booth at SueEllen's cafe and looked around. Saturday morning meant that a lot of his friends would be here for breakfast. He saw Caleb entering with his family and stood to go towards him, excusing himself from Deirdre.

Caleb Logan stepped to one side after a word to his wife. Hannah smiled and greeted Frankie, then directed the two boys to a table.

"Frankie." Caleb waited. "I know this isn't just a social hello. I can tell. You have your working face on."

Frankie blew out a breath. "It's not. I wish it was. We need to talk sometime soon, Caleb. Something's going on with Deirdre. She was almost abducted this morning." Caleb looked at him, startled, then waited for him to continue. "I don't know how she did it but she had the man down before I caught up to her. She even managed to get the plate number." He shook his head. "She really didn't need my help."

Caleb snorted. "No, she wouldn't. Ben has trained her well, and with her trips overseas, she has picked up a lot more about self defence. I wish I could get her to agree to teach our young women some of her moves."

His eyes drifted to where Deirdre sat, a calm look on her face, watching them. "Why don't you bring her over for supper? Say around 4?"

"Hannah won't mind?"

"No. And neither will Seth or Noah. She teaches them in Sunday school sometimes and they adore her."

"All right. I'll check with her. If she can't, I'll be there."

Caleb moved away to join his family as Frankie slid back into the booth across from Deirdre. Her eyes moved from him to Caleb and back to him again.

"Okay, so what time is it you planned for me to meet with Caleb?"

He looked at her, astonished, then began to laugh. "How do you do that?"

"Do what?" she smirked.

"Figure out what was said across the room from you."

"Lip reading. I have friends who are deaf and they taught me."

"You really are scary, you know." Frankie grabbed up a menu. "Let's eat. All this activity has made me hungry."

She shook her head. "Men and boys - always a bottomless pit when it comes to food."

As they left the cafe, Deirdre stopped him with a hand on his arm. "Go home, Frankie. I have things I need to do, and you have to let me."

He nodded. "Can I pick you up about 3:30 to go to Caleb's?"

She sighed, then nodded. "If you must."

“I must.”

She pulled a face, then said, “You’re smothering me, Frankie. Don’t. I will walk away and leave.” At that, she turned and walked away from him.

He watched her leave, knowing he would see her later. Right now, he had some research he needed to do and headed home.

****

The Watcher stood across from the cafe, eyes on the two. He followed Frankie with his gaze until he saw he was headed away from Deirdre, then he shoved on his sunglasses and sauntered down the street after Deirdre, all the world like a tourist in town just for the day. He would follow her and when the time was right, he would find that information he needed. Time was running short but he couldn’t rush this. If he did, many more than just this one woman would pay.

Chapter 4

Frankie sat back from his computer and stared at the screen. He had never expected to find the information that he had by putting Deirdre's name into a search engine. He really didn't know how to absorb what he was reading.

He knew she had been all over the world, into troubled areas, but he didn't know that it had been through a mission that her parents had set up when she was a child. The Recovering People Mission sent aid and people into troubled areas of the world, war-torn areas, areas where natural and manmade disasters had struck. From what he was reading, Deirdre had been on many of those missions in the last few years.

He paused and wondered if this was what she had meant when she said she had a story to tell and it wasn't pretty.

As he looked back to his screen, it refreshed and a news article popped up. He pulled it up to read. His hands on the top of head, he read it through and then again. Deirdre - that explained why her name was different from her uncle and her father. He leaned forward and read the article again and then searched for more.

A sudden look at the clock and he knew he had to leave. He shut down his computer and stood. He had to be so careful that she didn't read him and that he had learned what lurked in her background.

He grabbed his keys and headed for his truck, eyes scanning the area out of habit. His eyes narrowed as he targeted in on a car parked across the street from his house. No one was around it, but he didn't recognize it. Out of habit, he got the plate number and wrote it down. He would pass it on later.

He knocked at Deirdre's door. As he waited, he again scanned the area. He didn't see anything but he had that creeping feeling that he was being watched and closely. He turned in a circle but saw nothing. So what was it?

Deirdre unlocked the door and beckoned him in. She returned to her dining room table, that was covered in papers.

"Okay, I'm back. So what is the situation over there?"

As a man spoke, Frankie realized she was on a speaker phone.

"Phil and Terry are headed out tonight, should be on the ground there tomorrow. Cal is already there. Communication is spotty at best given the infrastructure destruction. That cyclone hit hard."

"I know. The equipment and supplies are headed out when?"

"Some are already on the way. Those we could ship from the warehouse in Australia. Danny says what we can send from here will go tomorrow. He's working on getting the cargo plane loaded today, he'll grab some sleep, and then head out."

"Sounds good." Frankie noticed her rubbing her forehead. She had a headache and was beginning to look a bit stressed, unusual for her. "Where do you need me most?"

"Right now, here. Right here with your Mom and the other board members. I'll be heading out tonight if I can catch the right flight. You've been there. You know the area and the people. We need your expertise to direct us where we need to be working. I'm not sending you back there."

Deirdre stopped her pacing and stared at the floor, arms wrapped around her. Frankie watched, not sure how he should react or if he even should. She looked up and he saw the shimmer of the tears she refused to let fall.

"That's fine. I can't go back there. Ever. And it hurts. I can't get a flight tonight or even tomorrow. Not a direct flight and I'm not comfortable with layovers."

"It's not that far of a drive. I could send Timothy but I need him here directing the warehouse."

"I know, Dad, I know. I'll figure something out and let you know."

"I know you will, pumpkin. You always do." Her father's voice hesitated, then he spoke, "Well, we've made what plans we can for now. Let's have a word of prayer, DeeDee, before we say goodbye.'

Frankie's head went down automatically when the deep bass voice began his prayer. He felt a hand on his and grasped Deirdre's hand.

When she raised her hand, he could see that she had closed down part of herself again and steeled herself for what only she knew was ahead.

She looked at him, then at her table. "I need to put this paperwork in my briefcase and then pack a bag. Somehow or other, I have to get on the road tonight."

"What about the youth centre?" Frankie asked as she stacked the paperwork.

"I've called Peter. He'll take over for now. Unless you're volunteering?"

"No way." Frankie shook his head. "How be I be your chauffeur?"

She spun to look at him and began to shake her head.

"Listen to me. It will be late at night, you're already feeling like you're being followed, and I know you are. If I drive, it will throw them off hopefully. You can rest, catch some sleep, and be ready to go in the morning." He paused, then said, "Just where are we heading anyway?"

She started to laugh. "Franklin, what am I to do with you?" As he opened his mouth, she held up a finger. "No, don't answer that. I don't know if I really want your answer."

He began to laugh. "You do leave yourself open at times, you know."

She giggled. "I know. Now wait here. I'm going to grab my ready pack and throw in a few things." She spoke over her shoulder as she headed for her bedroom, "If you're going, we'll need to stop and grab your stuff. Answer that, will you?"

Frankie answers her phone.

"Hello? Who's this?"

Frankie recognized her father's voice. "My name is Frankie. I'm a friend of Deirdre."

"Frankie? Well, well." He could hear something in her father's voice, and he turned to gaze down the hallway. What had she said? "That

Frankie. Now, I feel better, knowing you're with her. I'm going to be honest and tell you something that has me bothered. I can't warn DeeDee. She needs protection. We just got a warning here at headquarters that she is being sought by some nationals from another country. They think she has brought back information somehow with her from her last trip that if known would bring down a corrupt portion of a government. She has no idea that this is going on. Stick with her, son. Don't let her out of your sight." Her father paused. "Now, if she's not in the room with you, tell her that I don't want her to come until at least Monday. I'm not getting out of here before Sunday night, Monday morning at the earliest."

Frankie continued to watch down the hall. "I will. I will also guard your daughter with my life if necessary."

Her father paused, then said, voice roughened with emotion, "Thank you. I pray it doesn't come to that. You're good for her. Ask her about her story sometime. You two are a fit. Ben's been talking."

The phone clicked in his ear, and he lowered the phone he held in his hand, standing there lost in thought. He started as a soft hand reached out and took it. He looked up. Deirdre stood there, watching him.

"It must have been Dad. He has that effect on people."

Frankie studied the woman ahead of him. He knew she was around his age, late 20s, early 30s. She was beautiful in his opinion. She was exactly what he had been looking for in a girl friend and maybe a wife. He had to be very careful that he didn't blow it, though, and he could very easily, given what he knew.

"Yeah, it was. He called to let you know you didn't need to come tonight. He can't get a flight before tomorrow night or Monday morning. He said you didn't to be there until Monday."

She shook her head. "I'll go tomorrow."

He stopped her with a hand on her arm. "We'll go tomorrow." At her look, he repeated, "We'll go tomorrow, unless you would like to head out after supper with Caleb and Hannah. It's not that far. We could be there by late tonight."

She stood and watched him, reading his face. She nodded and he reached for her bag and briefcase. Waiting for her to lock up her house, he again studied the area, looking for what he didn't know but her father had explained a lot. He now knew the danger but where it would come from or how, that was still the unknown.

He tucked her bags in the back of his truck, then helped her in and shut the door behind her. Rounding the front of the truck, he stopped and once again looked over the area. Someone was there, he could feel the eyes.

After a quick stop back at his place, he pulled up in front of Caleb's house. He laid a hand on her arm as she undid her seat belt.

"Wait a minute, Deirdre." She turned to look at him. "We still need to talk at some point about the danger you're in. We can't run from it forever."

"There's no we in it, Frankie." She stared at him, defying him.

"No, there is a we. I got involved by being there last night. I'm involved, whether you like it or not. You are not facing whatever is going on by yourself. I don't let my friends go through trouble alone. Go talk to anyone on the street. Talk to Ashling and Liam." He brought his hand up and brushed her hair back from her face. "No, I'm not going anywhere. And don't try to run. It won't work. I'll find you."

She shook her head. "Not if I have anything to say about it." She turned to look at Caleb's house. "Come. We need to go in. Let's put this aside from now."

She was out of the truck and halfway up the walk before he could respond. He hurried to catch up with her, stopping her just as she went to ring the doorbell.

"Our discussion is not over." He stared at her and she refused to look away. "It's not. We'll take it up again later."

Neither one had heard the door open. Caleb stood watching them, then shook his head. Here we go again, he thought.

"Would you two like to come in or just stand out here all night and stare at one another?" His amused tone broke through the silence.

Frankie flushed and tried to come up with some words.

Deirdre kept staring at Frankie. "We'll come in. Our discussion is over." She brushed past Caleb and went to find Hannah.

Caleb studied his friend. Frankie—street cop, wise in the ways of the streets, but Frankie—the man, finding out women were not so easy to read or get to do what they should.

Caleb tapped Frankie on the shoulder. "Come on, Franklin. Let's go find the girls and spend some time with my boys. They were very excited to hear you were coming, especially since you were coming with Miss D."

Frankie shook off his thoughts and turned. "Franklin, eh? She's got you doing that too!"

Caleb laughed as he closed the door behind Frankie. "Naw, it was Ben."

After a supper of hamburgers and hot dogs for the boys, Caleb took Deirdre outside to show her the work that was being done in their gardens. But what he really wanted was to talk to her about what was going on.

Caleb stopped and watched her. She had stooped to pick a daisy. "Deirdre, something's going on, isn't it?"

She stopped, refusing to look at him. "What would give you that idea?"

"Other than the fact that your uncle told me you confronted someone holding a switchblade, then Frankie gives me a plate number to run, you're not acting like yourself. Where would you like me to stop?"

"Caleb, you've been a cop for too long. As far as I know nothing is going on. What Ben said, it's part and parcel of the youth centre. As for now, I'm heading for home for a bit. Dad's heading overseas to the area where the cyclone went through."

She went to go past him, but stopped as he laid a hand on her arm. He waited. He knew from experience it took a while for her to respond, especially if she felt crowded or threatened.

She finally sighed and said, "I have no idea what's going on. I have had a feeling like I'm being watched but don't see anyone. There have been a couple of men looking for my hours at the centre. No one gets them. Even the staff never know when I'm going to be there, other than for the times when I have classes with the girls. That's what the staff is for—to do the day-to-day stuff." She looked up at him. "I really don't know, and I'm scared. It feels different this time. Frankie wants to stay close and I don't know if I can handle that again, if anything happens to him."

Caleb's eyes studied her, compassion filling them. She had become like a sister to him; her uncle and he were close. He reached out and pulled her into a hug.

"I know, Miss D, I know. We're praying for you. And keep Frankie close. He's got instincts that I wish I had. Let him in. He may be who God has chosen for you."

She hugged Caleb and then turned away from the house. "I need some space."

He watched with a heavy heart as she walked to the end of the yard and sat down in the swing Hannah kept there. There were things going on that no one knew about. He raised his eyes and scanned the area. He too could feel it, the eyes and the danger. He could almost smell it.

Hannah watched as he entered and sat at the table. She set a cup of tea in front of him and refilled Frankie's coffee cup.

"Is she okay?"

Caleb shrugged. "She's hurting in a way I haven't seen in years. Not since Finn."

Hannah nodded. Frankie's eyes flew between the husband and wife, who were communicating in a way he couldn't understand.

Hannah dropped a kiss on her husband's head and headed for the door.

"She wants to be alone, favourite girl," Caleb said.

"I know. She will be. I'm just going out to share a swing with a friend. No words are needed." The door clicked quietly behind her.

Caleb sighed, then picked up his cup of tea. "It's not easy loving them, Frankie, it's not easy. They have a depth to them that we can't understand."

Frankie's eyes didn't rise from his hands

Caleb looked at him, a humorous glint in his eye. "Not biting, I see." He laughed. "All right. I'll let it slide for now. But something is on your mind. Give."

Frankie nodded. "When I went to pick Deirdre up, she had been on the phone with her Dad. He said something about her not being able to go to the area where the cyclone had it. Then he called back. She had me answer. He doesn't know me, but he was very open." Frankie went on to explain what had been said to him. "So how does he know he can trust me?"

Caleb sought for the right words. "There are times when we don't and can't understand why people enter our lives. If we have been open to God, He shows us those we need at a particular time. You're it for Deirdre. Whether it's just for this, or as I suspect, you wish for more, God does this. Be there for her. Respect her Dad's wishes. Protect her. She'll fight you and fight you mightily. I can already see that's happening. She doesn't like to be put in a box and set behind a locked door. You're in the middle of a mighty powerful storm. Deirdre has been there. Talk to her." Caleb paused. "I'll need to follow up with what Brett has told you. And wait for Hannah to come up with a name."

Frankie nodded. "I figured you would." He glanced at the door. "I was doing some research on the youth centre and found a disturbing article."

Caleb waited. Frankie didn't go on with his words. Caleb sighed. "Ask her. It's her story and she needs to be the one to clarify it with you. There's a lot more to it than what that brief article has said."

He stood and walked to the door. "It doesn't look as if the ladies are coming in any time soon. Come on, I have something to show you."

Frankie pulled his truck to a stop in the driveway. Deirdre had been quiet on the drive. His attention had been on the traffic surrounding them, watchful. Given what Brett Johnson had told him, he had not relaxed his guard. He knew Caleb would be looking for anything, likely calling Eddie in to help. Ben wouldn't be asked, Caleb feeling he was too close.

He looked over at Deirdre. She was staring at the house, making no effort to get out.

"Deirdre." She didn't respond. "Deirdre, we're here. You want to get out, or would you like me to drive around for a while longer?"

She shook her head and then looked at him. "It's okay, Frankie. You don't have to. It's always so hard to come here. Just too many memories of things that went wrong."

Frankie waited.

She sighed, then looked down at her hands. "I should tell you before we go in, and it's just so hard." She stopped, then swiped at the tears on her cheeks. "I know you have probably been searching for answers. I would have if it had been me." She turned pain-filled eyes to him. "Yet you have said nothing. Why?"

He reached for her hand and clasped it in his rough scarred hand. He rubbed his thumb along the scar on the back of hers. "It's your story. You needed to tell me when you were ready. Both Ben and Caleb told me you had a story and that you would tell me. That's all they said, other than Caleb warned there was more to it than what the newspaper articles said."

She thought about that. "I have some very good friends. They are right. There's a lot more to the story than what was written." She looked at the door. "Let's go find some coffee somewhere. Dad and Mom aren't expecting us yet."

He shook his head. "No, first you need to go see your parents. Then we can talk. I'll make us some coffee, we can sit in the dim light in the house or under the moon and stars outside. Your choice." He got out and came around opening her door. "Come on, darling one. Let's get you inside."

She stepped down and then surprising him, wrapped him in a hug. "Thank you."

He reached for their bags and her briefcase, than catching her hand, led her to the door. It was unlocked. She pushed it open and told him softly to set the bags to the side of the hall.

She wandered through the house, looking for her parents. All was quiet. She guessed they had gone to bed. She sent Frankie to the kitchen, telling him where to find the coffee. She grabbed her bags and headed up the stairs. Her mother was just coming down the hall. They hugged, spoke for a minute, and then Beth headed back to bed. Deirdre dropped her bags in her room, then stood, drawing in a deep breath. This would be hard. There were things not even her parents knew about what happened. Here and now, she was ready to share with Frankie. She prayed for the words and wisdom, then headed back down the stairs.

She found Frankie standing, coffee mug in hand, looking out the large window over the sink.

She grabbed her favourite mug and filled it. She looked at the window, then at Frankie.

"Inside or outside?"

He turned, watching her. "It's not cold out. Come, let's go out. Your parents have a really nice deck and furniture."

She nodded. Once on the deck she headed for a chair but a hand on her arm stopped her.

Frankie draped his arm across her shoulders and led her to the love seat. "Here. I want to sit with you beside me. I won't let you put space between us."

She studied him, then nodded. Okay, so what was really going on, she thought. She really didn't know what to think.

They sat for a while, drinking their coffee and just enjoying the sounds of the night.

Finally, Deirdre reached forward and set her mug down. She ran her hands down her jeans, hesitant to start. Frankie let his arm rest along the back of the seat, just touching her shoulders.

She spoke, "I was married, Frankie, married at 19 and widowed the same day." His hand dropped to her shoulder and rested there.

"Tell me about him." His voice was soft, hiding the emotions that were within him.

"At the time, I thought he was wonderful, the love of my life. He worked for our mission. He had been overseas and came home, surprised me when he asked. We had been dating and had briefly talked about getting married. Mom was not happy. Dad was not either but he agreed. We didn't do the whole bit, the large wedding, the large reception. I didn't even want a wedding dress. Mom and Dad were really disappointed. Looking back I guess I should have suspected something. Too young and naive." She stopped and swallowed. "This is the really hard part."

Brett stood in the kitchen. He had come down, knowing his daughter was home. Beth said she hadn't headed to bed yet. He wasn't meaning to eavesdrop but the voices carried softly over the night air. He knew he should just walk away but he needed to know what she was saying, how much she really knew. When his daughter began to speak again, he listened until he had heard what he needed to hear.

"We were supposed to fly out that night. Finn was heading back to an area where we were setting up training for disasters. He wasn't scheduled to be back for two months and surprised us all when he came back. There was something different about him. If I hadn't been so blinded at the prospect of being married, maybe I would have probed further. He wouldn't say what was wrong." She stopped, swallowed, then continued, "We had arrived at the hotel. We were heading into the hotel, then there was a drive by shooting, at least that's the official word. It wasn't. Finn had been targeted. I had no idea why, then or now. Two other people died that day. Finn had seen something and shoved me away from him. I got to walk away but my newly married husband lay dead on the pavement."

Frankie's arm came around her and pulled her close. She buried her head in his chest, tears soaking into his shirt. "The police didn't think it was a random act but they couldn't prove it. The men who did the shooting disappeared. Families were left to mourn."

Frankie's chin rested on her head as he hugged her. He couldn't speak. No wonder he had been told the story wasn't pretty.

"Did they ever find them?"

She shook her head. "No. They tried and couldn't. They suspected that they were from overseas and had headed out again as soon as they had done what they had to do." She stopped. "That's why I feel like I am being watched. I think they want what Finn gave me. He gave me nothing. I have gone through his stuff, what I have left, and have nothing."

Frankie thought about it. "Let me take a look when we go home. Maybe I can find something. Being on the streets, you learn how to hide things so they aren't found."

She pushed away from him and stood. "Sure." She watched him. "Come on. Enough gloom for the night. I"ll show you the guest room. It's just off the kitchen. Morning will be here soon enough and we always go to the early service."

"Like how early?"

"It's at 9:30. You'll love it."

Frankie groaned and then followed her in, watching as she locked the door. With a quick good night, she was gone. His sleep that night would be troubled, he knew from experience. He would get what sleep he could and be ready to protect this lady. No one had to ask him. It would get done.

****

The Watcher stood in the darkness of the trees across the street. He had had a feeling they would come here when he heard about the cyclone, and he was right.   Now it was a waiting game.   His experience here had taught him that she would be almost impossible to reach, surrounded by her family. He could wait but he couldn't wait long.

Chapter 6

Frankie heard voices in the kitchen the next morning as he awoke. After dressing, he stopped, then dropped back to his bed. He needed time with God this morning. He felt like he was in the middle of a tornado and he had no idea where it would drop him off.

As he opened his door, he heard laughter, then voices again.

"Don't tell me. You didn't, did you?" He heard the dismay in Deirdre's voice.

"Sure. Greg asked me the next time you were in town if we would. I told him yes."

"Timothy!" Frankie could hear the frustration in her voice. "I told him no more. I wasn't going to!"

Frankie arrived in the doorway in time to see a young man, around their age, shrug. He caught the resemblance to Ben and wondered if this was his son. His eyes went to Deirdre and he started to laugh, then struggled to keep it off his face.

Timothy shrugged. "What was I to say? You know they like to hear your voice."

"Timothy!" A wet rag was launched at him and caught him in the face.

He howled with pretended rage and went to throw it back at her, then stopped, and stuck his hand behind his back.

Frankie's head turned as he watched the woman who stood in the other doorway. This had to be Deirdre's mother but he saw no resemblance to Deirdre.

"Okay Timothy, what did you do this time?"

"Me? Nothing."

Beth waited until he shrugged, then admitted he had promised that he and Deirdre would sing the next time she was in town.

Beth shook her heard. "That's not a good promise to make. Deirdre has the right to decide if and when she wants to. This is not the right time for that, this trip." Then she turned to Deirdre. "And you, stop picking on the boys."

A howl of outrage came from Deirdre. "He started it."

Beth started laughing. "You two will never grow up. Timothy, you will need to talk to Greg and let him know she can't this time. Deirdre, you have company standing behind you. Perhaps if you stop fighting with your cousin, you could introduce us."

Deirdre's face went into her hands. "He really isn't, is he?"

This sent her mother and cousin into fresh gales of laugher. Frankie just stood there, a delighted grin on his face. This was a new side to Deirdre that he hadn't seen. He rather liked.

Without turning, Deirdre waved a hand at her mother. "This is my mother, Beth, Franklin. That brat over there is my cousin, Timothy. Benny doesn't acknowledge he's related to him when Timothy acts like this."

At her mother's shocked voiced "Deirdre", Frankie started to laugh and came into the room.

"It's okay, really it is. I've seen her deal with the youth at the centre. I would say, Timothy, you got off very lightly."

Deirdre swatted him as he walked by him. He just laughed and took the mug of coffee he was handed. He was seeing a whole different side to her. He loved it.

Frankie settled himself into the pew. He looked around. It was an older church, pews instead of chairs, beautiful stained glass windows. Deirdre had dropped her stuff by him and then left. She returned shortly and sat beside him. Timothy had dropped down to the pew on his other side, and Beth and Brett were on Deirdre's other side.

He listened to the hymns, not the worship songs he was used to. This was different. He tilted his head to listen. He could see why Timothy and Deirdre would be asked to sing. Their voices blended in a magical way. He could listen all day.

"We'll be looking at Psalms 107:29 in particular this morning: He calmed the raging storm, and the waves became quiet. First let us look at the storm on Galilee. The storm raged, the men were frightened, the Christ was sleeping. How would you have felt? Think about that." The minister, Greg Frankie thought it was, went on to talk about that storm and the way it was calmed.

"My friends, we all face storms, whether of our own making or not. The same Christ who calmed that storm will calm yours." As Greg went on, Frankie felt Deirdre shiver. His arm went around her and he drew her close. Brett, sensing movement, peeked over his wife's head, took a look, sought out Frankie's eyes, and then frowned.

Frankie stood at the end of the service, Deirdre beside him. He looked around. He didn't know the people, but he felt the evil presence near him. Who was it and why?

Deirdre looked around. She felt uncomfortable here today, as if she was out in the middle of an open field with no shelter. She tugged at Frankie's hand and when he looked at her, she pointed to a side door. They excused themselves and they walked out.

"What's up, Deirdre?"

"I don't know. I just don't know. Something's happening here and I don't know what."

Frankie scanned the area and then headed for his truck. "We need to get you out of the open." As they walked across the street, Frankie's head shot around at the sound of an engine revving. Scooping Deirdre up, he ran for the side of the street and safety just before a gray car sped by.

He set her on her feet and hugged her, her arms tight around him.

"Tell me that really didn't happen, please."

"Sorry, darling, but it did. Someone is really after you and they have followed us here." Frankie looked around and then saw Brett watching from the other side of the street. He lifted his hand and Brett nodded. Good, he thought, he knows something is going on.

"I think we need to head back to your home and go through Finn's stuff. There has to be something there."

She sighed. "I know. I just want to help out here."

"I think your Dad will say no and send you away. I'm not sure where you will be safest."

She shook her head. "I don't think I will be safe anywhere." She stepped back, resigned as to what was needing to be done. "Let's go break the news to Mom and Dad. This is why I don't come often. I feel like I am bringing trouble to their door."

"And it has been how long?"

She shrugged. "Eight years, I don't know, ten maybe?"

"Oh, honey, no wonder." His words stopped, and she turned puzzled eyes on him.

As Frankie expected, her mother didn't it take it well, but there was something there that was different. It wasn't that she was going home instead of staying. She just couldn't define what it was. Brett just nodded. He had a good idea that something had happened that morning that was sending them home.

"Call me when you get home, Frankie." Brett had pulled Frankie aside. "Tell me what you can."

Frankie studied the older man, then nodded. "I will. Some of it has to come from Deirdre. She has never told you the full story, I don't think."

Brett sighed, then said, "No, she hasn't. I did some investigating at the time but came up empty. I never felt comfortable with the official version."

"I wouldn't have either."

****

The Watcher let some traffic pass, then pulled into the lane behind them. Good. He had them on the run. That's when mistakes would happen and he

53

would finally get the information he needed. It had been way too long.

****

Frankie pulled off into a restaurant parking lot and turned off his truck. He scanned the area, then spoke.

"We need to eat." When she didn't speak, he reached out and touched her face. "Deirdre. I know we're on the outskirts of town, but we need to eat. We need to talk. You haven't talked to me all the way back."

She shook her head. "I don't know, Frankie. I just don't know." She reached for her door, and he stopped her. He shook his head.

"Wait, let me come around. From now on, you don't go anywhere on your own." As she started to protest, he continued, "No, whoever is after you is getting bolder. Time has to be getting short for them. So for now, consider that you have a boyfriend. That would be me." Her eyes shot to his, and he smiled. "Yes, me. We'll figure it out as we go." He paused. "We'll need to watch you at the centre. We both need to be there but we'll have to talk to Caleb, see what he can come up with." As she shook her head, he said, "Either Caleb or Ben. I think you would prefer Caleb."

Her eyes slid shut and she nodded. "Anyone but Ben. I love my uncle, but I really don't need to be smothered so much. It's bad enough now. I sometimes think he knows more than what he's saying"

Frankie studied her and then his eyes shifted to the vehicles around them. "I am sure he does.

54

Caleb certainly seems to. If he does, Ben does. And more than likely Eddie."

She hesitated and then spoke, "Thank you, Frankie. You have never pushed. I need that."

He came around the truck and then taking her hand walked towards the restaurant. He felt like he had a target on his back and the hair on his neck bristled. Scanning the area, he kept his body between Deirdre and the driving area. He didn't want to risk another incident like this morning.

Neither had much of an appetite and they were soon walking back to Frankie's truck. Hand clasped tight in Frankie's, Deirdre moved as close to him as she could get. She felt safe with him but there was something in the air. It was getting dark, and she just wanted to be home, locked in her house and safe. But even there, she didn't feel safe.

Frankie stopped as a dark form stepped around from his truck. He started to tuck Deirdre behind him when he felt a blow between the shoulder blades and he was propelled forward into his truck and then held there. He could feel the prick of a knife at his neck.

Deirdre caught back a scream. Screaming would do no good. The patrons of the restaurant could not help and by the time help got there it might be too late.

The form came from around the truck and stopped in front of her.

"Where is it?" A guttural voice sounded, in it a tone that sent shudders through her.

"I don't know what you want." She tried to get a look at him but he was in the shadows and she couldn't see him well enough to identify him. "I don't have anything you want."

A rough hand reached out and caught her arm, the fingers squeezing together in a tight band that hurt. "Yes, you do. That husband of yours had it and gave it to you."

Deirdre kept shaking her head. "No, he didn't. He didn't give me anything. I would have known if he had."

Frankie tried to turn to watch her, but the knife dug deeper. He could feel the trickle of blood starting.

A muttered word in another language, and one at Frankie's back stepped back a bit. The knife loosened and he could breath a bit better. He was able to turn to watch Deirdre.

She was calm, steady. No fear radiated from her, but he knew she had to be afraid. He watched the two men, looking for an opportunity to down them and get Deirdre away.

The conversation continued between them. The one near Deirdre watched her, then his eyes lifted to the traffic around them. He turned and studied the vehicles. A word to his companion, and Frankie was forced to move away from his truck. Deirdre was roughly shoved after him. He reached for her hand and her fingers clung to his. They were then forced into an SUV, Deirdre in the front seat, Frankie behind the driver. There was no chance they could get away.

Frankie watched the area they were traveling through. He knew it and knew it led to a wilderness area. He didn't like this at all. He turned to watch Deirdre. Her face was still calm. How she could be so calm, he didn't know. He felt panic rising within him. Then he stopped. He was not alone. God was there in this storm. He had control. Frankie sat back,

attempting to relax and plan.   God knew and God
would provide a way.

Ben was worried. He paced around the outside of Deirdre's house. She wasn't home. Brett had called, letting him know they were on their way and to watch out for them. He hadn't said much as he was already at the airport heading away from the country.

Ben then turned to the study the house. It looked okay, windows and doors seemed intact. He pulled out his keys and searched for the one for Deirdre's front door. He hoped she was really inside and had not heard the doorbell, but he had that feeling in his gut that said otherwise. He opened the door, stepped in and turned off the alarm. He then paced through searching. She wasn't there and her briefcase that she always keep by her desk in her office was missing.

His heart sank. That meant they weren't home.

His phone rang. It was Eddie, another senior officer and close friend. Ben had called him to go check on Frankie.

"Ben, no sign of Frankie. His truck's not here and his house is still locked up solid. His neighbour said he hadn't been home since yesterday afternoon. She saw him leave and hasn't seen him again."

"That's what I was afraid of. Deirdre's not here either." He thought for a minute. "Call Caleb. He'll need to know. I have a feeling there is more involved than just a stop for a meal. Brett, Deirdre's dad, called as he was running to catch his flight. Sounds like there's been a threat come through to the office on her. He was going to have Timothy forward it to me." Ben stopped and stared around the kitchen. Nothing was moved, but it felt off, like someone had been through. "Eddie, something just doesn't feel right in the house. I can't pinpoint what. Deirdre is very particular with her stuff. It looks okay but I have that feeling."

Eddie's voice came through the phone. "I know. I do too. Frankie's too wise a street cop to get caught out. But then again, he's a man in love and that changes things." Eddie then spoke again. "I'll have Katie and Mike come out and take a look around. They'll come in as friends, but let them in through the garage. That will hide what's happening."

Ben's voice was amused as he responded, "A man in love, eh? Yeah, I guess you could say that. Deirdre's fighting back against that." His voice sobered. "I just wish I knew where they were. I don't like this."

Eddie's voice came back through. "Where's your faith, Ben? Aren't you always telling me God's in control? He is in this. No matter what happens."

Ben shuddered at the thought. "I know, Eddie, I know. Tell Caleb to call me."

****

The Watcher turned and looked around. He didn't know who that was who entered her house. He hoped that he would not find the information. He would need to be stopped. He knew his men had found the two and had them with them. This was up to him. He stepped quietly through the yard, up the steps and to the door. It swung silently open and he stopped and waited. He stepped in and waited. He could hear movement in the house, and he crept towards it. He stopped once more, barely moving.

59

He stepped forward again and as the man's body turned towards him, he struck. The man went down with just a whisper of a sound. The Watcher looked around and then crept back out. He would stand and watch and wait. His men would soon let him know where they were.

****

Eddie met Caleb on the sidewalk leading to Frankie's house.

Caleb looked at the house, then around the neighbourhood. "I just wish this would stop. We've had too many in the last year.:

Eddie nodded. "I know. It's going to hit the men hard. He's one of us." He turned to face the house. "We'll have no end of volunteers to search. If they have been taken for whatever reason, those involved will wish they hadn't. Deirdre is one of us too. She's Ben niece, but she's Frankie's girl."

"Has it gone that far?"

"Not officially, but I know Frankie. In his mind, she's his. She'll take longer to make that decision."

"I think she already has. She's just too afraid of what happened in the past to expect to have happiness with someone else. Come on, let's go search his house. I doubt we'll find much but at least we'll know."

Caleb's phone rang as they were walking through the downstairs. As the voice at the other end spoke, his eyes closed and then he grabbed for Eddie's arm. Pulling him with him, he locked up Frankie's house.

"What's up?"

60

"Ben. Katie and Mike found him down in the house. Katie's on her way to get Marg. Mike has called in for more men to come help him."

"Did she say how bad?"

Caleb shook his head. "I'll meet you there. Once we know what's going on, I'll want you at Deirdre's."

Frankie watched as the SUV stopped in front of a house. It was isolated but he could see lights not that far away. He scouted around the area with his eyes, taking in what he could in the dim light. Trees were close but the underbrush was cleared. There were a couple of outbuildings and he thought he saw light reflect off another vehicle. His heart sank. How were they to get out?

The doors opened and they were pulled from the vehicle and then shoved towards one of the outbuildings. It was unlocked and they were pushed inside. The door swung shut and he heard the lock click. He stood and stared around. There were a couple of windows and the door. The floor was dirt, he could feel the cold and dampness through his feet.

He heard Deirdre moving around the building. When she stopped in front of one of the windows, he went towards her. Her posture was stiff and he could feel the anger vibrating within her. His hand went to her shoulder.

"I am very ticked off right now, Franklin."

"Just ticked off?   I'm just a touch mad myself."

Her elbow caught him in the ribs. "You know what I mean. I could be really angry but that solves nothing." She turned slightly. "How's the neck?"

"It's okay, just a little prick."

"It looked a whole lot worse than a little prick."

He felt it. It was tiny and when he got out of here, he would have it looked at if he needed to.

"So what's your plan?" Deidre asked as she continued to move around the room.

"I have no idea as yet. Do you have one?"

"Of course." He stopped and stared at her. "Of course, I do. I've been in lots worse situations and with much meaner men. Follow me and I'll get you out."

Frankie shook his head and then turned her to face him. Standing with his hands on her shoulders, he spoke, "Deirdre. Please. Don't do anything foolish."

She shrugged off his hands. "I'm getting out of here and out of here tonight. You can come or stay, whichever you want."

He watched as she dug down in her pocket and pulled out something. She showed him what looked like a knife but then she headed for the door. Inserting it into the lock, she wiggled it and then he heard a click.

"Is that legal here? I highly doubt it. And I don't even want to know where you got it. Well, maybe I should find out, if it was here in our country."

"Probably not, but it looks like a pocket knife, so I can get away with it. No one but you knows what it really does. And no, I didn't get it here." She pushed the door open and looked around. "Come on, we can get out of here now."

He crept through the door behind her and she closed and locked it after them. Then he watched in amazement as she headed for the SUV. A few minutes later, she was once again by his side. She stopped at the second vehicle and then she led him towards the woods.

"Deirdre, what did you do?"

"Something my beloved cousin taught me. I let the air out of all their tires and took the tire valve caps." She grabbed his hand and dropped something in it. Sure enough, that's what was in his hand.

Frankie laughed softly. "I still wouldn't want to meet you in a dark alley. You're too scary." He looked behind him. "I just wish I knew if we had time to get away."

"We do. They're planning on leaving us there overnight and then questioning us in the morning. Whoever hired them will be here some time tomorrow morning. We have time as long as we move quickly."

"How do you know that? They were speaking another language."

She shrugged. "I pick up languages very easily. Give me a month in a country and I speak like a native. It's a gift but can also be a curse. Come now, we need to get moving. And yes, before you ask, I have been in that country long enough to pick up the language."

Frankie stopped her. "Did they take your phone?"

She smirked. "No and I bet they didn't take yours either. They certainly aren't from here. That's the first thing they should have done."

He pulled out his phone as they walked forward. "No service here. Let's go."

"Can you hotwire a car?"

He stopped and stared at her. "Hotwire a car? Really? And I suppose you can?"

She nodded and he just stared at her, mouth open. "Of course, I can. But you didn't say if you could if we found one."

He shook his head, grabbed her hand and pulled her with him. "I tell you. You're very scary. I must remember not to get on your bad side. And yes, I can hotwire a car. Now who taught you? Timothy?"

He felt her head shake and he stopped once again to stare at him. "Who then?"

"Well, I guess you could say Raffaele, then Pietro, then Thomas."

He held up his hand and she giggled. "Enough. I gather these are all men from your adventures?"

"No, just boys, usually under the age of 10."

He shook his head and then started forward again. "You're scary. Your friends are scary. I'm never going to be safe around you or them. No one will be safe around you."

Her laugh warmed his heart even as he feared they never make it out of the trees alive.

Chapter 8

Marg met Caleb at the Emergency Department door.

"How is he?" He could tell she was frightened for her husband but her demeanour was calm.

"He's awake. The Emergency doctor is with him right at the moment. I'll take you back soon."

"What happened, Caleb? He said he was worried about Deirdre and left. Then Katie called and came to get me."

"He was at Deirdre's, found something I gather and then had called for Katie and Mike to come over. He was attacked while waiting for them. He doesn't remember much other than being in her kitchen and then waking up here."

Marg's eyes slid shut. "Thank you, God. I was so scared."

Caleb nodded and then turned. "Come on. I'll take you back. The doctor said he could go home tonight."

Caleb watched as his friend held his hand out to his wife, then he turned and walked away. He was headed for Deirdre's house. Maybe they had come up with something.

Eddie met him in the living room.

"Nothing. Absolutely nothing."

Caleb looked around and drew a deep breath. "No sign of either one of them, I gather."

"No, and they're not answering their phones." Eddie looked around. "I have had enough of this. Three was plenty and now we're into four."

Caleb smiled and nodded. "I know. Our friends just seem to be attracting trouble."

"If it's in the water, I'm giving that up. I'll drink juice instead."

Caleb laughed at Eddie's grumbling. "No, it might be in the air, and you can't stop breathing that."

Eddie glared at him, then laughed. "I know, you're right. I just wish I knew why."

"So do I, Eddie. Katie and Mike are finished?"

"They are. They didn't find anything though. If the place was searched, it was done by an expert who took ample precautions." Eddie shook his head. "I just don't get it."

"Me neither, Eddie. Ben's fine. Marg was there to take him home."

"Did he remember anything?"

"No. He's angry. And worried. He said he would be calling Beth tonight."

"Will Brett come home?"

Caleb thought about that. "I really don't know, Eddie. I really don't know." He hesitated, choosing his words. "I never liked how Deirdre was left on her own all those years ago. She ran, but they let her."

"Did they ever figure out if Finn was the target or one of the other men?"

Caleb turned to stare at Eddie. "Now that's an idea of where to look. Find out everything you can on Finn. There was just something that has never satisfied me with that."

"That I can do, Caleb. If you can get me the country he came back from, I may have a friend over there who can search out information there."

Caleb nodded. "That I can do."

"Meanwhile, it's not that late. I'm going to take a drive around the area of town where they would have come back through. Maybe I'll find something."

Caleb watched Eddie walk away. He was burdened for his friends in a way that he had not been in a long time. What storm, Lord, he asked, what storm is gathering, ready to hit our town and my friends?

****

The Watcher stood in his house and looked around. Finally, he had her where he wanted her. She would tell him where to find the information he was looking for. But first, a celebratory dinner was being prepared for him. A good night's sleep and he would head out to where she was being held. The man with her was not important. His minions would dispose of him without a second thought.

****

Frankie stopped and looked around. His sense of direction was keen and he knew now where they were. Just ahead would be the parking lot they had been abducted from.

"Isn't that where this all started?" Deirdre's voice was quiet beside him.

"It is. We need to wait, though. I don't want to rush to my truck just in case they did find out we're gone."

She shook her head. "Trust me. They won't. In their country, a locked door stops people. They don't break out and run."

"No, it's only scary people like you who do."

She shoved him and then pointed. "Look, someone has stopped near your truck."

Frankie peered through the darkness and then grabbing her hand, pulled her closer to the truck. "I think that's Eddie."

"Eddie?"

He nodded. "Eddie. I've trusted him with my life before. If we could only get his attention somehow."

Deirdre looked around. "I can."

Frankie shook his head and looked at her. "No."

She slipped her hand from his and was gone before he could stop her. He watched as she changed her gait and seemed to shrink. This girl's good, he thought. She really would survive on the streets. I think she's even better than Ashling, Liam's wife.

Eddie tried the doors on Frankie's truck. Locked. He cupped his hands and peered inside but it was too dark to see much. He turned as a woman approached him.

"Can I help you, ma'am?"

She mumbled some words and Eddie stepped closer.

"It's Deirdre. Frankie's behind me somewhere. Here's his keys. Grab our stuff as if you were sent for it, then leave and park at the gas station two blocks down. We'll find you." Deirdre limped her way past him towards the restaurant, as if that had been her goal all the time.

Eddie turned to watch, then looked down at his hands. Sure enough, he had keys in his hands.

Frankie watched in amazement as Eddie unlocked his truck and pulled both their bags and the briefcase out, locked the vehicle again, and then headed for his car to leave. He felt his pockets. She really had picked his pocket for his keys. He was almost afraid to think of what she would do next.

He felt her come up beside him and waited.

"Eddie's meeting us down the block at the gas station. We need to move now."

Frankie's hand went out and stopped her. "When did you pick my pocket?"

He caught a flash of a grin and a shake of her head. "You never felt a thing, did you? I did about ten minutes ago."

Frankie stared at her, shook his head and then caught her hand. "Come on, let's go home. And I want to know what other skills you have that you haven't shared with me."

"I have plenty. When you get caught in trouble overseas, you learn quickly to adapt and figure out how to survive. These are survival skills I've had to learn."

"That's it." Frankie declared. "I'm never letting you go overseas again. At least, not without me."

Eddie eyed the two as they shut the doors of his car behind them. "Are you both all right?" At their nod, he pulled away from the station and headed back into town. "Caleb is going to want to see you. I'm taking you there."

His eyes searched Deirdre's face in the rearview mirror. She was tired and dirty, more than likely hungry, he thought.

"Deirdre, Ben went to your house to look for you. He thought someone had been through it and called in one of our teams. While he was waiting, he was attacked." At her gasp, he continued, "He's fine, other than a headache. Marg was taking him home. He didn't see who it was though." His eyes questioned her silently.

She shook her head in denial. "I don't know, Eddie, I don't know who it would have been."

He nodded. He pulled into Caleb's driveway, turned off the ignition, and then turned to them.

"This situation is escalating. We need to figure out who. The why is easy. Someone wants something you have. It has to be something of Finn's."

Deirdre's eyes slid shut as she nodded. "I know. I don't have anything of his left. I never had much of his anyway, just some books and a few trinkets. We were too young to have gathered much."

"There has to be something we're missing. We'll keep you safe and figure it out in the meantime."

Caleb met them at the door, scanning their faces. He felt relief wash through him that they were okay.

"Come on back to the kitchen. Hannah has some soup and sandwiches ready. We hadn't eaten earlier. The boys ate and she put them to bed."

Hannah gave Deirdre a look and then turned to Caleb. "They're cleaning up first before eating and being questioned."

Deirdre shot a surprised look at Caleb, caught his small smile at his wife, and then felt better knowing he wasn't angry. She followed Hannah up the stairs to a guest room.

"There's a shower in there and I'll find you some clean clothes."

"Actually Hannah, if one of them could grab my bag from Eddie's car, I have clean clothes."

Hannah nodded and headed back down the stairs.

Fifteen minutes later, feeling much cleaner and more like herself, she opened the door to the room and stepped outside. Frankie was leaning on the wall across from the door, waiting for her. He had had a chance to clean up as well. He looked at her, then opened his arms and she walked into them. He hugged her tight, without saying a word, then turned her to walk down the stairs. They needed food first. Then the questioning would begin. He was really looking forward to seeing the looks of Caleb's and Eddie's faces when he told them how they had got away. It would be priceless.

Hannah set soup and sandwiches before them, then seated herself at the table.

Caleb went to ask something, then caught his wife's eye. He smiled and nodded. Yes, he could and would wait.

When the two finally pushed away their bowls and plates, Caleb looked around the table. Now would come the hard part, trying to figure out who and why. And Hannah had not yet given him a name.

"Who wants to start?" He eyed Frankie and Deirdre.

They looked at each other. Frankie's eyes grew big as Deirdre started to laugh.

"You don't know this lady, Caleb. She's scary. She's got scary friends. Don't meet her in a dark alley." He shuddered dramatically.

"Behave yourself. It wasn't that bad, not as bad as you're making out."

Frankie nodded his head. "Oh, yes, it was. You are very scary."

By this time, the eyes of the other three were bobbing between the two. Caleb finally held up a hand.

"Please, guys. I would really like to know why Frankie thinks you're so scary, Deirdre."

This sent Deirdre off into fresh gales of laughter.

Frankie looked at Caleb and shook his head in a sorrowful manner. "She is scary, Caleb. I could have used her on the streets. There wouldn't have been a speck of trouble." By this time, Deirdre had pillowed her head on her arms on the table, shoulders shaking.

Eddie was starting to smile. Having dealt with her and Frankie's truck, he wasn't going to be surprised with what was coming, he knew.

Hannah watched the two closely, sensing there was more going on that what showed on the surface. She was glad. These two were just so right for one another.

"Frankie."

"Okay, Caleb, but don't say I didn't warn you that she's scary. She takes switchblades off teenagers without much of a protest. She carries a knife, or what she says is a pocket knife, but she can pick locks with it and then lock it again as if it had never opened. She blames her cousin for teaching her how to disable a car. She actually removed all the tire valve caps from two SUVs. Two, not just one! She can hotwire a car and says it was kids that taught her. She can pick a pocket and no one even knows. She's scary. Her friends are scary."

By this time, Frankie's narrative had the other three in laughter.

When he was finally able to talk, Caleb turned to Deirdre. "Scary, eh? Did you really do all that?"

She nodded, her eyes sparkling with mirth. "All except hotwire a car. We didn't need to."

"I forgot." Frankie spoke up. "She can even learn a language in a month."

They turned to stare at her and she shrugged. "It happens. Now, about today. We had headed home, stopped for something to eat, and then when we were walking back to Frankie's truck, we were stopped. Frankie needs to get his neck checked out. One of the men held a knife to him and I know it cut into the flesh. We were taken to a house about an hour away, middle of the woods. They locked us in an outbuilding and then disappeared. Their conversation went along the lines of 'We'll leave

73

them here, he'll be out tomorrow morning, we'll question them then, they can't get out of here.' Well, locks don't hold me in. Stop laughing, Frankie. As Frankie said, I picked the lock, got us out, locked the door so they wouldn't know until they unlocked it, stole the tire valve caps (they won't be going anywhere any time soon), and walked back to the restaurant. I walked up to Eddie, gave him Frankie's keys, he got our stuff, met us at a gas station, and here we are."

Caleb and Eddie were staring at her, mouths open. Hannah had laid her hand on Deirdre's arm and was watching Frankie. Frankie was sitting there, shaking his head, still somewhat in disbelief. Yes, she thought, Deirdre is so good for Frankie. He is coming alive and losing that beat-up look he had had for so long. Thank you, Lord.

Caleb swallowed, and then said, "That's what really happened? You just unlocked the door and waltzed out of there?"

She smiled at Frankie and then looked at Caleb. "Just about. Except Frankie keeps saying I'm scary. I'm not. I know people who are a lot scarier."

Caleb looked at Eddie, who was staring at Deirdre.

"You know people who are scarier than you?" At her nod, Eddie looked at the ceiling. "Heaven help us if they're in this town. And does your uncle know?"

She reached over and patted his hand. "They're not. I left them overseas. And yes, he does. He helped teach me."

At that, they all broke up in laughter.

Sobering, Caleb watched her. "Someone was looking for something in your house. Do you have any idea why or what?"

She thought about that, then shook her head. "I have very little in my house. After seeing how little my friends have overseas, things aren't important to me. I have some keepsakes, mainly from my trips and gifts those friends have given me. I don't have anything of Finn's if that's what they were looking for. Come to think of it, he really didn't give me a lot or write a lot." She looked sad at that.

She looked at Caleb. "I will need to go back over the house again, I guess."

"You will, but it can wait until tomorrow. Right now, I would say you two need some sleep and I know I could use some."

Timothy stood in his parents' kitchen the next morning. His aunt had sent him home. She told him he needed to be here. He wasn't as sure though.

He turned as he heard his mother enter the kitchen. She stopped, then crossed the room to hug him.

"I'm so glad you're here, Timothy. It's time you came home." She stepped back to look up at him, taking in the dark brown hair and hazel, almost brown eyes. He looked so much like his father at that age.

"I'm glad. Aunt Beth really laid it on the line. I think they are really regretting the way they handled it with Deirdre all those years ago."

Marg nodded. "I'm sure they are. They handled it very poorly. I'm just glad she came to your Dad and I."

Timothy drew in a breath. "How's Dad this morning?"

"He's got a headache but he'll be down shortly. He says he has to go in, even though Caleb told him to stay home today."

"He would." Timothy looked down at his mother. "What would you say if I told you I was moving back here, looking for something to do here?"

Marg studied her son, then smiled. "It would make your Dad and I very happy.   But most

importantly, it has to be what God wants you to do.
Is it?"

He nodded. "I'm getting to that point. That's
part of the reason I came. I want to be here for
Deirdre. What do you think is going on?"

Marg sighed, then sat at the table with the cup
of coffee she had been fixing. She patted the table
beside her and Timothy sat with his own cup. "I
don't really know, son. I think it has to do with Finn
but it could be something from one of her trips. She
has gone to some pretty hard areas of the world.
Why would Brett even let her when he won't go to
them himself?"

Timothy stared across the kitchen, not sure
how to express himself. He saw his father standing
quietly in the doorway, not entering so as not to
disturb the conversation. "Uncle Brett has changed.
I can't explain it. It's like he's going through the
motions and not really focused on who goes where.
Aunt Beth is different too. I just can't figure it out."

Ben entered the room, dropped a kiss on his
wife's hand, laid a hand on his son's shoulder, then
sat at the table as well. "He has, Timothy. I have
noticed that the last few times we've talked. I can't
get a straight answer from him. I'm not sure if he
even knows why or how."

After they had spent some time in family
prayer, Ben stood and looked at his son. "I think you
should go spend some time with Deirdre." As
Timothy went to protest, Ben held up his hand. "I
know, she has Frankie, but she needs family as well.
You are probably the one closest to her. She needs us
right now. Frankie does, too. He has never said
much about his family, so I know if he has some, he's
not close to them."

Timothy nodded. "I'll head over there, unless Mom wants some time with me."

His mother smiled. "With what you said about moving back here, I'll have plenty of time. Go, spend some time with Deirdre. Get to know Frankie. He's been beat up by his time on the streets and I suspect long before that, but he is softening. Your cousin has worked wonders in directing him back to God." Marg paused, then said softly, "And I think that's what you're looking to do, renew yourself."

"I am, Mom, I am. See you later."

Frankie stood in Deirdre's kitchen and looked around. She was right. She really didn't have a lot of what he always called stuff. She had some nice pictures, some ornaments that obviously meant something to her, and not much more.

Deirdre looked around her living room. Eddie stood watching her.

"Can't see anything obvious?" He asked.

She shook her head. "No. I really can't. Finn was overseas a lot the last year or so before we married so we never had time to collect things. We had planned on living overseas for about six months, then moving back here." She walked over to the bookshelves and pulled out a photo album. "This is the only album I have that has anything in it from that time. You're welcome to take it and look through it if you think it will help"

Eddie took it from her and briefly glanced through it. "Thanks. I'll do that, then get it back to you."

She shrugged. "No rush. That's a time in my life that has come and gone. Going back over pictures and whatnot won't bring it back."

Frankie's puzzled eyes met Eddie's over Deirdre's head. They both wondered at her words.

After a tap at the door, Timothy entered. He greeted the two men and gave his cousin a hug. "So, what are we up to today?"

"Not stealing tire valve caps, I hope." Eddie's dry tone brought on the laughter.

Timothy looked at his cousin and groaned. "Don't tell me. You really didn't, did you?"

She nodded and held up eight fingers. He shook his head. "That was a joke, Deirdre. I never ever thought you would do that."

Frankie spoke from the doorway. "If she hadn't, we may not be standing here today. Your cousin is very scary."

Timothy took a look at Frankie, then Eddie, and finally his cousin. He smiled and shook his head. "She is. Very scary."

Deirdre slapped her cousin's arm as Eddie headed for the door. "I had your truck brought back to your place, Frankie. Keys through the mail slot, but I gather you have a friend who could pick the lock and hotwire it for you." On a laugh from the men and a squeal of outrage from Deirdre, he shut the door.

Frankie looked around the living room after Eddie left, then turned his gaze on Timothy. Timothy was turning an object over and over in his fingers. "What's that?"

Timothy looked up. "I really don't know. I found it in our warehouse one night, and just never threw it way."

"Can I see it?" Frankie took it from Timothy and looked it over. It was a piece of silver, he thought, engraved. There seemed to be an edge that wasn't smooth and he needed to get a better look at that.

Deirdre had come to stand near him. At her surprised gasp, he looked at her. She was pulling a necklace from around her neck. It held a similar object. She removed it from the chain and held it out to him. He looked at both of them, examining them well.

"I need a piece of paper I can lay these down on." Timothy handed him a sheet of paper from the printer, and Frankie headed for the kitchen.

Laying the two objects on the paper, he slid them close together. He twisted them one way and another, then they clicked together. He concentrated on them and then looked up at the other two.

"This may be what they are looking for. We need to get this to Eddie or Caleb. Timothy, it won't look strange if you go there, looking for your Dad. It would be expected that you would be meeting him for lunch or something seeing as you're in town. Deirdre and I can't be out and about much until we catch those men."

Plans were quickly devised and Timothy sent on his way. Deirdre looked at Frankie and sighed, "Now what?"

"We wait and see what that brings. In the meantime, we are going to search your house, and I mean search. Every book and picture will be looked at. There has to be something here."

****

The Watcher stood in the doorway of the outbuilding, anger and rage evident on his face. Where were they? He had been assured they were here and could not escape. The men he had hired were useless, he thought, absolutely useless. They had them in their grasp and let them escape.

"Find them and bring them to me. As long as they can talk, bring them to me. The man, I don't care about. Finish him off if you have to. Bring me that woman."

The two men looked at each other and then at him. They were dumbstruck that the two had escaped. The door was locked, windows not disturbed, no holes anywhere they could get out of.

****

Eddie tapped at Caleb's door and then entered, closing the door behind him. He sank into one of the chairs in front of Caleb's desk and sighed, tapping the folder he held.

Caleb waited, knowing Eddie would speak when the time was right. Finally, he asked, "What did you find out?"

"You're not going to like it and I am not going to like having to totally destroy a young woman's memories and life."

Caleb watched his friend. Whatever he had found out lay heavy on him.

"Which do you want to start with? I can handle the not liking it. Tell me and then we can figure out how to tell Deirdre."

Eddie opened the folder, studied the contents, then handed the closed file to Caleb. "Read this and then we'll talk."

Caleb shot him a glance as he accepted the folder. He opened it and began to read. Eddie watched the distressed look cross his friend's face and raised his heart in prayer. This was going to hurt, no matter how they approached it. Someone had been keeping some terrible secrets that would blow apart a world or two in their friends' lives.

Caleb finished reading it, then laid the folder down on his desk. His eyes slid closed. Eddie was right. This was life changing.

"Did you have any idea when you started looking?"

Eddie shook his head. "None. Whoever did the initial investigation swept it under the rug. Makes me wonder if money changed hands. I had to do some hard digging to get this much."

Caleb shook his head. "I have no idea how we are ever going to approach this with her. It was totally destroy what she has believed for years and totally change how she looks at herself."

"I wish I could get my hands on him. They have absolute proof he died in that shooting but he took two other men with him and destroyed their families as well." Eddie stopped. "I just wonder if his parents knew. Deirdre doesn't seem to talk much about them and I can't find much on them in this country in the last 10 years."

Caleb eyed him and then spoke, "I have a contact at the federal level. Let me call him. He might be able to get us more information than we can lay our hands on. Let's keep this between us until I hear back from him. This is really going to hit Ben hard."

Eddie rose and then spoke, "It will. I just don't understand her parents. I wouldn't have let a girl of mine run like that."

Caleb shook his head. "Me either, even if she is scary."

Eddie laughed. "Frankie sure knows how to play that one. She's good for him. I don't think I've ever seen him so lighthearted."

"That she is. He's also finding his way back to God. That goes a long way."

Eddie nodded. "I'll keep digging. If I find out anything more, I'll call you."

Ben stood at the door, just ready to knock as Eddie opened it. "Wait will you, Eddie? Timothy has just brought in something I think you will both to look at."

Caleb looked up as Ben and Timothy entered. Eddie shut the door again and approached the desk as Timothy laid down an envelope.

"Frankie figured this out. He saw me with one of these, realized Deirdre had one, played with them and they went together. I have no idea what they are."

Caleb opened the envelope and slid out the joined stones. He studied them.

"Ben, Eddie, any idea?"

Ben shook his head. "All I can think of is a map, but that really doesn't fit what we're seeing."

Eddie studied them closer. "I think you're on the right track, Ben. They seem to be map when together. When separate, they are really meaningless.

It almost seems, though, that there should be another piece to it."

Caleb looked closer. "You could be right. Who do we have that is skilled in this? Whoever it is, get it to them and warn them I'll fire them if they even think about talking about it."

"That I will." Eddie picked up the envelope, slid the stones back in and left.

Ben and Timothy spoke with Caleb a bit longer, then Timothy left.

Ben hesitated, and Caleb watched him.

"Sit, Ben. Tell me what's up."

Ben sat and looked at his hands. "I really don't know, Caleb. I can feel something but I don't know what it is. Just this sense of impending doom."

Caleb nodded. "I know. That worries me. And no, Hannah has not given me a name yet." He paused. "It's more than that, isn't it?"

Ben nodded. "There is. Timothy is talking about moving back here and he loves working for the mission. He said Beth pushed him to come home and that's not her." He looked up at Caleb, distress in his face. "I just wish I knew what was going on. Deirdre's in trouble and now my own son is not being open with me, not like he usually is."

Caleb watched his friend. "I don't know what to say, Ben, except we'll pray and pray hard. God is still in control. He'll watch out for them." He smiled. "Besides, you have a niece who's very scary."

Ben laughed. "Who told you that? Let me guess, Frankie. He's just beginning to know that girl.

She has had experiences she has never talked about
and learned things you and I would never ever had
thought a woman should know."

The Watcher stood across the street from Deirdre's house. She was there. How she got away he couldn't understand. She had gotten out of a locked building and appeared back here as if nothing had happened. He needed to get to her but now she had two with her. He really did need what she had. Time was running out and running out quickly.

****

Frankie watched as Deirdre wandered her house, touching pictures and then objects. She just couldn't settle down.

"Deirdre." She looked at him and he patted the couch beside him. "Come, sit down. You're going to wear a hole in the floor otherwise."

She shook her head. "I can't. I'm still trying to figure out who those men were."

"No, come, sit."

She grudgingly did, crossing her arms in an angry manner. He angled his body so he could watch her.

She sighed and then uncrossed her arms. "I'm sorry. That's not a good attitude. I shouldn't take it out on you. I just want to go back to what it was last week. Being safe. Working at the youth centre. Living my life the way I want."

Frankie nodded. "I know you do, and you will." He watched emotions flickering across her face. "We'll get back there and soon. Caleb and Eddie are really good at digging."

"I know they are and so in Ben, but I don't want Ben involved. He's too close."

"What about Timothy?"

She thought about that and then looked at him. "There's something going on there. I have no idea what but for him to be here while the mission is working a crisis, that's not normal."

Frankie thought about that. "I would tend to agree with you. It's not in his character. But something had triggered him coming home and I am going out on a limb and says it's permanent. It feels like he has given up on the mission and is coming back here, not to lick his wounds but to go on with his life."

She laid her head back and then nodded. "I think you're right. He and I grew close when I came back here all those years ago. He definitely wants to talk with me but doesn't know how to approach it."

Frankie reached for her Bible on the end table. "Tell me again about those verses, the ones about calming the sea and about finding comfort and rest. You have helped me to find them. I think you need to find them yourself."

She turned her head to study him. He was right. She was growing tired in her heart and soul. She needed what resting in God would bring. She reached out her hand to him and thanked him.

Eddie tapped at Caleb's door and then entered. He sank heavily into one of the chairs.

Caleb finished his phone conversation and then looked at Eddie. His heart sank. He could tell he wasn't going to like what he would hear. A prayer rose to heaven as he waited.

"Do we need to pull Ben in?"

Eddie looked at him, then at the ceiling. "Read what I have and then decide. I'm thinking we'll have to but I'll let you make the call."

Caleb reached for the file and opened it. Eddie was right. Ben would need to be involved but it was going to really hurt.

"Your source is sure he's back here?"

Eddie nodded. "Same flight, two rows back, aisle seat opposite side. He paid dearly for that seat. He was watching her then."

"And he's in town?"

"He couldn't make the same flight she did that day. He tried hard. He flew in the next morning. He has brought two men back with him. I would suspect they're the ones who they had the run-in with. Nasty characters. If they catch up to Deirdre and Frankie again, it won't go so well. They dislike being bested but to be bested by a woman, that pretty much writes her obituary."

Caleb shuddered. "Then we'll have to make sure they stay safe. But where?"

"I know. It seems all our safe houses are known. Frankie might be safe on the streets, he has so many contacts and friends. Deirdre, she might be or she might not be. Depends on how scary she is."

Caleb shook his head. "I still can't believe what they were saying. I thought Frankie was good, but is she that much better?"

Eddie thought about that. "She has spent time in all those countries, in some pretty rough and rotten areas. It is completely possible that she has learned survival skills we would not even consider necessary here. She's quiet, doesn't say much but there's a hard layer in her that shows every once in a while.   I would say that it's about to be shown. Ben has said she can put a man down without really even trying."

Caleb studied the notes and then sighed. "We're going to have to talk to them but we'll need a plan first. Otherwise, she'll run and take Frankie, or he'll run and take her. We also need to watch for Timothy. If it was found out he had one of those stones, they'll be after him too."

"It just keeps growing, doesn't it? And you're sure Hannah hasn't given you a name?"

Caleb shook his head. "Not this time. The Lord's being silent with her."

"Which one of us gets to break the news?"

Caleb smiled. "You?"

"That's what I was afraid of. I get to go talk to a scary lady."

Caleb laughed as Eddie walked away, and then sobered. Things were taking a turn and he didn't like the way they were turning. His phone rang and he was delighted to hear his wife's voice. They spoke for a few minutes, then her tone changed.

"You have a name, don't you?"

"I do, Caleb, I do. It's just going to hurt so much when it comes out."

"Tell me."

She told him and he closed his eyes. She was right. It was really going to hurt. The name she gave was the same as the one Eddie had found.

Eddie tapped at Deirdre's door. Frankie checked to see who it was and then let him in, scanning the street as he did.

Deirdre stepped in from the kitchen, drying her hands on a towel.

"You don't look very happy, Eddie."

"I have some news, and I am not sure how to tell you."

"Are my parents, Ben and Marg, and Timothy all right?" At his nod, she continued, "Then what you have to say may not be as important as you think it is."

"Oh, it is. Come, sit, Deirdre. This will take a bit."

Deirdre watched him with apprehension, then sank to the couch. Frankie sat beside her, arm on the back of the couch for support. She watched Eddie as he tried to find words.

Eddie stared at her, grief tracing his face. "I really don't know how to begin, Deirdre. What I have to say will dramatically change your life." He paused. "What I am about to say we have verified with more than one source. This should have been done years ago and wasn't."

Deirdre shared a look with Frankie, then stared at Eddie. "What is it, Eddie?"

"How much do you know about what Finn was doing for the mission that last year?"

She shrugged. "Not that much, I don't think. He never really said and I was too busy in school to ask much. Why?"

"We have discovered that Finn was involved in black market trading of relief supplies. He was being bought off too by corrupt government officials and we suspect doing a little blackmailing on the side.

"That stone that he gave you has a clue to the information. Timothy found the second one in the mission warehouse, where Finn should never have been." Eddie paused. The hardest part was coming, and he could already see tears in her eyes. He saw Frankie's hand come down on her shoulder.

Eddie continued, "Now this is the really hard part. I know you have always wondered who the real target was. It was Finn except they didn't want him dead. They wanted the information he had hidden on those stones. We're not sure yet if there is another one or not." He paused. "There's no easy way to say what I have to say. You didn't have much of a wedding, did you?" She shook her head. "Didn't think so. A lady like you deserves all the bells and whistles, even back then, instead of a little tiny wedding like you had. I hate to tell you what I must." Eddie paused again. "Your minister was not a minister. He was an actor Finn hired. Your wedding certificate, it's a fake. You were never married, are not a widow. He was using you to get out of this country. He had plans to leave you at the hotel once you were checked in and disappear."

Deirdre's eyes were wide with shock and her hands covered her mouth. To think that this is what Finn had brought her to. Not married. Not widowed. Living a fake life. Frankie's hand was heavy on her shoulder. What must he think, she thought? He was becoming such a part of her life.

She stood and paced the room, thoughts running rampant through her mind. All these years, to come to this? And the men from overseas? Who hired them?

"Who hired them?"

"What?"

"The men. Who hired them? Someone from here or from overseas?"

Eddie was amazed at how quickly she got to the centre of it all. "That we are still working on, but they do not come from that country. It looks, from what my contact says, that time is running out and without the information Finn had on them, they will be facing multiple charges. Whoever has hired them will be facing multiple charges as well as murder charges."

Frankie shuddered. "And they really don't care then if Deirdre dies, so long as they don't?"

Eddie shook his head. "No, they don't. We still have to identify who is in charge here but we do know he returned on the same flight as you did, Deirdre, and tried to book a flight back here on your flight."

Deirdre stopped pacing to stare at him. "So now what? I obviously can't go back to the youth centre or church. I'm not going around my parents or Ben and Marg."

"Caleb feels Timothy may be a target as well if they have found out he had one of those stones. Timothy will be tucked away somewhere safe today and no one will know where."

"So where do we go?" Frankie asked.

Deirdre spun to look at him, shaking her head. "No way. I'm on my own with this one. You're not coming."

Frankie shook his head. "Nope, you're not scaring me today. You're stuck with me. Where you are, I'll be. I need you to remind me how to ride out a storm."

Deirdre kept shaking her head.

Finally, Eddie spoke up. "Actually, Caleb does plan for the two of you to be together. Where, we'll still trying to figure out. We could always send you back to the street, Frankie. Deirdre would protect you in those dark alleyways."

Frankie snickered as Deirdre spun to confront Eddie. "Not you, too. I am not that scary."

"Hey, I'm just repeating what I've been told."

At another snicker from Frankie, Deirdre spun and narrowed her eyes at him. "No more comments from the peanut gallery."

"Seriously, you two. We need to make some plans and make them now. We know the one who is after you is in town now. He has the two thugs that nabbed you here in town. He will not hesitate to harm or even kill anyone who gets in his way. We want to tuck you away somewhere and we have to figure it out. You won't be going to the youth centre. You won't be going to church. You will be staying away from your family. There's no give or take in that. They will use any of the venues to get to you."

Deirdre shivered and then sat down beside Frankie again. "I just can't take all this in. You are absolutely sure about Finn?"

At Eddie's nod, she hid her face in her hands. "Talk about betrayal. He never really intended me to go with him, did he?"

"No, he didn't. But I don't think he ever intended to die that day. He likely thought he had time to get away and didn't realize they were so close. I don't think we'll ever completely understand his motivation."

Frankie studied the woman sitting beside him. He knew he wanted her in his life all the time. He had come to love her heart and her mind. "So, Eddie, where do we go from here?" he asked.

"Right now, we keep you here. We have officers outside and around the block. Frankie, if you need anything from your place, give me a list. I'll make sure you get it. It's not safe for you to be going back there. Deirdre, I need you to pack an emergency bag. I won't tell you what to take. You know better than me. You've been through this too many times before."

She nodded. She then spoke, "Who tells my parents about Finn? Do I or do you? They never really gave me a lot of support at the time and I can't figure out why. Ben and Marg were more support than them."

"We'll look after it for you, Deirdre. We'll have officers from their town go and talk to them. Your Dad is still overseas. We are going to try and keep him there. Your Mom we'll have placed somewhere safe. I know they have people who can run the mission while they're away."

Deirdre snorted. "Like they have ever been given a chance." The men looked at her. "My parents never leave the mission together. There is always one or the other in charge. Not ever do they leave anyone else in charge. That's the way it's always been. That's why I left and came to Ben and Marg. They have time for each person in their lives. If you're going through a storm, you need someone there with you. I didn't have that at home. I do here."

Frankie was pacing. He knew Eddie and Caleb were working on a safe place, but how safe would it be? He could hear Deirdre in the kitchen. He wandered that way and stopped to watch her.

She looked up. "Here's a sandwich. I figured we may as well eat. Who knows when we'll next get a chance."

He studied her, then walked towards her. He took the plate from her hand and set it on the table, then reached to pull her into a hug. She stood stiff at first, then her arms came up and she hugged him back. He could feel the tears through his shirt. She just needed someone to hold her and let her mourn. She had much to mourn. Eddie had really thrown a lot at her today.

She stepped back, swiping at her eyes. He reached around her, wet a cloth and then gently washed her face. His hand lingered on her cheek, then she turned away.

"Eat up. Who know when Eddie will be back to take us who knows where."

"You need to eat too. I won't if you won't." Frankie watched until she finally made herself a sandwich and dropped herself into a chair. He poured them both cups of coffee and then sat down. He reached for her hand as he said a blessing on their food.

She tugged at her hand when he was done but he didn't release it. She looked up at him. "Don't say anything, Frankie. Just don't say anything."

"I don't intend to. The only thing I was going to say is what you tell me. God is here in the storm. He has called us to come and find rest in the midst of the turmoil. Will you remember that and run to Him?"

She lowered her eyes and then sighed. "Yes. It's just so hard."

"I know, darling, I know. Now eat up before you need to get scary with the bad guys." That earned him a smack on the arm.

****

The Watcher studied the house. He knew they were in there. He had not seen them leave. There were, however, police officers all around. There would not be an opportunity for him or his men to get to them. He would need to wait for that. But time was running out. He needed that information and quickly. Those two would pay for this delay and so would anyone else who got in his way.

****

Frankie sank down into a chair in the dim light of the living room and rested his head back. His gaze went to Deirdre. She had finally curled up under a blanket on the couch and dozed off. His heart broke for the woman he loved. She had been dealt such a blow or two today. He prayed for healing for her, for comfort, for strength, for protection. He prayed for safety for her family. He prayed for wisdom and safety of the law enforcement teams that were working around the clock. He felt like he was in a free fall with a parachute that may not open until too late.

Deirdre stirred slightly in her sleep. He could tell it wasn't restful. His eyes slid shut and he slept as well. He had been running on empty he felt for so long and he just couldn't not sleep.

Frankie stirred as he heard Caleb and Eddie enter. Ben was with them. Ben stopped by the couch and stared down at his niece. Frankie saw the sadness in his face and understood that he had been told about Finn.

Frankie headed to the kitchen with Caleb and Eddie. They spoke in low tones, then turned as Ben entered the room.

"Are we set?" Caleb asked.

"I think so." Eddie looked around. "Are you two ready to go?"

"About as ready as we can be." Frankie hesitated. "Before we go, can we pray?"

The four men bowed their heads and Ben led them to God's throne. Frankie walked away from that prayer humbled by the power of God he could feel in the room. Who knew what was coming next but God did and God was in control.

Ben touched his niece's shoulder and called her name. She stirred and then sat up. He sat beside her and gathered her close for a few minutes like he would a daughter. They had a few minutes of soft whispered conversation. Then Ben stood.

"We're set. The plan is in place?"

"It is and hopefully we can throw off those men until we can find them."

Lights went off in the house and Frankie and Deirdre were led out through the garage to a car waiting inside. Two officers who resembled them in height and build went into the house and then out the front door with Eddie and Caleb. They hustled them to a waiting car and then left, escort cars in place. Ben waited patiently. They were in no rush.

Finally word came from Eddie that they were being followed. Ben climbed behind the wheel of Deirdre's car.

He turned to the two. "Down on the floor on the back seat. We want it to look as if it's just in case someone has remained behind. No one will question me taking your car, Deirdre, if you're on the run, which is what we have tried to put across. They know I was with Caleb and Eddie and that they left with you two."

Ben backed out of the garage and then hit the remote to shut it. He looked around, didn't see anyone and drove off. He seemed to be driving around in circles but in fact he was watching for tails. Not seeing any, he headed for his next destination, the impound yard at the department. He drove up to the gate and then punching in his password, entered. He drove to the very end of the lot and stopped.

"Just stay down and wait," he cautioned. "We still don't know if they followed us."

Frankie moved restlessly. Crouching in the back seat of a car didn't sit well with his almost six-foot frame. Deirdre reached out for his hand and he clasped hers in his. How long they had waited, he didn't know, but finally Ben moved.

Ben turned slightly to speak with them. "You are going to get out on the passenger side and get behind that truck over there. Wait for me once you do. I'm going to move Deirdre's car and park it well out of sight. I'll be back." He looked around again, and then said, "Move."

Frankie slid the door opened and grabbing his pack, pulled Deirdre with him and out of sight. He hoped Ben was right and no one was around. He could feel the hair on his neck rising once again. Not now, Lord, he prayed. Let us please get away. Keep us safe. He could feel Deirdre's hand on his back. They waited.

A soft sound came to them and they tensed.

"Frankie, Deirdre." It was Ben. "It looks clear. Come on, let's get you out of here." He led them to another vehicle, an older beat up sedan. "Don't worry about the looks. It's got lots of power under the hood." When they were inside, he spoke, "Stay down on the floor until we get out of here. There's a blanket to cover yourselves with."

Frankie reached for the blanket, then his hand stopped. "What else is back here?"

"Just a couple of garbage bags stuffed with paper to keep it light. Part of the disguise."

Frankie grumbled under his breath. Deirdre laughed softly.

"Behave yourself, Franklin, or I'll find my scary friends."

Ben shook his head at their nonsense. They did need some levity in the situation but he really wasn't sure if this was the time.

He pulled up to the gate and punching in code once again, pulled through. He scanned the area. So far, so good. It didn't look as if anyone had seen them. Now to go to Part B of Caleb's plan.

****

The Watcher stood in Deirdre's house. He had managed to get in and had walked through the entire place. She was not here. It didn't look like she had been for a while, but his men were adamant they had followed her here. And that man was with her as well. He had stood and watched. He was sure that it was not them who had been taken away with the escort. Who had taken her out of his clutches once again? Fists raised to the heavens, he cursed. Someone would pay and pay dearly. Now, who would he start with?

****

Ben pulled up to the curb in front of a coffee shop and looked around. He didn't see anyone but he would wait for a bit.

"You can pull the blanket off, but stay down as much as you can. Be ready to cover back up if you have to."

"What the plan, Ben?" Frankie wanted to know.

"You'll find out soon. Caleb should be here soon. First, let me have your phones. They're finding you when they shouldn't be. Next, your backpacks will be staying in this car. We have other ones for you to take with you."

Frankie nodded. "That makes sense. They've been in our homes. They could very easily have planted tracking devices. I am assuming you swept for bugs?"

Ben nodded, barely visible in the dim light. "We did. We didn't find anything."

Frankie thought about that. "Then it is likely our phones. I wondered why they didn't take them from us. That just never made any sense."

"No, it never did. I'll have one of our techs go over them. Here, put these in your shoes." Ben handed over tiny devices. "They'll let us track you, but they won't be able to. We won't lose you." Ben sighed. "Deirdre, how sure are you that the men are from overseas?"

She stared at him as she thought about what he asked. "Their accents were right on. I guess it doesn't mean they're from overseas. I assumed and now that assumption is coming back to haunt me. Do you have proof they're not?"

"That's what we're running with right now. Whoever is after you is not from that country. It wouldn't make sense for them to have hired men from overseas and brought them here. It would make more sense to have found thugs here and then used them. We're working on that angle."

"Whoever they are, they certainly are stereotypical. But it has never made sense. Why target us?"

"We've determined that you're the target. Frankie is collateral. They won't really care if either of you live once they get the information they need."

Deirdre shuddered. Frankie reached for her hand as she said, "That is just plain sick."

Car lights crossed their vehicle and Frankie reached to pull the blanket over them once again. Ben pulled away from the curb and followed the car.

Frankie could smell the water as they pulled in. They were near the lake. Ben climbed out of the car and walked away. They heard his footsteps come back and then the back door of the car opened.

"Come on, you two. We have another mode of transportation waiting for you."

Frankie looked around as he turned to help Deirdre. He kept hold of her hand as they followed Ben towards the dock. A small cabin cruiser was waiting there.

"No, don't tell me. You're really not, are you?" Deirdre's face was pale. "I can't do that."

Ben looked at her with compassion. "You can and you will. It may be the only means we have to keep you alive." He sighed and looked up. "I know how hard it will be but you need to. Besides you can put on your scary face and scare all the fish away."

Frankie laughed softly at her outraged cry, then watched in amazement as she straightened her shoulders and walked toward the boat.

Ben watched her. "Marg and I have never been able to figure out her fear of boats. She can swim, canoe, kayak, but don't ask her to get on a boat. She flat out refuses, or did until today." Ben looked at Frankie. "She's doing it for you, to keep you alive."

Frankie stared at Ben, then at Deirdre. He nodded. That made sense, she would do whatever she had to for those in her circle of family and friends.

"We're taking you across the lake to an island. We're hoping this way, they don't find you. But they always seem to. Eddie will be with you. We've also had a couple of fellows come in from a neighbouring department to help. That way it's not obvious we've pulled men from ours."

Frankie thought about that. "What about the youth centre? Who's keeping it going?"

"The board met. They have asked Peter, her assistant, to step up for now. He's good with the kids, almost as good as she is. He's really ready to take over if she ever decided she wanted out."

"Can't see that happening," Frankie replied.

"I know her. She's distancing herself, getting ready to step back. It's how she works. Come on, let's get you away from here."

****

The man stepped from the shadows and watched as the boat pulled away from the shore. He had found them. He just didn't know where they were headed. It had to be somewhere along the lake shore. He would search until he did find them. Then he would let the Watcher know. They would pay a handsome price for their trouble.

Frankie wandered through the cottage they had been tucked away in. He still didn't feel safe. He knew Deirdre was still sleeping, he had checked on her about an hour ago. Eddie was somewhere around, likely outside doing his rounds. The two officers assigned to them were also around. He knew them slightly but not well. He prayed Caleb hadn't made a mistake in bringing them in.

Frankie finally sank into an easy chair and stared at the fireplace. It was a warm day but he envisioned the flickering flames that could illuminate that area. His head went back and he found himself lost in thought.

What had happened to his father? He just disappeared one day. His mother never talked about him much. Then one day, he came home to find his mother was gone as well. At least she left him a note, telling him she had to leave, that there was something only she could take care of. He always wondered where she was and if she was okay. There were times he felt very lonely. Maybe that's why he had been such a good cop on the street—he knew how they felt. He decided that when this whole thing going on right now was over he would try and track her down, just to make sure she was fine.

He turned his head as he heard a door shut. Eddie had come in from the outside and stopped to pour himself a cup of coffee. He looked over at Frankie, then poured a second one. He handed it to him, then sat down in the other easy chair.

"Everything okay?" Frankie asked, watching Eddie closely.

"So far, it seems to be. But I just don't know. Something feels off."

Frankie nodded. He knew that feeling. "I have the same feeling."

It had been a long day. Night had fallen. Deirdre looked around the cottage and sighed. This just wasn't home. She wanted to be home so badly, to go back to her kids at the centre. She just wanted this to be over and who knew how much longer it would continued. She watched Frankie and Eddie talking in the kitchen, solemn looks on their faces. They were worried, but hadn't talked to her yet about their worries. She looked around once more and then grabbing her Bible headed for the bedroom she had been assigned. Spending time in the Bible and prayer just seemed to be the right thing to do.

Frankie looked up as her door clicked shut. He hadn't been avoiding her but he just wanted to know what was going on and what Caleb and Ben were planning. Eddie wasn't saying much but he did say they were working on the mystery and had good leads. He hoped that soon they would uncover who was behind the abduction and make an arrest.

Eddie stretched. It had been a long day and wasn't over yet. He was still waiting to hear from Caleb or Ben. Like Frankie, he wasn't too sure of the other officers—he had never worked with them before and these were friends he was trying to protect.

One of the officers entered. "All clear, so far. How did you want to work the night shift?"

Eddie thought and then said, "If we take two hours shifts, we'll all get some kind of rest. I'll take the first watch. You two get some sleep. It's going to be a long few days and we need to conserve our energy."

The other man nodded and then looked around.

Eddie spoke. "There's a bedroom at the end of the room. It has twin beds. You two can have it. I'll bunk in with Frankie when I need to."

Frankie watched as the man headed for the bedroom. He could feel a presence around him that he didn't like.

Eddie's eyes fell on Frankie and he stopped. "What's up, Frankie?"

Frankie shook his head. "I don't know, I really don't. Just that feeling. I used to get it on the street."

Eddie nodded. "You never lose that sense even when you stop being a street cop or undercover. It's yours for life. I have the same feeling, that something is about to happen, and we can't stop it." He clapped Frankie on the shoulder. "Go, get some rest."

****

The two men silently beached their canoe. They had come prepared to take those two with them. It really didn't matter to them if others died in the process. It would be messy, but messy was how they lived. They gestured to each other and then approached the cabin, splitting up to each take a side. A quick movement and the guard went down.

They approached the cabin on silent feet and cautiously opened the door. The main room was empty. They crept in and listened at the doors. They opened one—Frankie lay asleep.   With silent gestures, they approached the bed.

Frankie's eyes flew open as he felt a presence in the room.   A quick blow and he was rendered helpless. One of the men slung him over his shoulder and walked cautiously back out.   The other headed for another room.   Peeking in he saw it was the officers, sound asleep.   He went to the next room, cautiously opening the door.   It was Deirdre's room. He once again approached the bed. She didn't stir. A quick movement with a cloth and bottle and he knew she wouldn't. He gathered her up and left.

****

Eddie stirred at hands shook him, pain radiating through his skull.   What had happened? Hands helped him to sit and then to rise. Once in the cabin, he sank into a chair, trying to figure out what was going on. He raised pain-filled eyes to see Caleb standing in front of him.   His eyes slid closed.   Not again, he thought, please not again.   My heart can't take it, not being able to protect my friends.

Caleb crouched in front of him.   "Eddie, are you okay? No, don't shake your head. It will make it hurt worse than it is. You had a heavy blow."

"Frankie and Deirdre?"

Caleb shook his head.   "They're gone. Whoever took them is good. Not a sound. We did find evidence in Deirdre's room that she was drugged."

Eddie stared at Caleb.   "I'm getting tired of this, Caleb. How are we supposed to protect them? We do our best and they still get found."

Caleb stood and nodded. "I know. I just wish I knew how. Ben's working that angle. I hate to tell him Deirdre's missing again."

Eddie drew a deep breath. "That is not going to be fun. How's the investigation going?"

Caleb was silent and Eddie just watched him. More was going on that what Caleb was ready to say. Caleb sighed and then turned to sit.

"It's really getting messy. The ones involved would not be who you expected." He turned to look at Eddie and started stating names. Eddie's face showed his shock.

"Never saw those coming."

"None of us did. This is really going to hurt when it comes out."

"What about the two officers from the other town? Are they okay?"

Caleb nodded. "They are. I don't know how they didn't hear anything though. They slept right through it until morning. They realized you hadn't come to wake them, went looking, found you and then Frankie and Deirdre missing. I was already on my way over when I got the call."

"You've done your best, Caleb."

"I know but it sure doesn't feel like it." Caleb was frustrated. He now had to try and track where Frankie and Deirdre were. They could be anywhere and his gut told him they were running short of time. "Hannah did give me a name."

Eddie stilled and watched Caleb. He could tell it was not what he would want to hear. At the name, his eyes closed. No, it wasn't possible. Caleb was right. This was really going to hurt and hurt bad.

"Come on, Eddie. Let's get you home and get your head looked at. It's going to be a long few days, I think."

"It will. I feel like we're in the middle of a cat 5 hurricane or and EF5 tornado. Just have to keep remembering that Christ calmed the storm on Galilee. He will calm this storm too."

****

The Watcher stood in the dimness of the hall and watched at the two who had tried to elude him were carried in and down the stairs to the basement. Soon, he would have want he wanted. Soon, he would be able to destroy those who had tried to stop him. Soon. He felt victorious.

Frankie moaned as he tried to move. His head hurt and he didn't remember running into anything. His eyes cracked open and shut again. The light was just too bright. He tried opening them again and this time he could focus. He looked around and then up. A basement, he thought. A room in the basement. There would be no way they could get out of the windows. They were small.

He rolled over onto his back. The pounding in his head was easing off some. He didn't see Deirdre. He sat up quickly and then regretted it at the fresh pounding behind his eyes. He scanned the room. She wasn't there. Where was she?

He staggered as he came to his feet, caught his balance and headed for the door. The knob turned under his hand and he pulled the door open. Cautiously, he stopped through. Deirdre was laying on the floor, not moving. Heart sinking, he stumbled to his knees beside her and reached out a hand. She was alive. Thank you, God, he whispered.

He looked around. He needed to find a way out of these rooms and soon. The windows weren't much of an option—they were small. The door opposite him was locked and he doubted that Deirdre would still have her knife, if the men had done their job right this time. Walls were solid.

He sank back to the floor near Deirdre, despair in his being. There was just no way out. He looked at the ceiling and prayed. God, You know where we are. You have a way out. Calm the storm within me and help me to think.

The sound of the door unlocking caught his attention. He turned. A larger man stood there. He recognized him as one of the men from before. Nothing was said as a tray of food was set down. The man's hard gaze locked with his own. Frankie could barely contain the shudder he felt at the evil in that gaze. The man backed away and locked the door once again.

Frankie laid his head back on the wall. At least for now, it looked as if they wanted them to stay alive if they were bringing in meals. He had no desire to eat. He raised his head and studied the tray. There were cups of fluid, what he couldn't tell from where he sat, but he wasn't prepared to even taste them and he wouldn't let Deirdre either.

Deirdre stirred. She had a dry bad taste in her mouth. She wondered where she was. It didn't feel like the bed she had laid down on last night. She sat up, then waited as her head steadied. She looked around and saw Frankie sitting beside her, eyes on her.

"Where are we?" She had to clear her voice to continue. "What happened?"

Frankie watched her, then sighed. "You're not going to like it. We're back in the hands of those men."

"How?"

"That's what I want to know. Something failed in the security somewhere along the line."

"So now what?"

Frankie shrugged. "I don't see a way out of here. Windows are too small. That door over there is locked. No other openings in the wall."

"Did you get a look at anyone?"

"Just the one who brought in a tray of food."

"Food?"

He nodded. "Food and drink. It looks as if they want to keep us alive, at least for now." He paused and then continued, "But we're not eating the food or drinking whatever is in those cups. I won't take a chance on them being drugged or poisoned."

"How long do you think we've been here, wherever here is?"

"Going by the sun, I'd say it's around 10 in the morning. So sometime after midnight I would suspect, maybe eight hours?"

Deirdre stood and walked around the room they were in and then into the room Frankie had awakened in.

"Frankie, come here."

Frankie followed her voice. She was standing at the far end of the room, running her hand down the wall. "It sounds hollow behind here. I wonder what's back here."

"It's a solid wall, Deirdre."

She shook her head. "No, it looks like it's just drywall. We could try some fancy moves and kick through it."

Frankie stared at her. "Kick our way through? Seriously? Deirdre, you have no idea what's on the other side of that."

She nodded. "I know, but we really could find out. It may be the opening out we need."

He shook his head, grabbed her hand and pulled her away. "We'll talk about that. By the way, do you still have your knife?"

She felt her pockets. "I do."

He stared at her again. "You do? They cleaned out our pockets." He stopped, then waved his hands. "I really don't want to know. Your scary friends again right?"

She smacked his arm. "My friends are scary. They have knowledge that they were willing to share. They're scholars in the university of life."

Frankie shook his head as he followed her from the room. "We'll think about that wall, scary one. Right now, come sit down. We need to pray. God will provide us a way."

Deirdre looked at him and nodded. "That He will. But are we prepared for the way He may take?"

Frankie's eyes sought her. He read in hers the realization she had come to. Like him, she wondered if they would make it out alive.

Deirdre suddenly felt for her shoes. "Do you still have it?"

Frankie looked at her in surprise.

"Do you still have it? What Ben gave us?"

His eyes brightened and he felt for his shoe. He nodded.

She sat back. "Good."

Frankie and Deirdre stared at each other. Caleb could track them but would it be in time?

Caleb stood looking around the conference room. It was a frenzy of activity. He had officers tracking the men they suspected of the abduction, other verifying facts for the case. Another two were on a computer, trying to trace the GPS units Ben had given them.

He turned as Eddie came up and stood beside him.

"I feel so frustrated, Caleb. This should not have happened."

"I know, Eddie. It shouldn't. Those two officers will have some hard questions to answer."

"How's Ben taking this?"

Caleb sought for words. "Not well, I'm afraid. His faith is shaking right now. I sent him home to Marg. I gather Beth is heading this way too. Haven't heard about Brett though."

"Brett. Now there's someone I would really like to talk to. He had better have some good answers when I do."

"All in good time, Eddie, all in good time."

Caleb moved away from Eddie towards the officers search for the GPS tracking.

"What do we have, Megan?"

"Provided they still have their shoes on, here's the address. They're not moving from there, but I am picking up some subtle shifting."

"Thank you, Megan. You may have just saved their lives."

Caleb turned and searched the room. Finding who he wanted, he crossed to the ETF leader. "Doug, get your men ready. Here's the address we think they're at." Caleb quickly scrawled it for him. "Get out there and let me know what you find. I'll be there as soon as I can get everything organized from here."

Doug nodded and then looked up. "We'll find them, Caleb. Frankie has been there more than once when we had situations in the down town area. We'll bring them home."

Frankie and Deirdre turned to watch as the door opened. They were resigned to whatever was happening. They just prayed their friends would find them quickly. The door swung back against the wall, and the two men who had abducted them stood there.

Deirdre's breath caught softly as the next man entered. Her fingers grasped Frankie's tightly.

Nothing was said as he studied the two. Frankie could feel evil shimmering all around his body. He knew Deirdre was tense, he could feel it. Why he didn't know.

Then, Deirdre spoke. "Meet Finn's father, Frankie. Stu McNabb."

Frankie shot a look at her and then back to the man.

"Still have your attitude, I see, Deirdre. Finn hated that about you."

Deirdre was shaking her head. "No, actually, he didn't. You did. You did because I refused to back down from you each and every time we had a confrontation. So tell me. Did you have your son killed? Were you the one who insisted on the wedding that wasn't a wedding?"

McNabb stared at her. "The wedding that wasn't a wedding? Oh no, my dear, it was a legitimate wedding."

Deirdre was shaking her head. "No, actually, it wasn't. Friends of mine have proof it wasn't. Finn was planning on running that day, and you knew it. You had him killed to stop him." She studied him. "Just how deep does this go?"

Frankie was worried. She was baiting the man and he looked as if he was ready to snap.

McNabb was shaking his head. "You know nothing, my dear. Absolutely nothing. Now, you are going to answer questions for me. The life of your friend there depends on it."

She was shaking her head. "No, I don't think so. I have no idea what you want. None whatsoever."

The older man stared at her. She stared back. This was the father of the man she thought she had loved and who she thought had loved her. It was all a sham. She could see the changes in him, changes wrought by evil and greed. She was not ready to go down without a fight, and she knew Frankie was the same.

Caleb stood near Doug. "You're sure they're in there?"

"Pretty sure. The vehicles you had tagged are there. Megan says the GPS is still reading here. We'll have to go in to make sure."

Caleb nodded. "I have warrants on the way, just to be nice and legal. I don't want any loopholes to trip us up."

"Wise move. I'll give you a heads up when we're ready to move in."

Ben stopped beside Caleb. "Any word yet?"

Caleb shook his head. "You shouldn't be here, Ben."

"No, I need to be. That's my niece in there. I'll stay back out of the way, but I need to be here."

"Has Beth arrived?"

"Not yet but she was almost here. Timothy came home. He refused to stay away."

"I thought he might. He's too much like his father. How's Marg handling it?"

Ben gave a small smile. "She's on her knees, Caleb. She's on her knees. She's also called the prayer chain and set that in motion."

Caleb nodded as he looked around. Eddie was headed his way.

"I'm sorry, Ben." Eddie's voice broke into Ben's thought. "I wasn't able to stop them."

Ben turned to study his friend. "No, you couldn't, Eddie. There are only two men here on earth who can, and they don't appear willing to stop this. God is allowing it to happen, only He knows why."

Ben stopped, unable to continue. Caleb and Eddie shared a glance, then turned to watch the activity quietly unfolding in front of them.

Frankie was pulled to his feet and shoved through the door into the adjoining room. The door slammed shut. Deirdre watched, then turned eyes to

McNabb. She was getting really frightened but struggled to control it.

"Don't worry, my dear. He will be fine."

Deirdre shook her head. "I doubt it. I'm beginning to see just how depraved you are."

The man's lips curled back in anger, then he smoothed out his face. "I don't think so. I am not depraved. I just want what is mine."

The two men entered and Deirdre caught just a glimpse of Frankie's crumpled form. Please, Lord, let him live. I don't care about me, but let him live.

"Stand up, my dear. You have some questions to answer."

Deirdre looked at him and shook her head. "I have nothing to answer. I don't have whatever it is you're looking for."

He stared at her, anger beginning to rise within him. He motioned to the two men, who hauled her to her feet and held her tightly.

"That, my dear, was a mistake. You will pay for your defiance."

He stepped towards her. "Where are the stones?"

"What stones?" Deirdre was good, she knew how to keep a calm, clear face in times of danger.

"You know exactly what stones I want."

She shook her head. "I don't have them. I have no idea where they are."

He stared at her, then motioned to one of his men. Deirdre had a feeling things were just about to get worse and she wasn't going to like them much. Her heart lifted to God for strength and protection.

Doug headed back to Caleb. "We got imaging up. We have four in the basement right now. The fifth one has come back upstairs." He listened to his radio for a minute. "No, we have three upstairs now. It's your call, Caleb."

Caleb studied the house, and then nodded. "When you're ready. It's your call as to when and how but we need to do this."

Caleb hadn't asked about the other two, Doug noted. He was worried. Imaging was showing that the two forms in the basement weren't moving.

Doug's team moved in silently and quickly. They breached the doors and were inside before the three men knew what was happening. A flurry of activity and the three were handcuffed and being led out of the house.

Stu McNabb stared in hatred at Caleb. "This is unwarranted. I'll have your badge and your job."

Caleb held up his warrants. "We wouldn't have these if it was unwarranted. The judge agreed with us. We have you on solid evidence, McNabb. Get him out of here."

Caleb strode towards the house. The ETF team was finishing clearing it. Doug appeared at the door and yelled for paramedics. Caleb stepped to the side to watch, Eddie coming up beside him.

"I am praying that means they're still alive, Caleb."

"Me, too, Eddie. Where's Ben?"

"He waiting by your car. He won't come in until and unless you call him. He doesn't want anything to be said that would hinder your case against McNabb."

Caleb nodded. "Let him know I'll be back out as soon as I can. Round up your evidence teams, Eddie. I know you have them waiting back there."

Caleb stepped into the opulent house. He looked around and felt sorrow building up in him. Money that should have gone for good had ended up in the pockets of a greedy, depraved man. Lives had been changed and ruined because of him.

He looked up to see Doug approaching, a grim look on his face. His heart sank. Were they too late?

"They're alive, Caleb. They're alive but not in great shape. I was just coming to find you."

Caleb followed Doug down the stairs and into the rooms in the basement. He stopped as he saw Deirdre's crumpled form on the floor. She had taken a beating and a bad one he assumed. He stepped around the paramedics working on her to the doorway of the next room. Another team was working on Frankie. He could see he had been beaten severely as well. They were getting ready to place him on the stretcher when he heard his name called.

He turned and walked back to where they were working on Deirdre. He heard a whimper from her as her hand was moved, and tears started to trickle down her face. He crouched down beside the head paramedic.

A gasp from the other side caught his attention and he looked. The younger paramedic had a look of horror on his face. "They really didn't, did they? They really didn't break her fingers?"

Caleb's eyes shot to her right hand. Dave, the senior paramedic, was gently holding her wrist and cradling her hand. He nodded. "They did. I want to get my hands on them." Dave looked sick at what he was seeing. Caleb knew he had served overseas as a medic and had seen things he wouldn't talk about. This was really hitting him hard. "I need a splint, then we can get an IV started, get her loaded and on her way."

Caleb reached to brush a tear from Deirdre's face. He really didn't know how he felt right now. He stood and looked around. If there had been something to kick, he just might have kicked it. He struggled to control the nausea he felt. He watched as the team carried Frankie past and up the stairs. He knew he needed to go too, but he wanted to wait for Deirdre. He wanted to be the one who talked to Ben.

Ben stood and watched as they loaded Frankie's stretcher in the ambulance and then left, police escort in place. He turned to watch the house, waiting for Deirdre to come out, waiting for Caleb to come to talk to him, just waiting. His heart sank as he tried to imagine what was going on. No one was saying much. He lifted his eyes and prayed harder than he had in a long time.

Eddie stepped through the door and came to stand by Caleb. He studied the men working on Deirdre and then saw the splint on her hand.

"No," he said. "They didn't, did they?"

Caleb nodded. "They did. Dave figures two fingers and at least one bone of the third. How she stood that, I'll never know."

Eddie looked sick and he had to turn away. They had both seen some very cruel things on the job, but he thought this just might be the worse. "How do we tell Ben, and then her family?"

Caleb shook his head. "I have no idea, Eddie."

He watched as they carried her up the stairs and through the house to the stretcher waiting outside. He stepped past them and saw Ben headed for him. He reached out and stopped Ben with a hand on his chest.

Ben stared past him at his niece, then at Caleb.

"She's alive?"

Caleb nodded. "She is. She's had a bad beating, as has Frankie. There's something else, though, Ben." He stopped unable to continue for a minute. Ben's eyes bore into his. "They broke fingers on her hand, more than likely to get her to talk."

Ben's eyes closed, then an angry look covered his face. He pushed past Caleb to where his niece lay. He reached out a hand and touched her hair. At a word from the paramedics, he stepped back and watched them move to the waiting ambulance. He followed and climbed in before the doors closed, without speaking a word.

Caleb watched, then turned to Eddie. "Go, follow them. Stick with him. I don't know what he's thinking."

Eddie nodded and headed for his car. This was one of the hardest times he could ever remember. He knew Marg and Beth would be brought to the hospital. Timothy would be as well.

Caleb finally was able to make his way to the hospital. He was bone-deep weary, almost ready to drop in his tracks. Today had been one of the hardest days he had ever faced. He searched the waiting room and saw Hannah with Marg and Beth. Timothy sat near them. Caleb saw his brother, Joshua, there and knew Hannah had called him to come sit with Timothy. He nodded. She was wise, his wife, knowing what to ask for and do almost before he had framed the thought.

Eddie met him and motioned him back outside.

"What's the word, Eddie?"

Eddie stared across the parking lot. Officers were milling around inside and out, there to provide support for their own. "Frankie is still unconscious.

They did a number on him, that's for sure. Bruised, if not fractured ribs. His left wrist is fractured. The doctors think he has a concussion. They're waiting for imaging results."

"And Deirdre?"

Eddie had trouble speaking, then drew in a breath. "How can they treat a woman like that? The doctors said much more of a beating, she would be dead. Even now they're not sure what effect the beating will have. Her hand—they have her in surgery right now trying to do reconstruction on it. They have no idea if they can fix it or if she'll have good movement in those fingers." He stopped, having to control his emotions. "Who in their right mind does that?"

"They're not in their right mind, Eddie. That's the problem." Caleb looked behind him into the Emergency department. "Where do they have Frankie?"

"Room 6 right now." He stopped. "Deirdre's dad is on his way back. Beth figures he'll be here tomorrow."

Caleb nodded. "Thanks. Go home, Eddie, go home to Peggy. You need some rest. Spend time in prayer with your wife."

Eddie stood for a time, then nodded. "You need to rest too, Caleb. Hannah's here. Go, be with her."

"I will, once I find out how Frankie is."

Eddie started to walk away, then stopped and turned to face Caleb. "She can't have said anything. Most people, including men, would have caved at the first bone. They were at two and a half fingers with her." Having said that, he turned and walked away.

Caleb stared at him, lost in thought. He was right. She hadn't given them what they wanted. He shook his head. Frankie, you have a very special lady there, I hope you know that.

Later, Caleb stood at Frankie's bedside. He had been moved to a private room. His face was battered as were his hands. His left wrist was in a cast. Caleb studied his friend. Once again he was struck with how man's depravity would show itself. Lives lost, beatings, theft, greed. When would it end?

He knew there would be a guard at Frankie's door. He still wasn't sure they had everyone involved in custody. There had been many volunteers. His department was reeling from this. Men and women both had volunteered to watch Deirdre's room. He knew men and women were in the waiting room. He still felt helpless.

He went to find Ben. Ben had refused to go home. He had sent Marg, Beth and Timothy back home. Beth had not argued and Caleb found that real strange. He knew if that had been Hannah, nothing and no one would have made her leave.

He found Ben outside, sitting at a picnic table provided for the staff breaks. He sat across from him, not saying anything.

"Why, Caleb? Why?" Ben anguished voice caught at Caleb.

Caleb shook his head. "It's coming together, Ben. We're working through it all. There was a lot of evidence gathered from McNabb's office today. We need to work through that." Caleb stopped speaking. "It's going to get a lot messier, Ben."

Ben nodded. "I know."

Caleb stood, laid his hand on his friend. "I won't tell you to go home; I know it won't do any good. Get some sleep if you can. Call me if you need to. I'm heading home but I'll be back in the morning." Caleb walked away before Ben could speak.

Morning came too soon as far as Caleb was concerned. He was at the office almost before he felt he had slept any. The investigation was really ramping up. His team was good and they were ferreting out information McNabb thought he had hidden away permanently.

After spending time with the investigators, Caleb headed for the hospital. This was going to be one of those days, and Caleb didn't feel ready for it.

He went to check on Frankie, figuring this was going to be the easier of the tasks. He nodded at the officer at the door and then pushed the door open to enter. He stopped at the side of the bed and watched his friend. Still out of it, he guessed, or sleeping, he couldn't tell. He winced at the bruising and cuts he saw. He thanked God that Frankie was still alive.

He turned and walked away towards Deirdre's room. He once more stopped at a bedside. Deirdre was heavily sedated he knew for the pain. He studied the bandages on her hand and wondered if they had been able to reconstruct it sufficiently so she would regain use of it. He studied her face next. He stayed there for a while, then walked away, walked towards the waiting room, a sense of foreboding in his thoughts.

He found Ben standing by himself, staring out the window. Caleb stopped beside him.

"How is she? I was just in there and she's still out."

Ben nodded. "They have her sedated, partly for the pain." Ben's eyes filled with tears. "I can't imagine the pain she must have been put through.

The doctors said they were able to pretty much reconstruct the hand back to what it was. The little finger, they're not sure about. But one thing is for certain, she'll always have trouble with that hand. They didn't think there was nerve damage but they have to wait for the swelling to go down." Ben stopped speaking. "Why, Caleb? Why did those monsters think it was so worth while?"

Caleb shook his head. "I don't know, Ben. We're trying to get that information, but we're in early stages yet. I'm sorry about Brett. I had no idea when all this started that he would be involved."

Ben's eyes slid shut in sorrow. "I didn't either. I knew he had been changing over the years, not the same as when we grew up. When Deirdre went through what she did and came to us, he never came after her. He never called. Never wrote. Just went on as if it didn't matter. I guess it really didn't. Eddie was over late last night and let me know how that part of the investigation is going. I've stepped back from it so I won't compromise any of it. You were wise not to involve me in that part." Ben stopped, then turned to face the waiting room, his eyes seeking out his sister-in-law. "What part did Beth have?"

"We're still working on that part as well. Once we can get it all figured out, then we'll move with charges. Unfortunately, we have to arrest Brett now. I have officers waiting here with the warrant."

Ben nodded. "I'm surprised he would even come, given what's happened."

"He has to. He needs to save face. He doesn't know what all is out in the open." Caleb watched his friend. Sorrow coursed through him as he thought of what was coming. Nothing could prevent the end to the steps Brett had put in motion years ago.

A figure at the waiting room door had Ben stiffened. Caleb looked up and saw it was Brett. Beth went to him, spoke to him and led him down the hall. Marg looked over at Ben and then came to him. He wrapped his arm around her.

"How is Beth taking this?"

"Strangest thing, Ben. She's not concerned. It's as if Deirdre is a stranger's child. Doesn't make sense."

Caleb had a thought and excused himself. He went to find Eddie; he knew he was around here somewhere. A few words and Eddie had left, on his way to do some more research. Both had suspicions and Eddie was determined to prove them.

About thirty minutes later, Brett and Beth returned from their daughter's room. Caleb studied them. There was just something not there. They didn't have that concern about them they should.

Brett spoke with Marg and then turned to Ben. He stopped in front of Ben and reached out his hand to shake hands. Ben took one look, his fist came back, and Brett sprawled on the floor. Movement stopped in the waiting room, then Caleb reached down and hauled Brett to his feet.

"That was from your brother, not from a cop. This is from a cop." Caleb drew Brett's hands behind him and slapped on the handcuffs.

"What is this outrage?" Brett demanded.

"Well for starters, you're under arrest for conspiracy to commit murder, kidnapping, financial fraud, wire fraud, theft. I'm sure we'll find a few more charges before we're done"

Brett spluttered as he was led away. "I don't think so."

Beth watched dispassionately as he was led away. "I guess you'll be wanting to talk to me, too. We might as well get it over with." She followed her husband from the room.

Marg and Ben stared after them, then at each other. What had just happened?

Frankie rested his chin on the side bar of Deirdre's bed. It was four days later and she was gradually awakening from the medications she had been on. He himself still felt rocky. Two concussions in a short period of time was definitely not recommended.

His hand reached for her unbandaged hand and held it. This was the woman he had been waiting for. He thanked the Lord that He had spared her life.

Deirdre's eyelids flickered, and her eyes opened. Her sight was unfocused for a minute, then she frowned as she looked around. Her eyes went past him, then came back. She frowned as she studied his face.

"Who did you go twenty rounds with?" Her voice was rough, barely above a whisper.

He smiled. "Probably the same ones you did." She tried to lift her right hand and he reached across and stopped her. "Don't move that hand too much. They're waiting for it to heal more before they put it in a proper cast."

She frowned once more as she looked at it. "What happened to it?"

"You don't remember?" As she shook his head, he sighed. "The two goons with McNabb had a little fun with your hand. They decided to start breaking your fingers."

Her eyes flew to his. "I don't remember. Then again, maybe I don't want to. I imagine it must have hurt."

He laughed softly. "That, my darling, would be an understatement. The doctors are confident they've been able to reconstruct the fingers."

"So why else am I here?"

"Shock, dehydration, pain management. They were really starting to work you over before they decided to go for your fingers."

She loosened her left hand from his grip and touched his face. "Looks like you didn't fare as well, either."

"Not really. Concussion again, fractured ribs, bruises, muscle trauma, broken wrist. But we're alive. God brought us through that storm."

"That He did, my love, that He did." Her voice faded and she slept. He sat watching, her hand in his until he was asked to leave so the nurses could take care of her. He would be back and soon.

Caleb looked around at the people gathered around the yard at Ben's place. Eddie and Peg were there. Joshua and Laycee, Leith and Regan, Liam and Ashling, Timothy. He knew Hannah was somewhere but their boys were with a friend. Ben and Marg had wanted to do this, have their friends over, just for a time to heal and pray. His eyes focused on the swing on the deck. Frankie was sitting there, his arm around Deirdre. Now that was a story in itself. Who would have thought that Frankie would have found such a wonderful soul mate, one to spend the rest of his life with, one who understood where he had been and where he was going? Only God.

The meal over, Caleb went to lean against the deck railing and faced his friends. This was one story that had so many twists and turns, he wasn't sure if they had unraveled them all.

He studied Deirdre. Her face was peaceful and calm. She had an inner strength he found in few. Her head was leaning back on Frankie's shoulder, his arm around her. He scanned the others, all focused on him.

Caleb started. "This is one story I'm not sure if we will ever totally unravel. It starts way back when you were small, Deirdre. Did you ever suspect your parents weren't your parents?"

She stared at him and shook her head. "Never."

"They weren't. They weren't able to have children on their own. They contacted a baby broker, what we would call a black market adoption today.

He found them a little girl who matched them in looks. That was you. From what we have been able to determine, you were on a boat with your parents, it capsized, but somehow you survived. You were rescued, found yourself in this man's hands, and then on to Brett and Beth. That's why they didn't come around for a couple of years and let on that Beth was pregnant. Ben, you may recall they never really told you where the "baby" was born, did they? They didn't want you to know Beth wasn't pregnant.

"Then they started their mission. It started out on the right feet but somewhere along the line, Brett was corrupted and began stealing and selling the donations. Beth knew and at times helped. They made sure one or the other of them was always on site so no one would have access to the financials. They kept two books. Timothy, you were catching on. That's why Beth insisted you come back home.

"Stu McNabb was the silent partner in the criminal activities. He had been a childhood friend of Brett. Brett had lost track of him until he showed up one day and threatened him. Brett caved and brought him in on the crimes. Stu had the idea that if Finn and Deirdre were married, Brett wouldn't cause any problems. Problem is, Finn really didn't want to get married. So he arranged a fake wedding, making sure it was kept small. He was planning on disappearing once they were registered at the hotel, but his father suspected something. The shots were to be warning shots only but the shooter had his own agenda and killed Finn. McNabb realized that he was under watch and had been very careful since then to watch himself.

"Finn had given you that stone, Deirdre, as a safety precaution. He planned to find you and get it back. The one you found, Timothy, McNabb dropped one day he was in the warehouse.

"The two men McNabb hired were from here. He had connections to some gangs and specifically searched for these men, thinking the language would throw everyone off. Frankie is right, Deirdre, you are scary. Your language ability helped to crack the case.

"That's about it, I think. Still some odds and ends to sort out but we pretty much have the case against them in order. And yes, they were tracking your phones and had inserted GPS units in your backpacks. That threw them when we traded them out. It was just a pure fluke that they found you. They were searching around the docks, thinking you may try to flee by boat, and saw you."

Small talk followed and then the friends started to disperse. Caleb went looking for Frankie and found he and Deirdre standing in the back yard, near the roses.

"Frankie, can I have a word?"

"Sure." Frankie shrugged. "It's okay if you talk in front of Deirdre if you want to."

Caleb studied his friends, then nodded. "About your father. I found out and have confirmed he was one of the men gunned down that day. He was going under a different name. I have spoken with people who knew him. He was trying his best to clean up and come back to find you. Your mother had found out and that's why she left. Your mother was in a bad motor vehicle accident on the way to confront him. She had to have a lot of plastic surgery. She didn't feel she could come back around you, not when she had been gone for so long. Eddie tracked her down." Caleb paused, looking at the business card in his hand. "Eddie has spoken with her. She gave him her card, told him if you ever felt ready, she would like to hear from you. She's really not that far away from you, never has been."

Frankie's eyes slid shut. Deirdre's arms came around him in a hug. "Thank you, Caleb. It hurts but now I know. Thank you, my friend."

Caleb walked away. Sometimes, he just hated that part of his job that meant he had to hurt people.

Frankie stayed silent. Deirdre watched him. He finally turned to her.

"Well, my darling, it's been quite the few weeks."

She nodded, waiting for him to continue.

"Will you go out on a real date with me? No police escorts, just you and me?"

She nodded. "I would like that. Now about the youth centre."

"What about it?"

"I'm stepping down from it. I can't continue there, not any more. Peter's ready and able to take over. I'll find something else to do, something I will enjoy so much more."

"A wise move, my darling. Come, let's get you home. Caleb wants me to come in and start desk duty tomorrow. He never did accept my resignation."

"I'm glad he didn't. You're too good a cop."

"So, will you teach me your scary moves so I can scare away thugs in a dark alley?" He laughed as she punched him in the stomach. "I love you too, my darling.

Epilogue

Frankie was nervous and that was not like him. He wiped damp hands on his jeans and then rang Deirdre's doorbell. It had been four months since their adventure ended. They were still waiting for the trials, but it looked as if McNabb and Deirdre's adoptive father would be going to prison for a long time. Her mother would be on probation for her part, due to a plea bargain. The mission they had started had been closed down, it could not continue.

Deirdre opened the door and stood in front of him, breaking into his thoughts. Yes, Lord, thank you for this lady.

He reached for her hand and she closed and locked the door behind her. They had spent many hours together, alone and with family.

He walked her towards the park in her neighbourhood. It was small but beautiful in lay out. It had become part of their routine, to walk there at least two or three times a week.

He drew her close to him and then down to sit on a bench. He wrapped an arm around her and then just sat.

"Who would have thought all that would have happened to us?" Deirdre's voice was hushed.

"I know. You were so right about the storm. We were both going through a bad one. God calmed it for us, brought us safely to shore."

She nodded. "Now what, Frankie? Where does God lead us?"

He thought about that. "Only He knows where He wants us or where we can serve. There will be many more storms in life but we know Who calms them. I can't imagine a life that didn't have One like that in it. When I thought I had lost you that day in the basement, I was devastated. I tried so hard to get back to you. God spoke through the pain. He let me know we would both survive, that He had plans for us we have no idea of."

He turned his head to watch her. She was staring out across the park, a thoughtful look on her face.

"You're right. Even with what I was facing, not knowing if you were still alive, He was there, right beside me. He could have stopped what was happening but He didn't. He calmed the storm within, not the storm without. Sometimes that's what He does. He doesn't want us fearful, not at peace. That's not who we are to be."

Frankie nodded. "You're right. He gives what we need at the time we need it. I have spoken with my mother in the last week. It was hard but we're talking."

He looked over her head and then back down. "Deirdre, I have come to know you over the last few months, have come to love who you are. You're not the scary person I tease you about being. I love that part of you, that part that makes you unafraid and able to keep your head and think in a crisis."

She had turned her head to watch him.

"Will you marry me, will you help to be my anchor, help to keep me grounded and safe?"

Her eyes filling with tears, she nodded. "I will. I love that about you as well. You are my protector, the one who keeps me safe."

He leaned over to kiss her, then leaned back. "Did you really say yes?"

She shoved him. "Keep that up, buster, and I'll get scary again." She held up her hand. "Now, let's go get that dinner you promised me. You driving or am I?" His keys were in her hands.

He laughed and hugged her as he reached for them. "Don't ever change, my darling, don't ever change. And if the Lord blesses us with a family, you can teach them to be scary too."

Deirdre smacked him, then leaned in for a kiss. "That, my love, I can do."

Dear Readers:

The Storm is written. How much of a storm are you facing this day? Do you trust the Christ to calm the storm? Do you trust Him to calm you instead?

Frankie is a beat-up street cop, worn out and ready to turn his back on everything. Deirdre enters his life and changes how he views himself and how he sees God as viewing him. God really does want us to trust in Him, to find that rest we need, to find the calm in our storms of life.

This book is dedicated to those of us, every one of us, who have fought through a storm and emerged victoriously through Christ's power. We don't need to wonder how it happened. That's where our faith comes in—that it will.

As always, I pray that this book has challenged you in your walk with God. It has me. I also pray that you really will learn to let God have control of your storms in life, to lay your worries, cares, stresses, and burdens in His outstretched hands.

Ronna

The Anchor

Haven of Rest Trilogy
Book 2

by

Ronna Bacon

Hebrews 6:19

This hope we have as an anchor of the soul, a hope both sure and steadfast and one which enters within the veil

Isaiah 43:2

When you pass through the waters, I will be with you; and when you pass through the rivers, they will not sweep over you. When you walk through the fire, you will not be burned; the flames will not set you ablaze.

Dedication

This book is dedicated to my Anchor, my Heavenly Father.   He is the one who keeps me safe and on track. Without Him, I would be adrift on the seas of life.

Table of Contents

Prologue

She watched in horror, hands clapped over her mouth, as the dark form stood over the fallen girl. The moon was mostly hidden by the quickly moving clouds. She could feel the rain coming. The form looked around in a furtive manner, then reaching down, gathered the girl into his arms and moved away, towards the quarry.

She followed, knowing that she couldn't help but she needed for know for sure the girl was dead. She thought she know who the man was, but she was still unsure.

The dark form stopped at the edge of the quarry and laid his burden down. He stood, searching the darkness. Was that a noise? Human or animal? He hated the dark. He hated that the woods were so close to him.

She watched as his foot nudged his burden towards the edge. She closed her eyes, a whimper coming from her as she knew what was coming.

He stopped, foot under the body. Yes, he heard a noise. Where was it?

She dropped to the ground, hiding. She didn't want to be seen. Her breath coming in gasps, she tried her best to control it. Peeking out, she saw him walking away. The form on the ground was no longer there. She buried her head in her arms and let silent sobs come. She knew who it was and who the girl was. How could she ever stay in this town now? To stay meant certain death, yet she didn't know how she would ever leave. Where would she be safe? If he ever knew she had seen him, her life would be forfeited. Why had she ever agreed to meet her friend out here tonight?

Timothy Johnson was headed into the local grocery store and stopped when he heard his name called. He turned to see his friend, Frankie Brennan, running towards him. They shook hands, stood talking for a minute, then headed into the store.

"So, what exactly did Deirdre send you for?" Timothy was amused. His friend's fiancee was trying to get him to eat more healthy and had sent him to a store with a list. Frankie was not particularly happy. He hated shopping.

"I have a list, I think, somewhere." Frankie dug through his pockets and pulled out the piece of paper Deirdre had slapped into his hands earlier. He smiled as he remembered the fierce look on her face but the twinkle in her eyes.

Timothy shook his head. Frankie had it bad, he thought. Street cop turned detective and he was not so hard as he pretended. His cousin, Deirdre, had been good for his friend. As Frankie read over his list, Timothy hazel's eyes moved over the shoppers in the fruit and vegetable section. They stopped and rested on a young woman, light brown hair in a braid down her back. She looked familiar. She was studying the apples as if they were the most important duty in her day.

"She wants me to buy apples." Frankie sighed. "She's trying to change my eating habits?"

Timothy laughed. "She is, but it's for the better. Come on, let's get your apples. I need to get some vegetables, too"

Frankie gave him a sorrowful look. "Not you, too. Here, I thought you would support me."

Timothy just laughed again and walked towards the fruit. Frankie stopped by the apples and studied them. He really didn't like apples, but if Deirdre insisted, he supposed he would have to get them. He really had no idea how to judge an apple, though.

"She wants small red delicious apples. These are not small." A voice came from his right.

Frankie turned to look at the young woman, who was staring at the apple in her hand.

"Excuse me?"

"Mrs. B. specifically said small red delicious apples."

"They have smaller ones in bags, I think, over there." Frankie pointed, all the while studying her. He didn't know her, he didn't think.

"No, she was specific. They couldn't be in bags. I have to hand pick each one. These are not small." She reached for Frankie's hand and slapped the apple in it, then walked away.

Timothy was watching, trying to keep a straight face. She was back; Rachel Andrews was back in town, and she hadn't changed.

Frankie stared at the apple in his hand and then at Timothy. "What am I supposed to do with this?"

"Buy it?" Timothy was trying hard not to laugh at his friend, but was not having much success.

Frankie's eyes narrowed at Timothy. Just as he went to speak, a hand reached out and took the apple from him.

"You don't like apples. Put it back." The apple was plopped back on the pile, and Rachel walked away, leaving Frankie staring after her.

Timothy started to laugh. Frankie turned to him, staring as if Timothy had helped set him up.

"Come on, my friend. You need to shop. Deirdre will be waiting to see if you really did follow her list."

Frankie shrugged, then walked towards the back of the store. Timothy watched him, then turned to study the area around him. Rachel was now by the lettuce. She looked up and, with a smile, gave him a wink. Yes, Rachel was back and hadn't changed. It was good to see her. He would need to find out where she was living now.

As they were leaving the store, Frankie turned to Timothy. "So, who was that?"

"Who?" Timothy asked innocently, but with a sparkle of amusement in his eyes.

"That female who informed me I didn't like apples. And how did she know that, anyway?"

"That was Rachel Andrews, an old friend. She moved from here just after high school." Timothy studied the sky. "She's friends with Deirdre."

Frankie looked at him. "That explains that. Deirdre has a wicked sense of humour."

"So does Rachel."

Frankie locked his groceries in the trunk, then turned to Timothy. Just as he was about to speak, they heard the sound of squealing tires and shouting from across the parking lot. Frankie took off at a run. Timothy quickly dumped his groceries in his front seat and followed.

Frankie crouched down by the younger woman who was by now sitting on the ground, assessing her.   She seemed unhurt but looked familiar. A man stood nearby, gesturing wildly.

"He tried to run her down. She barely got out of the way." He stared at the woman, then at Frankie. "He really tried to run her down. Where are the police when you need them?"

Frankie stood and pulled out his badge. As Timothy came up, Frankie moved the man away so he could talk with him. Timothy looked down, then with a small cry, crouched down. It was Rachel.

"Rachel."   He waited.   "Rachel, are you okay?"

She didn't move, didn't look at him. Her gaze was fixed ahead of her. He reached and slipped the back pack from her shoulders.

He reached out and touched her face. No response.

"Rachel, are you okay?" he asked again.

Her eyes turned to him, a tortured look in them. The red and blue emergency lights from the arriving cruiser flashed across her face. "He knows. He knows I'm back."

"Who knows, Rachel? Who knows you're back?"

She shook her head. "He knows." As she crumpled forward, Timothy caught her and then gathered her up. He stood, looking around, then headed for his car.

Frankie was at his heels and caught the keys Timothy tossed to him and grabbed Rachel's backpack. He cleared the bags of food from the front seat and stepped back. Timothy gently sat Rachel in his car and then fastened the seat belt. She had not stirred at all. He crouched down once again so he could watch her. He tucked the backpack at her feet.

"What happened, Frankie?" Timothy's eyes did not leave his friend seated in his car.

"It's the strangest thing. She was walking across the parking lot and a car headed right for her. She just managed to get out of the way. The witness wasn't sure if she had been hit or not, it was that close." Frankie stepped back to take a better look at Rachel. "Is she okay?"

Timothy shook his head. "I really don't know." He stood, then looked at Frankie. "I had no idea she was back, so it must be fairly recent. Deirdre never said anything, and I know those two have kept in touch."

"Did she say anything?"

Timothy nodded, thinking of the words she had said. "She did. She said, "He knows. He knows I'm back." I have no idea what or who she means."

Frankie looked over at the patrol officer taking the formal statement from the witness. "I'll want to talk with her when she's able." He looked back at Rachel. "Does she have any family here she can go to?"

Timothy shook his head. "Her foster parents took an early retirement and moved away 10 years ago. Her sister and brother aren't here either. I'm not sure where either of them are now. I have no idea where she is living or where she's been."

"She should be checked out at Emergency."

Timothy again shook his head. "She won't go. I know her. She will flat out refuse and walk away. Then, you'll never find out anything." He studied the white, drawn face of his friend, eyelashes dark on her cheeks. "Mom will want her to come to their place. She has always had a special spot in her heart for Rachel." He closed the door, then stood looking through the window.

"What are you thinking, Timothy?" Frankie studied his friend, knowing something was going on.

Timothy shrugged. "It's just so strange. Who would want to harm her?"

Frankie shook his head. "I don't know her, not as well as you do. What happened around the time she left?"

Timothy started to shake his head, thought, and then said, "I can't really remember much. I'll talk to Mom and Dad. Maybe they will remember."

Frankie nodded. "I'm about done here for now. I'll catch up with you later tonight or tomorrow. Maybe by that time, your friend will have said more."

Timothy shook his head. "I wouldn't plan on that. She was always quiet about things. She never said much."

"I'll talk with your Dad as well. Or Eddie. One of them will likely remember."

"Caleb knows her from high school. He might have an idea." Timothy referred to the local police chief, Caleb Logan, a good friend of both of them.

Timothy stared at the keys in hands, his thoughts going back in time. Why had Rachel left? She just packed up one day and was gone. She hadn't said a word to any of her friends, and her parents really hadn't either.

Frankie watched his friend's face. Something was bothering Timothy. Frankie could see the puzzlement in his eyes. There was more there, though, than just that. Frankie took another look at the young woman in the car, then back at Timothy.

He wondered just how close they had been as teenagers.

Timothy finally shook his head and looked up. He took a deep breath and then said, "I'll see what I can find out and call you later. Be careful what you say to Deirdre. For some reason, she was always protective of Rachel. I never knew why. If she knows Rachel was almost run down today, she'll want to be with her all the time. Rachel can't handle that, unless she has really changed."

Frankie watched his friend's face, noting the flickering emotions on it. "I will."

Timothy walked around his car, opened the door, and hesitated. He started to say something, stopped, and then climbed into the car. Backing up, he lifted a hand and was gone.

Frankie headed for the patrol officer to see if there was anything different in the statement than what he had been told earlier. He hoped he was wrong, but he had that feeling again, a feeling of being watched when he was with Timothy and Rachel. His heart raised in prayer, he knew they would need God's guidance and protection once again. When would this stop, he wondered?

****

He stood on the sidelines and watched. She was back in town. How much did she know? Had it been her all along that he heard that night or had it just be sounds from the woods? He needed to find out but how he would go about it, he wasn't sure. He needed to find out where she lived. That would be his first step and then he could plan from there. It figured that street cop had to be there so soon. And that friend of hers. If he got in his way, he would have no choice but to remove him.

154

Timothy pulled his car up behind his mother's. Good, he thought, she's home. She'll know what to do with Rachel. Turning off the ignition, he turned sideways to study his friend. She had not moved from where he had placed her nor had she awakened. This just felt so strange. It wasn't the Rachel he remembered. What or who had her so frightened, he wondered.

Timothy sat and thought for a moment, trying to puzzle it out, then shook his head and climbing out of his vehicle, walked around to open the passenger door. Rachel didn't stir as he reached to undo her seatbelt, then gathered her up in his arms. He shut the door with his hip, and then headed for the house. As he approached the wooden, carved door, it opened and his mother stood there.

"Timothy, who do you have?"

"Remember Rachel Andrews? Someone tried to run her down in a parking lot today. She fainted. Knowing her, I didn't take her to Emergency. There's something going on with her, Mom. She's scared."

Marg looked at her son, then down at Rachel. As Timothy paused beside her, she reached out a hand and touched Rachel's hair.

"Take her up to the spare room, honey. I'll be right there."

Marg followed Timothy up the stairs and pulled back blankets on the bed. Timothy laid his burden down, and then with a touch to her face, stepped back and stared at her, studying the changes he could see in her face. He turned to his mother.

"It's really strange, Mom. Just out of the blue it seemed."

Marg studied her son. She nodded and then said, "Go on down. I'll just get her settled and I'll be down in a few minutes."

Timothy hesitated, then nodded and stepped from the room. He waited in the hall for his mother. He could hear Marg moving softly around in the room. When she came out of the room, she stopped and looked at her son. Timothy stared back. Marg nodded and then headed back down the stairs for the kitchen. Timothy followed slowly, knowing he couldn't wait in the hall for Rachel to awaken but not wanting to leave.

Marg poured them both cups of coffee and then checked the meal she had in the crockpot. She didn't know what time Ben would be home but she always had something ready for him. She then turned and studied her son. There was more going on that what he had said. She breathed a prayer for guidance and words. *Lord, he's still hurting from when she left and said nothing. Help him to cling to You. I fear for what is coming in the next while.*

Marg sat, then laid her hand on her son's. Timothy didn't react or move. Marg once again studied him, then nodded. *Now to find the words.*

"Timothy, it's been a lot of years. Things have changed around here. You've changed. Rachel will have changed." She paused. "Did she ever say anything before she left?"

Timothy shook his head. "No. One day she was here, the next day no one knew where she was. Her parents or her sister would never say. By that time, Gideon had been gone himself for a couple of years." He looked at his mother, puzzlement in his eyes. "Did you ever hear anything?"

Marg shook her head. "No. I know your Dad had gone to speak with them, but he said they

156

wouldn't say anything. The last I heard about her parents and sister was that they have moved to the west. Gideon, I don't know about. He just seemed to disappear."

Timothy nodded, then looked at the clock. He reluctantly pulled himself to his feet. "I have that meeting tonight I can't get out of or I'd stay. Will you call me if she wakes up?"

Marg nodded as she watched the conflicting emotions on her son's face. "I will. But I doubt she'll be awake much before morning. There's a lot more going on with her than just the almost hit and run."

Timothy dropped a kiss on his mother's cheek and then walked away. Marg sat for a while, and then went back to check on Rachel. She was stirring.

"Rachel, do you want something?" Marg kept her voice low.

Rachel shook her head, then stopped, her hand going to it. "I could use something for pain, maybe. Where am I?"

"It's Marg Johnson, dear. You used to spend a lot of time with me."

Rachel squinted against the light as Marg handed her the tablets. "I did. Thank you. I just don't know how I got here today."

Marg gave a soft laugh. "Timothy brought you." As she went to continue, she hesitated. Rachel had sunk back to the bed and was asleep again. Marg brushed the hair from her face and studied her young friend. There had been a lot of hard years, she thought. Lord, please bring healing to my friend, she breathed.

Late that night, Ben stood watching as Marg checked on Rachel and made sure she was settled for the night. Leaving the door cracked open a bit, Marg followed Ben down the hall.

"Did you find out anything more, Ben?"

Ben shook his head. "The witness didn't really see much and didn't get much of a description."

"I'm glad Timothy brought her here, but I just have questions."

Ben wrapped his arms around his wife. "I do, too, sweetheart. I do too. I just wonder where she's been."

Ben felt uneasy. He hadn't gone to bed but had gone downstairs to his study. He sat with just a small light on, waiting for what, he wasn't sure. He had enough light he could see his Bible that he had picked up on his way past his desk.

He heard the soft sounds of someone coming down the stairs. It wasn't Marg, so it had to be Rachel. He looked at the clock—3 a.m.

Stopping at his study door, he watched. Rachel had her backpack and, after hesitating, she headed for the kitchen door.

"It won't work, Rachel." Ben spoke softly behind her as she reached for the lock.

She froze, fingers on the metal.

"Running never works. What is it you're running from?"

She remained silent, back stiff.

"Let us help you, Rachel. You're more than welcome to stay here."

Finally she moved, giving a small shake to her heard.

"You're not just scared, you're scared and running." Ben looked down and then back at her. She hadn't moved. "I always thought you ran all those years ago because you were scared. It wasn't because of who and what your parents were."

She shuddered and then her fingers turned the lock. "I can't. I just can't." the words barely audible to Ben.

"Why not?" He stayed where he was, not daring to approach.

She gave another small shake of her head. "He knows I'm back. He'll be watching. You'll be in danger."

"Who knows?"

She stood, once again not moving. Then, as she pulled the door open, she said in a very low voice, "Did you ever find out how Mary died?"

Ben stopped. Mary. Who was Mary?

She was gone before he could stop her, before he could offer her a ride to where she was going.

Rachel was running again, this time to her own place. She was tired of running from the unknown. That was what had brought her back to town. She was ready to fight, to get her life back. She wished she knew where Gideon was. She really needed her older brother right now.

It seemed a long way in the dark back to the store where she had left her bike. She stowed the lock and then was gone. It wasn't a wise move, she knew, as it was dark, but she wanted to be at home, safe behind her own locked doors.

****

He stood and watched the Johnson house. He knew she was in there. He just couldn't walk in, not to a police officer's house. He would have to wait until she left. He was getting angrier by the moment. She just had to come back. But did she really know what had happened? So he watched. He had tried to track where she was living but he could find no trace, no sign of any place in her name. So where was she living?

"What do you mean, she's gone?" Timothy stared at his father as he calmly told him that.

"Just what I said. She's gone. She left around 3 this morning." Ben watched his son, knowing something was going on.

Timothy ran his hand through his brown hair. "That was stupid. Someone tried to kill her yesterday."

Ben held up a hand. "First, when you find her, don't tell her that this was a stupid move. If she slugs you, you deserve it. It was her decision to make, not yours. Second, I talked to both Frankie and the patrol officer. It is unclear if she really was targeted or just in the wrong spot at the wrong time."

"She wasn't just scared yesterday, Dad. She was absolutely petrified. I have never seen anyone like that."

Ben nodded. "I understand how you feel, but without any evidence or any input from Rachel, they can't go any further with it."

Timothy was frustrated. "I know. I just wish she had stayed. She didn't say anything?"

"Not really." Ben was not about to tell his son what she had asked about Mary. He wasn't sure even who she was talking about.

Timothy turned to leave, then stopped. He couldn't just walk out and look for her. He had work he had to do, a full day. When he moved back home a few months ago, after leaving the mission his uncle and aunt had started and then lost, he had started up his own business of elder care. He had seniors he had to look after.

He felt his Dad's hand on his shoulder. "We'll find her, Timothy. One of us will find her."

Timothy nodded, then walked away. Ben watched, then headed for the department. He had work to do, but he wanted to talk to both Eddie and Caleb, and maybe Frankie, to see if they could help shed any light on what had happened.

None of the men were sure what Rachel had been referring to when she mentioned Mary. Ben set the idea he had aside as he had other investigations on the go.

Rachel looked up at the sound of a vehicle, then reached behind her for the loaded rifle. She stepped back and into the shadows at the edge of the forest. Someone was approaching and until she knew who, she would not allow herself to be seen.

It was a police cruiser. She watched. Timothy emerged from the passenger's side and she turned her eyes to the driver. Caleb Logan. So he did go into law enforcement. That was not a surprise. But what were they doing here? And how had they found her? If they found her, could he?

Caleb turned at the sound of a rifle bolt. He watched as Rachel came from the shadows, rifle in hand.

"What are you doing here, Caleb?"

"Nice way to greet an old friend, Rachel. We came to see you."

She snorted. "Yeah, right. This rifle's for my protection. There's wild animals around here, you know."

"I gather someone taught you how to use it safely."

She glared at him. "You haven't changed a bit, have you? Always assuming the worst about me."

Caleb held up a hand. "Wait, Rachel. That didn't come out right. I apologize."

She brushed by him, heading for the cabin. "Apologies like that don't count, Caleb. Apologies after assumptions aren't worth the breath it takes to make them."

Calleb's eyes met Timothy's puzzled ones. This was not their friend, Rachel. Something had happened, had made her hard.

She turned. "If you want coffee, I made some a while ago. I can't guarantee if it's still drinkable."

They followed her into the small, one-roomed cabin. She pointed to the table and then set mugs of coffee before them. Caleb looked at his and then at Timothy. He hated coffee but how could he tell her?

The mug disappeared from in front of him and a few minutes later a cup of tea appeared. He looked up at her but she had turned away. Timothy caught a smile before it disappeared, but Caleb missed it.

Rachel refused to sit, instead working at something on her counter.

Caleb finally cleared his throat. "Rachel, I just wanted to ask you about yesterday."

"What about it?" Her tone was curt and unfriendly.

"What happened?"

She shrugged. "From what I can remember, someone tried to run me down. Next thing I knew I was at the Johnson's." She spun, pointing a knife at him. "So, you tell me. You tell me who tried to run me down."

Caleb looked at the knife and then at her. "We don't know. That's why I wanted to talk to you, to see if you had any ideas."

She glared at him. "If I had, you would be the last to know. The police in this town, they never ever did help the likes of me." She stopped and then headed for the door. As she reached for the handle, she stopped again and then spun to face him. "Do either of you remember Mary?"

The men looked at each other, then both shook their heads.

"See what I mean? No one cares. Find out who killed Mary Emms. She didn't die naturally."

She almost ran from the cabin. Timothy started to rise, but a hand on his arm stopped him.

"Mary Emms?" Caleb looked puzzled for a minute.

"Mary?" Timothy thought about the name. "Sure, she's the young girl they found in the quarry, about 15 or 16 years old. The coroner's report said she fell over the edge."

Caleb stared at Timothy. Not again, he said, Lord. Please not again. I don't need another mystery to solve that involves my friends. Why me, anyway?

"Is Rachel saying it wasn't an accident?"

"That's what it sounds like."

Caleb rose and headed outside to find Rachel. She wasn't around. Timothy stood beside him.

"We'll come back, Timothy. Right now, it looks as if she wants us to leave. We must, you know."

Timothy nodded. "I want to talk to Dad and maybe Eddie. Do you think they'll remember?"

Caleb shrugged. "It's possible. I want to look into Rachel's parents as well. Come to think of it, they left town only about a year after she did. It was so quick and so strange that he had money to retire when they could barely keep a roof over their heads."

"What?" Timothy was shocked. He stared at his friend.

"You never knew?" Timothy shook his head. "They never had enough to pay their bills and buy food. Someone was always leaving food for them. It got so her parents just took it as their due. It left bad tastes in some mouths in this town. Her sister was the same. The last I heard, she had hit the streets, been arrested and then ended up dying in prison. I never heard what happened to her brother, though. He always had a good head on his shoulders and looked after Rachel."

Timothy looked shocked. "No, she never said. I knew she had had a hard life but never that. That's why Deirdre is so protective—she knew."

Caleb nodded. "I would say so. I would say your parents as well as mine helped out more than most of the town. Gideon spent a lot of time with Dad." Caleb hesitated, not sure how to continue. "I used to hear Mom and Dad talking after they thought Joshua and I were asleep. It always sounded as if there was some kind of physical abuse directed at Rachel. No one could ever get to the bottom of that rumour."

Timothy was silent until Caleb dropped him off at his car. He hesitated as he went to get out. "How do we pray, Caleb? How do we pray for her? How do we approach her?"

Caleb studied his friend. "Like you always did. Be her friend. Include her. Don't shun her. I think that's likely her uncle's place she staying at. I heard that he had willed it to her but I wasn't sure if that was true. Pray for protection for her. Pray for healing. She's hurting in ways we can't understand."

Timothy just shook his head. "I could use your prayers, my friend. This is really going to take a lot to work through."

"It will. You'll get there."

Timothy stared at his friend and then out the window. "I'm still thinking about what she said about Mary. It was an accident, wasn't it?"

Caleb looked thoughtful. "That's what we were always told. I'm pretty sure that's what the coroner's report said. It may be worth another look."

Timothy shut the door behind him and then stood looking around. He felt eyes on him, eyes from someone he couldn't see. He shuddered at the evilness he felt. What was it all about? Are you there, Lord? I have your protection, but I see rough seas ahead. Be my anchor. Keep me founded and safe.

****

He must know where she is, he thought. Where were they? Had she told them? Would they be coming for him soon? He needed to find her, to make sure it wasn't her that night, and if it was, to deal with her. She could tell no one. His life would be ruined if she did.

****

Rachel sank to the ground and leaned up against a tree, dropping her head to her knees. She listened and heard Caleb drive away. How had he tracked her down so quickly? She had left the cabin listed in her lawyer's name. She didn't want anyone to find her. Shudders shook her body, sorrow so deep it had no voice. She couldn't even pray any more, she felt. It was like there was this steel ceiling between her and God. She had hoped by coming here she might find peace again, find that anchor she had lost somewhere in the storms of her life in the last few years. She swiped at the tears that tracked down her face. She knew it would do not good to cry. Her parents had taught her that and taught her well. She wondered if they had ever made peace with God. She had been told they had died in a tornado not long after they had left here. Her father would likely have refused to believe that a tornado would dare come near him. Her sister she had visited in prison and then received word she had taken ill and died. Gideon, her brother, she had no idea where he was. She just wanted her big brother suddenly. She needed him and he wasn't here.

She looked up at the sky. "Why, God? Why? I need my brother and he's not here. Please find him, send him to me. Let that be a sign that You do hear and care. Help me to find the anchor I need."

She sat there in the silence, then heard stealthy footsteps. She shrank back into the bush and watched in silence. A dark clad, heavyset form moved past her, intent on reaching the quarry. It was him, she was sure. She whimpered in sudden fear, then clapped her hands over her mouth to still the sound. He couldn't find her. If he did, she wouldn't live. She knew it.

The form stopped, looking around. Eyes pierced through the underbrush directly at her. He listened and then moved forward again. Rachel sank back to the ground and once again hid her face. She was so afraid, the fear seeming to take over her body. She willed herself to stay alert, not to faint. She needed to leave here but where would she go? She had no other place to go. She didn't feel she could go to the friends she had so abruptly left. She knew Ben and Marg would gladly open their house, just as they had in the past. But how could she bring danger to them or Timothy?

She finally rose as dusk was falling and crept back to her cabin. Doors locked and barred, rifle by her side, she settled down for the night. She knew her sleep would be hit and miss, just like it had been for so long. Sometimes she just wished it was all over but first she had to see justice done. That was why she had come back.

Ben and Eddie appeared at Caleb's office door early the next morning. Caleb watched as they sank in the chairs in front of his desk and waited. How many times over the last a few years had they met like this? He really wished it would stop happening when it involved family and friends.

Caleb finally spoke. "I couldn't get any information from her about what happened. I tried. She is the same. She will only tell you what she wants to and that the bare minimum. If she could say nothing at all, she would." Caleb leaned back, studying the work on his desk that he needed to get through today. It could wait. "There's something going on. She's scared but it's a lot deeper than just fear. She is petrified. Why, I have no idea."

Ben nodded. "That's what Timothy said. I had doubted it the other night. Now I know differently."

Eddie spoke up, watching Caleb. "How well did you know Mary Emms?"

Caleb looked thoughtful. "Mary? I really didn't other than to know who she was in the youth group. She was two to three years younger than me."

"That's what Timothy has said, you mentioned, Ben. I did a little digging into her file. I wasn't too happy to see a lot of information was just

168

swept aside and not followed up. I also got a copy of the coroner's report.   Now that I can see a real problem with."

Ben and Caleb looked at him. "Who was the coroner?" Caleb asked.

Ben and Eddie once again shared a look, then Eddie spoke, "Dr. Young."

Caleb stared at them, then threw up his hands. "Of course, Dr. Young. Is it legit, the report?"

Eddie shrugged. "Who knows now. To make sure, we would have to do another autopsy. And that would be really hard to get court permission to do so without adequate evidence, which we don't have."

Caleb studied the wall behind the two men. He had learned much from them over the years. At times, he felt inadequate to be police chief but his credentials and experience said otherwise. Where did they go from here, he wondered?   How did they proceed? Lord, we're in that place again. You know what we're asking once again.

Timothy was tired. He hadn't slept much the night before and had spent the day dealing with issues for his elderly clients. He really loved working with them but today, his mind had been elsewhere. He found himself wondering where Rachel was and if she was okay. He paused, hand in the process of locking his office door. Did she have a phone? If not, he was going to get her one. With the little she seemed to have with her, he didn't think it likely.

He turned to walk around the building to where he had parked. He never went out the back door—it was too hard to lock. He really needed to get it looked out. Sudden movement came from his left and he found himself slammed into the building wall with an arm across the back of his neck.

"Where is she?" A harsh voice sounded in his ear.

Stunned, he couldn't answer and the arm pushed harder against him.

"Where is she?"

He shook his head. "I don't know. Who are you looking for?"

"You know who it is. We'll find her. If you get in the way, you're dead."

Another shove against the wall and the arm was gone. He could hear running footsteps as he dropped to his knees. His breath came in gasps as he struggled to his feet. He peered around. No one was there. He leant back against the building until he was breathing easier, then bent to pick up his briefcase. A piece of paper lay beside it. He picked it up and read it on his way to his car. He stopped. Why was

Rachel being threatened and who had written this note?

He paused as he unlocked his car door and looked around. He felt those eyes again, evilness in their gaze. Who was it?

Timothy handed his father the piece of paper he found. Ben was in his study at home, working on lessons for his Bible study group. He then sank into the chair by the desk.

Ben took the paper, watching his son as he did so. Timothy was starting to show the strain. He then glanced down at the paper and read it.

"What happened, Timothy? I know you just didn't find this by accident."

Timothy shook his head. He hadn't but he didn't think he was supposed to have it. He related to his father what had happened. Ben sat back and studied his son's face. He could see some faint abrasions where the rough wall had come in contact with the skin.

"Did you recognize the voice?"

Timothy thought, then shook his head. "I didn't. But there have been so many new people in town it could have been one of them. He sounded around my age or younger."

Ben nodded as he listened. This thing with Rachel was escalating. Now it had come to his own son in a way he had always hoped and prayed it never would. He had been so careful to keep his family and his work separate. That had changed. What was it that Rachel knew or who was it she knew? Was it really tied to Mary Emms or was it something else?

"I'll pass this on in the morning, son, but I doubt we'll get much off of it. They are too smart likely to have left any trace evidence."

Timothy didn't seem to hear his father at first, then shook his head to clear his thoughts. "Thanks, Dad. That's all we can do."

"So about Rachel. Is she at her uncle's cabin?"

Timothy nodded. "Not many people know she has it, I don't think. I didn't see that she has a vehicle or a phone. I'm going to track her down tomorrow and see if she at least has a cheap phone. If not, I'll get her one." He looked up as Marg appeared in the doorway. Supper was on and the discussion would have to wait until later.

****

He was angry, livid in fact, and the man in front of him stepped back. He had tried to find the information that was wanted and failed. Now he was in front of who was paying him and suddenly he feared for his life. He had no fear of anyone but the evil coming from this man was palpable in the room. He wished fervently he had never answered his phone that day. He had two choices: walk, no run, as far as he could, or find the woman.

****

Ben studied the note Timothy had found. Who, he questioned, would be after her? Something had happened all those years ago, he suspected. What was it? He laid the note aside and spent time in prayer. He could sense a gathering storm and wanted the Lord's protection on them.

Caleb looked up as Ben entered his office the next morning and then at the note he was handed. He listened as Ben explained what had happened and what he was suspecting. He nodded in agreement.

"Run with this. See what you can find out. Eddie I think was working the Mary Emms angle."

172

"That he was. I just hope we don't have another one of those situations again. I don't know if I can take it."

Caleb watched with compassion as Ben walked away. Ben had been through a lot in the last few months: his brother was now imprisoned for fraud and conspiracy to commit murder, his sister-in-law on probation for the same, the mission he had supported totally destroyed, and the niece he adored kidnapped, tortured, and left for dead. Now it was affecting his son. How much more could he take? Caleb continued to study the door Ben had walked through, then bent back to his paperwork. He would find time later today to track down Rachel again and talk with her.

Rachel stopped and watched as she saw Marg headed into a local store. She wanted to speak with her and thank her once again, but she knew the woman who owned the store. She wouldn't be welcomed there, she knew. She turned and headed away, unaware that more than one pair of eyes was on her.

Deirdre saw Rachel and, with a call, ran to catch up with her. They stood and talked for a few minutes. Finally, Rachel shook her head at something Deirdre had asked and walked away. Deirdre watched in dismay, wanting to go after her friend, but knowing she couldn't. She turned to walk away herself and found she was trapped by two arms. She looked up. Frankie. How did he know she really needed to talk to him at this moment?

Frankie took one look at her face and then led her to the local cafe. Once seated, he ordered for them, and then reached for her hands.

"What's wrong, sweetheart?"

Deirdre just stared at him, tears in her eyes. "It's Rachel. She just refuses to have anything to do with anyone. I can't get her to come and stay with me. She won't even meet me for a coffee. I just don't understand."

Frankie rubbed her hands as he watched her face and the emotions running over it. "She doesn't feel safe and she doesn't want to put anyone in danger. I know what you're going to say. I know how scary you can be." That earned him a small smile. "But she has been gone for what, at least ten years? She doesn't feel she knows who you are any more. I know you have kept in touch, but people can change and still write the words they want you to hear." He paused. "The only thing I can think of that might get through to her is Timothy, and only because he won't let her get away with shoving him away and blocking him out of her life."

Deirdre nodded. "They always did have a thing for each other, but neither would admit it. I think Timothy was getting ready to when she turned 18, but she was gone before he could. It took months for him to get over her leaving like that."

Frankie stared out the window of the cafe. "I never really got to know her that well. I wasn't part of your group back then. Did she ever give any indication that she was planning on leaving? And I don't think Timothy ever did get over her."

Deirdre thought back over the years. "She did. At one time, around when her brother left, she said he was the lucky one, he was getting out, and she wished he could have taken her with him. When I asked what she meant, she told me not to bother and then stayed away from me for a while. I always felt that her home life wasn't the greatest. She would have bruises she couldn't explain away when she was younger."

Frankie's eyes slid shut. It was what they had suspected. She had been abused as a child and no one helped. "That would explain why she left but not so suddenly." He paused. "Do you remember anything about Mary Emms?"

Deirdre shook her head. "No. She was more Rachel's sister's age, not ours. Other than her body was found in the quarry. I could never figure that out. She was terrified of the quarry, so why would she be there by herself at night?"

Frankie studied the woman he loved. "You may have something there. So tell me about the work you're creating for yourself?"

Talk drifted into new topics. Just before they stood to leave, Deirdre stopped Frankie. "So, you think Timothy still cares for Rachel?" At his look, she smiled. "Don't worry. I won't say anything but you confirmed my feelings about the two."

Frankie just shook his head. How did she do that? She picked up on little things in conversations that most others missed.

Late that afternoon, Caleb parked at Luke's cabin. He knew Rachel owned it now, so his thoughts were that she would be here. He knocked at the cabin door without an answer. He walked around the outside but saw no signs of Rachel. Hearing a small noise from one of the outbuildings he headed that way.

A small click stopped him and he slowly turned, to find himself once again staring down the barrel of a rifle. Rachel stood there, eyes watchful.

"You need to stop doing that, Rachel. You're pulling a gun on law enforcement."

"But you didn't identify yourself as such, so I am defending myself." She set the rifle back down by the door and returned to the building. He followed her. She had been working on what he saw was Luke's old motorcycle.

"He still had it?" Caleb was surprised. He hadn't seen it in a few years.

She nodded. "I've just about got it ready for the road. Then I want to work on his old truck there. People would pay dearly for it, it's in such good shape for a classic vehicle.

Caleb stared at her. "You ride a motorcycle?"

She turned to him, then laughed. "Luke taught me. I was trying to save up for one when I left and had to use the money to survive. He knew that and left me his." She rubbed the handlebar. "I miss him. He let me be a kid or teenager. He always had time and I could talk to him about anything."

Caleb nodded. Her uncle Luke had been just that. He would talk with any of the kids and he always kept their confidences. A little hint now and then to a parent and discipline was dealt out if needed. But he never ever tattled on them.

"I miss him. He always was interested in what any of us were doing."

Rachel took a look at him, then grabbed a rag to wipe her hands. Catching up her rifle, she headed for the cabin. "That's not why you're here. Let me clean up and I'll be back out."

Caleb took a seat in one of the chairs on the back deck. She was back shortly and handed him a mug of tea. She sat quietly and waited. Where does she get so much patience, he wondered?

"Why are you here, Caleb?" The words finally echoed through the forest.

"I just needed to make sure you were okay. People are worried about you." At her snort, he looked over at her. "People are worried about you. People I care deeply about are worried, and I would like to help them get over that worry. I need you to talk to me, to tell me what you can remember about Mary."

She shook her head. "Not happening, Caleb. It's bad enough I'm a target. I'm not making anyone else one. I don't have facts about that night, just impressions. I can't prove anything and to say anything means certain death." She looked over at him. "If Luke hadn't left me his possessions, I wouldn't even be here today./"

Caleb absorbed what she said, then nodded. "I hear what you are saying. But hear me. It is no longer just about you. The search for you has spread. Whoever it is knows you're back in town and is targeting your friends." She stared at him. "Timothy was approached last night as he left his office and roughed up a bit. He's fine but a note was dropped. That note is now evidence and I can't tell you what it said. But it clearly indicated that you were to be found and quickly."

Rachel stared at him in horror. What she had tried to avoid had happened. The danger was now affecting her friends. She swallowed hard and then turned her gaze to the forest around her. Was she even safe here?

She felt Caleb reach towards her, turn her hand over, and place something in it. She looked down. A phone. The one thing she didn't have.

She looked up and saw the friendship, concern and compassion in his eyes. "You shouldn't have, Caleb. I could have got one myself."

He shook his head. "It wasn't me. It was Timothy. He is that concerned about you that he went out and bought a phone so you would have a way of calling for help. He was even looking for a cheap vehicle for you."

She shook her head. "I can't take this. And I don't need a vehicle. I have two."

"I know that now. Timothy doesn't. He cares deeply about you, Rachel, and I would hazard a guess that you feel the same about him." He studied her, saw the faint blush, and then nodded. Hannah, his wife, was right once again. Only this time, he wished she would hurry up with that name for him so he could end this adventure today.

She looked down at the phone. Of course, Timothy had had to get a really nice one, probably with all the bells and whistles she would never use. Just a simple one would have done.

Caleb reached over, turned the phone on, and showed her the address book. Timothy had programmed just about every name he could think of into it for her. She smiled. That was Timothy, taking care of those around him.

They sat talking for a while longer, catching up on news of friends. Caleb noted that she was very careful not to say where she had been, and he wondered at that.

"Have you ever thought about a dog, Rachel?" Caleb studied the sky, watching the clouds move by at a brisk pace. The wind was picking up.

"No, I haven't. Why?"

"I just thought you might like companionship. A dog is good."

Rachel started to laugh. "And who's been trying to convince you of that?"

Caleb laughed as well. "Let's see. Joshua has a golden retriever and his wife has a Shetland Sheepdog. Oh and a cat that sings. Really, this cat sings and chirps like a bird." Rachel was laughing and shaking her head. "Then, Laycee's brother Liam, and his wife, Ashling, have a Sheltie. Her parents run a pet store in town and have a miniature macaw. Sally flirts with the customers. I would have loved to see the look on Liam's face that day. Laycee runs the local pet therapy group and Ashling does dog obedience training. They sometimes come across a dog that needs to be rehomed or even fostered for a few days. Just think about it okay."

She nodded. "I will. I make no promises. As soon as I can get things straightened out again, I'm gone."

Caleb studied her again. No, he thought, you're not. Not if Timothy has anything to say about it. "Just think about it."

He stood to leave, then stopped. "I don't know why you're a target, Rachel. I want to help. So does Frankie, Eddie and Ben. Timothy will put himself in the line of fire for you. It's who he is. If you can tell anyone of us something that can help us find whoever it is, please do." He stopped, then continued, "I don't know where you go to church, or if you even do anymore. Come back to worship with us. We have a new pastor since you were here. He's great. If you won't talk to one of us, talk to Greg or his wife."

She refused to acknowledge his words. He sighed, set down his mug and walked away. She is doing it again, Lord, shoving us away. Help us to help her. She is like a ship without an anchor, has been all her life. Show her the anchor you have for her.

Rachel sighed, picked up their mugs and headed inside. She laid the phone on her table and studied it, turning it over and over. Why, Timothy? Why did you have to go and do that? This will make it so hard to walk away again. Her thoughts drifted, and then with a sigh, she headed for the book shelf. Luke's Bible was there, and she knew she needed to dig it out and start reading it again. She was afraid, afraid of how it would change her. Afraid that she would read and have to confess what she knew.

Timothy paced outside the church. It was almost time for the service to start and he was hoping Rachel would show up. He didn't know for sure if she would and his feeling was that she likely wouldn't. He looked up and saw Rachel slowly walking towards him, uncertainty in her movements. He walked towards her. A little smile on her face showed him that she really didn't want to be there.

He stopped in front of her. "Hi."

"Hi, back." She looked around, avoiding his eyes.

"I'm glad you're here." He tilted his head to study her. No response. He sighed, reached for her hand and turned to lead her to the church. She pulled back but he refused to let go on her hand.

"It's not that bad, Rachel. Nothing like you remember. Our services are really relaxed now. Dad always sits at the back as he never knows if he'll get called out or not. I sit with them. Frankie and Deirdre do too."

She looked up at him. "It's been a long time, Timothy. I sometimes go where I live but not often. Most Sundays, I've worked."

He nodded, desperately wanting to ask her about that, but knowing the time was not right. "That's okay. God understands."

"Does He? Does He really?"

He looked down at her. She was staring straight ahead as they walked.

"He does, Rachel. He really does. He's not some faraway person who doesn't care. He cares deeply about you. He's my anchor, what keeps me safe."

She shuddered and then turned to him. "I don't know if I can go in there."

He stopped, looked at her, and searched for words. "Okay, we'll go in. If you want to leave, we'll leave and go somewhere and talk. If you want to go home, I'll take you home. No strings. Just my promise to take care of you."

She finally nodded and followed him, her hand still grasped solidly in his. She was glad he held it. She didn't think she would have stepped through the doors otherwise. Once in the sanctuary, Timothy saw Frankie and Deirdre about to sit with his parents. Frankie took a look at Rachel and then at him. He said something to Deirdre that made her look over with a smile and then she slid in next to her aunt. Frankie followed. With a hand on her back now, Timothy indicated Rachel should slide in next to Frankie and he himself sat at the aisle. Marg smiled over a hello at Rachel.

Rachel was uncomfortable. This was not her norm. She didn't do church much any more, not since the church here had turned its back on her. But this was not the church she remembered. The Johnsons must have moved churches. She studied the paper she had been given, a bulletin she thought they said, and then looked around. She knew Timothy was watching her. She felt uncomfortable as well under his gaze.

She finally leaned towards Frankie and asked, "Did you enjoy your apple?"

He shot her an astonished gaze and then fought to control his laughter as she looked at him with no smile on her face but a twinkle in her eyes. She sat back, satisfied.

Ben, feeling the wooden pew shaking, looked over at Timothy, who shrugged. Eyes running down the young people sitting there, his gaze stopped on Frankie. He shook his head. Now who was starting something? He happened to catch a look on Rachel's face, a sort of cat-in-the-cream look and nodded. Rachel had been up to no good, he could tell. He shook his head and said something to Marg, who leaned forward to look down the row. Deirdre studied her fiancee, wondering what had set him off, then looked at her cousin. Timothy was staring down at Rachel, unknown to him with his heart in his eyes. Deirdre's face softened, and then she reached for Frankie's hand. Yes, Timothy was in love. Now to make sure Rachel was in love with him.

Rachel listened intently to the sermon about hope, about an anchor. She had never had either and doubted she ever would. She was still, she had trained herself not to move or give away emotions. Timothy watched her and wondered.

Frankie shifted. He could feel it again, the evil he had felt when Deirdre was in trouble. Someone here was in trouble. He glanced at Rachel and knew it was her. Who was after her? He saw Timothy shift suddenly, then gaze around. This was not like him. He never let things distract him. Timothy gazed down at the woman beside him and then looked at Frankie. A shared look and a commitment to keep her safe was formed. How, neither of them knew.

Timothy stood at the end of the service, greeting those around him. He watched as Rachel still sat, lost in thought.

Frankie leaned over. "You have a wicked sense of humour and really good timing, you know."

She started to laugh. "That's what I'm told. The look on your face that day was priceless. I heard you grumbling, remembered you and knew you were Deirdre's fiancee. I just couldn't resist."

Deirdre was now laughing as well. "I wish I could have seen it."

"It was priceless, Deirdre. One of the best you or I have ever pulled."

Frankie looked between the two. "Now it's come out. A pair of practical jokers."

Marg spoke up from behind them. "Yes, both were bad. It's a good thing Deirdre didn't live here year-round. We would never have survived." At a squeal of protest from her niece, Marg continued, "Now, I have a picnic packed for us. If anyone wants to join us, meet us at the park."

Frankie stood and grabbed Deirdre's hand. "Let's go. I love your aunt's picnics. See you both there, Timothy."

Rachel stared at him, mouth open, then turned to Timothy. "Excuse me. Just like that, I'm going to a picnic."

Timothy stopped her with a finger to her mouth and grabbed her hand and led her out of the church. He looked around, the feeling of being watched and that feeling of extreme evil once again overpowering him.

He stopped and looked down at her. "No, you don't have to. It's your choice. I would like it if you would. If you would rather not, it's fine with Mom and Dad. I was actually hoping to ask you to join me for a meal on our own."

She was shaking her head. "No, Timothy. Please."

He stopped her once again and looking around, said, "It's okay. I won't push. But I know you would really enjoy the meal and the company today."

She studied him, then looked around. She didn't feel safe anywhere but she should be safe, shouldn't she, in a group with two police officers. She nodded.

"All right, for a while. Then I have to get home."

"How did you get here today anyway?"

She smiled. "I walked."

He stared at her as he went to close the car door. "You walked. Someone is after you and you walked to town." He went around and climbed behind the steering wheel. "Next time, please call me. I'll come get you."

She shook her head. "I almost have Luke's bike ready and then the truck is almost ready to go back on the road."

He stared at her again. "I forgot. He taught you, didn't he?"

She didn't answer. She was scanning the area around the car. She felt him. He was so near to her.

****

He watched as she drove away with Timothy. His rage grew with each day. The one he had hired had yet to come through. Why was it so difficult to grab her? He would have to deal with those getting in his way. But it would be difficult to do without his name being exposed. He would think about it some more and come up with a way.

****

Rachel stood beside Deirdre, watching as the men carried over the picnic baskets and set them on a

185

table under the trees. Marg had picked a nice area and was busy laying out the food. Deirdre watched her friend. She could see the changes in her. There was a hardness that never used to be there. Where did it come from?

Rachel turned and looked around, shivering, hands going to rub her arms. Deirdre's eyes narrowed and she glanced around. She's acting like I did. Is someone after her? She was going to have to have a talk with either her uncle or her cousin, or even Frankie.

Laughter was abundant as the meal progressed. Rachel joined in but not like she used to. There was a reservation about her now that Marg wondered about. She had been badly hurt while she was away from us or else it's coming back here that has stirred up memories she has tried to hide. She turned to watch her son. Timothy's gaze was on Rachel. Marg could see his feelings for Rachel in his eyes and prayed that he wouldn't get hurt again. She too shivered, thinking that she could feel evil gathering around them.

Rachel's gaze wandered the park as she listened to the talk and teasing. This family had not changed, despite what they had just gone through. They just opened up and let people in. Frankie was such a part of the family now. She longed for that, for somewhere she could belong, some family that would open their arms and hearts to her. God, are you listening? Do you even care? I have asked and asked to see my brother again and You have never brought him to me. If You care, please let me see Gideon again.

Her eyes once more searching the park, they stopped on a man walking towards them. He had a baseball cap on so she couldn't see his face. But the walk, the stance, it was so familiar. The face lifted as he scanned the park inhabitants. No, it couldn't be. God, did you hear? Did You really hear me just now?

"Gideon." The word was said softly and then Rachel was up from the picnic table and running towards the man before anyone knew what she was about. Timothy stood to go after her but stopped as his father laid a hand on his arm and he sat back down. Their eyes followed Rachel as she ran, stumbled and caught herself before she fell, and then continued. The man had stopped as he saw Rachel running towards him, opened his arms, staggered as her body slammed into his, and then wrapped his arms around her, his head going down on hers. Eyes at the table studied them, then studied one another.

Ben nodded. "I suspect that is Gideon. His walk is the same."

"Gideon!" Marg exclaimed. "Where did he come from?"

Ben shrugged. "I put out word I wanted to talk with him. I tracked him down to where he was last living. I didn't say anything as I didn't know if he would come."

Timothy studied Rachel and her brother. He then stood and walked away from the table. He needed time to digest this. Would she leave and go with Gideon or would she stay? He shivered as he once more felt evil around him. Who was it and where were they?

Gideon held his sister as she sobbed. It had been so many years. He had wanted to take her with him when he went but his father must have known. Gideon was locked out of the house, beaten by friends of his father, then taken and dumped in a town miles away. He was told that if he ever came back, Rachel would die. He had tried to keep track of her but when she left home at 18, he lost the trail. He was glad that Ben had tracked him down. He needed to talk to him but right now, his sister was his priority.

He finally leaned back and searched her face. He didn't like what he saw. Life had been rough for her. She deserved better. He bit back words he wanted to say, instead hugging her again. He felt it when her body started to relax. She was like that, strong emotions, then sleep. It was her way of compensating.

As he gathered her into his arms and turned to walk away, he saw the three men coming towards him. Ben he recognized but not the other two.

Ben stopped, studied Rachel in Gideon's arm, and then the face of the man himself. He nodded as if satisfied with what he saw.

"Welcome home, Gideon. Why don't you bring her back to our place? We're still in the same place. We need to talk."

Gideon stared at him, taking his measure, then nodded. "I will. I have my truck just over there."

Timothy stepped forward. "Let me have your keys and I'll unlock it for you. I'm Timothy by the way, and that's Frankie."

Gideon acknowledged the names, then handed his keys to Timothy. Cradling his sister close, he walked to his truck, waited until Timothy opened the door, and then gently set her on the seat, stopping to fasten her seatbelt. He stepped back, closing the door, and then looked at Timothy. There was more going on here than he knew about.

"What's going on, Timothy? Your Dad doesn't track me down over nothing."

Timothy studied the surrounding area. He still felt the eyes, the evil. "Something is. Your sister is on the run from someone here in town and we're trying to find out who. I suspect that's what Dad and Frankie will want to talk to you about." At Gideon's puzzled look, he continued, "Frankie's on the force and is also engaged to Deirdre."

Gideon pulled up to Ben's house and stopped. He stared at the house, remembering the times and talks he had had with Ben over the years. Ben had always listened to him and given advice that was needed. He looked at his sleeping sister and his heart broke. How much she had suffered over the years! He hadn't known why she had left town so quickly and for so long. And to think she was now a target of someone? He couldn't stay long this trip but he would find out what he could and try his best to help.

Timothy appeared at the passenger door and opened it. Gideon looked at him and then his sister and nodded. Timothy stepped back to let Gideon gather his sister up. He led him into the house and to the study where Gideon laid her on the couch and then reached for a blanket to cover her up. Gideon wasn't going far from her today, not if he could help it. He pulled up a chair beside his sister and sat, elbows on the chair arms, chin on his steepled fingers, watching his sister. There was so much he wanted to say to her.

He looked up as Ben, Frankie and Timothy entered the room. Ben handed him a cup of coffee and then sat, just watching and waiting. Timothy wandered the room for a few minutes before he too sat where he could watch the woman he was coming to love. Frankie sat, watching both Timothy and Gideon, eyes flicking every once in a while to where Rachel lay sleeping.

Gideon stared at Ben, and finally spoke. "What's up, Ben? You went to all the trouble of tracking me down. I know it's not for something simple or you wouldn't have left word for me to call you or to come back."

Ben shook his head. "It's not. It involves a lot, going back to when you were still at home." Ben hesitated, choosing his words with caution. "If you don't want to talk in front of anyone and just talk to me, we can do that. But, Frankie is part of our family now. He is also an officer. Timothy has a special spot in his heart for your sister. He always has been her defender. Now, about when you left and before. What can you tell us? I'll let you know right now, we've been doing some digging, have found out things, and I want to tell you how sorry I am that I never knew the extent of what was going on. If I had, I would have taken steps to get both you and Rachel out of there."

****

He stood across from the house, watching once again. She was always surrounded by them. How was he to reach her if she was never alone? And who was that man that just appeared today? He knew of no one who would come to her rescue. It was time to make further plans, plans that she would not like. If anyone got in her way, they would pay

190

Chapter 6

Timothy stopped his Dad. "Dad, will you pray first? God needs to be here in this discussion. I feel like we've been cast out into a storm without an anchor to hold us firm."

Ben nodded and did just that. When he finished, he looked around at the three men. He excused himself for a minute, went to find his wife and niece and brought them back to the room.

"I want Marg and Deirdre in on the discussion. They will help us in a way that a man can't." The three men were surprised but Timothy wasn't as much as the others. He knew how his parents worked as a team.

"Tell me about why you left home, Gideon. About why you never came back."

Gideon hesitated, needing to sort out his thoughts and words. He studied his sister's sleeping face. He didn't want to bring harm to her, but it sounded as if it was already there.

Ben watched his young friend, noting the changes time had wrought. His dirty blond hair had darkened and he had it cut short. His gray eyes were darkened with worry, grief, and something else Ben couldn't define. There was strength in his face and a certain hardness there. When he turned his head, Ben saw the scar on the jawline.

Gideon spoke, eyes locked on his sister, voice low and rough. "Why did I leave? Rachel. She's why I left. I wanted her out of that house. I was planning on taking her with me, even though she was only 16. I figured we could make it on our own. Dad used to beat both of us on a routine basis. We always felt someone should have known, should have stepped in, and no one did. I didn't say anything to anyone but had everything planned. The night I was ready to go, Dad locked me out of the house, had me beaten and dumped miles away. He threatened to have Rachel killed if I came back." He stopped, emotions clogging his throat. When he could, he continued, "I tried to keep in touch but couldn't. I was so afraid for her. Then I heard she had run away. I was glad but I couldn't find her. She just disappeared."

Ben nodded. He had managed to figure out part of it. The three younger ones looked shocked and horrified. They had no idea.

Gideon continued, "They went to church every Sunday. They pretended. They pretended to be so poor others helped them out. I saw their back account one day not long before I left. They had hundreds of thousands of dollars socked away. Dad was either blackmailing or being paid off. Probably both."

Frankie spoke up. "Did you not go to the police about this?"

Gideon snorted. "Why? There were police in pockets all over town. Who would I trust that could get anywhere without being killed? That's why I didn't come to you, Ben. I heard Dad talking about that one day. If you look back at some of the deaths, they weren't suicide, they weren't accidents, they were murders. Our good doctor was in the pocket too."

Timothy studied the brother of the woman he loved and then turned his eyes to her. She still slept. He felt sick at what Gideon and Rachel had gone through and to hear that Rachel had been threatened was even more disturbing.

Marg reached for Ben's hand and squeezed it. They had often discussed the different men and women on the force. This came as no surprise. Deirdre studied Frankie. Frankie looked horrified but determined to ferret out those men. She was afraid suddenly, afraid for all of them. She could feel the evil closing in, just like it had with her. But who?

Frankie spoke up. "Why would any father do that? I just can't fathom that."

Gideon spoke without taking his eyes from his sister. "Because he wasn't our father. He was our foster father. Lucy was their only child. Rachel and I are blood siblings. If he had let Rachel go at 16 with me, he would have lost a source of income from the government but he would also have lost a source of income from the town."

Silence greeted his words. Frankie reached out for Deirdre's hand. She had never known. Her heart broke for her friend. She looked at Timothy. Timothy's face was drawn and white but set. She didn't think she had ever seen such a look on his face, even with what they had gone through with the mission.

Marg gasped as tears came to her eyes. "We never knew, Gideon. I am so sorry. If we had known, we would have taken steps to have you both removed."

Gideon shook his head. "It wouldn't have mattered. If you had tried, he would just have moved to another town. I just thank God we were the last."

Ben spoke, hesitating at the choice of words Gideon had uttered. "The last. Does that mean there are others out there?"

Gideon shrugged. "When we were first placed with them, I used to hear them talking in the night. They spoke of other kids who had been in their care. It sounded as if they were dead. You should also know, they kept changing their names to keep from getting caught. They could buy all the good will and good reports they wanted to keep up fostering."

Ben spoke again after thinking this through. "I am to gather, then, that your last names are not Andrews."

"They are. I have the proof. I took it from them before I left. That's what probably set that whole thing off. They changed their names to match ours, but left the paperwork with the government in their old names. I have proof of that as well."

Ben sat back. This was a lot to absorb.

Marg stood and headed for the kitchen. She knew no one really felt like eating but they had to. She pulled out a container of soup she had. As Deirdre came into the room behind her, Marg turned, then went and hugged her niece. It seemed as if false names just kept coming up to haunt the family.

"I think if we do soup and some sandwiches, that will be enough for now."

Deirdre moved to make the sandwiches, then went to call the men to come and eat. They were all quiet as they ate. Timothy barely touched his food and then excused himself. He wanted to be close to Rachel.

As he went back into the study, he stopped. He could feel it, almost taste it. Where was the evil coming from? He changed directions and went out the front door. He looked around but saw no one. Frankie came out behind him.

"You feel it too, don't you?"

Timothy nodded. "I do. I used to wonder how you could feel it as you said you did. There is someone watching us, watching the house. How do we keep her safe?"

Frankie's eyes were scanning the neighbourhood. It was dusk, and the shadows seemed full of men watching. "I'll talk to Caleb and Eddie in the morning. Your Dad is just too close."

Timothy turned to look at him. "What do you mean?"

"I can see how you feel about Rachel. It's written all over you if someone knows how to read you. He knows. He cares about her like a daughter. We will need to protect both of you, but we also have to keep your Mom and Dad safe." Frankie turned back to the house. "Come on. We'll make some plans for tonight."

****

He stepped back more into the darkness of the tree. How did they know he was there? He could feel their eyes on him. He was sure they hadn't seen him follow them from the park, or anywhere else for that matter, but they always knew when he was there. How? Who was leaking his presence to them?

****

Gideon sank back into the chair by his sister. It didn't look as if she had stirred much but he knew she would soon and she would have a really bad headache. He was tired. When he got word Ben was looking for him, he dropped what he had on his desk and came. He needed to go back in a couple of days. He had a court case he had to testify at and some other cases he wanted to wrap up. Then he was moving back here. He wanted to make sure his sister stayed safe.

Frankie and Deirdre stopped on their way out. Frankie let him know with a look that he would be searching for somewhere to keep Rachel safe. Gideon nodded.

Marg came through with blankets and a pillow and an offer of a bed upstairs. He shook his head and told her he was staying where he was.

Ben stopped to watch the siblings. They were so much alike, he thought, stubborn, vulnerable. One could tell they were brother and sister. He searched for words and found none. He finally spoke to Gideon and then on a good night, headed for bed himself. It was early but it had been an emotional day for all. He needed to find Caleb and Eddie in the morning and talk to them. They really needed to do some digging. He would get what information Gideon had and work from there. His heart raised in prayer, he asked for the anchor they needed to keep them safe and for guidance in the coming storm. He knew it would be a bad one. He didn't like it at all that it involve his son.

Timothy carried a cup of coffee into the study and handed it to Gideon. He then sank into a chair with his own. Neither man spoke as the darkness grew. Timothy reached and turned on a table lamp, giving just enough light with what came in from the hall to make it comfortable.

Rachel stirred. Her head was pounding and she had no idea where she was. Panicked, she sat upright, and regretted it. Her hands came up to clutch her head. Hands found hers and then she was pulled into a hug. She leaned back. Someone else helped her to a drink and she swallowed the tablets they had given her.

Gideon's heart broke. He didn't remember the pain being this bad all those years ago. What had she suffered in those two years that he didn't know about? Timothy whispered softly, left and came back with an ice pack and a cold cloth. He wasn't sure which one would work, but he hoped one would. Gideon laid his sister back down and settled the ice pack at her neck. He prayed it would help.

He then stood and stared across the room. "Find them, Timothy. I hate to leave but I have to in two days. I have duties I have to take up but I'll be back within a week. Find the monsters." His head turned and his eyes bore into Timothy.

"You have my promise. We will do just that."

The men settled down to sleep. They didn't hear Rachel rise in the early morning, study both of them, and then turn and walk away. She grabbed her pack and headed home. She needed space to take in everything that had happened yesterday. She felt she would be safe at her own home.

Ben once again watched Rachel walk away, his heart breaking for the girl. When would she learn to trust others, trust God?

Timothy yawned as he waited for the coffee to finish brewing. Once it had, he grabbed the carafe and poured a cup of coffee. He really needed it this morning. A hand reached out and took the mug from his hand. He looked up. His father had just taken his coffee. Ben headed for the back deck. He just needed to be out in the open this morning. Timothy reached for another mug, poured his coffee, and poured a mug for Gideon. They then headed for the back deck.

Timothy listened as the two other men discussed the gardens and yards. His thoughts went to Rachel. She hadn't been in the study, so he had assumed she had found the spare room again and was fast asleep.

Gideon finally leaned back against the railing, crossing his ankles and using a hand to brace himself. He looked at Timothy and then Ben.

"I left the paperwork on the kitchen table, Ben. I hope it helps your investigation. If you need more, let me know." He caught Timothy's eyes on him. "I do fraud investigation, Timothy. When I left here, I was at loose ends. A couple at a church I happened to go to took me under their wings. He made sure I had college and then took me into his investigative firm."

"I'm sure it will, Gideon." Ben was waiting for one of the two to say something.

"Did she run again?" Gideon's eyes were on his mug.

"She did, about 5:30."

Timothy stared at his father. "She ran again and you let her again?"

"Timothy, she is an adult. She is not under arrest or in protective custody. If she wants to leave, she can." Ben's eyes were stern on his son. "You can't wrap her in bubble wrap and keep her safe. She will make her own decisions until such time as we need to step in as a police force."

Timothy shook his head and stood. Ben stopped him from leaving.

"No, Gideon goes. He's her brother and he's here now. It is right that he goes."

Gideon nodded at Ben and then turned to walk away. "I'll make sure she's safe and if I have to, I'll bring her back here."

Timothy watched him go, desperate to be the one, but knowing his father was right. Ben's hand rested on his son's shoulder in sympathy.

"We'll keep her safe, son. We'll do our best."

****

198

The Watcher's eyes followed the man leaving, then went back to the house. Who did he follow? Who would lead him to her.

He pulled out his phone. There was no message from the man he had hired. What was wrong with him? Did he have to do everything himself.

He turned, walked to his vehicle and left. He needed to find someone else to do his work and he knew just where to turn.

****

Gideon pulled his truck up his uncle's cabin. It looked the same, just neater. He could see Rachel's hand in that. He didn't see her but that didn't mean anything. She was here.

He stepped from the truck and looked around again, then moved to walk around the buildings. He stopped as he saw the motorcycle, put back together and ready to ride. Then he walked over to the truck. He had always loved that truck. Luke had taught him to drive with it. He wondered what would happen to it now.

He waited but Rachel didn't appear. He finally entered the cabin. He couldn't tell if she had been there that day or not. He found pen and paper and writing her a letter, sealed it into an envelope. He hated to leave without seeing her again. They had so much to talk about. But he understood her only too well. She would run and hide, she had been taught that only too well. His heart lifted in prayer, he finally shut the door and headed for his truck. He stopped and searched the area. He could feel the evil, feel it coming close to his sister, and yet he couldn't stay. He prayed that the men in her life right now could protect her until he got back.

Chapter 7

The two men stared at the tall heavyset man in front of them. Was he for real? He wanted them to kidnap a woman and maybe her boyfriend and bring them to him? And for how much? They shook their heads and walked away.   He came after them, shouting that he would give them more. Finally they stopped and turning walked back towards him. A fist flew through the air and the man lay on the ground. Curses followed them as they walked away.

Hours later, he had found the men he needed and given them their instructions.   Now he just needed to wait.   He had emphasized that time was running out and they needed to act now.   They nodded, took the printed information and pictures and walked away.

****

She had just missed him. Rachel stared at the letter in her hand. She had just missed Gideon. She had wanted to talk to him so badly and he was gone. He had left his address and phone number but it wouldn't be the same as talking to him in person. She felt all alone again.

She turned and gathered up the paperwork she needed. She was headed back to town. She needed to talk to Caleb, but she wanted to talk to him away from the department. Ben she knew would help her.

Marg paused as she saw the figure sitting on her back deck. Rachel. She had come back. Marg stopped to grab some juice bottles and headed out the door. Rachel looked up as Marg handed one of the bottles to her and gave a quiet thanks.

Marg sat and waited. She knew Rachel would talk when she was ready.

"I need to talk to Ben or Caleb, Marg. I need to give them what I have. I can't hide what I have any more."

Marg nodded. "Ben's on his way. He's made sure Timothy won't be here. You need to talk to Ben first and then if you want to, Timothy. Do you mind if Eddie comes too?"

Rachel looked at Marg. "Eddie?"

"Eddie was a patrol officer back when your parents lived here. He responded a number of times. He always felt there was more to what was said but not having proof, he couldn't do anything. He wants to help. If you don't want him here, he's okay with that."

Rachel shook her head. "I think I can remember him. It's okay." She paused and rubbed the scar on her arm. "I don't know how much good what I have will do. I couldn't get a lot. I was too closely watched."

Marg nodded and then looked down to the end of the yard. "Every little bit will help, dear. Give it to them and they will work with it. But even more, you need to give it to God. He's waiting for you to turn it all over. Let Him be your anchor."

Rachel looked up, frustrated. "Why does everyone say that, that God is an anchor? It doesn't make sense."

Marg studied her young friend. Her heart broke for what she saw in her face. "God is an anchor. What does an anchor do? It can either drive with the tides and gather garbage if it's not engaged right or it can hold you firm to where you are. Which do you want, Rachel, an anchor that drifts or an anchor that holds you firm?"

Rachel stared at Marg, then looked down. Marg had explained it in a way no one ever had. She had always thought an anchor was bad but now she wasn't sure.

A noise at the door had her turning her head. Ben came out and greeted his wife, then stopped by Rachel. He studied her, then reaching for her, hugged her. She was surprised. No one other than Gideon hugged her.

Eddie greeted Marg, then turned to Rachel. "Hello, Rachel. I'm sorry I couldn't stop it before."

She nodded. When the two men had seated them, she hesitated. The silence grew, but it was not uncomfortable. She knew they were waiting for her to speak.

Ben spoke. "Why don't we tell you what we have found out so far and then you can tell us what you have?" She nodded. As he spoke, her eyes grew round. They had found out so much, but there was still lots they didn't know. Motives and reasons that they hadn't even come to yet.

She reached for the papers she had dug up and handed them to Ben. "I can't say it, Ben, but here is some more information. I took a lot of beatings over the years. I wanted to kill them, I wanted them dead. God may punish me for that, but that's how I felt. No one should have to undergo what both Gideon and I did. You know where to find me when you want to talk to me. I just hope you find me before he does."

"Before who does?" Eddie asked.

She shook her head. "I'm not sure. I have an idea. All I ask is that you investigate the deaths of those two. They may not be dead after all."

She stood. "I know things are really going to get crazy and out of hand. I don't want anyone put at risk, but I need to stop this. Who knows how many more he has hurt besides Gideon and I?"

She walked down the steps and around the house. Ben, Marg, and Eddie stared at each other and then at the papers Ben held. What would they tell them?

Deirdre had tracked down Rachel and wouldn't take a no for an answer. Rachel followed Deirdre into the local cafe and to a booth at the back. Deirdre greeted friends on the way by but didn't stop to introduce Rachel. Rachel wondered at that.

Deirdre slid into the booth. "I know, you're wondering. A little bit of mystery goes a long way." Rachel stared at her, mouth open. "Close your mouth, you're going to catch flies."

Rachel laughed. "And are you going to share the reason?"

Deirdre smirked. "Of course. First we order, then we talk."

Orders placed, Rachel looked at Deirdre, waiting, smile in place.

Deirdre smirked once again, then sobered. "I know it's hard for you to come back. Having to meet a whole bunch of strangers won't help that feeling. We'll take it slow and easy and gradually introduce you to everyone in town."

Rachel choked on her soft drink. "Just like that, introduce me to everyone in town? And if I don't want introduced to everyone in town, then what?"

"By the time I'm done with you, you'll want that."

Rachel eyed her friend. "That's what I'm afraid of. I remember how you operated when you would stay here with your aunt and uncle. I'm not sure I'm up to that any more."

"Sure you are. You just don't know it yet."

Rachel shook her head. "No, I don't think so. There are too many people here I can't trust, who could have helped but didn't."

Deirdre tilted her head. "No, that wasn't right what happened. I just wish I had known." She stopped and changed topics. "I wish I could have seen the look on Frankie's face when you handed him that apple."

Rachel started laughing. "It was priceless. This crazy woman is muttering about apples, hands him one, then comes back and takes it away. Timothy was no help to him." The friends laughed and reminisced about other practical jokes they had played.

Deirdre looked up as they were deciding on dessert and smiled. Frankie and Timothy were heading their way. She slid over so Frankie could share her seat. Timothy stopped by Rachel and waited, not taking for granted that she would let him sit.

Rachel eyed Deirdre and then Frankie, finally looking up at Timothy. She pretended to think about letting him sit, and then slid over. The night had just gotten better. The two couples lingered over dessert and then left the cafe. Frankie and Deirdre wandered away, intent on one another.

Rachel stood uncertainly. Deirdre had picked her up and now she had no way home except to walk, in the dark. She was not happy with her friend. Timothy watched the emotions and thoughts flicking across her face. He was not happy with his cousin either. She would have a serious talking to as soon as he could.

Timothy reached for Rachel's hand and pulled her away from the cafe. She stared at him and then at their hands.

"Taking a lot for granted, aren't you, buster?" she asked, a laugh now in her voice.

He nodded, smiling to himself. "No, just walking with an old and cherished friend."

She would have stopped had he not held her hand and kept her walking. "Why, Timothy? Why say that?"

He led her to his car, opened the door and tucked her inside. Walking around to the driver's door, he prayed for the words he wanted to say. Once he was inside, he turned to her. She was watching him in the dim light from the streetlights.

"Because that's who you are, Rachel. You are an old and very cherished friend." He watched her face and her eyes. She had that look she always had when she wasn't sure someone was being honest with her. He sighed. How did he get her to understand his interest in her? "I have always treasured our friendship. You are a big part of my life. I would like to explore that more and see where we go. I don't want to lose you again."

She started shaking her head. "It won't work, Timothy. It just won't work."

"And why not? Because you say it won't? We need to get past what's going on now and then go from there. I won't let you run from me again, Rachel." He stopped. Staring out the windshield, he sought for words. "When you left, I was getting up the courage to ask you out. It really hurt when you left and didn't leave word where you were going. I wanted to come find you and bring you home to Mom and Dad."

Her hand came out to lay on his. "I never knew, Timothy. I never knew that. If I had, I might not have run." She stopped, tears clogging her throat. "But you didn't know my Dad. He was nothing like yours. I was scared for my life. I was scared for the lives of my friends. He had threatened you as well. He had threatened Gideon. I didn't know what else to do."

Timothy's hand turned so he could grasp hers. "I know. You had to make a decision and you did. I just wish I could have helped back then. Please don't run again. Come to one of us. Promise me this?" At her hesitation, he asked again. "Please, promise you won't run away. You'll run to one of us. I know Gideon is planning on moving back here, that's what he has said. Don't run before he comes back."

Rachel hesitated and then nodded. "I can't promise but I'll do my best."

****

The men watching them waited for the car to pull away and then followed them. Tonight should be the night they caught up to them and took them to the Watcher. But things weren't going their way. The car didn't head for the outskirts of town. Instead, it headed back to the suburbs. This was not going their way at all.

****

"Where are we going, Timothy? This isn't the way to my house."

"No, it's not. I'm taking you to my Mom. You need her right now."

She shook her head. "How do you know what I need? You're assuming a lot."

206

"I'm sorry. I guess I was. It's just that when I hurt, I need my Mom. I know you never had that. I want to share my Mom with you."

She studied him, then turned to stare out the side window.

"If you want to go home, I'll take you there. Please, Rachel, don't shut me out. Talk to me."

She finally shrugged. "I really don't care, Timothy. Do what you want."

He was hurt at her words. He knew he should have asked first. He pulled over to the curb and stopped, putting the car in park. He then turned to her.

"Talk to me, Rachel. Don't shut me out."

She remained silent, then sighed. "I know you mean well, Timothy. It's just that I've never had that kind of relationship that you have with your Mom, and it scares me." She motioned with her hand. "Well, what are you waiting for? Take me home to your mother."

He laughed, then reached over to plant a kiss on her cheek. He started up the car and pulled away, catching her in his side vision. Her hand was on her cheek and she was staring at him in astonishment. He gathered no one had ever kissed her like that before. He would have to make a practice of it, he guessed.

Sudden squealing of tires and a loud thump on the car sent it into the ditch. Timothy wrestled to keep control. Rachel frantically searched to see what was going on. Timothy was able to keep the car from overturning. When it stopped, he pushed at Rachel.

"Get out. Out your side. Quick. I don't think that was an accident."

Rachel grappled with the door handle and shoved it open, scrambling out and to cover. Timothy was on her heels. He grabbed her hand and pulled her towards the brush, hoping the darkness would cover their flight. He could hear the men at his car, searching for them. He knew they would soon be on their heels. He desperately looked for cover.

Rachel pulled his hand and pointed silently. There, up ahead, a shed. If they could make the men think they were in it, then maybe they could get away.

Chapter 8

Ben paced his study. Something had him worried. Something to do with Timothy. Was he okay? His feeling was that he wasn't. Marg walked towards him.

"Something's going on with Timothy. He's in trouble, Ben."

Ben gathered his wife into his arms. "I know, sweetheart. I can feel it." Both parents prayed, not knowing what was going on.

Frankie and Deirdre walked into the house. Ben and Marg turned, expecting to see Timothy with them.

"Where's Timothy?" Deirdre asked. "I thought he was headed here with Rachel."

Frankie stared at her. "And why would you think that? Rachel wouldn't be planning on coming here. And you really didn't leave her in a nice way tonight, walking off like that. I know you wanted to spend time with me, but did you think that she had no way home if she refused to go with Timothy? I thought Timothy had agreed to meet you there tonight and it was arranged with Rachel for him to take her home."

Deirdre had the grace to look ashamed. "I never thought. I just assumed she would go with him."

Marg looked at her niece. "Never, ever assume something like that, especially with Rachel. She doesn't like to feel trapped in anything."

Ben motioned to Frankie and the two men moved out to the kitchen.

"Do you know for sure Timothy was headed here?"

Frankie shook his head. "Not really. I know he wanted to bring Rachel here to Marg but we left before he talked to her. I don't like this, Ben."

"I don't either. We need to go looking for them."

"Before we do, Caleb wants to meet with us and Eddie in the morning. He caught me as I was leaving."

Ben nodded. "That we can do. Let's go searching."

Timothy stopped to catch his breath, wrapping an arm around Rachel. He searched the darkness around them. Where were the men? How close were they? God, are You there? Will You protect us?

A snapping of branches to his left and he pulled Rachel with him towards the town. He needed to get her safe. He wasn't far from his home but right now the distance seemed too great.

Rachel's breath came in gasps. She was scared but having Timothy with her helped. She blindly followed him, hoping he knew where he was and where he was going. He stopped again, in the shadow of a building and pulled her close, listening. Both tried to quiet their breathing. They could hear the men getting closer. Rachel buried her head in Timothy's chest and held onto him. She felt safe with him but the fear of the unknown was growing within her. She couldn't pass out, couldn't faint. She wouldn't do that to him.

Timothy listened. He couldn't hear anything. He was afraid to move, afraid if he did he would give away their location. His eyes slid shut as he felt the cold of metal at his temple and the clicking of a gun cocking. They had been found. They would not get away now. He looked around as best he could. Two shadows stood, one on either side of them.

Ben and Frankie stopped and scrambled from the vehicle. There was Timothy's car. Doors were open and there was no sign of them.

Frankie reached for his phone to make the call. Ben searched inside the vehicle, and then took the flashlight Frankie handed him. Searching the ground, he pointed.

"That way. It looks as if they were on the run."

Frankie nodded. "At least two after them. I don't see another vehicle though, do you?"

Ben shook his head. The fear for his son's safety was rising. They followed as best they could, trying to stay off the tracks they followed.

Frankie's heart was in his throat. He knew only too well what had happened. Whoever was after Rachel had found them. They had failed to keep them safe.

Sirens sounded behind them and blue and red emergency flashed through the night. Help had arrived but was it too late?

Timothy's breath caught in his throat and his arm tightened around Rachel. He was not about to let her go without a fight, but he had to be smart. A gun against his head wasn't going to make it easy. He heard the sirens and saw the lights. Help was on the way but would it be in time?

He felt Rachel shift in his arms, move more to his side. What was she planning? She was up to something. The gun at his head shifted slightly as the man turned to listen through the night. The other man had turned as well. He felt Rachel push away from him and towards the other man. He drew back his arm and wildly threw an elbow at the man next to him. Gunshots rang out.

Ben and Frankie slid to a stop. Gunshots! Where and who?

Frankie pointed and the men broke into a sprint. Who was there? Was it Timothy and Rachel? Would they be in time? They could hear sounds of running feet behind them.

Where were they? Ben and Frankie frantically searched. There was no sign of them. They could hear the footsteps behind them.

Frankie slid to a stop. There was a dark form on the ground in front of him. He dropped to his knees and reached to turn the form over. It wasn't Timothy or Rachel. He didn't know who this was. He looked up at Ben and shook his head, then stood, searching the night as best he could.

"Where are they, Frankie? Where are they?" Ben's voice was rough with worry. Where was his son?

"I don't know, Ben. They must have been here. The grass is trampled by more than one pair of feet." Frankie turned to the officers coming up. "Spread out and search. We're looking for Ben's son and his girl." The men nodded and then split up, searchlights breaking into the dark.

Timothy stared at the man who held the gun on him. He had forced them to move, to walk away from the building and the shelter they had sought. Who was he? He kept his arm around Rachel, trying to keep himself between the gun and her.

"Who are you?" he demanded.

The man remained silent, just staring at him, then at Rachel. He turned and listened to the noise from behind them as the search continued. He then turned back and motioned silently with the gun. Timothy refused to move. The gun was then pointed at Rachel. Timothy knew he had to do what he was told to, but he would watch, watch for a chance to at least get Rachel away.

He turned and grasped Rachel's hand, leading her forward. The man followed closely, gun still held at the ready. He could feel the trembling of Rachel's hand in his. He prayed like he had never prayed before. They were being forced into the unknown by someone unknown. But the Lord knew exactly where they were.

****

He stood watching, mingling with the growing crowd. What had happened? He had received word that his men had found the two and were closing in. Where were they? They had promised. Another broken promise! He turned and walked away, already plotting new ways to get those two.

213

Ben sagged back against his car, exhausted physically and emotionally. Despite the search by the men and women he worked with, there had been no signs of his son or Rachel. They just seem to have disappeared into the night. He could see the faint pink in the eastern sky. They had been out here all night.

Eddie approached his friend and leaned against the car. He watched as Ben turned and arms on the roof of the car, buried his head in his arms. He looked at the sky and whispered a prayer for safety for the two and for strength for Ben and Marg.

"Come on, Ben." He laid his hand on Ben's shoulder. "Let me take you home. Marg needs to hear this from you."

Ben shook his head. "No, I need to stay."

"No, Ben, you don't. You need to be with your wife." Eddie opened Ben's car door and shoved him in. "Come on, my friend. Let us help you."

Ben's steps were heavy and slow as he approached his door. Eddie had been right. He needed to be with Marg but he wanted to be on the front lines searching.

Marg stood in the open doorway, hand to her mouth, as she watched her husband walk towards her, defeat in his every movement. Tears gathered in her eyes as he stopped in front of her and then she was in his arms.

"Tell me he's not dead. Please, Ben, tell me he's still alive."

Ben sighed. "As far as we know, he is. We just can't find them. It looks as if they were chased and then the trail disappears."

Ben held his wife as she sobbed. He didn't see his niece standing in the study doorway. Deirdre was horrified. She knew it would be so hard on them. Her thoughts turned to her cousin. Lord, keep him safe.

Timothy stopped at the dock, staring at the small boat that was rising and falling with the waves. Where were they being taken? It was still dark. He turned to watch the man behind them. He motioned for Timothy and Rachel to get in. Timothy hesitated and once again the gun was pointed at them. Timothy helped Rachel to settle and then sat beside her, arm going around her. He felt the boat rock as the man sat behind them, and then the sound of the motor broke through the night.

They were forced out of the boat at a landing. Timothy felt disoriented. He wasn't sure where they were. The cabin loomed ahead of them, and Rachel's hand found the knob and opened the door.

Timothy spun to watch the man enter behind them. Desperately he searched for a way to get them free, to get them away from here. Shoving Rachel behind him, he rushed towards the man. The gun rose and fell. Timothy was on the floor, unconscious, blood trickling down his face. Rachel sobbed as she fell to her knees beside him and cradled him in her arms.

She stared at the man in front of them. "Why? Why are we here? Who are you?"

The man studied her in silence. A look of regret crossed his face. Rachel watched. He looked familiar, but then she shook her head. She didn't know him. She bent over Timothy's form, thinking she could protect him from further harm. She heard the man enter and exit the cabin and the sound of boxes being set down. His footsteps stopped beside her and a hand was laid gently on her head, and then the footsteps continued on to the outside. She vaguely heard the sound of the boat motor and then silence. She sat, her mind racing. They were safe. He hadn't killed them. But who was he? And why?

She laid Timothy's head back on the floor and stood, searching through the dark of the cabin. She walked towards what she thought was a table and hit the edge with her leg. A sound on the table and she reached for it. A flashlight. Strange. She flicked in on and the strong beam pierced the darkness around her. She saw the boxes on the table and moved to look inside them. Food and water. He had brought them food and water. He was taking care of them but why here, in this cabin? Why didn't he just let them go home? She grabbed a bottle of water, found a cloth and went back to sit on the floor by Timothy. Wiping at the blood on his face, she watched him. He wouldn't be awakening any time soon, she thought. She moved backwards until she felt the couch behind her. Her head sank and she was asleep.

Caleb stood in the conference room doorway and studied the men and women gathered there. There had been no lack of volunteers to search for Timothy and Rachel or to start going over the documentation Eddie and Ben had been gathering. His eyes sought out the white board and noted it was starting to fill up already with thoughts, ideas, and known facts. They were finally getting somewhere.

He turned as he heard someone come up behind him. It was Eddie and Frankie. He nodded towards his office and they followed him. Once they were all seated, Caleb watched them. The night had taken a toll on them, just as he knew it had on him.

His prayers went up for Ben and Marg. He could not even begin to imagine how they felt. If it had been one of his sons, he didn't know how he would cope.

"Where do we stand now?"

Eddie swiped his hands down his face. He was exhausted but refused to give in and sleep. "No sign of them. We brought in the K-9 unit but they lost the scent on the road. There was just too much there. Phil thought they might have headed to the lake but he couldn't confirm that." He stopped. "It's just so strange. It's like they were rescued."

Frankie nodded. "Those are my thoughts. Someone came along, shot that one fellow, and then took them away. But who and why?"

Caleb's eyes were on his desk. Hannah, this would be a really good time for you to come through with a name. But God is being silent with you right now.

"Has Hannah come up with a name yet, Caleb?"

Caleb shook his head. "No and I wish she would. Sometimes though I wish God hadn't given her this gift of speaking with her like that. It worries me."

Eddie studied his boss. The strain was showing. "He'll tell her when the time is right. Now, where do we go from here?"

Caleb thought about that. "How far back did we go searching into Rachel and Gideon's past? What do we know about their biological parents and how they came to be in foster care? Frankie, start searching there and see what you can find out." Caleb stopped and rubbed his eyes. "I guess I'll have to call Gideon. From what he said, I'm not sure if I can reach him over the next couple of days."

Eddie sighed, knowing their work was just beginning. "One step at a time, boss, one step at a time."

Timothy stirred. His head was pounding and he couldn't think why. He tried to open his eyes and even his eyelashes seemed to hurt. Much later, he stirred again. His eyes cracked open. The dim light even hurt and he closed his eyes again. Later, he stirred and rolled to his side. The headache wasn't quite as bad and he could finally open his eyes. He stared through the pain at the cabin, searching for the man who had brought them. Movement came into his vision and he rolled onto his back. Soft hands touched his face and he felt his head lifted and a water bottle at his mouth. He drank and then he was laid back down. He lay with his eyes closed for a few minutes, gathering his strength and then looked around again. Rachel sat beside him, hand on his chest, watching. A smile trembled on her lips. He reached and touched her face.

It took a few minutes but he could finally speak. "Hi."

She studied him, then rose, left and came back. She helped him to sit, steadied him, and then helped him to his feet and to a seat on the couch. She handed him some pain tablets and then the bottle of water. He drank as his eyes roamed the cabin.

"What happened?"

She shrugged. "You tried to tackle our kidnapper and ended up unconscious on the floor."

He decided that a nod wasn't the best move. "How long?"

"How long have we been here?" She shrugged. "It's about mid-morning."

"Do you know anything about where we are?"

She stared at him, then away. "We're in the middle of the lake, on an island. We have no boat."

"No boat. Okay." He studied her. "Let's think about this. How can we get away? Are we far from the shore?"

She shook her head. "I can see the shore from here."

"Can we swim back?"

She stared at him again. "No. You're in no condition to swim and the person with you doesn't do water."

He stared back, hazel eyes meeting gray. "You don't do water?" She shook her head. "So we need to plan. Can we make a raft?"

She snorted. "Sure, if you can find the rope to tie trees together. I don't do trees and I don't do water."

His eyes began to sparkle with mirth. "No water, eh?" He thought, "Is the water low enough anywhere we could walk out?"

"Timothy! We're in the middle of a lake. No, we can't just walk away. We can't make a raft."

"Can we take a door off then and use it for a raft?"

Her hands flew into the air. "Yeah, right. It would never hold both of us. You're in no condition to swim and I told you, I don't do water."

He shook his head. "When we get out of here, I want to find out why you don't do water."

"It's very simple. It's wet and it's cold." She looked around and then stood. "Do you want a sandwich? Whoever that was made sure we had food and water."

"That's what I don't get. It's like he rescued us and brought us here to be safe. Who was he?"

"I have no idea. I feel like I should know him, but I don't." She sat back down, eyes on her hands. "Timothy, how do we get out of here? Your parents must be frantic."

He watched her. "They would be. Dad would be trying his best to find us. Mom would be spending time in prayer." He looked at the ceiling, emotions overtaking him. When he could speak again, he said, "I hate that they are worried."

She nodded but remained silent. How were they to escape? Would there even be any escape?

****

The Watcher stood once again in the crowd, staring at the activity going on. The police hadn't found those two. Where were they? One of the men he had hired was dead. The other was long gone. Now he would have to go through the process once again. It was time consuming but also it mean more money. The anger continued to build and burn. When he got those two, they would pay.

****

Caleb rubbed his eyes. He was just too tired to continue reading but he refused to give up. He needed to find Timothy and Rachel. Eddie had been in and said Ben and Marg were coping but were devastated that Timothy was missing. He looked up at a knock at his door.

Frankie entered, closed the door, and then sat. He stared at the floor, trying to find the words he needed.

Caleb waited, knowing Frankie would speak when he was able.

Finally, Frankie looked up. "It's just so strange, Caleb. Why shoot the assailant and then kidnap them? It's just too bizarre."

Caleb nodded. "It is. Did you find out anything about Rebecca and Gideon's parents?"

Frankie sighed. "I did. Their mother died from an accident when Rebecca was only two or three. Their father was raising them, then the two of them just disappeared from his care and ended up in the care of the foster parents. I did find out something interesting. The foster parents used a long list of aliases. We're still trying to sort out how many and where all they lived before they moved here. It's a long, slow process." He stood. "Go home, Caleb. Spend some time with your wife and boys. I have a feeling it's going to be a while yet before we find them."

"I think you may be right. I'm about to go check on the work in the conference room and then heading home."

Timothy stood outside the cabin and stared around. There had to be some way of getting off the island. How though? He started searching, looking for a canoe, a kayak, anything that would work. His head was aching but not like it had been earlier. He had left Rachel curled up on the couch, asleep. He didn't figure she had gotten much sleep the night before.

He paced towards the water and stared across at the shore. So close and yet so far. How could he get Rachel out of here and to safety. There was the sound of steps behind him and he spun. He faced the man from last night. Today he got a clear look at him and it puzzled him. He looked familiar but why?

The man held up his hand before Timothy could say anything. "I don't want to hurt you. I am sorry I had to hit you last night."

Timothy stared at him. "Who are you?"

"That's not important. The important thing is to keep you and Rachel safe. I know who is after you and he will stop at nothing until she is dead. You're just collateral damage as far as he is concerned."

"Couldn't you have just gone to the police and told them?"

The man shook his head. "No, not knowing who I could trust, I couldn't."

Timothy shook his head. "There's my Dad, there's the police chief, there are detectives that are friends. You can trust them."

The man shook his head. "No. Not until I have all the evidence. I am working on gathering that."

"So, are you going to let us off the island?"

The man stared at Timothy, then his eyes shifted as he studied the shoreline. "No, not until I have a safer place for you."

"And if we don't want to wait for that?"

The man's gaze came back to him. The gray eyes looked familiar. Who did they remind him of, Timothy wondered?

"The man after Rachel has already hired more men to find you. If she hadn't come back, she would have stayed safe. But she came back."

Timothy looked behind the man. Rachel stood back a ways, listening. "Why am I not safe?"

The man didn't turn. He kept his eyes on Timothy. "Because of who you are. Because of what you saw. Because the man who is after you is pure evil." The man walked past Timothy. Timothy stood rooted in spot, then turned and ran after him. The man was gone. Where had he gone? He hadn't heard a motor.

Rachel stood beside him. "Where is he? He can't just have disappeared?"

Timothy shook his head. "No, he couldn't, but I don't see him. I don't hear a motor."

He looked around. "Is there a secret passage here somewhere? Do you know what island we're on?"

Rachel looked around at the lake and then the shoreline. She walked closer to the water and turned and studied the island.

Her eyes lit up and she turned to the end of the island. "Down there. They used to say at certain times of the day, you could cross to the shore, that the water was lower. I just can't remember what time of day they said."

Timothy grabbed her hand and pulled her towards the end of the island. He pointed.

"You're right. See. The water does seem lower." He looked down at her. "Okay, you who doesn't do water, ready to give it a try?"

She shuddered, then stiffened herself. "Let's go for it. It can't be worse than staying here."

They plunged on the rock pathway they could faintly see and followed it along. The water rose to their knees and then stopped. They knew that if the wind came back up, they wouldn't make it. They dropped to their knees as they reached the shore and turned back to look behind them. The water had already risen again. They had just made it. No one could explain why this happened but it did. God had provided a way for them.

Timothy drew Rachel into a hug and then turned her towards the woods.

"We need to keep moving. Do you have your cell phone?"

She shook her head. "No, mine was in my backpack, which is in your car. Do you have yours?"

He reached for his pocket. "I do but it looks as if there isn't very good service here. And it doesn't have much of a charge left." He looked around. "Come on, sweetheart. Let's keep moving. It will dry us off and hopefully we can find somewhere we can get better cell service." He reached for her hand, then stopped. "What happened to the one who doesn't do water?"

"I don't do water, not deep water. That wasn't water, that was just a puddle."

He laughed, then tugged her with him. It was hard walking, the ground very overgrown. They finally reached a trail and stopped. Rachel sank to the ground, exhausted.

"Can you get service yet?"

He shook his head. "Not yet. We need to keep moving. I don't feel comfortable staying anywhere for too long."

She sighed, then let him pull her to her feet. "If you insist, we must go on. I hope we can reach someone soon. I don't do dark very well either."

"You're just a fountain of information today, aren't you?" He laughed at her nonsense. "I'll do my best to get you home before it's too dark."

****

He stood once again watching. The activity level had increased but he could find out nothing. He stood among the news people. They didn't know much more than him and what they were saying was speculation. He had sent his two new hires out to try and find them. Who had taken them? He was running out of time and needed that girl's help if he was to survive.

****

Eddie's phone rang and he stepped out of the conference room to answer it. At the voice on the other end, he turned, ready to head back in but stopped. He listened, then looked around for Caleb. Finding him, he tapped him on the shoulder and beckoned for him to follow him. Caleb stared at Eddie, wondering what was up, but knowing Eddie wouldn't have asked him to come with him if he didn't have a good reason.

Eddie stopped the pavement of the parking lot and listened. When he pocketed his phone, he turned to Caleb.

"They're safe, Caleb. Praise God, they're safe."

Caleb's eyes slid shut and then popped open. "Where are they?"

"Timothy gave me a general idea of where they are. He is worried though that if we try to get to them, we'll be followed. He didn't say much as his phone battery was pretty much depleted."

Caleb's mind was racing. How could they get to them without being followed? He was sure that whoever was after them knew all their vehicles and their family vehicle.

"Who can we send that no one would suspect?"

Eddie thought, then turned to Caleb. "Greg. He would go for us."

Caleb nodded. "Let me call him. I'll need to know as much as you can give me as to where they are."

Greg readily agreed to find Timothy and Rachel. Caleb had thought his pastor would be willing to do that. Eddie took Caleb's phone and gave Greg what information he needed.

Caleb was already working on a place to take them. It wouldn't be safe to bring them back to Ben's or any of their homes. Where could he put them?

His phone rang. It was Greg. He had a suggestion as to where they might be safe. Caleb thought about it and then agreed.

Timothy pulled Rachel back into the trees and brush as they heard a car approaching. The car slowed and stopped. The engine was turned off and the lights extinguished. They heard the door open and then a voice called softly for them. Timothy listened and then drew Rachel forward with him. He knew that voice and knew they would be safe.

Greg hustled them into his car and starting it drove away. Timothy and Rachel watched as he seemed to be driving in circles.

Finally, Timothy just had to ask. "Are you driving in circles for the fun of it or are you trying to make us dizzy?"

Greg laughed. "Neither. I am waiting for Caleb to call with a place to stash you two. There's a tray of coffee and muffins on the floor back there, Rachel. By the way, I'm the pastor from the church, Greg Evans."

She nodded, then searched the floor and found the food. She kept a coffee and muffin for herself and then handed the tray over to Timothy. She wasn't used to this. The ministers she knew didn't do this. She listened as the two men discussed the sermons Greg had been giving lately, the ones on anchors and why and what they were.

She finally leant forward. "Mr. Evans."

"It's Greg."

"I'm sorry?"

His eyes met hers in the rearview mirror and he smiled. "It's Greg. The only one who calls me Mr. Evans is my wife when she's ticked off at me." Timothy snorted at that.

She studied him. "Okay, Greg. I don't understand. You've put yourself in danger for us. You're driving us around at night when you should be at home with your family. You've brought us food.

Why? What's in it for you? The ministers I know don't do this kind of thing."

Greg thought about what she said. "I know a lot of ministers like that. I don't believe that's how we are to be. Christ wasn't. Christ was there for each person who needed him, sinner or not. I have to follow His example, not matter the cost. There is nothing in it for me, per se. It is just knowing I have followed Christ is my reward."

She sat back and studied him again. He was just so different from what she had been raised with and what she had seen. Timothy had been nodding in agreement. This gave her a lot to think about, but first she had to figure out who was after her.

Caleb was waiting for the phone call. He, Eddie and Frankie had made plans. They weren't about to tell Ben until they had Timothy safe. Ben had wandered through the department minutes earlier, worn, tired, beaten down. He said Marg was taking it really hard.

His phone rang, and Caleb stepped away from the commotion in the conference room. He shut the door to his office and answered. It was Greg. He had them and was on his way to the safe house he had suggested. Caleb went searching for Eddie and Frankie. A quiet for and each one made their way out, just as planned. They went in separate directions. Soon they would find Timothy and Rachel and hear what they had to say but for now, they would take as many precautions as they could to prevent being followed.

****

Where were they going? All three had left by themselves. The investigation was still ongoing. He didn't think they had found them yet. Those three wouldn't just walk away and not search for them.

Who should he follow? Should he stay here? All he could think about was how short time was getting.

Chapter 11

Timothy stared at the building and then at Greg. "Really? You brought us there?"

Greg smiled. "Why not? Who would think to look for you here?" He stared at the old church parsonage. "I can't think of a better place to stash you two for now, until Caleb comes up with somewhere else. We use this for the visiting missionaries or as a temporary home for those needing it. Most people have forgotten about it."

Rachel stared at the building, then at the two men. They were being given safety in a building belonging to a church? She didn't like that. She didn't feel safe in a church.

Greg looked around and then said, "Looks okay. Let's go. The door is just there beside you, Timothy. Here's the key. Lock the door after you. Caleb will be along shortly. He has a key to the building as well and will find you. Here, take this flashlight. Don't put on lights."

Timothy shook his head. "I don't know, Greg. It still doesn't feel safe." He turned slightly so he could see Rachel. She was staring at the building as if she couldn't believe it either.

"No." Rachel was adamant. "I'm not going in there. He knows. He knows about it. He used to talk about it."

Greg shared a look with Timothy, then turned to Rachel. "Who knows, Rachel? Who are you afraid of that would know about this building?"

Tears in her eyes, she pleaded with Greg. "Please, take us somewhere else. We won't be safe here. I know we won't."

Greg sighed and then started up his car. "I guess we could find somewhere else. I just thought it would be a good place."

"Frankly, Greg, I don't think there is a really good place for us right now."

Greg pulled out his phone and tossed it to Timothy. "You get to call Caleb and break the news to him. We need to find some place fast. Driving around only increases the chances of you being seen."

Timothy spoke briefly to Caleb, then turned to Greg. "He wants us to meet him at the diner on the highway." Worry clouded his face. "I just don't know where we'll be safe. It seems....." His voice died away and the thought was left unsaid.

Greg watched their faces in the flickering lights from the passing vehicles. He was worried. He needed to get them to Caleb and then Caleb would look after them. He just hoped he could do it without them getting caught.

Caleb was frustrated. They had had it all set up for a safe house, and then Rachel had balked at going in. Then he thought about it. So far, her instincts had been right on. If it was who he thought it was after her, then she knew the man and knew just what he was capable of.

He pulled to the side of the road and pulled out his phone. "Eddie, we're not using that place. They won't go in."

"Doesn't surprise me. If you have lived here for any amount of time, you know about that house. Now where?"

"Good question. Any ideas?"

Eddie's voice faded for a minute, then came back. "I'm trying to think of someone who could take them in." Caleb could hear the sound of traffic passing him and then Eddie spoke again, "Rebel's Cabins."

"Sure, why not? I'm sure Abe will take them in. His cabins all have state of the art security because of who stays there." Caleb pulled away from the curb and searched the traffic around him. He couldn't get over the feeling of being watched, of evil hovering just outside his line of sight. "I'm headed to get them. Abe's Peg's nephew, isn't he?"

"He is. He'll be glad to help. We don't have to call first. I know he'll find somewhere to stash them."

Caleb pulled up to the busy diner and around to the back. He stopped and turned off his car. He waited. He knew Greg would take no chances. Few people knew that Greg had been in the army for a tour before he went into the ministry. That could work to their advantage. Caleb watched as a car pulled around to the back of the diner and then stopped on the other side of the garbage bin. The engine was turned off and lights extinguished. It was a waiting game, to see if either of them had been followed. He knew Frankie was parked at the front of the building and that Eddie had gone inside, supposedly to grab a meal for himself and his wife, Peg.

Finally, the doors of the other car opened and two figures emerged, to disappear in the darkness near the bin. Caleb heard the doors open on his car and the figures slipped in.

"Stay down, you two." He whispered. "Let's make sure we haven't been followed."

The other car pulled away into the night. Still, Caleb waited. Finally, he pulled out from the back of the diner and headed for the downtown area. He watched the traffic, searching for who he didn't know. Then, after a very circuitous route, he headed for the highway.

"Where are we heading, Caleb?" Timothy's voice cut through the darkness.

Caleb turned his head slightly at the voice. "I'll let you know shortly. First, your phones. Turn them off and drop them on the front seat." As they did so, he pointed to the floor in the back seat. "There's a pay-as-you go phone there. We've programmed in numbers you need and made sure that the location finder is off. No one but Eddie, Frankie, and I have that number." He could hear the exhaustion in Timothy's voice. "You two all right?"

Rachel snorted. "If you mean being kidnapped, kept on a island, having to watch an unconscious man to make sure he is still alive, escaping through water (and I don't do water), then through the bush, being taken to a house where we can't stay, and now in the back of a police cruiser? Then I guess you could say we're all right."

Timothy stared at her. "It wasn't my fault I didn't know what was going on."

"Only because you tried to play hero and attack our kidnapper. But there's something strange about that, Caleb. He provided food and water, and I am sure he put his hand on my head as if he knew me. He looked familiar, but I can't place him."

Caleb nodded. "We're in the midst of gathering a lot of information about you and Gideon and about your foster parents. Interesting reading. We're hoping that we can sort it all out in the next day or so."

Timothy stared out the window and then swallowed. "How are Mom and Dad?"

Caleb sighed, his heart hurting for his friends. "They're okay, but it's really hard on them. Deirdre is with them. Frankie was going to swing by later and talk with your Dad."

"Not telling us where we're going?"

Caleb shook his head. "Not until we get there. I'm still not sure if it will work, but we're trying, Timothy. You two have to do your part and cooperate." His eyes sought Rachel's but she refused to look at him. He was worried that she would take off and leave their protection.

****

The Watcher stood in the diner parking lot. They had been tracked to here. Now they were gone. Who had them? Where were they headed? He had to find them. He only had a few days left before the bottom fell out of his world.

****

Frankie tapped at Ben's back door and then entered. He thought Deirdre might be here. Ben was sitting at the kitchen table, a cup of cold coffee in front of him. Frankie studied his face and the new lines that were etched in it. He took the cup from in front of him, dumped it and made fresh. When he had poured their cups, he set Ben's in front of him, then pulled out a chair at the table and sat.

"Marg sleeping?"

Ben nodded. "Getting what she can. Deirdre went home earlier. She said she had some work she had to get down." Ben looked up, his eyes bloodshot and worried. "Any word?"

Frankie nodded. "Caleb has them. They're safe."

Ben's eyes slid shut. Thank you, Lord, he murmured. They're alive.

"Has he got any word on what happened?"

Frankie shook his head. "Not yet that I know of, other than that they managed to escape. Greg picked them up and then handed them off to Caleb."

"They're not hurt?"

"Not that I know of, but I haven't heard much other than they're safe." Frankie studied his cup. "Caleb won't say where they are, you know that, Ben. It's for your protection as well as theirs."

Ben nodded as he stared across the room. "I can handle that as long as I know they're alive." He hesitated. "I'll need to tell Marg. I can't keep that from her."

Frankie shook his head. "I'm not sure about that. We need to keep everything as it is."

"What can't you tell me?" Marg's voice came from the doorway.

Ben turned and then stood to gather his wife close. "Timothy's alive. He's with Caleb." He felt the relief run through her body, then she pushed away from him.

"What can you tell us, Frankie?"

He studied the woman who would soon be his aunt by marriage. "Not a lot, I'm afraid, Marg. They haven't said much. Caleb was headed somewhere with them. Greg had come up with what we thought was a great place but Rachel refused." He took a sip of his coffee before continuing. "I wish I knew who she was so afraid of."

Marg looked at him. "And you still haven't figured that one out?"

Frankie shook his head. "If you have any ideas, please share."

Marg's hands flew into the air. "It's her foster father. I never believed that he died in that tornado. He was too mean. He likely faked his death and has been hunting for her ever since. No one knew where she was. Ben and I tried to find her over the years." Ben's hand rested on his wife's.

"Marg's right, Frankie. I never believed the reports either. There were many rumours over the time they lived here. That's what I was working on and come tomorrow, I'm going back at it. I always felt there was more to the background than what was ever said or ever came out."

Frankie stared at the two. "You mean, you two have been sitting here, figuring it all out while we've been running like crazy to do just that?"

Ben gave a short laugh. "Not really. It's just we know the town and the people in it. You have to find the evidence to convict, that doesn't happen on rumour or innuendo."

****

The Watcher clicked off his phone. He was down to mere days if not hours to come up with the information. He had been warned. He had no intention of dying. That would be the girl who died, not him. He turned to the two men he had hired.

"Find them and find them tonight, by tomorrow afternoon at the latest. If you value your lives, find them."

The two men looked at him and then each other. With a shrug, they turned to leave. How did he expect them to find those two? They weren't from this town. If they had to, they would leave town.

Timothy peered through the dark at the house Caleb was pulling up beside.   Then he nodded. Perfect, he thought. No one would find them here.

Caleb turned off the ignition, then turned to Timothy. "We'll keep you here for now. Abe has very few guests at the moment, and they are off in the far cabins. He's going to put you up in the house. We need to lay down some ground rules that both of you have to follow.   We can't keep you safe otherwise."

Timothy nodded, then glanced over at Rachel. "She's asleep, Caleb."

Caleb peered through the darkness and then emerged from his vehicle.   At his nod, Timothy slipped around and gathered Rachel into his arms. He followed Caleb into the house and then down to a bedroom on the main floor. He tucked Rachel in and after studying her face for a moment, turned and followed Caleb back to the kitchen.

"I'll be back out sometime tomorrow or Eddie will." Caleb nodded towards the hallway. "Abe has set up a room for you as well on this floor, near the back of the house. The yard is totally fenced with a privacy fence so you'll be able to get outside without being seen. Get some sleep."

Timothy nodded, turned, and stumbled in his tiredness. Caleb watched until his friend had entered the bedroom he was assigned, then went to find Abe. A few minutes conversation, and Caleb was on the road back to town. He didn't think they had been followed but he really wasn't positive.   Nothing seemed certain any more.

Rachel awoke to the sun in her eyes the next morning. She stretched, then looked around, uncertain as to where she was. She sat up. It had been good to sleep in a bed last night. A duffle bag sat on the chair by the door. She arose, curious, and went to open it. It contained clean clothes for her. She was grateful to whoever it was that thought ahead. Her hands stopped as she was brushing her wet hair back into a braid. Is this what Greg had meant last night? Is this how a Christian was to act? She still felt lost, felt anchorless, but was beginning to see and finally understand what was being said to her.

She found the kitchen and saw that there was food waiting. She went straight to the coffee pot, poured a cup, and then wandered over to the door to look out. The fenced yard was large and well landscaped. Numerous seating areas were scattered throughout it.

She felt someone come up behind her and tensed.

"You can go outside, you know." Timothy's voice was amused. His voice ruffled the hair near her ear.

She shook her head. "I'm not sure. Is it safe?"

Timothy laughed and reached around her for the knob. "It is, very safe. Abe's father and his uncle set this place up with very high security. They had a number of diplomats and government officials come here for vacations."

Hand on her back, he ushered her through the door. "This will give us a chance to recover from the last couple of days. Caleb's working on solving what's going on. He said Dad, Eddie and Frankie were really pushing to get answers."

She looked around and then up at him. "Still, Timothy, how do we know they can't find us?"

He sighed, her question echoing his own thoughts. "We don't. No one can guarantee anything. But our friends will do their very best." He looked down at her. "Come on, let's take a walk around the yard, the person who doesn't do water. There's only water features, nothing like that lake."

"Timothy! That's not very nice."

He laughed, then clasped her hand in his and led her down the steps. They spent time wandering the yard, just getting to know one another without the stress of running from the unknown.

Abe stood at the doorway, watching them. He smiled. They look good together, he thought. Lord, help us keep them safe. He turned as one of his employees came into the kitchen and handed him a file. He studied it and then nodded. Things were starting to make sense. Now he just needed to get this to Caleb or Eddie. He sent his employee on his way, with orders to give it to only Caleb or Eddie. Soon, he hoped, like them, that they could send this two on their way without having to worry about their safety.

Caleb reached for the file Eddie handed him. He looked up at Eddie and asked, "Is it what we were looking for?"

"All that and much more. Abe's men are good."

"How is Ben making out on his investigation?"

Eddie paused and thought. "I think he's finding out some very interesting facts. One of them he did share is that Gideon and Rachel's biological father is still alive. He's trying to track him down."

Caleb stared at Eddie. "He's still alive? Do we know the story behind them coming into foster care?"

Eddie shook his head. "I don't think we have the whole story yet. Ben's pushing on that." He hesitated, then continued, "It's pretty certain that the foster father is still alive and is back in town."

Caleb stilled. "In town? Then that could explain everything." He thought for a minute. "Have someone research his financials."

"Already on it. I should have a preliminary report by late today or tomorrow."

Caleb nodded. "Let me know what you find out." He sat back. "I just pray we can keep them safe until we get everything run down and sorted out."

Eddie stood. "I know. I have that feeling though that we won't."

"I know and that worries me."

Abe turned as Rachel and Timothy entered the kitchen. He knew he had to go over the house rules and really didn't want to. They were stringent, but they had been set up that way for a purpose. That purpose had kept many men and women alive.

Rachel studied Abe as he told them the rules. She nodded, figuring they wouldn't be here that long anyway. They were a lot less strict than what she had been used to as a child.

Abe turned to Timothy. "Now, about your business."

Timothy nodded. "That has me worried. The seniors really depend on me."

"Caleb had talked to your Mom. She has gone in to help you in the office, I understand?" At

Timothy's nod, he continued, "She will do that for now.   As to the actual work, you have more volunteers than you have clients."   At Timothy's stunned look, he laughed. "Your Dad said he had officers coming forward to volunteer to help keep your company going. You're part of their family— they take care of their own."

Timothy's eyes slid shut in relief. That was one burden he was glad to share for now. "Thank you. Now if we could only find out who is after us."

"We have some ideas on that and Eddie, Frankie, and your Dad are working through a plethora of information."

Rachel started laughing and the men both looked at her.   "Who talks like that? Plethora? Really?"

Abe grinned at her. "Sorry, my mother was an avid reader and she used to teach us those words. She said we could always throw them into a conversation to stop the conversation in its tracks if it was going nowhere."

Rachel started laughing harder, then headed for the fridge.   "At least, let me cook for you, professor."

Timothy shook his head. It was good to hear her laughing.   He shared a glance with Abe and sobered at the look in Abe's eyes. Things were over yet, not by a long shot.

****

"We've found them."   The older of the two men stared at the Watcher. "It's going to be tough to get to them, but we'll get them."

"You only have two days to do so.   Don't fail."   The Watcher turned and walked away from them.   He would never show those two men his

241

emotions but he was scared himself. He knew he had to get to Rachel and get that information and possibly signatures from her. Time was running short.

****

"What do you have, Ben?" Caleb waved Ben into his office.

Ben sank wearily into one of the chairs. "I'm not sure yet how far this goes, but it goes far beyond what we thought. It's not just their foster father. It involves someone here in the town and it's looking as if it's someone in the town office."

Caleb's eyes slid closed and he shook his head. "It just never stops, does it? When will corruption ever end?"

Ben shot a glance at Caleb. "It doesn't, does it? I'm working on tracking down who it is and if they are still in office." He looked up at the ceiling. "I just wish it was all over. We keep praying for it to end and for God to protect them." He looked back at Caleb, emotions high on his face. "You know what it's like. You went through it with Joshua. I keep telling myself God's in control of it all. Sometimes I just wish He would be more open in sharing what His plans are."

Caleb nodded. "I know what you mean. His plans are not our plans. We have to keep that in mind. Maybe it's to show Rachel she really does matter to Him, to show her she has an anchor to keep her safe."

Ben studied his friend. "If you look at it that way, it puts a whole different perspective to it, doesn't it?"

"How's Marg?"

"She's doing okay. Working in Timothy's office is helping. She feels close to him there."

242

A knock at the door interrupted them, and Eddie entered. He sat in the other chair and looked at the folder in his hands.

"What's up, Eddie? I don't like that look on your face." Caleb knew he wasn't going to like what Eddie would have to say.

"I can tell you right now you're not. My research into Rachel and Gideon's past." He handed the folder to Caleb. "Short version: Their mother died when Gideon was about three and Rachel one or so. I haven't been able to determine if it was an accident or not, but she was run down while biking. The driver of the vehicle that hit her was impaired. Their father was raising them and working. He had found a really good babysitter for them, near their home. About three years after their mother died, he went to pick them up and there was no sign of the babysitter or the children. The police report that I got from then says there was no evidence to suggest foul play. But they found the body of the babysitter about two years ago dumped in the forest. No sign of the kids. Not until they turned up a year or so later in the care of their "foster family". We haven't been able to track down any paperwork at all establishing this couple as a foster family through the normal system."

"This is just getting more and more bizarre." Ben was shaking his head. "So they were never approved as a foster family, the kids were more than likely taken from the babysitter, and the babysitter murdered?"

Caleb tried to absorb the words he was hearing. It was just so difficult to take it in. "Keep working that angle, Eddie. Pull in who you need to. Abe's men might be able to help. They have resources we don't."

Eddie took a look at Caleb. "Hannah hasn't given you a name yet, has she?   It would be real helpful if she did?"

Caleb shook his head as he laughed. "No, she hasn't. I'll let her know you're getting anxoius."

Chapter 13

The men studied the house and the grounds. It was going to be difficult but not impossible, they thought to reach them. This place was like a fortress but fortresses could be breached.   They took the pictures they needed and then melted back into the surrounding terrain.   It was time to go plot their move. The Watcher was depending on them. He was paying them well to accomplish what he wanted. They conferred with one another and then set off for their vehicles.   Their thoughts were to return that night.

****

Timothy wandered through the house. He was unable to settle himself down to anything in particular.   Abe watched him, knowing the restlessness was not him but the circumstances they found themselves in. He had an uneasy feeling that something was about to happen. He prayed that the plans and security details they had in place would be enough.   But sometimes, no matter how much planning, how secure they thought they were, it was not enough. The line could be breached.

Rachel had curled up in a chair with a book, but she wasn't reading, just flipping pages every once in a while as if she was. Her mind was busy, trying to sort out the facts and emotions. There was just so much she didn't know. Her mind went to the man who had taken them to the cabin. Who was he? He looked so familiar, as if she should know him. She shook her head. She couldn't know who he was. It just wasn't reasonable that she would.

Night had finally fallen. Timothy headed for the kitchen. He wanted another cup of coffee; he wasn't ready to go to bed just yet. He glanced into the living room. Rachel was still curled up in the chair. He poured the coffee, and then taking a cup for Rachel, headed back towards her. She absentmindedly took the cup and sipped.

Timothy sat across from her, watching. She looked puzzled at something.

"What are you thinking about so hard?"

She shrugged. "I'm not sure. I've just got so much going through my mind right now." She looked at him. "I'm trying to sort out everything in my mind, but there's just too much to think about."

He nodded. "I know what you mean." He tilted his head to watch her. "What are your plans once this is all over? Will you stay here?"

She looked at her cup and didn't speak for a few minutes. "I'm not sure, Timothy. I would like to but I just don't know. I would like to be near Gideon."

"He's planning on moving back here."

She looked up, surprised. "He is?"

"That's what he said. I guess he can work from just about anywhere. His boss is in agreement."

"That's interesting. I'll have to think that through."

Abe passed by on his way out to do his rounds. "Everything okay in here?" At their nods, he reminded them, "If the alarm goes, head for that room over there and lock the door behind you. We'll come get you."

Rachel shuddered at the reminder. "I don't like the sounds of that, professor. Can we say we did and don't?"

Abe gave her a stern look. "No. If there is an alarm, I want you in there within seconds of it going off."

Rachel shrugged but wouldn't look at him. Timothy's heart sank. He knew what she was planning. She would run if the alarm went off. He just prayed he would know and could go with her. He didn't want her running away on her own.

Abe paused in his patrol. He could feel the evil, knew it was close, knew it was watching him. He turned, staring into the night, trying to pinpoint where it was. He keyed his mike for help and ran for the house. It was there. He prayed the two were in the safe room. The lights were off, and he was suddenly very afraid.

The lights flashed off and Rachel gasped. Timothy lunged for where she had been and grabbed her hand.

"Come on. We need to find that safe room."

She hesitated. "We can't. I can feel them here in the room."

Timothy pulled her with him towards the room. "Quick. We should have time."

A black figure stood in the doorway he was heading forward, the light from the emergency lights showing only the form. Timothy slid to a stop and then pulled Rachel towards the front door. He hoped they could get out in the time and find Abe or his men.

They wouldn't make it in time, Rachel thought. How could they? The form was too close and it was safe to say he wouldn't be on his own. Sobs caught in her throat. They were supposed to be safe here. What had happened? God, where are you? You're supposed to keep us from harm, aren't You?

Timothy pulled the door open and then shoved Rachel through, footsteps pacing heavily behind them. He couldn't take time to close the door; he could feel the evil at his back. He grabbed her hand again and searched the darkness. Where could they go? He raced for the edge of the yard, hoping that the darkness would cover their path. If it didn't, could he protect her? He could hear running footsteps heading for the house and then running footsteps behind him again. He stopped, searching for a place to hide. Rachel pulled at his hand and then took off again at an angle from where they were running. He followed, her hand tight in his. What had she seen that would provide them protection?

The large rock formation loomed in their path. Timothy stopped for a minute, listening, his breath coming in gasps, arm tight around Rachel. He could feel the pounding of her heart, the laboured breathing, matching his own. Were they safe? He heard measured footsteps pacing towards them and he pulled her hand once more to go forward. He didn't know where they were or where they could find shelter. God, are you there? Provide a way.

Timothy listened for footsteps. They had stopped. He couldn't tell where the man was or if there was more than one. He wasn't even sure that it wasn't Abe or his men. He grasped Rachel's hand and pulled her towards the dark, away from the compound. He needed to get her to safety. He could feel the evil around them. Please, Lord, lead us.

Abe stood in the house, lights once more on. Timothy and Rachel were gone. They hadn't had a chance to make it to the safe room. One of his men came up to him and spoke with him, then moved away. They just weren't sure which way the two had run and with little moonlight they would have to wait until morning to try and track them. Somehow, someone had breached their security to the power room, turned off the main switch, and at some point, sabotaged the generators.

Caleb stopped at the front door and watched the activity. His heart sank. They must be gone, he thought. Abe looked up and shook his head.

"What happened, Abe?"

"We're not sure. We were out doing rounds. Timothy and Rachel were here in this room. I felt something off, headed for the house and the power went off. The generators never kicked in and they should have. When we got here, the front door was wide open and they were gone."

Caleb stepped back so he could see the safe room. "They never got in there?"

"No. They should have had time and they didn't. The front door was wide open when I got back. It was not even five minutes, Caleb, just that brief span of time. Someone knows our setup. Someone got to them."

"Do we know if they've been taken captive or are just on the run?"

Abe shook his head. "We don't know. We'll have to wait until morning for proper light to try and track them. I just pray we're in time."

Caleb looked down at the envelope he had in his hand. "I was headed out here tonight to show them these photos. We have tracked down the two men that were hired to capture them." He pulled the photos out and showed them to Abe.

Abe studied them, then pointed at one of them. "This guy - he was out here a week or two ago, said he wanted somewhere safe to stay, that he was being threatened with death. He just didn't ring true with his words. I sent him on his way. He didn't get past the edge of the yard over there, where the gate is. What I don't understand is how did they figure out how to get through tonight?"

Caleb stepped back outside. "I can tell you. You have such a wide open range behind you, that's covered in rock formation, trees, etc. It is very easy for them to sneak in there during the day, wait until dark, and then strike. They could take out your power and generators. Were any of your men hurt?"

Abe started to shake his head, then stopped. "Now that you mention it, one of them had an accident this morning when he was checking out the area just to the left when you're facing the house. He's not sure what happened but he ended up with a concussion and a fractured arm."

Caleb winced, then said, "So we can assume then that the area was compromised. How did they know we had them here? We were so careful."

"I trust the men working for me. In fact, I trust them with my life. They are all highly interviewed and investigated before they come on staff."

"I know they are. I'm not sure how I am going to tell Ben and Marg that they're on the run again, that we couldn't keep them safe."

A grim look on his face, Abe spoke with force, "We'll be out there just as soon as we have any bit of light. Will you be sending out anyone?"

Caleb shook his head. "No, your men are good. Just watch them. And Abe, if you know of any of your people who had left in the last year or so, track them down. We need to clear everybody."

Caleb laid his head back on the headrest in his car. What had happened? How had they been found? He was positive that no one had followed him, that no one knew where they were. His thoughts went to Ben and Marg and a sadness filled him. How was he to break it to them? At this point, he had no idea if the two were even still alive. Lord, guide us. Help us to find them. Protect them.

He picked up his phone and dialled Eddie. When Eddie answered, Caleb filled him in. There was silence on the other end of the phone. Caleb could tell Eddie was running scenarios, trying to put the pieces today.

"I've got it, Caleb. Meet me at the diner like last night."

Timothy stopped again, trying to catch his breath. They couldn't keep running like this, not in the dark and not knowing where they were going. Rachel dropped to the ground and with knees drawn up, laid her head on them, trying to breath easier.

"Did we lose them?" she whispered.

"I don't know. I don't hear anything." He looked around. "Do you have any idea where we are?"

"No. I thought you did by the way you were running."

He dropped to the ground as well. "I just hope we've lost them. We need to keep moving though."

"We can't see where we're going. We could be near the quarry and I have no desire to walk off the side of that." Rachel shivered as she thought of that. "I can feel them, Timothy. I can feel the evil from them."

Timothy nodded, then rose and once again grasped her hand. "Come on, let's keep moving."

The men were not that far behind them. They knew they would soon catch them. If only they hadn't run so far. They would have a long hike to the vehicle they had hidden.

Timothy looked around.   Where could they go? He searched the sky and getting his bearings for direction, headed off again.

Rachel stumbled and her hand loosened from his. He turned and helped her up again. They had to find shelter soon. She couldn't go much further.

Chapter 14

Caleb climbed from his car in the early light. He was exhausted and he still had to talk to Ben and Marg this morning. Eddie walked towards him.

"What do we have?"

Eddie nodded at the roof of the building next door. "Security cameras. I went back over the footage. Found our guys. They were here just after we left. I still haven't figured out how they knew, though. We've kept it to just us four as to who knows."

Caleb nodded. "Somehow, word is leaking and I know it's not one of us four." He sighed. "Do we have any leak in the department or is someone hacking in to the system?"

Eddie looked around, then went towards Caleb's car and searched around it. He beckoned Caleb over and pointed. "There. That's how they knew. How did they get their hands on this?"

A small dart protruded from just above the license plate, barely visible. Caleb bent over to look at it and nodded. "I wish I knew. Blackmarket more than likely. Get the team out here. I'm not moving my car. We'll need to check all of ours."

"You're heading to Ben's." It wasn't a question but a statement.

Caleb studied the area around him as he pondered his next move. "I'll have to. I hate this. We had them safe and someone was one step ahead of us. Find him, Eddie. Find out who is really the one we want. I don't think it's their foster father. He's just a pawn in a bigger game."

"I agree. We've been digging deep, but we'll dig deeper." He paused, then continued, "I think we're going to find once again it's someone we least expect."

Caleb agreed. He turned to study the area around the back of the diner. "How did we miss this, Eddie?"

"Whoever is planning this is good. I still suspect a link to us somehow."

Caleb turned and studied him. "I have a bad feeling you're right. I just wish it was all over and Timothy and Rachel were home safe."

Ben watched as Caleb walked up to the door. His heart sank at the look of defeat on Caleb's face. He didn't often look that way.

Caleb looked up at Ben standing on the front step. "Ben, I'm sorry."

Before he could continue, Ben stepped down, turned him around and walked them away from the house. "All I want to know, is Timothy still alive?"

Caleb nodded. "As far as we can determine, he and Rachel are. Someone tracked us. We had them at Rebel's and the security was breached. They didn't get a chance to get to the safe room. Abe figures they're on the run somewhere back of his place."

Ben stopped and drew in a deep breath. Caleb saw how tired he was, how drawn his face. Ben was trying hard to keep strong but even his strength was being tested. "They're in God's hands, Caleb. It is His will. I know Timothy has that strong anchor of his faith. Rachel, I don't know her well enough to say if she does or not but I pray that she does." He glanced back at the house. "I don't want to tell Marg, but I'll have to. This has to have been the hardest thing we have ever gone through."

Caleb reached out a hand to Ben's shoulder. "Before you do, Ben, let's pray. Let's cover them with God's protection."

Marg watched the two men. She knew. She just knew her son was not safe. No one could ever doubt that a mother knew what was up with her children. She turned and headed for her prayer chair, as she called it, her rocking chair she had used for years. Dropping heavily into it, her head bowed and tears ran down her face. But she could feel God's peace flowing through. At Ben's step on the hardwood floor, she looked up and smiled. He drew her up into his embrace and together they prayed. Whatever happened, it was in God's hands as Ben said.

Timothy paused. They needed to stop somewhere. He looked down at Rachel. She couldn't go on much further. The rising sun showed pink and purple in the east. He studied the area around him. He just wished he knew exactly where they were. He had a vague idea.

Rachel sank to the ground. Her strength was gone. She didn't think she could take another step. Her head sank to her upraised knees.

"Have we lost them, Timothy? Or are they closer than we think?"

He dropped to the ground beside her. "I just don't know, Rachel. I hope we have lost them, but I can feel the evil behind us. I think they're close. I just pray that we can outrun them and get to safety."

"Do you really think God cares that much, Timothy? Does He really?"

He tiled his head so he could see her face, partially covered by her hair. "He does, Rachel. He cares that much."

"It sure doesn't feel like He does."

"I know. We have times when we feel like that, that we feel abandoned and adrift. But we're not. It's like a boat swinging at the end of an anchor chain. We can swing and turn and feel loose but God has us in His hands." He continued to watch the area around them. He just wished he knew exactly where he was.   He also knew they needed to find fresh water at the very least.

He stood, then reached down his hand. "Come on, Rachel. We need to keep moving. I hope Abe and his men or Caleb are behind us."

She looked up at him, frail and tired in the dawning light. She reached for his hand and let him pull her to her feet.   "Which way now, Timothy? Can't we just go back the way we came?"

He started to shake his head, then looked behind him. Why not, he thought? They wouldn't expect them to do that. A sound came from their left and he pulled Rachel with him towards the rocks behind them. He shoved her down and then crouched in front of her. They could hear the footsteps and the low conversation.   At least two men, Timothy thought. If they would just leave, then they could head back towards Abe's.   He could feel Rachel's hand on his back, grasping his shirt.

The footsteps faded in the distance. Timothy sank to the ground and leaned back on the rock. They would have to wait for a few minutes. Would they be able to get away?

****

The Watcher was angry. They had almost had them last night but they had escaped. Who was helping them? He was getting pressure to bring her in. There was not a lot of time left for him. If he failed, his own life was forfeit and he had too much to live for. He was just so close to finally getting what he had been scheming to get for so many years.

****

Caleb stood at the white board in the conference room. There had to be something they were missing, some link they hadn't come across yet. What was it or better yet, who was it? He took the file he was handed and looked at it. He sighed. Still another dead end. Then, he reread it. His finger stopped and he read over what had caught his attention. He spun around, looking. He headed for Frankie.

"Frankie, take a look at this. New research they've dug up."

Frankie searched Caleb's face, then reached for the folder. He read and then going back, stopped where Caleb had stopped. "Is this for real?"

Caleb nodded. "It appears to be. We'll need to verify it. Find your best person and get them on that." He looked around. "Have you been able to connect with Gideon?"

Frankie shook his head. "Not yet. His boss says he's been out of town working on a case and he can't reach him. He did give me Gideon's number and I only get voice mail. Hopefully, he'll get back to us soon, but better yet, we'll have his sister safe and sound."

"That would be nice. Keep up the good work, Frankie. You, Eddie and Ben are really working overtime on this."

257

Frankie stared at the wall. "I just don't get how Ben and Marg are just able to let it go like they do. I know they're worried, but they have such a peace."

"That's what God can do—give us peace in our storms. He can become our haven, our anchor. When times are good, we don't need that. When the storms come, that's when we are tried and tested and find out how great our God really is."

Timothy cautiously stood and looked around. He didn't see or hear anyone. He stepped around the rocks and studied the ground. He wished he knew how to read tracks. He had never needed that gift before. Rachel touched his back, and he jumped, not expecting that.

"They went that way.   Let's go this way. Maybe we'll find Abe or Caleb heading our way."

Timothy stared at her.   "Just like that, you know what way to go."

"Luke loved the forest. When I was young and could spend time with him, he used to show me. I hope I haven't forgotten too much."

"Okay, the one who doesn't do water, you can teach me as we go along." Timothy stopped, and then pulled her into a hug.   She stiffened for a minute, then hugged him back.

When she stepped away, she studied his face, then turned and walked back the way they had come. He took a deep breath and then followed. Rachel was becoming very important to him. He never thought he would ever find someone he would even consider spending the rest of his life with but when they were out of this and things were back to normal, he wanted to get to know her better, to take her on walks and out for dinner. Lord, is she the one You planned for me? If so, please keep her safe.

Rachel drew a deep breath. Timothy had surprised her. She was not used to hugs. If anything, beatings had been the norm in her growing up years. She was saddened at that thought. Yet, she could remember hugs from a man, she thought her father. He had loved her and Gideon so much. Where was he, she thought? Why did he let us go?

The two men stopped and studied the area around them. They were lost. They were city dwellers, not country people. They had no idea where they were or where the two they were following had gotten to. They turned and trudged back the way they had come. Would they be able to find their way back? They heard voices ahead of them and stopped, then crept forward as silently as they could. Who was ahead of them? Did the voices belong to the ones they were trailing? They stopped at the top of the rise and searched, eyes piercing through the rising light.

Ben turned to look for Marg and Deirdre and watched them through the glass in the back door. Marg was moving among her gardens, taking time to enjoy her flowers. Deirdre stood in the middle of the yard, looking lost but determined to do something. She said something to Marg, who turned and then walked towards her. An arm around her niece, she led her to a swing to one side of the yard. Ben's eyes slid closed, and a tear trickled down his cheek. Lord, it hurts so much. It hurts that I don't know where he is, if he's hurt. You do. Keep our hearts at peace, no matter what happens, Lord, even if it's the worst we could think of.

Rachel stumbled and went down on her hands and knees. She didn't think she had the strength to get back up. Timothy reached for her and pulled her up.

"Here, hold my hand. You need to. Let me help you."

She stared at him. No one wanted to help her in the past. Why now? She shrugged and turning walked forward.

Timothy stared after her. What would it take for her to accept his help? He sighed, then followed after her. He searched the area, recognizing bits and pieces of the area from their flight. It had been dark but little things had stood out. There was the funny rock over there, that looked like a bear cub. His foot slipped and he barely caught himself from falling forward and into Rachel.   They needed to find somewhere to stop and rest but where?

Rachel stopped finally to catch her breath. She knew they were getting close to Abe's again but she could feel the evil behind them.   She turned slowly and scanned the area. Nothing stood out to her. She looked over at Timothy. He was worn out, just like her. He had to be as thirsty as she was. She was afraid to stop for long. She just knew the men were behind them.

She turned to walk forward and screamed. One of the men stood in front of her. She spun. The other stood behind Timothy, gun to his head. Her heart sank. All that and they were caught. Timothy's eyes were steady as he stared at her. Somehow they had to get away again. How though?

Timothy stood, gun to his head, and watched Rachel. He could see the panic she was trying to push back down. He was pushed forward from behind. As he came to Rachel, he reached for her hand. Her fingers clung to his. Somehow, he had to get her out of this. But how? If they were close to Abe's, would he be around looking for them? He thought they would but he didn't know for sure where they would be looking. Their flight last night in the dark had sent them on a random path. They just had not had time to think.

Caleb turned as Eddie came up beside him. He was once again in the conference room, watching, waiting, hoping that they would find anything, even a small lead that would help. Eddie studied the white board, then reached over and wrote something at the bottom. Caleb stared at it and then at him.

"Seriously?" At Eddie's nod, Caleb shook his head. "I didn't see that one coming. The tracks were really well hidden."

"They are. We're still digging. Gideon was finally able to call. He can't leave where he is, no matter how much he wants to. With the weather, they're not letting any flights in or out and he said the traffic was nothing but a bottleneck. He'll get here as soon as he can. He's got an idea he wants to run with. We can't stop him. He's a civilian and her brother."

"No, we can't. He might find out something more than we can from the financials. That's what he does - forensic auditing. We could use him on the force."

"We could. Why don't you offer him a position when he comes back?"

Caleb smiled. "I just might."

"Has Hannah come up with a name yet?"

"No she hasn't. She's been away with her parents and the boys. They'll be home in about a week. And she hasn't said anything when we've talked." Caleb looked around at the activity going on. "I hope the one she comes up matches what we've discovered. If not, then we have a whole lot of work left to do."

Eddie nodded glumly. "That's exactly what I'm afraid of. Your wife is spot on with the names and if she has a different one, then we're in trouble."

Caleb laughed. "I know we are. Just keep digging. We'll get there."

"That we will. When this is done, we will all need a vacation. We'll also need to put up a sign at the entrance to town that says we've had enough."

Caleb shook his head as Eddie wandered off. He knew Eddie was joking but he felt the same. He reached for his phone as it rang. To his delight, it was Hannah. He stepped away from the conference room to talk with her and catch up on the news.

"I miss you, Caleb. So do the boys." She sighed, and Caleb heard it in her voice. He knew what was coming.

"You have a name." It was a statement not a question.

"I do. I don't like it but it is what the Lord have given." She hesitated for long moments and Caleb's heart sank. That meant it really did bother her and he knew then it was a new name, not one they had been looking at.

"Who is it, my favourite girl? You never have to be afraid to tell me."

"This time, I really don't want to. I really don't." Caleb could tell she was in tears. "I just wish someone else had this gift."

"Is it really that bad?"

"Yes."   When she said the name, Caleb slumped back again the wall. Hannah was right. It was really bad.

They talked for a few minutes longer, and then Caleb tucked his phone away. He stared across the corridor at the blank wall. How were they ever going to find the evidence? The tracks were well hidden and had been well hidden for many years. He sighed, looked up with a quick prayer for guidance and went to find Ben, Eddie, and Frankie.

Abe watched as the men shoved Timothy and Rachel forward. He knew he had his own men on the other side of the trail, but he could tell one wrong move and one of the two would be hurt, if they even survived. They had been that close to getting them to safety. He looks up and saw Joseph, one of his best men, on the other side of the trail. They stared at each other, then Abe nodded. Joseph had an idea and Abe had learned to let him run with his ideas. They were always excellent. He was one of the younger men on the team but came from a background of training. Abe also knew that Caleb wanted him on the force and that Joseph was really considering the move.

The man behind Timothy spun at a noise behind him.   He stared at the man dressed in camouflage who stepped out of the woods. When the man spoke, Timothy's heart jumped with relief. They were safe. Rachel moved closer to him, not sure of what was happening.

"You know, you're not getting out of here." Joseph's voice was calm and matter of fact.

"We are." The taller of the men snarled back. "We have what we want and we are leaving."   His gun came up to point at Joseph.

Joseph studied the man. It was what they thought. These men were not amateurs, even though they were out of their element. Now, how to get Timothy and Rachel away from them. He knew Abe was close by and so were a couple of the other team members.

The man in front of him kept backing up. Timothy and Rachel were forced forward and away from Joseph. There didn't seem to be a way that they could escape.

Joseph spoke again. "You really aren't going anywhere. There are men surrounding you."

"The man doesn't count. It's the woman we want. We were paid to bring her to the Watcher."

Abe listened to the conversation. Who was the Watcher? He knew it would take a lot of patience and negotiations but he feared they would never get to a resolution without someone getting hurt.

Joseph spoke again. "Then, you'll need some way to get out of here. My team members won't let you by, I can guarantee you that."

The man sneered. "We'll get by." He continued to back up, forcing those behind him down the trail. "You won't hurt these two."

"And a trade won't work?" At the man's vigorous shake of the head, he continued, "Then, let me get you out of here. I'm tired of working here. I could use a new boss."

Timothy stared at the man, dumbfounded at what he was hearing. How had Abe ever hired him? He felt Rachel's hand clutching tighter.

The man thought, then nodded. "Ditch all your weapons."

When Joseph complied, he was motioned forward. "You go first, hands in the air. Find us some transportation and then you drive."

Joseph strode past them and down the trail. He couldn't show his relief that his plan worked. He only hoped that Abe had caught on to what he was up to. He didn't know where it went from here.

Abe watched as Joseph led the group down the trail, then bowed his head. With Joseph in the group, at least they had a chance. He dropped down to the trail and met his team mates. A quick conference and they scattered. Abe pulled out his phone and made a quick call to Caleb. Things were still in motion though and out of their hands. Please, Lord, keep them safe.

Timothy watched closely, hoping to find a way to escape once again. He could feel the fatigue weighting down his body. He stumbled and caught himself before he fell and dragged Rachel down with him.

Joseph stopped by a vehicle. "We can take this one. It's the easiest one to get away with."

"Search it." Joseph stared at the man. A gun went to Rachel's head and she whimpered. "Search it and get rid of any tracking devices."

Joseph did a search, knowing Rachel's life was in his hands. He also knew there were tracking devices placed where no one would find them. He held up his hands when he was finished. "I've found what I can."

The man's eyes narrowed and then he pointed the gun to Joseph. "You drive. I'll be sitting right behind you, so don't try anything."

Once they were in the vehicle, Joseph started it and headed for the compound gate. His eyes roamed the area and he caught a glimpse of a team mate watching from near the gate. Once through the gate and out to the road, he was forced to drive towards town. Once in town, he was directed to an area he really didn't expect to be going towards. His eyes sought Timothy's in the mirror and noted that Timothy's eyes were surprised as well. He could also see that Rachel was asleep, Timothy's arm around her to keep her safe.

Caleb went to find the other three.

"Abe called." Ben's eyes sought his. "They're alive and so far okay. They are in the hands of the two men but one of Abe's men is with them. He's convinced the captors that he wants a new job."

Eddie looked at Caleb, and then the ceiling. "He convinced them he wants another job? Just like that?" He just shook his head.

"What's our plan now, Caleb?" Ben's look hadn't changed.

"Abe said they can track the vehicle as long as they don't change to another one, and he's afraid that's what the plan is. Joseph will do his best to keep them safe."

Caleb looked around. "It's time to end this. We need to come up with some plans because one plan just won't do. Get with our best people and start planning. Ben, I need you to work on finding information on that name. Dig into whatever you have to and pull in whoever you have to."

Caleb's phone rang. It was Abe.

"Bad news, Caleb. The vehicle's stopped. We're at it. They're gone. It looks as if it was just a ploy to get out of the compound."

"That's what I was afraid of. Is Joseph still with them?"

"As far as we can tell, he is. They're watched so close, he wasn't able to leave much of a sign for us."

"Thanks, Abe. Do what you can to find them."

Ben sank into a chair. "They're not there?"

Caleb shook his head. "These guys are smart. They seem to be one step ahead of us all the time."

Ben looked around. "Is there a leak again?"

"I hope not, not when it affects our own."

****

The Watcher hung up his phone. His men had them and were on their way to the meeting place. It was too bad they had to pick up that other man, but they would deal with him. He won't be alive much longer to tell who they were.

Timothy hadn't been able to awaken Rachel when they changed vehicles. He sat next to her on the back seat of the truck, arm once again holding her close to him. His eyes moved constantly, searching for a way out. Joseph drove once again, in a seemingly endless, meaningless circle. God, are you there? Timothy's heart cried out. Where will this end?

Joseph was finally directed to a warehouse outside of town. His eyes met Timothy's and he saw the surprise in Timothy's eyes. This was not what they had expected. Driving the truck around to the back of the compound, he waited until a garage door was opened and then drove in. He searched the dimness, looking for a way out. He knew his team would be searching but it seemed helpless. It was up to him and Timothy to protect Rachel, and he didn't think Timothy had much left to give.

They were forced out of the vehicle and then to the office of the garage. Timothy sank down on the torn couch, Rachel beside him. Joseph sank down into a chair. The door closed behind the men. Timothy went to speak but Joseph shook his head. He didn't trust that they couldn't be heard.

Caleb looked up as Eddie entered his office.

"I've had a thought, Caleb. What if we went to the news with an update? You know they're covering the story."

Caleb sat back and thought about that. "We could, but I'm not sure if that would work and not backfire on us. The media has a way of doing things that often lead to bad situations getting worse. Let me think on it."

Eddie nodded. "That's what I thought too. It's getting hard to know who to trust in this town."

Caleb smiled. "I know what you mean."

Eddie looked towards the door. "It's just so frustrating. We had them safe and someone got to them."

Caleb watched him, knowing he wanted to say more. When Eddie didn't, Caleb spoke. "I know how frustrating it is. This time, it's one of our family of officers that's affected. We need to resolve this but I can't see how soon we're going to be able to."

Eddie's eyes turned back to him. "I just hope we do soon. It will kill Ben and Marg if Timothy doesn't make it home safe."

"It will certainly test their faith. All we can do is pray and keep on doing what we doing."

Timothy and Joseph looked up as the door opened. Rachel shrank back against Timothy, not sure what was happening. Joseph was pulled to his feet and out the door by one of the men. The other closed the door and stood in front of it watching them.

Joseph was shoved through the back door of the building and towards the back of the lot. He turned just as he felt a crushing blow to his head. He collapsed and lay still. The man with him looked around, then dragged him behind the dumpsters. He would be found but not before they had left. He had been ordered to kill him but his own personal code wouldn't let him. No one would know, he knew. He looked around. He felt someone watching him. Who was there? He could see no one in the dark.

The door opened and the man in front stepped aside. Rachel and Timothy watched as the first man entered. Joseph was not with him. Where was he?

Timothy could feel the fear radiating from Rachel. Lord, he prayed, please protect us. Help us to get away.

The two men conferred quietly and then the men left. Rachel sat watching the door, then got up and moved around the office.

"Timothy," she whispered. "What did they do?"

Timothy stood and went to her. "I don't know. I just pray they didn't kill him."

Rachel spun slowly in a circle, studying the office. "We need to get out of here."

"I know we do, but how? I don't think we're going to be able to get past the door." Timothy looked around as well. "There are no windows and no other entrance."

"I'm not staying here. I need to get away." She was starting to feel the panic building inside her.

Timothy stepped in front of her, hands on her shoulders. "Rachel, please, you need to stop. We'll find a way."

She looked up at him, then shook her head. "So far, it's not been happening. Who do you think it is?"

He shook his head. "I have no idea. It has to be someone with lots of money. These guys here don't come cheap."

Something caught his eye and he moved away to look at it. A fire extinguisher. Could they use that? He held it up, and Rachel shook her head.

"That won't work. It only works in the movies."

"So, we'll pretend we're in the movies."

"And if it doesn't work?"

"Then we'll have tried, at least. I'm not waiting around for whoever is paying these guys to show up." He stopped and watched her. "You know that they mean to kill you, don't you?"

She glared at him. "You just had to mention that tiny little fact, didn't you? I don't plan on getting killed, but I don't see how we can use that." She pointed to the fire extinguisher.

They heard the door knob rattle and raced to get back sitting on the couch. The first man entered and dropped a bag of food on the cluttered table. He didn't say anything, just stared at them.

Timothy looked at the food and then at the door. He wondered if they had been heard talking. He had no appetite to eat. Rachel opened the bag of food and then closed it back up again. She didn't feel like eating either.

Timothy stood and paced as best he could. After a few minutes, he stopped by the desk and idly looked at what was there. He reached for a piece of letterhead that caught his attention and then read what was on the paper. His eyes stilled, and then he looked at Rachel. This couldn't be about her, could it? That name too. What connection was there between it and Rachel? He paused to look again at Rachel. She was leaning back on the couch, eyes closed. He couldn't tell if she was sleeping or not.

The door rattled and the first man entered. He stared at them, then silently motioned them forward and out the door. Rachel walked towards the centre of the building, then her steps slowed and stopped. Timothy halted his steps right behind her and his hands went to her shoulders. She stared at the man standing there.

"So, it has been you all along." The scorn was evident in her voice. "I thought as much. Timothy, I'm sure you remember my foster father. I won't introduce you as I have no idea what name he's using now, he's used so many over the years."

Timothy's hand tightened on her shoulders. She was baiting the man. He could feel the anger and dislike, almost hatred, building beneath his hands.

The man studied her. "I see your attitude hasn't changed a bit, has it? Still need to have it beaten out of you." He approached her. "You have cost me a lot of trouble, time, and money. Between you and your brother, you have done a lot of harm."

Rachel refused to step back from him. "I look at it this way. You deserve everything you get. And you will pay for all you've done."

The man began to shake in rage and came at Rachel with an open hand. It was just Timothy's hands on her shoulders that kept her on her feet.

She tasted the blood on her lip, and then looked at him. "Always a bully, aren't you? You'll never change."

As the fist was raised again, Timothy stepped forward and shoved her behind him. The man stopped with his fist just shy of Timothy's face. He peered around him with a look of hate.

"You're not just dealing with me now. There are others involved."

Rachel stared back at him. "Of course, there are. There always are. You're a bully, and bullies never act alone."

Timothy once more stepped into the line of the fist. This time it didn't miss and he felt the strength of it rock him backwards. If she kept this up, that man would kill her.

The man stepped backwards and then started pacing.

"So," Rachel asked in a deceptively mild voice, "who do we call you now? It certainly won't be Dad."

The man stared back at her. "No, it won't be. I can go back to my real name finally. It's Bill Waters."

Timothy's mind raced. He knew that name and it wasn't in a good way. But where had he heard it before?

"Well, then, Bill." Rachel's voice dripped with sarcasm. "What exactly is it that you think I have?"

Bill Waters stared at her, hatred in his eyes. "You have a locket that belonged to your mother. In that locket is a paper with an account number on it. If I don't access it in the next two days, that money is gone."

She shook her head. "Sorry, Bill, I don't have that locket any more. Your daughter stole it from me years ago."

Bill stopped and stared at her. "No, she didn't."

"Well, yes, she did. Anything I had when I came to your house, your wife or daughter took. I was left with nothing. Gideon was the same."

Bill glared at her, his mind racing. He knew neither one of the females in his house had had the locket. So where was it?

Joseph drew himself up to his knees, hands going to his head. Where was he? He peered around through pain-laden eyes and remembered. He had no idea where Timothy and Rachel were. He stumbled to his feet and across the lot to the gate. Strange, he thought, it is still unlocked and there doesn't seem to be any workers around. He staggered as he walked, trying to get his feet and legs working as they should. He finally came to a coffee shop and after fumbling with the door, made his way inside. The workers looked at him in horror, then one of them rushed to his aid. He told them little of what happened to him. Instead he asked them to call Abe. As he waited, his mind cleared. There had to be something about that warehouse or factory or whatever that building was. Who was it connected to?

Caleb's phone rang as he was sitting down to a late dinner.

"We've got Joseph." Abe's voice was rushed. "I don't know the details but he's alive. No sign of Rachel or Timothy with him. I'm on my way to get him. Are you home?"

"I am. Bring him here. I'll call the other three."

Joseph sank gratefully on to the couch and reached for the water bottle Caleb handed him and then the pain tablets.

"Thanks, Caleb. I don't know how I made it to that coffee shop. It's all kind of a blur."

The other men had seated themselves, waiting for Joseph to speak.

He swallowed, then looked around, centering his gaze on Ben. "I'm sorry. I couldn't get them out. They separated us. I ended up outside by the dumpster." He looked down. "They were fine when I last saw them. Exhausted, hungry, but alive." He looked up and stared at Ben. "I'm so sorry."

Ben nodded, pain showing in his eyes. "I know. It's nothing you could have helped. These men are smart. We just need to be smarter." He looked down at his hands, flexing his fingers. "Tell us what happened. Tell us where you were taken. Tell us what you can remember about the men."

"Do you have a map with you, Abe? I think I can remember where the buildings were."

Bill paced the cement floor of the warehouse. He didn't like being here. He would rather remain behind the scenes but he knew Rachel would never give up what she had to anyone else. He studied her as he passed her. She was different. She was not longer the meek, scared girl that he had had in his hands. Something or likely someone had changed her. She never had backbone before, so why now?

He stopped behind them and watched Timothy. Timothy stood alert, but relaxed. His face showed his exhaustion as did the slump in his shoulders. Bill knew it wouldn't be easy to interrogate Rachel like he would need to with Timothy there. He turned and paced towards the back of the building. His phone rang and he grimaced as he saw the number. He spoke briefly, turning as he did to watch them. The two men he had hired stood and watched, not missing a lot.

He motioned to the older of the two men as he hung up his phone. They conferred for a few minutes, then both turned to watch Rachel and Timothy. Word had come and they needed to move them. They just needed for find a safer place.

The man walked forward and shoved Timothy and Rachel towards the large shop doors. Once outside, they were directed to a van and shoved inside. The younger of the men followed them in and the door closed behind them. Bill took the passenger seat as the older man climbed behind the steering wheel. Timothy couldn't see much from his position on the floor of the van and it was impossible for him to figure out direction from the way the van was turning corners.

Rachel leaned against Timothy's arm.   She was really scared right now. She knew just what her foster father was capable of.   She had heard them talking in the past about the children who disappeared in their care. Where were the bodies, she wondered?   There was no doubt in her mind they were dead. He wouldn't hesitate to kill either one of them, she knew. She felt Timothy's hand grasp hers in a steady strong grip. Lord, she prayed, You know where we are. I just need to learn to trust You, to trust You to keep me safe. It's so hard.

Caleb stood in the doorway of the warehouse. They were too late, likely just by minutes. He was frustrated. He turned to look around the outside area and saw Ben walking towards him.

"Caleb, where are they?"

Caleb shook his head. "Not here. Someone has to be watching us to know what is going on. We've kept this too close to just us four and Abe and his men. So who is watching us?"

Ben stood looking around the warehouse, then focused on the office. "There, the office. Maybe we can find something there."

Caleb nodded.   "I'm sure we'll find something. They're starting to get sloppy. Joseph should be dead and he's not."

Eddie stood behind them. "I know of a fellow who takes contracts for abductions like this. He has a strange code. He won't kill anyone at all.   He'll deliver the person but if someone gets in his way, he doesn't kill them. He'll dispose of them in a way that won't kill them."

"Can you find out if he's here and who hired, Eddie?" Ben spoke without turning.

"I should be able to." Eddie walked away.

Ben and Caleb stepped into the warehouse as one of the crime scene team member came up to them. She handed Caleb an evidence bag containing a necklace.

"Where did you find it?"

"It was on the floor by the couch and had to have just been dropped there today. There was no dirt or dust on it. If it had been there for any longer, it would have been seen and picked up."

"Did you open it?"

The woman nodded and handed him another bag. It had a small piece of paper in it. "These look like an account number of some kind. I can run it when we get back to the lab."

Caleb nodded. "Call me directly when you do. No one else."

Caleb and Ben walked towards the office in the building, meeting Frankie headed their way.

"Take a look at this, Caleb."

Caleb took the new evidence bag and read the letter inside. Ben read over his shoulder. Caleb nodded. "That's who we're looking for. Get on it, Frankie. I think we should have enough to go for warrants. I would go with Judge Lane this time, though."

Frankie stopped, looked at him for a minute, then nodded.

"Well, now we know." Ben stared around. "How long will it take?"

"Hopefully, not long. Judge Lane is good. He'll get the warrants for us as soon as he can."

Rachel's hand clung tighter to Timothy's as the van stopped in a garage. It was too dark to see where they were. They were pulled out and roughly shoved towards a door at the side of the garage and, once outside, towards a low building at the back of the yard. Lighting was limited and they could see little. The younger man stood with his back to the outside of the door and waited. The older man and Bill Waters had gone into the house.

Timothy looked around the building. There were no windows and only the door that was guarded. There was no way out. Rachel came up beside him.

"What do we do, Timothy?" Her voice shook. "There's no way out. They won't be able to find us."

Timothy drew her into a hug and laid his cheek on her hair. "I know, sweetheart. God knows. We have to trust."

She hugged him back. "I'm scared, Timothy. I know what Bill is capable of. I'm sure he killed kids in his care. I saw him dump a body years ago. It was Mary."

Timothy's heart broke for the woman he loved. "Oh, sweetheart, I'm so sorry. I didn't know but I wondered why you asked about her."

He felt her head nod. "That's why I ran. He knows."

"Did you have the locket?"

She nodded and whispered, "I dropped it in the office. I just hope the police find it first."

Timothy raised his head and looked around. He had to get her out of that building but how. He had seen the look in Bill's eyes. Rachel would not be walking away from him this time, and neither likely would he. Keeping an arm around her, he led her to a arm chair and pushed her into her.

"Sit here. I'm going to see if there is any way out at all."   He waited until she finally gave a reluctant nod.

He walked around the interior. It was as he feared. There was just no way out but for that door. It was a strange building, he thought, with just the door and no windows. The door opened to the outside, not the inside, so the option of hiding was out. He ran his hand through his hair. Lord, I'm out of ideas. I just don't know how I am going to get Rachel out of here.

He heard a voice: It's not your place to do that, it's Mine. I will look after the two of you.

He paused. God had spoken, and He was right. God was in control, no matter how it looked. He paced back to where Rachel was sitting and crouching down he looked up into her face.

She stared at him, tears tracking on her face. He reached up and rubbed at them.

"I know you're scared, sweetheart. So am I. Just remember that God has the ultimate say in this. If it means we wake up in heaven with Him tomorrow, that's okay with me."

She studied him. "How can you be so calm about this?"

He smiled at her in a gentle manner. "Because God has told me He is in control. Things don't always work out how we want or plan. God has a plan for each of us. That's where our faith and trust come in. It's difficult to give up control to Him but at some point we have to."

She watched his face, then reached out to touch his cheek. "I wish I had your faith. I'm learning but I don't think I'll learn enough in time."

She glanced at the door. "Bill will be coming back at any time."

Timothy nodded. "He is. But while we're waiting, give me your hands. We'll spend it in prayer."

Caleb looked up from the file he was perusing and studied the white board in the conference room. Names had been eliminated and there were just two left. One was Rachel and Gideon's foster father, Bill Waters. The other was the one Hannah had given. When he had written it down, surprise and consternation had spread through the room, then heads had bent once more to find the evidence and track the investigations through to the end. Caleb turned as he heard footsteps behind him.

Gideon stood in the doorway and reached to shake Caleb's hand. "Where do we stand?"

"Definitely not where I wanted to be. We are still looking at properties but we have pretty much narrowed it down to two. I have officers out now scouting them to see if there is much activity."

Gideon nodded as he moved in to read the white board. He really shouldn't be there but Caleb was not about to send him away. If he had his way, Gideon would be on his force soon. He heard more footsteps and turned to see Eddie headed his way.

"Found him. He's here in town and was hired by Bill Waters. But the money transfer didn't come from him."

"Our other name?"

Eddie nodded. "We have him fast for that. There is no way he can get away from that."

Frankie spoke up from across the room. "We have a location and the warrants are on the way. Judge Lane was very pleased to sign them for us. He was not happy when we gave the name." He looked past Caleb and stopped speaking.

The men turned to stare at the older man standing in the doorway. Ben's eyes traveled from him to Gideon and back. He shook his head. He thought he was seeing things.

The man spoke. "I am looking for Chief Logan. I was cleared and told I could find him here."

Caleb went forward. "I'm Chief Logan. How can I help you?"

Gideon froze in place at the voice, then slowly turned. He stared at the man and then stepped forward. At his movement, the man's eyes turned to him, stared at him and then slid closed.

Gideon stopped in front of him. "It can't be. We were told you didn't want us and then that you were dead. Rachel never believed it. She always thought you would come and save us."

The man looked at Gideon, tears in his eyes. "I never stopped looking. It was only in the last three months that I found out you two were both alive and were near here. I have searched the country many times looking for you both. My world disappeared with you two."

The four officers looked at each other in puzzlement. What was going on?

Gideon took another step forward and then was pulled into a hug by the man. "Son, I have wanted to find you so bad. Now I have."

Ben stepped away, emotions overcoming him. Caleb approached him. "Is that really his father?"

Ben nodded. "You can see the resemblance. I often wondered if he was still alive. I am sure Bill

Waters will have a lot of explaining to do. He has stolen years from this family."

Frankie came back through the door. "I have the warrants."

Caleb looked around. "Eddie, find who we need and let's get going. Did they determine which property?"

"No, they're still working on it. I should hear by the time we're ready to go."

Caleb and Ben approached Gideon and his father. "Mr. Andrews, I'm sorry Rachel isn't here."

"Please, call me Shane. Mr. Andrews was my father. I know it's not your fault. I have quite a story to tell but we need to find my girl first, and I understand one of your men's sons. Ask me anything you want about Bill Waters, though. I probably know him best of all of you from tracking him down through the years."

Timothy turned as the door opened and Bill Waters walked in, followed by the two men. Another man hovered back in the shadows, silent but watching. He went to stand by Rachel.

Bill stopped in front of her and glared down at her. He reached to pull her out of the chair, and Timothy stepped in front of her. Bill moved back. He was angry that Rachel had a defender. She had never had one in the past, except for Gideon, and he had dealt with that one. He had not seen him back in town since he chased him away.

He motioned and the two men moved forward. Gripping Timothy's arms, they pulled him away from her. Rachel watched in horror as he was dragged from the building, struggling all the while to get loose and back to her. Her hands started to shake and then she straightened up. She was no longer afraid of Bill. He no longer had the power to beat her down in spirit or in mind. She looked up at him as he once again stopped in front of her. She could feel the hate radiating from him and something else. He was afraid. Someone had made the bully afraid. Her eyes flicked to the man standing just outside the door. It had to be him, but who was it? Who had this kind of power?

Bill pulled Rachel to her feet, shoving the chair away. He then stepped back from her.

"Where is the necklace?"

She stared at him, refusing to answer.

"Where is the necklace?" His voice rose in anger.

She saw his fists raise and lifted her chin. She would not answer.

Caleb studied the house and buildings through the night vision goggles he had been given. "There, back by that building. I can see a man standing outside."

Doug, the Emergency Task Force Leader, nodded. "He seems very intent on what is going on in there." He searched the area, knowing his men were in place. "We're good to go when you say."

Caleb removed the goggles and looked around him. He knew Ben was standing back by the vehicles with Gideon and his father. Frankie and Eddie were just behind him, Frankie with the warrants clasped in his hand, ready to serve.

"Is all the activity so far centred around the building at the back?"

"So far it seems to be." Doug stopped. "Wait. They're coming out. We need to move now."

"Go for it."

Caleb watched as the dark-garbed ETF officers moved in quickly. The four men they had been watching were down on the ground and arrested in short order. As they were walked towards the watching cruisers for transport downtown, Caleb moved forward. He studied each man as he was walked by. At the fourth man, he held up his hand for him to be stopped.

"Judge Lee. I should have known."

"You have nothing on me." The man's face was drawn into an ugly snarl.

"I'm afraid we do. We have a multitude of evidence that has been dug up in the last 24 hours and we're still digging." Caleb looked up at the sky and then back down. "This time, you'll be the one behind bars and for a long time."

He watched as the man was shoved into a cruiser and driven away. He turned to Doug as he came up, shaking his head.

"What makes a man do that?"

"Greed, plain and simple." Caleb looked beyond him. "Tell me, do we have Rachel and Timothy?"

Doug looked around him. "No. I don't get it. They should be here and they're not. I've called in for the K9's to come."

Caleb stopped moving and closed his eyes. "Where are they then, if they're not here?"

Doug shrugged. "I suggest you use your warrants to search the other property. My men are going through these buildings." Doug studied the sky. "I just hope the rain holds off long enough for the dogs to work."

Caleb watched through the glass as Frankie sat down at the table in the interrogation room, placing a file folder in front of him. Ben was in the conference room with Gideon and Shane. He had prayed they would find them safe but they hadn't. God, where are they? Right now, You seem to be silent on this. Please speak.

Bill Waters glared at Frankie and refused to talk. He hadn't asked for a lawyer, but Caleb knew he would soon. Frankie came out of the room and then stood by Caleb.

"He just won't talk. He's running scared."

"Of Judge Lee. Have the other two men talked?"

Frankie shook his head. "They asked for lawyers right away and we're waiting on them to arrive. I've asked our best people to interview them." He looked around. "Eddie is with Judge Lee?"

Caleb smiled. "He is. Eddie's fighting mad and the Judge won't stand a chance. His lawyer's out of town and Judge Lane has set his bail extremely high. He is very angry and you don't anger him."

Frankie nodded. "How's Ben?"

Caleb sighed. "He's hurting. We were so sure we'd have them home by now. Time's running out, Frankie. If they're out there in this rain, I don't know how they'll survive."

Caleb's phone rang. It was Doug. "Tell me you have good news."

"I wish I could. The other property's been searched but they weren't there. We've gone over the first property with a fine-tooth comb. Nothing."

Caleb looked up as Frankie held up a finger. "Just a minute, Doug. What's your idea?"

Frankie stared at Caleb, then swallowed past a lump in his throat. He could barely speak. "The quarry. The first house is near the quarry. Have they checked there?"

Caleb's eyes slid shut and his heart sank. "Did you get that, Doug?"

"No. What was that?"

"Frankie suggested the quarry. It's near the first house." Caleb could feel the tension through the phone.

"The dirty little...." Doug's voice dropped. "I'm on it. I just pray they're there and still alive. This rain is going to make it hard to find them."

"If you need more people to search, I'll send them."

"Not to search but have the EMS on stand by near the quarry."

Doug and his men scrambled down the path to the quarry. It was starting to get slippery from the heavy rain. A quick conference at the bottom and they spread out, careful to search every inch. If Rachel and Timothy weren't on the bottom, then they would have to start searching the walls and that would be impossible in the rain. Doug's radio crackled and relief flooded through him. They were found. He sent the woman officer beside him back up to get the paramedics and ran towards where they were.

He slid to a stop, almost falling on the wet rocks and mud. "Please, tell me, are they alive?"

"Not by much, but they are. I would say another hour or even less and we would be doing a recovery, not a rescue."

Doug looked around. He knew he'd not get cell service down here but he refused to leave until the paramedics had them up top. He watched through the teeming rain as Rachel and Timothy were stabilized and then strapped into wire stretcher baskets to be carried to the top. Many hands came out to help carry them. Doug stepped over to speak with the lead paramedic.

"Who does this, Doug?" Dave was angry. These were friends that this had been done to.

"Evil, depraved, greedy men." Doug's eyes followed the stretchers as best he could. "Talk to me. How are they?"

Dave stared at him, hardly knowing what to say. "I don't know if they'll even make it to Emerge, they're in that rough of shape. Timothy's not as bad as Rachel. She was really worked over."

Doug nodded. "It's not the first time her foster father's done that to her, from what Caleb has told me. Thankfully, it's the last."

"How did they even get to be foster parents?"

"That, from what little Caleb has said, is a story in itself." Doug walked towards the slope leading up to the road around the quarry. "I guess Rachel and her brother were stolen from their father when they were little. He's been searching for them for years and just found out where they were a few months ago. He's with Gideon now at the station."

Dave was silent, then he shook his head. "I still don't get it. I hope the key gets thrown away on them."

"It will be. Do you also hear that we arrested Judge Lee as well?"

Dave stopped, then shook his head again. "Where does evil stop?" He headed for one of the ambulances to make the trip to Emerge.

Doug slipped behind the wheel of his vehicle and reached for the towel he kept in the back seat. Drying off his face and head as best he could, he reached for his phone, went to dial, and then stopped. His heart raised in prayer, he sought for the words he would need to give to Caleb and then Ben. He had sent one of his men to find Marg and take her to Emerge, another he had sent for Eddie's Peg, knowing Marg would need her friend.

"Caleb." His voice broke, and Caleb's heart sank. He was headed into the conference room and paused just inside the door. The three men waiting looked up, apprehension in their faces.

"Caleb, is Ben with you?"

"He is, and Gideon and his father too."

"Put your phone on speaker, please." Doug could hear the echo as Caleb did so. He watched traffic as he headed towards the hospital as fast and as safely as he could. "Ben." His voice cracked, and Ben's head dropped to his hands. "Ben, we have your son. He's alive. Gideon, we have Rachel. She's alive too. They should be at Emerge now. I'm almost there myself."

Chapter 19

Eddie stood at the window, watching Bill Waters. The man was getting restless, constantly moving. His lawyer was speaking with him, trying to calm him down. It wasn't working.

Caleb stopped by Eddie.

"Any word yet?"

"Doug spoke briefly with the doctors. It will be quite a while, he said. Neither one is in great shape." Caleb paused. "I just pray we're not looking at murder rather than attempted murder charges."

Eddie nodded, not trusting his voice. "I wonder what Mr. Waters will have to say. He was pretty cocky there, figuring we wouldn't find them until too late." He stepped to the door, then paused and turned. "This sure does try your faith."

"It does, Eddie. It really does."

Caleb watched as Eddie entered the room and then sat, not saying a word. He continued to sit in silence, just watching the man across from him. Eddie's good, Caleb thought. Building the suspense. Waters shifted in his chair, eyes roaming the room.

Finally, Caleb saw Eddie speak. As he continued with his words, the face on the man across from him changed. The anger, fear, and absolute disregard for human life became evident. He jumped to his feet, chair flying back to hit the wall. His lawyer tried to calm him with no effect. Finally, Caleb sent in officers to restrain him and take him back to his cell.

Eddie stepped out, followed by the lawyer. Caleb knew the lawyer slightly, not as well as some of the others in town.

The lawyer paused, looked at Caleb, then shook his head. "I can't do it. I can't represent him. When Eddie was speaking to him and I heard what he was accused of, I just knew I couldn't. I don't think he's going to find a lawyer in town that will touch him. Ben's too well liked and too well respected. He and his family have been for years."

He walked away as Eddie and Caleb stared after him and then at one another.

"I wonder how Judge Lee will find representation here in town. But he likely has a lawyer somewhere else he'll call in." Caleb turned to stare at the men and women hard at work. They had many investigations ongoing but most had been dropped so they could work on finding Timothy and Rachel. He was proud of his officers. They had all given so much. He would need to come up with a way to say thanks. He would talk to Hannah. She always had good ideas.

Ben stood at the entrance of the Emergency Waiting Room and searched for his wife. Spotting her, he headed that way. Marg saw him coming and was up and in his arms. Sobs wracked her body. When they had lessened, Ben moved her over to sit.

"Have you seen him?"

"Not yet, Ben. They were working on him. The doctor said he'd be out as soon as he could and then we could go in." Marg's eyes drifted to Gideon and his father. "Who would have thought that Shane would show up after all these years. I often wondered what had happened to him."

Ben nodded. "He has a story to tell and we haven't been able to hear it yet. Soon, I suspect he'll share. Have they said anything about Rachel?"

Marg shook her head. "No, not yet, but from what Doug said, it's not good. Greg called. He's out of town at a funeral but will be back tonight. He'll come as soon as he drops off Mary and the kids."

Ben's arm tightened around his wife. "We have such support, not just from those I work for, but from the church. God will hear our prayers"

"He'll hear but whether He answers the way we ask or not...." Marg couldn't continue.

A hand was placed on his arm and he looked up to see Deirdre standing beside him, holding out a cup of coffee for him. As he took it, she sat beside him. She knew Frankie was around somewhere and would soon come to find her.

Caleb walked into the waiting room and scanned the area. Ben and Marg were seated at the far end, Deirdre and Frankie on one side and Eddie's Peg beside Marg. He searched for Gideon and found him sitting, almost by himself, with his father beside him. He walked over to him and took the chair beside him, sitting silently with his new friend.

"Why, Caleb? What was the purpose for all this?" Gideon's voice showed his fatigue and despair.

"Money. Your mother was an heiress and she didn't tell anyone. Somehow the Waters found out and wanted that money. She had hidden the account number in the locket and they were desperate to get their hands on it. We have the information and our department lawyer is in touch with the bank and courts. We are seeking an extension, given the extenuating circumstances, to closing the account. We'll likely get it." Caleb looked at Shane. "Did you have any idea, Shane?"

"I knew. Elizabeth wanted it kept quiet and for us to live on what I made. We were doing okay when she died. She wanted the money to be kept in trust until Gideon and Rachel were old enough to be given it." He laid his head back on the wall and closed his eyes. "Now, I suppose you're going to tell me her death was not an accident at all."

Caleb looked with compassion at the man. "I have someone looking into just that. Did you know they found the babysitter's remains about two years ago?"

Shane shook his head with sadness. "No, I didn't. I am so sorry for the family." He stood and walked outside, overcome with emotion.

Gideon looked after his father and then at Caleb. "We have a lot of healing to do, not just physical." He looked at the door to the exam rooms. "I wish they would come tell us how they are."

Caleb nodded, then sat with his eyes closed. The exhaustion had gone deep this time, more so than any other investigation he had been involved with, even when his brother, Joshua and his wife, Laycee, girlfriend at the time, had disappeared. He opened them again as he heard movement in front of him.

An emergency doctor had come out and pulled up a chair in front of Gideon and Shane. Silence dropped into the room. The grim look on his face didn't sit well with Caleb. Please, Lord, not that.

The doctor studied the two men in front of him. He had been told that Rachel had not seen her brother for years until just a few days ago. Her father, she didn't know that he was here and had been looking for her since she was a toddler. He wished he had better news to share.

He looked down, then back up at the apprehension in their faces. He spoke in a quiet manner.

"She's still alive. I don't know how. She shouldn't be, by all rights. The exposure has not helped the beating she took. Gideon, I heard you were in foster care. Did beatings happen before?"

Gideon couldn't speak, overcome with the emotions of never having been able to defend his sister. Finally, he could speak. "He seemed to have it in for her. The first few years were okay, I guess, no beatings, just being deprived of things. Then it escalated when she was around 10. I guess she found some backbone and refused to back down from him. That's when the beatings started. They just escalated over time. I couldn't stop them." Tears streamed down his face. "I tried so hard to stop him. He got that he would wait until I left and then beat her. I was going to take her with me when I left at 18. He found out, had me beaten and then dumped miles away. I was warned if I came back to get her, he would kill her. I used to find men watching me. I just didn't dare come around her. I knew he had friends on the force here. I didn't know who so I was afraid to come to them. I was watched so closely that I didn't even dare go to the police in another town. I just didn't trust that they would not contact one of his friends."

The doctor nodded. He had heard variations of that over the years. He looked at Shane. "You're her father?" At his nod, he continued, "I am so sorry you have had to come back to this." He paused, collecting his thoughts before he continued. "We have the exposure to contend with, and that is no small thing. Our estimates are that they were there for at least three to four hours and in the rain for about half of that. That has led to hypothermia. Rachel's health condition doesn't seem to have been great before that. I would suggest she had been really stressed before this happened and it shows. She wasn't strong to go through what she has." He paused again and looked past them at Caleb. "Now this is the hard part. I never like this part, telling family what their loved ones have suffered. Rachel was beaten and beaten severely. There are internal injuries that we have to deal with. Her liver has been damaged, her spleen for starters. We are running tests now to see what else is going on internally. She more than likely will have a concussion, how severe we can't tell. There is also some damage around her face. She has facial bone fractures that will require surgery." He stopped, unable to continue at the sight of the men's faces. "We are prepping her for surgery. Hypothermia or not, we need to deal with the internal injuries and internal bleeding. I'll be back in about an hour."

Caleb stood and moved away with him, back to the exam room. "Can they see her before surgery? Regardless of how she looks, they need to see her."

The doctor looked back and then nodded. "I'll see what I can do. She's in exam room 3. Go ahead. I'll be in shortly"

Caleb stood at Rachel's side, his heart breaking for her. The bruises and cuts on her face were brutal. He hoped they could put the monster who did this away for good but he no longer had as much faith in the system as he used to have. If things had been different and she hadn't been taken from her father, how would her life had turned out? Not battered and scarred like this for sure. He raised his heart in prayer, thanksgiving that she was here, petition that she would live and heal.

Caleb then turned and looked around for Timothy's room. The charge nurse directed him to a room just across from Rachel. He stepped inside and stopped as he watched the nurses working around him. The physician looked up and nodded. When he was able to, he stepped away and came to speak with Caleb.

"Walk with me, Caleb." John Thompson was a member of a Bible study group Caleb belonged to. "I'm heading out to talk with Ben and Marg."

Caleb stopped him before they had gone far. "Tell me, John. How is he?"

John shook his head. "He's alive. I need to speak with Ben. He's looking at needing surgery and I need consent."

Ben looked up as he saw John Thompson and Caleb headed their way. He spoke with Marg, who glanced around him, fright in her face.

John crouched down in front of them after shaking Ben's hand. He studied the faces of his friends and prayed for the words he needed.

"Timothy is rough shape. The soaking he got has led to hypothermia. That we're treating now. I won't go into the whys and hows, just that we are. That is the least of what we are dealing with. I can tell he put up a good fight to get back to Rachel. It took a lot to put him down." He looked down, then back up, catching Ben's eyes. Ben had a good idea of where this was headed. "I won't go into the full details at this point. We are needing to take him into surgery at some point tonight. He really should be transferred to a trauma centre but we can't get the chopper in and I won't send him by land ambulance. It's too long a ride, especially in weather like this. For starters, he's been beaten. His right lower leg is broken. His jaw is broken. He has assorted cuts and bruises. So far, we don't see any sign of a concussion or internal injuries. The hypothermia I mentioned is compounding these injuries. As soon as we can, we'll get you back with him for a while."

John stood and Ben stood as well and moved away with him, holding out hand.

"Thanks, John. I know there is more you're not saying and I appreciate it that you didn't mention it in from of Marg or Deirdre."

John watched him closely. "There's no much more. It's the exposure that we're worried about. It's affecting how quickly we can treat his other injuries."

Caleb stood in his office, behind his desk, contemplating the pile of work awaiting for him. He sighed and sat, knowing only he could go through it. He picked up the first folder, then set it back down. There was still something bothering him about what had happened. He still felt that there was someone in the department who had leaked information to Judge Lee. He went to find Eddie and spoke with him. Eddie stared at him, then nodded. He would scour everyone in the department and find out who was connected to whom. There was a connection, they just had to find it.

Caleb sat back down in his chair and once again studied the pile in front of him. It wasn't going to get done on its own. He had made a good start on his desk work when Eddie tapped on his door. As Caleb looked up, Eddie entered and then closed the door behind him.

Eddie sank into the chair. "I hate this job at times."

Caleb waited. Every once in a while, Eddie reacted like this. Caleb knew not to take it personally.

"Who did you find, Eddie?"

Eddie stared at him glumly. "I already know you won't like it. Hannah has probably already told you who it is."

Caleb smiled and shook his head. "No, she saves that for the big guys. So who do you have?"

Eddie scrubbed at his face. He was exhausted and feeling just a bit short tempered. Finding this was enough to almost destroy his faith in mankind.

"Here, you read it. I just can't speak out the name."

Caleb studied him even as he reached for the folder. His heart sank. He knew before he even looked that he wouldn't like it. He opened the folder and he didn't think his heart could fall any further.

"Go find him. Bring him in, even if he's off duty. Make some excuse. Find Frankie too. He may still be at the hospital with Deirdre. We need him here."

Ben and Marg stood at Timothy's bedside. He had been through surgery and brought back to an ICU bed for monitoring.   John had told them that he would likely go to a ward in the next day or so. The hypothermia had not caused a lot of issues, which they were thankful. The leg had been set. The jaw had been reconstructed and wired. They were just so thankful God had spared him.   Ben's arm came around his wife.

"He's alive and going to get better, Marg. God spared our son."

She nodded and wiped at the tears on her face. "I just wish I knew why they had to go through this. Why God felt it necessary."

"God's ways are not our ways, Marg. We may never know.   It may be that Timothy had to go through this to get Rachel back to her faith or for her father and Gideon to find her. It may be that God protected someone down the road that we'll never know about. That's why God is God."

"I know that in my heart, Ben, but sometimes I have trouble with my head getting around that. My faith has been shaken."

"So has mine, Marg. It had to have been. But we have dug deep and found deeper faith. God has granted us that." He looked around and then drew up a chair for Marg. "Sit, dear. I'll be back in a minute. You need something to eat and drink and I do too."

Ben stepped out of Timothy's room and looked down the hall towards where he knew Rachel lay. Her brother and father stood in the hallway, staring intently into the room. As Ben moved towards them, he saw nurses and John Thompson running for her room and the call overhead of a Code Blue. He stopped, leaned on the wall, and let the tears fall. Please, Lord, please not that. Please spare her. He looked up and moved to stand with Gideon and his father.

Gideon and Shane stood and watched the harried activity in Rachel's room. She had seemed fine, then the nurse had asked them to step outside for a minute. Next thing, nurses were running for her room. Finally the activity eased and John Thompson stepped back and watched. He wrote on the chart he was handed, then stepped back, stethoscope going to her chest. One of the nurses headed for the desk and they could hear a page overhead for the surgeon on call.

John stepped back out and over to the two watching. He stopped and then glanced back at Rachel.

"How is she?" Gideon spoke first.

"We almost lost her." John watched her. "There's a bleed somewhere we need to find."

"Bleed? What's that?" Shane's voice shook.

"She's bleeding somewhere in the abdomen. In medicine, we call it a bleed. We need to find it and stop it. We have an ultrasound tech coming to do a scan and we'll likely do an X-Ray as well. If that doesn't show anything, then we may go to a CT scan. I have the surgeon on call coming back in. He's the one who did the surgery last night. You can go back in for a few minutes, then I'll have to have you wait down the hall."

John nodded to Ben and walked away with him.

"How bad, John? I know it's worse than what you've said."

John hesitated. "I can't go into particulars because of patient privacy, but she may not even make it with surgery. If we can't find the bleed, we can't stop it."

Ben slumped against the wall. "I thought we had them back."

John laid his hand on Ben's arm. "You have Timothy. We're fighting to keep Rachel. She's got too much to do and give to go home yet."

Caleb looked up as Frankie came into his office and sat.

"What's up, Caleb?"

"We have found another name. Eddie's bringing in that person right now. I wanted you here because we have more investigation to do and you've been involved since this started." He stopped. "Any word on Timothy and Rachel?"

"Ben said Timothy was okay. They're planning on moving him to a ward in the next day or so. I haven't heard on Rachel this morning. Gideon said when I last spoke to him that they were worried about her. The doctors weren't sure she would even make it through the night."

Caleb studied Frankie, remembering what he and Deirdre had gone through and knowing how close it had been for them losing Deirdre. He looked up as Eddie tapped at his door and then entered. He looked at the man Eddie had with him and his heart sank. Why this one?

Frankie looked between Caleb and Eddie and knew something was up. He looked at the man with Eddie in surprise. What did he have to do with all this?

"Why Roger? Why did you do it?"

Roger Lee looked at him and sneered. "As if I'll ever tell you."

Caleb pointed at the extra chair. "Sit." When Roger didn't, Eddie shoved him into it, just a little bit rougher than he needed to.

Roger continued to stare at Caleb.

"What did you find out, Eddie?" Caleb spoke without taking his eyes off Roger.

"Where would you like me to start?" Eddie responded. "With the juvenile record he acquired in Oak City, I don't know how he ever made it on the force here. Assault and battery, theft, grand theft, break and enter, blackmail." Eddie's voice continued to list crimes and dates, Roger's demeanour not changing at bit.

Eddie continued. "It says here that Judge Lee persuaded the presiding judges or arresting officers to drop the charges. I looked quickly at the financials." He looked up then at Caleb, then at Frankie, and finally Roger. "Your uncle paid them off so you would have a clean record. He paid to have all of these hidden. If I hadn't known what to look for, I wouldn't have found them."

Roger's cocky attitude changed. "I want a lawyer."

Caleb stood. "That you will have. Lock him up, Eddie. We'll sort through the charges but they will include conspiracy to commit murder and kidnapping."

Frankie watched in shock as Roger was led away. "So we did have a mole after all."

"With the way someone was always one step ahead of us, I knew there had to be someone. So did you. Eddie started searching this morning, going over everyone in the force, including you, Ben and I. I searched Eddie's record. We needed to be able to prove we weren't involved."

Frankie nodded. "If you have nothing else at the moment, I thought I'd head back to the hospital, spend some time with Deirdre, Ben and Marg."

"Go. Keep me updated."

Chapter 21

A week later, Timothy sat at Rachel's bedside. He was sore but the leg and jaw bones were starting to knit together, he was told. He was already tired of the diet he had to be on but faced a few more weeks of it. He would never again complain about a meal, if he could help it. He watched the face of the woman he loved. Bruises were dark purple and green and yellow but were finally starting to fade. The stitches were due to come out in a few days. A plastic surgeon had already been around at her father's request and that surgery was planned for as soon as she was well enough. He was just waiting for her to wake up.

Rachel's head turned and she grimaced with pain. She couldn't ever remember so much pain, not with any of the beatings. So why was so different? She didn't have the strength or desire to open her eyes, even though she could hear someone calling her by name.

Timothy watched as she drifted off again. He would soon need to leave to go back to his room. They only allowed him so much time with her. He waited but he guessed it would be another day before she would speak with him.

A few hours later, Gideon stood where Timothy had sat in his wheelchair. Shane stood at the end of the bed, watching his daughter. His heart breaking at the sight, he wondered how he could ever have prevented this. He knew there was no way he could have but it still hurt.

Rachel's eyes flickered and then she opened them. Squinting again the light, she decide a frown hurt too much. Her eyes wandered the room, stopping on Gideon. She reached out a hand and he took it.

"Rachel." He couldn't speak for the tears in his throat. "Welcome back."

"I'm not sure I want to be here. Everything hurts so much." Her voice came out raspy with disuse.

"We're glad you are. We almost lost you."

Fright was in her eyes and she frantically searched the room. "Where are they? Where's Timothy?"

Gideon laid his hand on her shoulder. "Timothy's fine. He's recovering. The men? They're in custody. We still have to hear the whole story, but Caleb has promised me he'll tell it soon. We need you to move a little bit further along the road to recovery first."

"He won't come back?" He could hear the fear in her voice.

"No, he won't ever hurt you again." Gideon's tears flowed down his face. "I tried, Rachel. I tried so many times to get you away, to protect you. I just couldn't. The day I left, I was taking you with me. He kept me from that."

Rachel reached for her brother's cheek. "I know, Gideon. I know you did. He was too much of a beast, too much of a bully." A sound at the end of her bed caught her attention and she stared at the man standing there.

Shane's heart was broken hearing his children talk. Why, God, why?

Rachel licked dry lips as she watched the man. She knew him. "Daddy?"

He nodded, then came to take Gideon's place. "I'm so sorry, baby. I tried to find you for so many years." He gathered her hand in both of his and dropped a gentle kiss on her forehead. "I wanted to find you, to bring you home."

Rachel was crying and he reached to gently brush away the tears. "I looked for you, without knowing who I was looking for. Every man I saw I wondered if it was my Daddy." Her words stopped as she drifted off to sleep.

The men stood and watched for a while, then stepped out of the room. Caleb was waiting. He had news to share with them but the moment was not right. He beckoned them with him and took them to the cafeteria. He would feed them first, then talk.

"Okay, Caleb. You've fed us. Now, what's up?" Gideon eyed his friend, his father surprised as the casualness of the words.

"Don't worry, Shane. It's okay. Gideon's a friend and I don't stand normally on a lot of formality with friends. Unless it's necessary. This is not." He looked at both of them. "I have news of Elizabeth's inheritance. It's yours, Shane, yours and your children's. It's how she had laid it out. Just a few days before she died, she changed the paperwork so it was iron clad that it could only go to you three. If it didn't then she had set up a foundation for it. Waters would never have been able to get his hands on it even with the account numbers. There were too many security checks and balances in place." Caleb handed him the folder he held. "There's the information you need. The lawyer in charge said for you to call when you're able. They understand that you can't right now. Apparently, Elizabeth must have had a premonition or something like that and made arrangements for something like what happened."

Shane shook his head. "She was an amazing woman and an amazing mother. Rachel looks so much like her."

Caleb studied Shane. He had so many questions he wanted to ask him but didn't feel he had the right to. That was Gideon's place. He stood and stared down at the table for a moment, then looked up. "I just wish we could have gotten to them sooner and saved them from the brutality of those men."

Shane shook his head. "You did everything and more that you could, you and your friends and officers. God allowed this, for what reason we may never know."

Caleb nodded, then gathered up the remnants of his meal to dump in the garbage on the way by. He stood in the bright sunshine outside the hospital, gazing around. So much had happened. People were going on with their lives around them and he had two friends and their families whose lives had changed in such a dramatic way. Thank you, Lord, for your protection. Send your healing. Let them feel the touch of the hem of the garment.

Shane headed back up to Rachel's room and stopped at the open door. Timothy sat beside her, watching her as she slept, her hand in his. He hesitated to enter but Timothy turned, having heard him. Shane entered and once again stood at his daughter's bedside.

"Has she been awake?"

Timothy shook his head and then moved back from the bed. "No, she's sleeping. It's what she needs." He turned to study Shane. "I'm glad you're here. She's needs her father."

Shane nodded. "I just wish I could have stopped this years ago."

"It was out of your hands. You did what you could to find them. Waters hid them well, in plain sight too."

Shane looked at the younger man. "Your parents have done an amazing job with you, Timothy. They have raised you right." He looked between his daughter and Timothy. "You're just right for her." With that, he turned and walked from the room. He needed to get some air and he also had an idea that had been forming when he heard about Elizabeth's inheritance still being there.

Rachel stirred. She was sure she had heard her father's voice. Her eyes opened and she looked around. There was a form standing by her bed, watching her. She tried to focus but the form kept wavering. She blinked. It was who she thought. It was her foster mother. Apparently the rumours that she had died were false. Rachel's fingers reached for the call button as she watched the woman. The woman's hand reached for her face and Rachel cringed.

"I am so sorry, Rachel. He was always a brute. I loved him at one point but he destroyed that. He destroyed our daughter. But he is still my husband. I can't let you destroy him by sending him to prison." She reached into her pocket and pulled out a syringe. "He beat me too. But somewhere deep inside I still love him. This will stop you from sending him to prison." She turned to move around the bed to where the IV was and stopped.

Eddie stood at the end of the bed watching her, a female officer in hospital scrubs standing beside him. Eddie's glove hand reached forward and took the syringe. He studied it and then the woman. He nodded to the officer, who moved to handcuff the woman.

"Nasty stuff, what you planned. I had a feeling you were in town." Eddie looked at Rachel who was staring at the woman in horror. "You were planning on giving her some of your own pain medication. Then the nurse, the doctor, and the hospital would have been blamed for the overdose. More lives would have been ruined, and you wouldn't have cared." He jerked his head and the officer led the woman away.

Eddie moved to stand closer to the head of the bed. "I'm sorry she got this close, Rachel. We've been watching for her."

"She was really here? I didn't dream it?" Eddie shook his head. "She was almost as bad. Not with the physical beatings but the emotional trauma she directed at us." Rachel looked up. "Is this it, then? Is she the last?"

Eddie gave a small laugh. "I hope so. You've had enough in your short life."

Two weeks later, Caleb looked around Ben's home. It seemed to be packed with people. He knew Ben and Marg were in the planning stages for something for the force but today this was about family and friends.   His eyes searched the room, setting first on his wife, Hannah. His two boys were somewhere around, likely outside with the dogs. They had been begging for one and Caleb and Hannah had finally agreed between the two of them that the time was right.

Next his eyes settled on his brother, Joshua and his wife, Laycee, then her brothers, Leith and his wife, Regan, and Liam and his wife, Ashling. He knew Ashling's parents and brother had been invited but had been unable to make it. Then his eyes drifted to Eddie and Peg. He gave thanks for the friendship Eddie had given over the years and the dedication to his work. Caleb often told Eddie he was like a terrier, that once he grabbed onto an idea, he didn't let go.

Next, he studied Frankie and Deirdre. Frankie sat with his arm around his fiancee, their wedding mere weeks away. Frankie had been one of the best street/undercover cops Caleb knew and now that tenacity and thirst for justice had transferred to the detective bureau.

Ben and Marg were next.   Their faces still showed the stress and strain from what their son had gone through but Caleb could see that they were stronger than they had been before. Their faith had been tested and remained firm.

He then watched Gideon and his father, Shane. Shane had found a house here in town and was working at setting up a foundation with the inheritance from his wife. Gideon and Rachel were in full agreement. He hadn't announced what the foundation was but Caleb knew that announcement would be soon. Shane had talked it over with him and Caleb had agreed to be on the board. It was something their town needed.

Gideon, Caleb watched closely. He knew Gideon had to deal with what he had gone through and that he couldn't get his sister away from the Waters. Greg, their pastor, was working with him. It was coming. He could see it in the way he looked and in how he moved. Gideon was also moving back to town. His employer was in full agreement that Gideon could work from there on the investigations their firm handled. Caleb had had hopes of recruiting him for the force but Gideon had shaken his head and said no. He was happy where he was, but would help on investigations as he was needed. He had resources even Caleb's people didn't have access to.

He shifted slightly and watched Abe Finlay. Abe was dealing with not being able to protect Timothy and Rachel at his compound and then having one of his own men abducted and assaulted. God was working on him, Caleb knew. They had had some good conversations over the past few days. Abe was becoming another good friend, in law enforcement but a different aspect.

He shifted his stance once again to watch Timothy and Rachel. Timothy had sat on the love seat and tucked his crutches underneath it. He was healing physically but mentally and spiritually he was still hurting. It would come, Caleb knew. They had a big God who was there and could heal. Timothy sat with his arm around Rachel, holding her as tight as she would allow.

Now, Rachel, Caleb thought. She is a strong woman. Given what she has gone through all her life and what she just went through, Caleb knew she was struggling but she was finding her way. Having both her brother and father back in her life was going a long way towards that. She was also in counselling with Greg, who although he couldn't say much had indicated he almost couldn't keep up with what she was learning.

Caleb looked down at the floor, gathering his thoughts. This was always the tough part, the part that would hurt, the explanation of why not fully satisfying all the questions. Where did begin? He looked up to see Ben studying him from across the room. Ben always seemed to know when he struggled for words.

Caleb looked around and then spoke. "This is a real tough one to sort through, my friends. There are still some investigations ongoing and those results will take time. We'll have them for when the trials start in the next couple of months. The judges here want quick resolution so the town can heal.

"Shane, it goes back to your wife, Elizabeth. We have determined that her death really was an accident, that the driver who hit her when she was biking was impaired. I'm sorry for your loss.

"From there, we go to the Waters. Suzanne was a distant cousin of your wife's, third or fourth I think we finally figured out. She knew about the inheritance and that it came to your wife. Her own family had been disowned years ago because of the crimes they had become involved in. She always thought the money should be hers. She tracked your wife down and waited and watched. She and Bill took an opportunity provided one day when your babysitter and the kids were outside. We have learned that Bill killed the babysitter and dumped her body where it was eventually found. They moved constantly when the kids were young, changing their own names, but leaving the Gideon and Rachel's names the same.

"Why they settled here in Riverville, they're not saying. Our guess is that they knew your family was from here and they were thumbing their noses at you. Hiding in plain sight. Bill had borrowed money over time from a loan shark, who under duress from Judge Lee, had sold him that debt. Judge Lee also knew of the inheritance and had been pressuring Bill over the last couple of years to find the account information and give it to him. They had planned on splitting it and both leaving town. Neither realized that they wouldn't have been able to get their hands on it. Between Elizabeth's preparations and the original will, it could only pass on to her direct line. If that wasn't possible, it would be turned over to a foundation trust. We are also working to determine if there are any more bodies associated with them, given what Gideon and Rachel remember.

"The two men they hired—police forces in the area have been searching for them for years. They were assailants for hire. There are so many charges in so many jurisdictions that it will take months, if not years, to sort out. Abe, Joseph took an awful chance that day but their code wouldn't let them kill anyone. Assaults, bribery, kidnappings, but not death.

"Shane, we also know it was you who took Rachel and Timothy to the island in an attempt to save them. You were acting on what you had learned and you didn't know who you could trust, given the parties involved. We also know it wasn't you who killed the man in the alley, it was Waters.

"Judge Lee's nephew is facing charges as well. He was our leak in the department. It's a shame. He would have made a good officer but chose not to.

"Rachel, the one you felt watching you—that was Bill Waters. He was here in town and saw you one day just after you arrived. He had always wondered who it was that saw him push Mary Emms into the quarry. He suspected it was you, just because it was close to Luke's cabin. He wanted to come after you for that, not just the inheritance.

"We have determined that Mary Emms was actually the Waters' daughter and had been adopted by the Emms. Ironically, she had been removed from them because of child abuse allegations. Somehow they all ended up in this town. Bill and Suzanne recognized her although she apparently never recognized them. She had a happy life with the Emms. Bill killed her to make sure Suzanne never got out of line." He stopped, having to compose himself once again. He scanned the room and saw the looks of horror and disgust on the faces. He stopped at Rachel's. She had compassion on hers. He would need to talk to her later, to see what she was feeling.

"It all comes down to greed and depravity. Man wanting what isn't his and not caring who or what gets in his way. I am glad, Rachel and Timothy, that you are here today. You're battered and worn but God protected you and brought you back. Your experiences are not what any of us would have chosen for you. God did, for His own reasons. That's where faith comes in, and we all struggle to understand. I can see He has given you His peace."

Caleb stopped and looked around once more, emotions almost overcoming him. He treasured these friends. They had been through so much. They could have been torn apart but they became closer. Their shared experiences would help one another. His eyes searched for his wife, and there they stopped. He moved to stand beside her and wrap her in his arms.

"What's up, favourite girl? You have a look on your face I haven't seen before?"

Hannah stood, relishing the strength and comfort she always found in her husband's arms. Her eyes sought out Abe.

"Something is going on with Abe's sister. I don't know what but God has impressed on me that she is in trouble, somewhere. Caleb, I wish He had given this gift to someone else."

Caleb dropped his chin to her head and then nodded. "He chose the best for that gift, Hannah. Use it for him."

They stood and watched as their friends slowly drifted away. They did too, leaving only Timothy and Rachel together.

Rachel finally stirred and stood. "I need to get going. Dad and Gideon are waiting." She stood watching him struggle to his feet and tuck the crutches under his arms.

He approached her, then balancing on his crutches, reached out a hand and traced her cheek. She leaned into it, eyes on his. His forehead came forward to lean on hers.

"Some day, I will kiss you. Now is not the time." He sighed, then said, "Life is getting back to normal. Will you go out with me, be my girl?" He felt her nod and reached to hug her.

He watched her walk away, knowing that their time would come. Right now, she needed to be with her father and brother. They had healing to do, as individuals and as a family, many years' worth.

Ben stood in the dimness of the dining room and watched his son. His heart was full that Timothy was here but hurting for what he knew his son was still going through. Lord, he prayed, be with him. Be that anchor he needs and that Rachel needs. They have been tested and come through the testing victorious. He felt Marg's hand on his, drawing him away. Timothy needed to fight this through on his own.

Epilogue

Four months had passed. Timothy and Rachel's physical injuries had healed and they were working on the other hurts. Trials had come and gone and those responsible were now behind bars and would be for a long time.

Rachel stood outside her uncle's cabin and looked around. For years, it had been her sanctuary. She had never known that he was not a relative but just a good friend from days gone past of her father's. He had known who she was and had done his best to protect her.

She had chosen to live here. Gideon and their father had tried to convince her to move to town, but she had held her own. This was where she wanted to be, where she had felt safe.

She turned as she heard steps behind her. Timothy walked towards her, a smile he reserved just for her on his face. Thank you, Lord, for bringing him into my life. Without him and his strength all those months ago, I would never have survived. He was my anchor then and drew me to You, my anchor always.

She walked into his open arms and hugged him back. He then led her to the chairs at the back where they sat, holding hands and just enjoying the quiet of the day with the noise of the woods in the background.

Timothy turned his head to study Rachel. He could see the peace she had found in her face. He could see the scars, fading from the surgery, but still there. She had a strength about her that he seldom found. He knew she was the one God had for him. Did she feel the same?

Rachel's head turned and her eyes met his. She saw the peace Timothy too had.

"Thank you, Timothy." Her voice was low and he had trouble catching her words. "You are my anchor. But more than that you have shown me who my anchor should be."

He smiled. "You're welcome." He watched her, gauging her mood. "So will you go for dinner with me? A really nice dress up dinner."

She glared at him. "If it means a dress, then no. I don't do dresses?"

He laughed. "You don't do water, and you don't do dresses. I can see life with you will be interesting."

He laughed at her outraged howl. "What do you mean, life with me?"

He stood and drew her to her feet. Hand in hand, he walked her back around to his car, and tucked her inside. He crouched beside her . "I have put you in my chariot, my love. I don't have a white horse to carry you away, but will a white car do?"

She looked around and nodded.

"Rachel, you have come to mean so much to me. My life would be empty if you weren't in it. Will you be my girl for life, share your life with me, be my anchor here on earth?"

He watched as tears filled her eyes. She nodded. He reached to give her a gentle kiss and then leaned back. "Thank you, my love."

He stood, walked around the car, and then slipped behind the wheel. "When? You know our families will be looking for a date?" He pulled out his phone, found the calendar app, and handed it to her. "Pick a date, and I'll be there."

She studied his phone, then said in a quiet, sad voice, "It won't let me pick the day I want."

Timothy stopped the car abruptly and looked over at her. "What do you mean, it won't let you choose the date?"

She looked up, a mischievous smile on her face. "It won't let me choose yesterday."

He stared at her, not understanding what she had said.

"Let me repeat myself. It wouldn't let me choose yesterday."

Understanding dawned and Timothy started laughing. "Yesterday, eh?" He reached over and kissed her again. "That soon?"

She nodded. "That soon. We've been through so much together, Timothy. We understand each other on a better, but different level than most couples. Dad and Gideon understand. Dad actually questioned me the other day if you had been brave enough to ask me to share your life. Stop laughing!"

Timothy's laughter rolled through the car again. "He didn't, did he?"

"And so has your mother. Your Mother! Your Dad just gives me that look that means have patience."

Timothy reached for her hand and then for the glove compartment. He pulled out a small box and opened it. "I've had this for days now. I wasn't sure how long it would take for us to realize that we need to be together. I know most women prefer diamonds." He stopped and looked at her. "To me, rubies suit you. Proverbs 31 verse 10 says, "Who can find a virtuous wife? For her price is far about rubies." Your price to me is way beyond rubies. This is the closest I can get."

Tears filled her eyes as she held out her hand and he slipped the ring on her finger.

"You have made me feel that I am precious, Timothy, in a way that I have never ever felt. Thank you." She stopped. "As we go forward, keep us anchored to God. That is your duty as head of the house, to set the example."

He nodded as he watched the one he loved. "That we will, my love. That we will." He paused. "Now, to get serious. What about a date?"

She stared at him and began to laugh. "I guess yesterday won't work, huh? We'll talk about it."

Dear Readers:

The story of Timothy and Rachel has come to a close. I pray that you have been touched by their story, by their desire to find that anchor that holds them firm. One of the hymns I used to love to sing as a child was "We have an anchor that keeps the soul, steadfast and sure though the billows roll". God is our anchor. He keeps us grounded and in one spot—in His care. We face billows and storms and at times it really feels as if our anchor is moving and dragging through the garbage at the bottom. That's when we have to say, God, You are my anchor.

Timothy and Rachel faced their trials and fought through them. We do the same every day, facing our own trials that many around us never ever know about. That's when we go to our knees and spend our time with God, in a quiet place with Him, and come out renewed and strengthened.

My father was a merchant mariner during World War II. He never talked a lot about it but I know it affected his life in ways we cannot imagine if we have never been through what those courageous men and women fought through. He knew what it meant to be anchored and safe on his ships. He also knew what it meant to be anchored and safe with God. His example is what I go back to. He wasn't perfect, we had our differences, but I never ever doubted his love for me or his faith in God. I miss his "You did a wonderful job" when I have accomplished a task around the house—putting down flooring, installing toilets and vanities, swapping out lighting (yes, I have done all that and more, by myself).

Even as my earthly father would say those words, I can hear my Heavenly Father whispering them to me. I can hear His "Well done".

Once again, this story has been given to me by God. These are His words, although framed in my sentences. This is the story He has chosen for me to write. My prayer, as always, is that when you pick up one of my books, read through it until the end when you finally find out who the villain is, would be that you are challenged to draw closer to God. We stumble, step away, turn our backs but He is ever so faithful and loving. We face the consequences of our choices but one consequence we never face is that He removes His love and caring. That doesn't happen. With this book, I pray that you find the Anchor that is God.

And as always, a big thank you to Faye Silvestro Kubassek, who takes the time in her busy life to read and critique my novels. Love you, my friend and sister in Christ. Your support over the years has made such a difference in my life. And I really hope I didn't make you cry at the end of this book, once again. And a huge thank you to my oldest niece and a wonderful lady, Angela Marie Gilfillan Smith. Thank you for taking the time from your so busy life, working and raising your two daughters and your son. All these years later, I still remember sitting at the dinner table at Bible school, getting called to the phone to hear your Grandma B tell me I was an aunt for the very first time. Love you so much.

God bless each one of you.

Ronna

The Haven

Haven of Rest Trilogy

Book 3

by

Ronna Bacon

Dedication

Dedicated to all those who are seeing their own haven of rest in this busy stressful world.

Matthew 11:28:   Come unto Me, all you who are weary and heavy laden, and I will give you rest.

Table of Contents

Prologue

He was back. She found feel his eyes on her no matter where she went. If she moved towns, he was there. She just couldn't lose him. He was everywhere around her. His notes that he left told her she was his. He had threatened her family. She was scared. How could she escape him and who could she turn to for help?

He watched her, chuckling to himself in glee as he saw her fear. He would bring her down and she would be his. No one would laugh at him any more when he strutted around town with her as his wife. They would look up to him.

He turned and his eyes followed her as she walked away, her faint limp a reminder of the lengths he had had to go to already to make sure she knew she was his.

Soon, my pretty, he thought. Soon.

She looked back over her shoulders, searching for the eyes watching her. Where was he? She knew he was here. Somehow, she had to get away from him.

Chapter 1

Gideon Andrews followed his friend into the Crazy Quilt Cafe. He knew they ate here a lot but he had never made it inside since he moved back. He looked around, liking the clean lines of the decor. His friend, Doug Foster, waved at the man behind the counter, then headed for the tables at the back. Gideon could see other members of the Emergency Task Force or ETF that Doug headed up as well as a couple of paramedics already seated there. Dave Allison he recognized and given enough time he would come up with the rest of the names. They slid into chairs, Doug leaving the one across from him empty, Gideon at the end of the table.

"What would you like, Gideon? Anything you get here is good."

"What's the special?"

"What day is it?" Doug asked the group in general. At the response of Friday, he said, "It will be haddock and fries. They always do a fish on Friday, rotating the specials each day."

"That sounds good." Gideon turned to look for the waitress to order, then noticed Doug holding up his hand.

Doug looked at him and laughed. "Don't worry. Mac's got your order."

Gideon stared at him. "I see. Hand signals still work?"

Doug laughed again. "In here they do. Mac's gotten quite proficient over the years. If you come in next Friday and don't say anything to him, you'll be given a plate of fish and chips without even asking."

"That good, is he?"

Doug nodded, then turned at a question from one of the other men.

Gideon's eyes strayed around the cafe, watching the various customers. He watched as a woman headed towards their table, mugs in one hand and a coffee pot in the other. He tilted his head. She wasn't dressed as he would imagine a waitress would be, dressed instead in khaki cargo pants, cream Tshirt, and hiking boots. He watched as a customer near him reached out and stopped her.

She stopped and stared down at the man. The look on her face was calm, but he could see the distaste in her eyes. He vaguely remembering hearing Doug mention that Rebecca Brogan was joining them. He glanced at Doug and then back to the woman. This must be Rebecca. He caught her words as she spoke in a low tone to man.

"I'm not your waitress. In fact, I don't even work here."

"Well, you have the coffee pot and mugs. Of course you do."

"Sorry, buddy, I don't"

She moved to walk away and his hand came out and grasped her arm. Gideon could see the woman with him cringe at that movement and speculation grew within him.

"I say you do, my darling. So, let's have you pour the coffee and take our orders."

"Mister, I'm not your darling. I don't expect your wife appreciates you calling other women something that should be reserved just for her. Secondly, take your hand from my arm. You won't like the consequences. You will be wearing a hot pot of coffee and the table right behind you has a number of police officers sitting at it who are more than likely watching you right now."

He scoffed. "Yeah, right. I've heard that before."

"And the owner is watching you right now as well. If you continue, you will be asked to leave. By the time you get to your car, the call will be out and not one restaurant, including the fast-food ones, will even let you in the door, let alone serve you. Mac will also give the police department a call with your plate number and you'll be escorted from town."

He stared at her. "Not happening, my darling. No one has that kind of power."

She snorted. "Do you really want to find out?"

By this time, Gideon was out of his chair and beside her. He reached for the coffee pot and then with a hand on her back, said, "We've been waiting for you. Lieutenant Foster is getting a little peeved that he can't get his coffee until you're sitting with us. I don't think we should keep him waiting any longer."

She flashed him a quick thank you and then moved away. Gideon watched her walk towards the table, then turned to the man and said something forceful in a low tone. The man looked up in anger, started to respond and then kept quiet. Gideon feared for his wife and two girls, knowing the anger would be directed at them.

He paused and again spoke. "If I hear of any harm coming to your wife or girls, even just a simple accidental bruise, I'll be all over you."

The man sat back, finally getting it that he couldn't bully his way through the meal. His wife shot Gideon a quick look of thank you, then lowered her eyes. Gideon prayed that she would find the strength to get out with her girls and get to safety.

Rebecca slid into her chair and set the mugs on the table. Gideon poured the coffee and then walked away to put the pot back. Doug watched Rebecca and then Gideon. He had missed what had happened but he knew something had. Rebecca looked upset and he could tell Gideon was barely containing a fine rage.

Gideon's hand brushed Rebecca's shoulder as he sat back down. She looked up with a quiet thank you, then concentrated on her coffee. Mac soon had their plates of food in front of them.

Doug looked over at Dave with a puzzled look on his face. Rebecca seemed different today, not like she had been for the last couple of years. Dave shrugged, noting the difference as well. Talk soon resumed around the table, although Rebecca didn't participate at first.

Doug finally looked at her and said, "Are you available for the weekend after next? I'm thinking we need to do some new photos of the guys."

Rebecca looked up and shook her head. "Nope. I'm out of town."

"What! You can't!"

She watched him, seeing the twinkle in his eye, and narrowed hers. "Abe can take care of that."

"Yeah, right. He'd cut off all the heads."

Rebecca laughed. "That he would. But that weekend is my weekend away. Has been for years."

Doug looked surprised for a minute, then he nodded. "The race. Which is it this year, bike or foot?"

"I'm not sure. Depends on the ankle. I'm set for the photo shoots though. If the weather cooperates, I'm hoping to get some really good action shots. Peter needs some new ones for his website and his promotional material."

Dave looked over at that. "It's still bad? Did you get the brace?"

"Change the subject, Dave. Not going there." Rebecca didn't look at him, just kept her eyes on her plate.

"Ok. Change of subject. What are you riding now?"

She looked up at him, smiled, and then nodded at the window. "Right there."

Dave turned and then whistled. "Sweet. Love the colour."

Gideon glanced through the window at the jade coloured motorcycle sitting there. She rode a bike? He turned and studied her. She was beautiful, he thought, with her red-gold hair cut in layers of waves and ending at her jaw. He knew her eyes reminded him of the brilliant blue of a summer sky. He mentally shook his head. No, he couldn't go there. He had caught the gold band on her hand.

"It is. You'll have to come for a ride some time. I really wanted the lemon yellow. Abe said he wouldn't be seen on the road with a bike that colour."

Doug stared to laugh. "Okay, what colour did he get?"

Rebecca smirked. "Orange. He wanted purple. I refused."

The men laughed at that. Gideon had to think that one through.

"Dougie, Mac has your pie ready."

Doug looked up and sure enough, Mac was holding up a piece of pie. "Dougie? Only because you're my cousin, Rebel. And I still haven't figured out how you know when Mac is holding up my piece of pie when your back's to him." He stood and walked over to get it.

Rebecca reached over and switched their cups. Dave started to snicker, knowing what she was up to. Gideon just watched, knowing this must be a common joke between the two. She then stood, waved good bye to the table, and was gone before Doug sat back down. Gideon could see her backing out her bike.

Doug took a swig of his coffee and choked. "Rebel!" He looked for Rebecca as the men around him laughed.

"She got you again, my friend." Dave was highly amused.

"She did. I don't know how she drinks hers without any sugar." He shook his head in disgust. He then stared at Dave, who had sobered. "It's been too long, Dave, since she did that."

Dave nodded. "Way too long."

Doug and Gideon remained at the table after the others left. Mac came to join them, bringing fresh coffee.

"How's Rebecca?" he asked.

Doug looked at him, then shrugged. "I don't really know. She never says much. Especially not now."

Mac nodded. "It's understandable. She has had a great loss, losing Nick so soon." He paused. "She never said why she wanted so badly to move from here?"

Doug sat back and stared at him. "I could never figure that out. I know Nick wanted to stay here but he agreed to move when Rebecca pushed."

Gideon spoke up. "You know, don't you, Mac?"

Mac looked at him and nodded. "I see you have picked it up in just a short time."

Doug looked between the men, puzzled. "Picked up on what?"

Gideon kept his eyes on Mac. "She has a stalker, doesn't she, and has had for years. That's why she left. He probably threatened her family."

Mac nodded. "You know. You can read it and you deal with it in your line of work. You just went through something similar to that with your sister."

Doug stared at them. "Wait a minute." He waved his hands and then shook his head. "A stalker and she didn't say anything?"

Mac looked at him. "That's right, Doug, a stalker. I only know because she found a letter here one day from him. I made her tell me. She refused to tell anyone else. Your dad knew because I told him." His face grew sad. "She thinks Nick was killed by him but she can't prove it. It was written off as an accident."

Doug's eyes slid shut. "I went with Abe the day he went to bring her home after she called to say Nick was dead and she was on her own. I had never seen her like that. We were told she had been hysterical but when we got to her, she refused to talk, refused to respond in any way. We just packed her up and brought her back without any protest. That never happens with her. That's why we all call her Rebel. No one ever said they suspected anything but an accident with Nick. So what do we do?"

"We do nothing. We treat her no differently." He nodded at Gideon. "Now this fellow, he can do what we can't. We wouldn't have gotten away with what he did today, taking the coffee pot from her and moving her away. She would feel smothered by our care. And we would smother her. She's family and we take care of our own family."

Doug sat and stared at Mac. All these years and Rebecca had said nothing. He thought he knew her well and she had been hiding a secret like that. Hiding the fear that her stalker had killed her husband and destroyed that part of her life. Why, God, why did You let this happen? His eyes moved to Gideon, who was staring out the window to where he had last seen her.

An idea formed and he looked over at his uncle Mac. Mac was watching him and seemed to be reading his mind.

"Gideon, have you settled on any place to live yet?"

Gideon looked back from the window and shook his head. "No, not really. I could stay with Dad, but we're still working on getting to know one another again and we need space. Rachel and Timothy are getting ready to move into their new house, now that Joshua and Leith have finished the renovations. So no, right now, I'm still at the bed and breakfast."

"Why don't you go stay with Abe Finlay? He has lots of room in the house and he also has cabins he used to rent out?"

Gideon stared at him. "With Abe? Why would I do that?"

Mac smiled, knowing what Doug was getting at. "With Abe? I think that's an excellent idea. Call him."

Gideon stared between the two men, knowing they were up to something but not quite sure what. "Sure, why not?"

Abe showed Gideon the suite he could let him have. Doug had called him earlier, asking him to give Gideon one near Rebecca. Abe wondered at that but knew Doug was looking out for Rebecca and had a good reason for asking.

Gideon looked around the room and like what he saw: bedroom, sitting area, ensuite, large walk in closet. Abe had mentioned that their internet was very secure, stemming from his work with the government. He had provided a nice-sized desk in the room with a comfortable desk chair. Gideon turned and reached to shake Abe's hand.

"I like this. I like the area around you too. It's not boring."

Abe started to laugh. "No, it's definitely not boring. You just have to make sure my guys know where you are so they don't take you down as an intruder. There are some who will try even then."

Gideon smiled. He had come to know Abe over the last few months and felt he was a good friend. "Let them try is all I can say."

Abe continued to laugh as he led Gideon back down the stairs and explained the security system to him. "Did you get any supper?"

Gideon shook his head. "No, I had planned on grabbing something back in town."

"Joseph cooked tonight, we take turns, and he always makes more than enough. Come on, we'll get you some leftovers that won't taste like leftovers."

Gideon stacked his dishes in the dishwasher when he was finished and then grabbed his cup of coffee to follow Abe out on the deck. Abe flicked on a series of light that were low wattage, just giving enough light to see without being glaring. Abe stopped as he stepped outside and then went forward. Gideon could see someone sitting out there.

"Rebecca, how long have you been out here?"

She shrugged, then moved to set her Bible on the table beside her. "I just needed some time out here." She grimaced with pain as she moved her legs.

Abe stared at her. "Which one?" She just looked at him. "Which one?"

"The left one."

"Did you eat?"

She shook her head. "I didn't feel like it."

Abe turned and brushed past Gideon to return to the kitchen. Gideon moved the ottoman in front of her and sat facing her, setting his coffee on the floor.

"Let me see your foot."

She stared at him and refused to move.

He sighed. This was not going to be easy. "Let me see your foot. If you don't lift it up for me, then I am going to reach for it and bring it up."

She stared at him again and finally lifted her left leg. He cradled her ankle in his hands. She had changed to sweat pants and an oversize T-shirt that had a picture of an old-fashioned camera with a stylized Rebel's Studios across it. He pulled off her sock and studied her ankle.

"Didn't ice it, I see." She moved to draw back her foot, but he kept a firm hold on it. Abe handed him the ice pack and elastic bandage and then watched as Gideon gentle wrapped the foot. Abe was puzzled. Rebecca never let anyone touch her for more than a few seconds and here she was letting a stranger wrap her foot.

He handed her the crackers he had brought out as well as her pain medications and a bottle of ginger ale. She set aside the crackers and medications but opened the ginger ale.

Abe sat in a chair near his sister, casually watching her. She acted differently with Gideon, even more so than she had with Nick. She had not been one in the last few years that liked any physical contact but there she sat, foot up on Gideon's knee with his hand holding the ice pack on it. His eyes turned to Gideon. Gideon was talking with her, just about things in random, not making a big deal that he held her foot. Abe knew then that God was behind this. God had brought Gideon into Rebecca's life. He prayed that she would be drawn into that haven of rest she so desperately needed. He got up and walked away. He wasn't needed here.

Rebecca tugged at her foot and Gideon turned to look at her. Her face was pale and distressed.

"Gideon, I need to get up. I think I'm going to be sick."

He stood, gathered her into his arms and strode into the house. "Which way to the bathroom?"

She pointed and he carried her through, then gently sat her on the floor. He waited, sitting on the floor, back to the vanity cabinet as she retched, then searched the cabinet for a cloth. Turning on the taps, he waited until the water was the right temperature, soaked and wrung out the cloth and handed it to her. He then searched for mouthwash or something she could use to rinse out her mouth and handed her a glass.

She glared at him. "Go away!"

He shook his head. "Not happening." He grinned as she glared even harder.

Abe had come to the open bathroom door looking for them, having heard them come back in. He stopped as he heard their conversation. No, Rebel wasn't getting her way this time. He heard the sobs as they started, and his tears flowed too. She had not wept for Nick, he knew, and she needed to. Tonight, Gideon's care had gotten through her barriers and broken down a few.

Abe stood back as Gideon came through the doorway with Rebecca in her arms and pointed towards her room. He went ahead and drew back the covers. Gideon laid her down and pulled the covers up over her. She was asleep, spent from her tears. He stood watching her, then turning, followed Abe out of the room.

Abe stopped in the kitchen and turned to face Gideon, leaning against the cabinet, arms crossed. Gideon stopped, hands on the back of a chair, then he ran a hand through his short, dark blond hair.

"I'm sorry, Abe. It was like it was Rachel all over again, back when we were teens. I just reacted."

Abe studied the man in front of him. He knew his story and his sister's story. *God, You prepared this man for my sister. He knows what to do, how to help. Thank you.*

"Gideon, I can't begin to understand what you have gone through. God does and He has prepared you for this. Not one of us has been able to get through her barriers. She has not yet wept for the loss of her husband of three months." Gideon's eyes slid closed as Abe spoke. "All of us have tried at some time or other. Today, Doug said she let you deal with an obnoxious man. She never does that. We call her Rebel because that's who she is. She has never let us smother her and we have all tried, me, our cousins, our father, our uncles, our friends. We would have just taken her to the bathroom and then walked away until she was over being sick. You didn't and you didn't let her chase you away." Abe stopped, tears gathering in his eyes. "Please, Gideon. We need you here. You are what she needs. God has placed you here."

Gideon studied him. "Then, I will stay. I don't know how I reached her. I just reacted as I would have with Rachel, had Rachel been here."

Abe nodded, walked towards Gideon, hesitated, then laid his hand on his shoulder. He walked past to go check on his sister and then to his office. He needed some God time.

Gideon headed for the outdoors. He should be going back to town to gather his belongings but he didn't want to leave. He felt he needed to stay here. He walked down the steps and to a bench that sat at the back of the fenced yard. He looked up at the night sky with all the stars shining down on him.

God, where are you? I know You're close. Thank you for providing rest for us. Draw us, especially Rebecca, into that haven of rest You have provided. She needs it, dear Lord. I can feel the evil near her. Give me the wisdom and the strength for the coming days, that I may be used to fight this and bring her through safely.

He sat for the longest time, until he realized he was starting to get cold. He walked back through the house, stopping to listen at Rebecca's door. It was quiet. His steps then led to his own room, where he sank down on the bed, and slept.

Abe stood at his office door and watched as Gideon had paused at Rebecca's door to check on her and then walk by to his room. He too could feel the gathering of storm clouds, of the evil near his sister. He didn't know if he had the ability to fight it or if even his team of highly trained professionals did, but as his eyes sought Gideon's closed door, he knew who God would use. He too then turned to seek his night's rest.

****

Where was she? She always came to town on a Friday night and came to the diner. She was acting out of character. He had to find her. He searched the restaurants and coffee shops. She wasn't there. He turned and faced the direction of the compound where she lived. She must be there. How would he get her from there?

Chapter 3

Gideon stretched as he stepped out onto the back deck. It was still early, the sun barely peeking over the horizon, pink and purple stripes mingling with the white clouds. It was going to be a hot day again. He took a sip of his coffee and grimaced. Whoever had made this didn't do coffee well. It's the weekend, he thought. For once, I'm putting work aside. Now he just had to find a way to fill his day. His father, he knew, had had to go out of town today and Rachel and Timothy had had plans. That left him at a loose end.

He turned as he heard the door behind him and Abe stepped out.

"Morning." Abe's voice still had the early morning growl to it.

Gideon nodded, then spoke. "I'm heading into town shortly to get my things from the B&B. Are you going to be around later?"

Abe nodded. "Saturdays are usually low key around here, unless we have a job we're on. Then it can get harried. There are times when most of us, if not all of us, are off site."

"We'll need to sit down at some point and figure out schedules. I'm usually around but there are times I have to travel for the investigations or for court."

Abe turned at the sounds in the kitchen. "Rebecca's up by the sounds of it. Thanks for last night. None of the rest of us have ever gotten through to her."

"When did she begin to change?" Gideon's question caught Abe off guard and he turned to stare at him.

Abe had to think about that. "Maybe when she was 16, 17 for sure. I know it was before she finished high school." He stared at Gideon, trying to figure out why he had asked. "Is there a reason you're asking?"

Gideon studied the door to the kitchen, then turned his eyes to the yard. "That's about when I thought. We're looking for someone around her age or just a bit older. I have a friend who does profiles. At some point, when I have sufficient material, I'll go talk to her."

Abe shook his head and waved a hand. "Whoa, what are you saying?"

Gideon looked at him. "You don't know?" At Abe's negative shake of the head, he continued, "We need to talk at some point today, without Rebecca around. It's serious."

Abe nodded, then headed for the door. "She has a photo shoot today. Talk her into taking you with her."

Gideon laughed as he followed him. "Just like that?"

Abe nodded. "You can do it."

Rebecca turned from the counter as they entered. "Who can do what? Or should I even be asking?"

Abe smirked. "Gideon has never been on a photo shoot. I think you should take him with you today."

Rebecca studied her brother and shook her head. "The shoot was canceled. I got the message this morning."

Abe stared at her. "They canceled. I thought they really wanted the shoot."

"They do but one of the kids is sick."

"What will you do then?"

She shrugged. "I'm not sure." She turned to walk away. "Don't do it, Abe. Don't start planning my day."

Gideon watched her walk away, then looked at Abe. With a smile, he stated, "That went well."

Abe glared at him. "I was trying to help you."

Gideon laughed. "You were. It just didn't work." He turned and went to find Rebecca.

Tapping at her bedroom door, he waited until she turned from the desk she had been standing at. She moved towards him and then stopped.

"I'm at loose ends today, and it sounds like you are too. I need to pack up my things from the B&B but that won't take long." He studied her face. He could see a bit of relaxation showing in it. It didn't seem quite as strained as yesterday. "Would you do me the honour of spending the day with me? Bring your favourite camera. I know some places I don't think you've ever been to that have fantastic views."

She watched him, blue eyes meeting gray. Then she shrugged. "Sure, why not? I don't feel like spending it around here."

He held out his hand and she reached for it. "Okay, so let's go find your camera and then we're off."

Abe stood, dumbfounded, in the kitchen doorway. Rebecca never let anyone hold her hand, not since Nick. Gideon had reached something inside her that no one else had reached. His eyes shot upwards and he breathed a quick prayer of thanks. Was she on her way back to the haven?

He stood outside the house, watching. He knew she was to do a photo shoot here today. So where was she? She was late, and she was never late. He cursed, shaking his fist at the sky. He turned and walked away after waiting for her. He needed to find her. He would have to teach her a lesson for not showing up when and where she was scheduled to be.

Gideon shoved the last of his duffel bags into his trunk and shut the lid. He watched Rebecca through the back window. Her head was turned as she looked out the side window. He could see the sadness in her body language, and it broke his heart. He didn't know her as well as he did her brother, but she was someone he wanted to count on for a friend.

He slid behind the wheel and sat for a moment before he started the car. Rebecca turned to watch him.

"Are you sure you want to spend the day with me, Rebecca? It was a suggestion but if you had something you would rather do, that's fine."

She shook her head. "No, I would like to. I need to start doing things outside my comfort zone, and with you, for some reason, I think I can do that. Don't ask me why. The guys in my life have a tendency to smother me or walk away. You do neither."

"Rachel wouldn't let me smother her and I was forced to walk away from her, not by her choice or mine. I tried over the years to change that but it never worked out the way I thought it would. Why would I treat you in a way that would make you less than who you are or walk away when you need me? It's not happening."

She searched his face and liked what she saw. He was being honest with her and with himself. "Then, thank you for being you." She looked around and shivered. "Can we leave? I feel something in this town that's not nice."

Gideon shot her a quick glance, then shot his gaze around the area. He knew what she meant. He could feel the evil closing in. He just prayed that he would be strong enough and quick enough to prevent any harm from coming to her.

Late that afternoon, Rebecca slid into a booth across from him at the cafe. Mac watched them, then nodded to himself. Gideon was the right choice for now. Please, God, he prayed, keep him in her life She needs him. I haven't seen that glow on her face in years.

"You need to stop, Gideon. I can't laugh any more."

He just grinned at her. His goal that day had been to make her laugh and he had succeeded much better than he thought. Wandering through the trails of the natural habitats in the area had been an adventure. He was eager to see the photos she had taken.

Mac came over at that point and slid into the booth beside Rebecca. He didn't say anything, just sat there. Rebecca turned to her uncle and studied him.

"You're up to no good, Mac. You have that look."

He shook his head. "Nope, not me."

"You know you are." She looked over at Gideon, then said, "That guy over there said he'd feed me and hasn't since mid-morning. What do you think about that?"

Mac looked at Gideon too, then grinned. "Then I guess he should. Your orders are in and will be here in a few minutes. I just wanted to sit with my niece for a few minutes."

She shook her head. "Nope, you're up to something, I can tell. I'll find out, eventually, some day, may be."

Mac shook his head. "No, I don't think you will, not this time." He stood and went to get their food orders. He set them down in front of them, stood for a moment as he was going to speak, then walked away.

Rebecca studied him. "He's not acting like he normally does. He's not usually that quiet."

Gideon looked over at Mac, then back at Rebecca. "He seems to have a lot on his mind. Eat up. We still have those pictures to look at."

****

He saw her. Here she was in the cafe. But who was she with? A stranger in town, but he didn't seem like a stranger. He thought he should know him. But she would pay for her betrayal. Being seen with someone else was not allowed. He had plans to make. He walked away from the stool at the counter he had been sitting on, leaving his meal untouched. He stood outside, looking in and watching the one he claimed as his.

Gideon reached for her hand as they walked back to his car. Hers nestled into his hand and she relished the strength she found there. Was he someone who could help her find and defeat the demon who had taken so much from her over the years? She had come to realize during the night that she had been letting him win and she didn't want that any more.

Gideon's eyes roamed the parking lot. He could feel the evil around him. He hadn't been able to protect his sister, but his prayer was that he could protect this woman, who in such a short period of time had become important to him. He didn't know if he believed in love at first sight but he just might be convinced it was possible. Knowing she had been widowed made it important that he tread carefully and slowly. He tucked her into his car and then stood, once more searching the darkness around them. There was someone there, he just couldn't see him.

He shut the car door and then walked around to the driver's seat, eyes scanning the area once again. He could feel it, just not see it.

Rebecca watched him as he slid behind the wheel and then backed out to drive away.

"You can feel it too, can't you?" She asked him, apprehension in her voice.

He glanced over at her, then returned his gaze to the traffic around them. "There's someone there. We need to talk, Rebecca. We need to figure out who it is. That means we have to bring in Caleb. And I know your brother isn't going to sit back."

She sighed. "I know he won't. It's just I've never talked about it, not really. Uncle Mac found out years ago. Nick never knew. I just couldn't tell him."

"How long, Rebecca?"

She shuddered, not wanting to think of how long it had been. "Since I was 17. I have tried to figure out who, but I just can't. The things he has said, he knows where I am, who I'm with. He's been watching me for years."

Gideon reached for her hand and held it tight. "We'll figure it out. First steps first, though. Caleb, and more than likely Ben and Eddie, and your brother and his team I know will want to protect you."

She turned to the window, tears in her eyes. "I just wish we didn't have to go to Eddie. Peg's my aunt, my mother's sister. She has asked over the years what has been wrong. That monster knows who all my family is. He has threatened each one of them."

Gideon's heart broke. "That's how it was with Rachel. He threatened me with her and threatened her with me." He paused, then continued, "You've kept everything over the years?"

She nodded. "My first instinct was to get rid of them but then I figured at some point I might need them for evidence. I have them in folders, sorted by year, at home."

Gideon's eyes watched the road around them. "Let's wait until tomorrow. I know it's Sunday but we'll see if Caleb at least can come out in the afternoon." He looked over at her. "We'll get there, sweetheart. We'll find this man who has held you captive and free you."

She turned her head to look at him. "That's exactly how I feel, like I have been held captive."

With a quiet good night, she headed for her bedroom. She needed rest if she was to face the monster tomorrow. Please, Lord, she cried. Help me to be strong. Help me to get through this. I am so tired of the stress, of the running.

Gideon watched her door close, then turned to go find Abe. He tracked him down in his office, working. At Abe's invitation, he entered and sank down in one of the chairs. Abe watched him, trying to guess how the day went.

Gideon stared at his hands, not sure how to open the conversation he knew was coming. He just prayed that Rebecca would forgive him. He looked up to find Abe watching him, apprehension in his gaze.

"Was it that bad of a day?" Abe asked, half in fun.

Gideon shook his head. "No, it was a great day. Rebecca seemed to let go of what's been weighing her down. It was fine until we left the diner and were walking to the car. I could feel someone watching us and it felt evil."

Abe stilled. This was how both Frankie and Timothy had described what they went through, that evil watched them. How on earth did it affect his sister?

Gideon looked up. "Has she ever talked about Nick's death?" Abe shook his head. "I pulled in a favour and got the report. The case has never been closed. They are still looking into it."

Abe's eyes slid shut. "I didn't know that." Glancing at the door, he continued, "Does Rebecca know?"

Gideon shook his head. "I'm not sure. She has told Mac that she didn't think it was an accident, that he was killed." He looked once more at the door, hesitant to continue, hesitant to destroy the friendship developing with Rebecca. "We need to meet with Caleb at least and likely Ben and Eddie. There is a huge issue that we need to address, and I won't go behind Rebecca's back to do so."

Abe looked at the door and then back at Gideon. "Let's talk to Caleb at church tomorrow and see if he can come out during the afternoon."

Sunday afternoon found Caleb, Ben, and Eddie sitting on Abe's back deck. The sun was hot but it was shaded enough that they were comfortable. Abe came out with a tray holding their coffee. He looked behind him, knowing Gideon had gone to find Rebecca.

Rebecca emerged carried a stack of folders that she set down on the table. Gideon added some he was carrying. The four men looked at them, then at the two. Caleb's heart sank. Here we go again, he thought. We just can't catch a break. Lord, we need Your wisdom, guidance and protection once more.

Rebecca sank down on the love seat and hesitated. She turned to Gideon, shaking her head. "I can't do this. I just can't."

Gideon's arms wrapped around her and he pulled her back against him, seeking to ease the shuddering. He looked up at the men watching him, knowing how hard it was going to be to vocalize what was going on and how hard each man would take it.

With a prayer for guidance and wisdom, he nodded at the folders. "That is evidence Rebecca has been gathering for years. I have added what I have learned in the last few days." He searched the faces.

"Rebecca has had a stalker for years, since high school. He has followed her no matter where she went. She has kept every letter, every picture he has sent.   I have dug up some information regarding some of what she has there, as well as obtaining the reports from Nick's death." He paused, not knowing how to continue.

Abe stared at his sister, then went to sit beside her. "You never said a word, Rebel. I never knew."

Tears gathered in her eyes as she reached for him. "He threatened to kill you, Abe. I couldn't let him hurt you again."

Abe hugged his sister tight, then as her words, sunk it, he leaned back to look at her. "Again? What do you mean?"

She spoke, her words muffled against his shoulder. "That accident on your bike in college?" He nodded. "It wasn't an accident. He sent me pictures weeks later of you before and after. He was watching you."

Eddie looked at her, then at Ben and Caleb. Reaching for the folders, he saw Rebecca had labelled them by years and found the year he wanted. Opening it, he searched through and found the pictures she mentioned. He handed the folder over to Ben, whose face had whitened at the thought. Caleb looked over the pictures, then looked at Rebecca. How had she kept it quiet for so long? Then his eyes found Gideon as he watched Rebecca, heart in his eyes. Rachel had keep similar secrets.

"You still never told me?"

Rebecca shook her head.   "You don't understand. Read the letters. Look at the photos. Then you'll get it." She jumped up and ran down the stairs, heading for the end of the yard. Abe stood, hand on his head and watched her go. He took a step to follow, but Gideon's hand on his arm stopped him.

"Let me. You're too close. She's been hiding this for years to keep you safe." He nodded at the folders. "Start going through those. See what you can dig up." He turned and walked slowly after Rebecca, not wanting to spook her more than she was already.

Abe turned to Eddie. "Peg never knew?"

Eddie shook his head. "No, she didn't. I would have known had she, and I would have been dealing with this years ago." He looked at the stack of files, then at Caleb. "Another one! When will we ever catch a break?"

Caleb studied him as did Ben. "I suggest we take this material back to the office and set up in the conference room again. We're going to need to sort through it all first." He looked at Abe. "Don't let her go anywhere on her own. Not one place."

Abe stared at Caleb. "She won't. She'll complain about being smothered, but that's what will happen until we find this creep." He turned to stare down the yard at where Rebecca and Gideon sat. "Gideon is the one who finally reached through all those barriers. None of the rest of us could. Doug mentioned that something was up but didn't say what."

Ben spoke up. "Mac has known something was up for years. He's dropped hints but never came right out and said anything. He didn't want to break her trust on this."

Caleb nodded. "He has to have known but with little to go on, we couldn't do much. Rebecca would never had said anything."

****

He stared around the park near the river. Where was she? She always came here on Sundays and she wasn't here today. He turned and searched along the river banks and then the parking lot. Not here! When she became his, she would learn she didn't dare deviate from the normal routine.

Chapter 5

Ben looked up from the pictures he was studying as Caleb stopped beside him.

"This guy is sick." He laid the photos back on the table and leaned back. He pointed to the folders laid out across the tables. "He's been at this since she was 16, contacting her at 17."

Caleb picked up one of the pictures. It showed Rebecca at 18, graduating from high school, cap and gown in place. "He is. We need to stop him." He laid the photo back in the pile and looked around. He sighed. "I've gone over the report on Nick's death and spoken with the officers involved in the investigation. I don't know who Gideon has contact with but he dug up a lot more than that department ever did."

Eddie had approached and then stopped as he heard the distress in Caleb's voice. "Rebecca was right."

Caleb nodded. "She was. Someone tried hard to bury it. Gideon's good. I wish he would come on the force. We could use him." Caleb handed over a folder he had been holding. "Here, Eddie, I'll let you follow up on this." He didn't release the folder right away as Eddie took it. He studied him. "Is Peg okay?"

Eddie nodded, sadness in his face. "She's getting there. Rebecca's one of the only girls in the family and has always been special to Peg since her mother passed away. Peg stepped in to help Mick raise the kids, as much as she could." He stopped, overcome with his emotions. "I just wish she had said something."

"She was scared. When you're scared at 17, you don't react the same. From what I've been reading, he's done a good job on that level." Frankie spoke up for the first time. "I saw it all the time on the street. There was nothing in any of those letters that said who he was nor was there enough to even charge him for anything other than harassment. We want him for more than that."

"Run with that, Frankie. See what you can find." Caleb turned to walk away but stopped when Ben spoke.

"Tell Hannah it would be really nice if she got a name today."

Caleb turned to look at him, a smile cracking through the grimness on his face. "I'll tell her but I don't think she'll have it today." Hannah, his wife, was known for God giving her the names of the villains, usually someone they least expected.

Gideon looked up from where he sat at the table with his breakfast as Abe entered the kitchen. Abe looked rough, as if he hadn't slept much, and Gideon didn't expect that he had. It had been a week since the knowledge broke that Rebecca had had a stalker for years.

"Where's Rebecca?"

Gideon leaned back so he could look down the hall. "She's still in her room. I haven't heard much movement from her yet."

Abe poured his coffee, stared out the kitchen window for a few minutes, then came back and sat down.

Gideon watched him, knowing he was running through plans and scenarios.

"How do we stop him, Gideon? He's gotten so close to her at times." Abe stared down at his coffee.

"We never let her go anywhere on her own, not until we catch him. Someone is with her at all times. You, me, your men. Caleb is ready to bring in off duty officers, particularly the women. We'll do our best to keep her safe, but it may not be enough."

Abe looked up at the passion and leashed anger in Gideon's voice. "You really have come to care for her, haven't you?"

Gideon's eyes met his, not backing down. Abe finally nodded. Gideon took another look down the hall, then spoke. "If it comes to it, Abe, I'll marry her. Yes, I care deeply for her and she should have been told first, but circumstances are not sane or normal."

Abe studied the man across from him. "Do it, if it comes to that. You have my blessing. Just watch your back. He's likely seen you together and you're now a target. He won't hesitate to remove anyone who gets in his way."

Gideon nodded, looking towards the hall as he heard Rebecca's bedroom door open. "By God's grace, we'll be safe. We just have to remember that we're in His hands and He knows the ending. I see Rebecca coming back into the haven. We need to get her all the way back, and this may be God's way of doing so. She's not going to back away any more."

Abe stood and headed for his office. "No, she won't. I'll look over the schedule and see who I can free up to help."

Rebecca stepped into the kitchen and looked around. She looked tired but there was something different about her. Gideon watched her as she moved to get her coffee and then some breakfast.

She went to sit down the table from him, but when he reached out his hand for hers, she set her plate beside him and sat, her hand nestled in his. She studied his eyes for a minute, then picked up her fork.

"What plans do you have for today?" he asked. He had already spoken with his boss and cleared his desk so he could focus on Rebecca. His boss had offered to help in any way and was already working on trying to find out who the stalker was.

She shrugged. "I don't have much on." She stopped, staring across the room, then looked at him. "I'm closing down the photo studio. I just can't do it any more. It was Nick's dream, not mine, and it's time to let it go. I have canceled any future bookings, except for the race tomorrow. That I love to do and I won't miss it. The website has been shut down."

"What will you do now?"

She shrugged. "I have enough photos I could do a coffee table photo book, but that's not what I want to do. A friend who's a publisher has been after me to do that." She stared down at her plate, then pushed it away. He could see the tears pooling in her blue eyes. "I don't know anymore. For so long, I have hidden, felt chased, and I don't know who I am any more."

He reached for her hand and absently rubbed his thumb along the back of it. "You have time. You don't need to rush into anything." As the tears started to fall, he pushed back his chair, then reached and pulled her to him. "It's okay, sweetheart. We'll get it figured out." His head on her hair, he didn't see Abe come back to the doorway, stop, and then walk away. His heart was breaking for the woman he loved, and he didn't know how to fix what was wrong.

She relaxed against him, feeling safe for the first time in years. She had never felt this safe with

Nick, but he hadn't known what she was going through. She had never told him. She wondered what kind of marriage they would have had, if it would have been strong enough to get them through what life threw at them. She leaned her head back to stare at Gideon, studying his profile and the strength that was evident. Is he the one, Lord? Is he really the one who will stop this nonsense and bring this creep to justice? Is he Your chosen one for me?

Gideon turned his head at that point, and she read what was in his eyes, what he wouldn't say. She laid her head back down, knowing she was as safe as he could make it for her. Troubles would beset them but he would stand strong and firm, first in his faith, then as a man, to keep her safe.

Gideon set her on her feet and then stood. He looked down at her, then said, "Come on. We're going to town. There's something we have to do."

She looked up at him, blue eyes beginning to sparkle with mirth. "There is?"

He nodded, a smile breaking out on his face. "There is. And we have to go today." As she hesitated, he spoke, "Go. Get ready. Put on your prettiest clothes. I want to take my girl out for the day."

"Your girl, huh? That's taking a lot for granted."

"Is it?" He watched her face and saw the softening there. "No, I don't think so."

She turned and walked away at a rapid pace. Gideon felt eyes on him and turned to find Abe watching him. Abe didn't say anything, just nodded and walked past him.

Rebecca stood at her dresser. She was ready to go, dressed in a skirt and soft sweater, with sandals on her feet, dressed how she very seldom did but today she felt cherished and a lady. She hesitated before she walked from the room. She studied her wedding band and remembered the feelings when Nick had placed it on her hand. The plans and dreams they had had, torn away too soon. She hunted for the ring box and then slipped the band from her hand and after placing it away, closed the box. Tears in her eyes, she tucked the box in a drawer. A chapter of her life was over and a new one was starting. She touched the picture of Nick she had on her dresser, then picked it up. Studying it, she wondered what kind of man he would have been. He had had such great potential. She looked up and said a silent prayer. She tucked the picture away as well and turned to walk from the room.

Abe watched Gideon standing on the front porch. His keys were in his hands and his eyes on them. Gideon had changed to a suit, dress shirt and tie. Abe nodded. He was treating Rebecca as she so deserved to be treated. He watched as she stepped out on the porch and took the hand Gideon extended to her. Gideon had reached something in her that few had, and she responded. He treated her like a lady. Abe couldn't remember the last time he had seen her dressed up and going out. Jeans, dress slacks, yes, but never a skirt. Thank you, Lord, he murmured. He turned to go find Joseph and Matt. They would be following them today.

****

There she was, walking down the street of town. She wasn't even in the right town. She should be in her studio working. She had people depending on her. How dare she? How dare she let them down? Something else he was going to have to straighten out when she became his. His eyes turned to the man

364

with her. The man was going to have to be dealt with
and soon. He was with her too much.

****

Rebecca shivered and looked around. She
could feel the eyes on her again, but couldn't see
anyone. Gideon's hand drew her closer to him. He
could feel the eyes too, and searched around not
seeing anyone. He did get a glimpse of Joseph and
Matt and smiled to himself. Abe was already starting
to watch, to guard.

Caleb looked up as Ben and Eddie entered his office and then sat. He could tell from the looks on their faces they had news.

"Talk to me. What have you found out?"

"This guy's good." Ben opened a file he held and studied it. "He's hidden well. We're going to have to go over everyone that she's had contact with in high school. That's where it starts. He's either her age or just a bit older."

"That is he." Eddie searched the file he held, and then handed it, open, to Caleb. "Read that."

Caleb read it and his face paled. "He was that close to her?"

Eddie nodded. "I wouldn't be surprised if it was more than once. He's someone here in town, who knows her routine, her family and her friends." He paused, looking for words. "The tone of the notes is escalating. In the first ones after Nick's death, he taunted her, as much as admitting he took him out because she "belongs to him and no other". We need to find him and find him fast."

Caleb nodded. "What else do we know?"

Ben shook his head. "Not a lot. We're still digging through what Rebecca gave us. He had her work email, used it. I wouldn't be surprised if he has hacked into it somehow too, to know where she'll be or else he has some way to access her computer. His voice is never heard though. She has no voice mail, no series of hangups, no words spoken to her when she's out and about. He's being very careful.

"Gideon was passing all this on to a profiler he knows. He thought he should have something preliminary back by tomorrow at the earliest and a full profile by next week. He's made arrangements not to work for the next few weeks so he can stick close to her."

Caleb nodded. "Abe is making arrangements as well to have his men follow them whenever they go out. We can't keep them under lock and key. It just won't work. I've had volunteers come to me as well. The female officers we will need to use."

Eddie stared at his hands. "I just wish she had said something years ago, like when it first happened. We could have spared her so much heartache."

Ben shook his head. "It's like with Rachel. They play with the girls' minds and make them think they are unworthy and deserve what is going on. It takes someone strong enough to show them they are. That's what breaks the cycle and the bonds."

Caleb sat back and thought. "We need her computer to search it. Can you arrange that, Ben?"

Rebecca sat across from Gideon in the upscale restaurant he had taken her to for their meal. She shook her head. "Gideon, you need to stop. I can't laugh any more."

He grinned at her. "Sure you can." He sobered then. "It's too good to see you laughing. You're so beautiful."

She blushed and looked down, startled at his hand reached across the table and was laid on hers. She looked up.

"You are very beautiful. You deserve so much. I would like to be that man who cherishes you all your life." She studied his face, his eyes. "It may be too soon, but please, will you think about it?"

She looked down as tears gathered in her eyes, then back up, shaking her head. His heart sank. He had blown it. "It's not." Her voice was soft. "It's not too soon. You are the one I have been waiting for, to rescue me from this."

He sat back and stared at her. "You just had to say that in a restaurant, didn't you? When I can't reach over and kiss you?"

She started to laugh at his nonsense. "Of course I did. Why would I be sensible? That's why I'm called Rebel."

Their meal finished, they strolled down the street. Joseph and Matt followed fairly close but with enough distance to give them privacy.

"Abe was right." Joseph shook his head.

"About what?"

Joseph nodded towards the two ahead. "He's a man in love. He's not watching for what's going on around him."

Matt shook his head. He was older than Joseph and had been through wars overseas and on the home front. "No, he's watching. I can tell by his posture. He's not missing much at all. He's got the ability to do both, watch her and watch for danger. Not many men I have met have as good an ability to do that as he does."

Joseph studied Gideon and then saw what Matt had picked up on. "I wonder how he does that. Is it something learned or something innate?"

"Knowing what he went through, I would say both." Matt studied the store Gideon had opened the door to. "Yep, a man in love all right."

Joseph looked and started laughing. "I wonder if Abe knew this would happen today?"

Matt starting laughing as well, even as his eyes searched the area. "Not likely. So which one of us goes in after them?"

Joseph snickered. "You can."

Rebecca looked at Gideon as he opened the store door and ushered her in. He held up his hand to the clerk heading his way, who stopped, nodded and stepped back. He then turned to her, holding her hands. "If I'm rushing you, tell me. We can slow down. But I do love you and want you to be with me. Another reason—your stalker is getting close. I can't protect the way I want. Will you?" He held up her left hand. "I think you're ready. You've put Nick's ring away."

She studied their hands and nodded. "I am. I have been saying good bye to him for months now. Yes, I will."

Matt stood back and watched them. He smiled to himself. Nope, I doubt Abe ever saw this coming this fast. Lord, it has to be you. Help us keep her safe.

Gideon turned and led her to the counter. She was surprised at the stone he asked to see but knew he had his reasons and would tell her when the time was right. He made his choice, slipped it on her finger.

He turned and saw Matt standing behind him with a grin on his face. He shook his head at him.

Gideon stopped in town and motioned Matt to drive up beside him. He told him to go home, that they would be along shortly. Matt shook his head.

"Go home, Matt. We're going to be all right. Tell Abe I sent you home." He was gone before Matt could follow.

"So, who gets to tell Abe we lost them?" Joseph was in awe of the moves Gideon had taken.

"I guess I do." Matt stared at where the car had disappeared so quickly. "Man, I want to learn his moves. They would come in very handy."

Abe stared at Matt and then Joseph. "You lost them. He just drove off and you lost them? How?"

Matt shook his head as he listened to Joseph snicker behind him. "I have no idea. One minute he was there, then he was gone. We need him on our team."

Abe shook his head. "Really? That's all you have to say, we need him on our team."

"All kidding aside, Abe, he's really good. I don't know who trained him but they have moves I haven't seen before. He'll take care of Rebecca. I have a suspicion where they were headed."

Abe searched Matt's face and saw something there that made him narrow his eyes. "And that would be?"

Matt laughed and shook his head. "Nope. Not going there. I'll let Gideon explain."

Abe's eyes then turned to Joseph, who was vigorously shaking his head. "Nope, I'm with him."

Abe shook his head and sent them on their way. What was going on?

****

Where was she? She was always at the seniors' home on Monday nights. She never missed. He wandered the halls looking for her and couldn't find her. Had she not come back to town? Was she on the run again? He would track her down.

Chapter 7

Gideon stopped in front of a house, turned the car off, then turned to Rebecca. She studied the house, then looked at him.

"Really? Taking a lot of granted again, aren't you?"

He laughed, then sobered. "Never, sweetheart. I will never take you for granted. All we have to do is go in and talk to him."

Her eyes narrowed, she glared at him. "Never? And I suppose you don't have a folded up piece of paper in your pocket?" Her mouth dropped open in a very unladylike manner as he grinned and pulled a piece of paper from his inside suit coat pocket. "You don't, do you?"

He laughed at the expression on her face, then sobered. "Only if you agree. I talked to Greg. He will marry us tonight and we can then go on to where you're doing your photo shoot tonight, or we can just leave and still go on to the photo shoot early tomorrow morning. It's your choice, Rebecca, yours and yours alone. Whatever you decide, I'm fine with."

She studied the house before her, chewing on her lower lip. It was such a big decision and she didn't want to make one she would regret. Okay, Lord, I'm at a crossroads here. Do I make the decision tonight or do I wait? I just feel so lost.

Gideon watched the conflicts chasing across her face and it saddened him. He shouldn't have pushed her, but he felt the evil moving in quickly and he so wanted to stand in the way, to be between her and it.

She looked at him and then back to the house. She finally spoke. "We're here. At least we can talk with him and get his and Mary's counsel."

Gideon felt relief at her decision. He went around and helped her from the car, walking towards their minister's door. Greg didn't seem surprised to see them, inviting them in to the living room where his wife sat.

Abe came in from the back deck as he heard Gideon come into the kitchen. Gideon had changed to jeans and a T-shirt and was making himself a coffee. He glanced at Abe, then back at his cup.

Abe stood, leaning against the counter, saying nothing, just watching. Gideon didn't rise to the bait, knowing what Abe was up to.

Gideon looked behind him at the door. "We're heading out tonight for the photo shoot. She says she usually leaves early the morning of and maybe this way we can throw the stalker off."

Abe turned to look at the door and then back at Gideon. "Leaving tonight, are you? Anything you want to share?"

Gideon just grinned and shook his head. "I'll let Rebecca tell you. It's her story."

Abe stared at him, mouth open. He couldn't believe that Gideon had refused to tell him.

Rebecca rushed into the kitchen, dropped a kiss on Abe's cheek, and then pulled at Gideon's hand. "Let's go. The traffic will be bad enough now, it's only going to get worse."

Gideon followed her, catching up her bag with his. Rebecca hesitated, looking at him. At his nod, she turned back to hug her brother.

"It's okay, Abe. Gideon will take care of me." She stood hands on his arm. "And you're not very observant tonight, are you?"

Abe stared at her, then as her left hand tightened on his arm, he looked down. Surprised he looked up, seeing tears in her eyes. He hugged her and then stepping back, looked at Gideon. "Take care of her, Gideon."

Gideon nodded, then waited for Rebecca to walk out ahead of him. He stuffed their bags into his car and then walked to shut the door behind her. He stood looking around and then walked back to Abe.

Abe stood at the foot of the stairs. "I've already sent Matt and Joseph ahead. They'll be waiting for you. Ian and Murphy will head up there early tomorrow. Caleb has asked if we can have someone search her computer. They think he has a spy program on it that was locked into her work calendar. They also think he has hacked into her work email. Make sure she doesn't access either her website or her email."

Gideon turned back to look at the car. "She's already shut the website down." At Abe's look of surprise, he continued, "She's shutting down her photo studio. She told me that today. She's ready to move on, as to what she doesn't know yet."

"The studio was always Nick's idea. She was never crazy about it but kept it up after he went in his memory. I knew she would give it up sooner or later. Take care of her, Gideon. She's in your hands and God's. Welcome to the family."

Gideon studied the man standing beside him. Abe's eyes were locked on his sister's. "We didn't meant to exclude you from tonight."

Abe nodded. "I know. We'll have a celebration when we get her stalker. It's best to keep it low key for now. Though in this town, it's almost impossible. They're already talking about you two being together so much. One look at her hand and word will be out."

"Can't keep a secret, huh? Can't keep the hand hidden?" At Abe's grin and negative shake of the head, Gideon laughed. "We'll manage."

****

He waited in the early dawn hours, just down the road from the compound. Where was she? She always left early in the morning of the race. Today was the race, and she would be there. But where was she? He watched a truck pull away. It wasn't her. No other vehicles left. She wasn't going? He ran his hand through his thinning air. She couldn't do this to him. She always went to this race. Now what did he do? It was too late for him to go. He didn't arrange his transportation to there, just to here.

****

Gideon stared around the staging area for the race. So much activity and Rebecca seemed to be in the very centre of it. He stayed as close as he could. He knew Matt and Joseph were mingling close and that Ian and Murphy had arrived and were around the edges of the crowd. He didn't realize it would be this big. He turned at Matt came up beside him.

"Surprised you, didn't it?" Matt eyes were constantly on the move.

"It did. I didn't think it was this big." Gideon stared around, eyes stopping on Rebecca as she stood and talked with the race organizer. "She never said how big it was."

Matt nodded. "She's been doing this race for years. She's usually in the foot or bike race. Her ankle won't let her any more."

374

"Her ankle!" Gideon turned to Matt. "What happened to it? I heard Dave ask about it, saw it that night, and she has never said a word."

"You don't know?" Matt was surprised and turned to study his face. When Gideon shook his head, Matt continued, "She was hurt when Nick was killed. Her ankle was broken in a number of places and required plates and screws and lots of healing time. She's never really said what happened."

Gideon's stomach turned at the thought of the pain that had been inflicted. "She never said how it happened! Did you know she has a stalker?"

Matt's mouth opened and closed a couple of times as he took in what Gideon was saying. "A stalker? No one ever said anything." He spun to canvas the crowd in a new way.

"No, she has never told anyone. Mac's the only one alive who has known for years. Her dad did. We've talked to Caleb and he and his men are working on it. My boss is working it as well. We have avenues the police don't have."

Matt's eyes narrowed as he turned them back to Gideon. "Those avenues! Yes, those avenues! I want to find out how you ditched us last night. So does Joseph."

Gideon laughed. "I'll be glad to share, some time."

Rebecca's hand slipped in his at that point, and he tightened his on hers. Matt stared at her and then at him.

"Anything you two would like to share?"

Rebecca blushed as Gideon laughed and held up her left hand.

Matt nodded and grinned. "I knew it. Joseph said it wouldn't happen that quick." He sobered. "The stalker. That's why."

Rebecca shuddered. "Yes, Matt. The stalker. Although I don't think he's here today. I don't have that feeling of evil I do when I think he's around."

"He may not be but we will be treating it as if he is. When you go out on the location shoots, two of us go with you. Don't argue."

Gideon was impressed with his wife's skills with the camera. It was a long, hot, dusty day, but she was confident she had the shots she needed for the new promotional material.

Matt stopped beside him as he leaned on the car, waiting for Rebecca to finish and pack her gear.

"We'll go in a convoy, Ian ahead of you and we'll be behind you. I just don't have a good feeling heading back that way."

Gideon nodded. "I know. It's so frustrating, that we can't pinpoint who is it."

"We'll be ready to go when you are."

Rebecca finally walked towards him, fatigue in every step. He reached for her camera bags and set them into the trunk. "You have everything?"

She nodded. "I do." She stepped into his hug. "I don't think I can do this any more. I'm just too tired."

Gideon held her. His heart broke for her, for the fatigue she felt. He knew it was from more than just today. "Give it time. You've got so much going on right now. We don't have to rush with any decisions that you make. Although we could use a good photographer when we do surveillance."

She leaned back to look at him. "Seriously?"

He laughed. "Seriously. But right now, we need to get on the road. Before we do, I want to pray for us, for the guys with us, for your brother and for those who are working to find this creep."

****

Where was she? She was always back by this time. He couldn't have missed her. He made sure he was here early enough that he didn't. He couldn't get close enough to really get a good look. Then he saw her. How did she get back without him seeing her? He watched as the new man in town draped her arm over her shoulder and walked with her towards the house. Yes, he was definitely going to have to deal with him and soon.

Caleb entered the conference room and looked around. The white board wasn't as full as he had expected it to be. This guy was difficult to pinpoint. He found Ben working through a pile of photos.

"What do you have, Ben?"

Ben sat back in his chair and studied the pile of photos he had been going through. "This guy is good. He doesn't leave in a lot of details but we can tell where and when they were taken. It's frightening to think he's been following her so closely."   He looked around for what he wanted and found the list he had been complying.   "Something interesting. There is always a gap every year at the very same time.   It's like he's away or out of town for some reason."

Caleb sat in the chair beside Ben and reached for the list. He read it over. "What's your feeling on this?"

"I think he's been away somewhere getting treatment.   It's always the same length of time, always the same time of year. Given what we can deduce from his mental state so far, I think he's been in an institution somewhere. Do we know of anyone in town who fits that description?"

Caleb thought about it and then shook his head.   "Not off hand.   I'll have Frankie put out feelers. He can probably find out more than we can from his sources on the street."   Caleb paused. "What do you think about him living in shelters or on the street?"

"That's a possibility. Someone else to check with would be Ashling Bradley.   She has lots of friends on the streets.   Deirdre might be another source, though she works with youth. They may have said something to her at some time."

Caleb nodded. "Make the contacts, Ben. We need to find this guy."

Ben shifted in his chair and looked sideways at Caleb. Caleb waited, wondering what was coming.

"Have you hear the latest scuttlebutt?"

Caleb shook his head.

"Gideon and Rebecca were seen going into a jewelry shop the other day over in Oak City. Peg saw them and is waiting for the announcement of the engagement."

Caleb laughed. "You mean, she just hasn't gone and asked them? This must be so hard for her, to have to wait."

"I'm sure it is. Eddie said she was ready to head out there today, if Rebecca had been in to see her."

"Where is Eddie?"

"He came across something he wanted to run down. He said he'd be back soon."

Abe turned as Rebecca stepped out on the deck. "No more letters or emails?"

She shook her head. "There never was at this time of year. It's like he was where he couldn't get to me. I always waited so desperately for this time of year."

"How long did it last?"

"Usually about three weeks. I always felt like he was out of town." She shivered. "This year, he's still around. I can still feel him when I go to town"

Abe nodded. "Don't ever go alone. If Gideon or I are not available, get one of the guys to go with you. I know you don't like the restriction, but Rebecca, we need to do this. He's increasing in his intensity and he will try to grab you at some point. I would rather he didn't succeed."

She sighed. "I know. I just can't wait for it to be all over." She stopped, then asked, "Why has God allowed this? Why me?" She walked down the steps and away from him.

Gideon had been standing there. "She's hurting. I just wish I could make it all better."

"We're trying. Caleb said they aren't getting too far. This guy has hidden himself well."

Gideon stared down the yard at his wife. "She's getting restless. I don't like that. Without the photo studio, she's at loose ends." He looked around. "Who's free today?"

"Ian and Murphy. You thinking of going somewhere?"

Gideon nodded. "I want to take her out for a meal. Somewhere other than here. Set something up with them and let me know." Gideon walked down the yard to his wife. His employer had been in touch. They were making much headway, but he had some research he needed Gideon to run for him. Gideon wanted to spend the day with his wife before he had to lock himself to his computer.

It was getting dark as they headed home from their meal. Abe had sent them to a small town about thirty miles away, hoping that they would be safe. Ian and Murphy were just ahead of them, Gideon could still see their vehicle in the dimming light.

Headlights appeared in his rearview mirror, approaching fast. The vehicle was not slowing down.

Gideon knew there was a curve up ahead and he couldn't take it any faster than he was going. A sudden jolt and the wheel spun in his hand. He desperately tried to correct but something gave in the steering and he had little control. The car flew off the road and careened into the trees. He felt the sudden stop and then nothing.

Murphy looked back. Where were the headlights from Gideon's car?

"Where are they? They weren't that far behind us."

"No, they weren't." Ian spun the wheel and headed back the way they had come. No sign of them. He spun the wheel again and headed the other way.

"There. Off the road."

Ian slammed on the brakes and parked. and the two men ran for the car, crumpled and on its side in the ditch. Murphy tried to open the driver's door but it was jammed. He could hear Ian on the phone with emergency services. The area soon teemed with personnel as red and blue emergency lights flickered in the dark.

Door open at last, paramedics could begin their assessment. Murphy and Ian stood as close as they could, eyes scanning the area. This was no accident. The crumpled rear end showed the damage done by another vehicle.

Gideon was lifted out and onto a stretcher. Murphy moved forward, almost in the way of the paramedics. When told to move back he held his ground. He could see them working to release Rebecca. His heart was sick, not knowing how she was.

"Murphy, it's Abe. You're not here. What's up?"

"Abe. They were run off the road at the curve. We didn't see a thing. It was timed too well. They're getting ready to transport soon to the hospital."

"I'll meet you there. Shane and Rachel will be there too." Abe's phone cut off and he was gone.

Murphy climbed back in his car and followed as the ambulances pulled away. Ian was with Rebecca. They didn't see the car hidden off the road, or the man that stood watching, gleeful in his deed he had done.

Caleb stood watching as Abe paced the waiting room. Shane and Rachel were seated near the door. Timothy came up to him.

"So what happened?"

Caleb shook his head. "Murphy said they were run off the road deliberately. He was just enough ahead of them not to see anything." Caleb looked at Timothy. "You haven't been told, but Rebecca has a stalker. We figure it was him."

Timothy stared at Caleb. "A stalker!" He shook his head. "Who would have guessed!"

Caleb moved to the exam room area. He had police officers stationed at their exam rooms and he knew Murphy was with Gideon and Ian with Rebecca. He entered Gideon's room and found Frankie there as well. The Emergency doctor was assessing him for injuries and Caleb could see the IV already in place. He watched as Gideon stirred, moving slightly in the bed. He moved forward as Gideon became more agitated.

"Rebecca! Where's Rebecca? Where's my wife?" Gideon was desperately trying to climb from the bed. Murphy had thrown himself across Gideon's chest and Frankie his legs just to keep him on the bed. Caleb reached across the bed to help hold the arm with the IV as the doctor barked for a sedative and the nurse ran to get it. It was taking all four of them just to hold him down.

Shane looked up as he heard the commotion and saw the nurse running for the medication cabinet, unlock it and grab what she needed before locking it up again. She disappeared into Gideon's room. He felt a hand on his shoulder. It was Abe.

"Any word yet, Shane?"

Shane shook his head. "I would say my son is awake and causing a ruckus, but I don't know for sure how either of them are."

Abe stared at the closed exam room doors. "Rebecca was with him, he had wanted to take her out for dinner. Most of the damage was on her side of the car. Murphy said it looks as if Gideon tried to control the car but that for some reason he couldn't. He's going back out there in the morning with Eddie to take a look."

****

He watched the newscast of the accident. Gideon Andrews and his wife, Rebecca? His wife? She was his. She wasn't supposed to be with him. She was supposed to be at home, waiting for him. So why wasn't she? He was really going to have to lay down the rules when she became his.

383

The Emergency doctor stepped back and wiped the sweat from his face. It had taken time for the sedative to work, and Gideon had fought them all the while. He looked up at the three men standing there.

"What just happened here?"

Caleb studied Gideon's still form. "He was deliberately run off the road tonight. Rebecca, his wife, took the brunt of it. There is an ongoing investigation that we can't disclose the details of, but his wife has been threatened. This gentleman or one of his colleagues will be with this man and others of their colleagues will be across the hall with Rebecca. There will also be police officers at the room doors. No one goes in or out that isn't cleared by me personally." Caleb looked at the doctor. "It is a matter of their life or death if what I say is not followed. They are now in protective custody."

The doctor nodded. "I need to go speak with his family, I guess. If that's his wife across the hall, I can't speak with her and she is his next of kin."

Caleb nodded. "Frankie will go with you. We're not taking any chances that someone can get to them."

The doctor stopped and stared at him, then swallowed. "You're really serious, aren't you?"

"I am." As the doctor left Caleb moved back to the bedside. He stared down at his friend, seeing the bruises forming, the cuts. He turned to look at the door and then back at Gideon. "There are no burns."

Murphy looked at him. "No burns?"

"No. Did the airbags go off?"

Murphy stared at him. "No, now that you mention it. I didn't see that they had. Are you telling me they were sabotaged?"

"That's what I'm saying." Caleb had his phone out and was ordering that the car be moved to their compound. It would be gone over with a fine tooth comb. "I have a feeling we'll find more than that tampered with. It's either they were tampered with or the airbags just failed or it was the angle they hit at."

He headed across the hall to Rebecca. Stepping inside he saw the physician was John Thompson from the church. John looked up and nodded, then continued his assessment of Rebecca. When he was done, he moved back to stand by Caleb.

"Accident or not?"

Caleb shot him a look and then looked back at Rebecca. "Any sign of harm from the air bags?"

John shook his head. "And there should be. I would say they didn't go off."

Caleb sighed. "That's what I was afraid of. How is she?"

John hesitated, then said, "Cuts, bruises Her wrist is sprained. From what Ian has said about the car, it is only the good Lord's protection that they weren't hurt worse."

Caleb nodded. "Ian or one of Abe's men will be with her all the time. I have men at the door. I'll bring in a female officer as well. We've put them into protective custody for now. Rebecca's life has been threatened, and tonight shows that Gideon's is as well." Caleb stopped speaking as he watched Ian step towards the nurse.

Ian reached and stopped her from touching Rebecca. She turned on him with words of venom and hatred directed at Rebecca and struggled to release her arm from his grasp as he moved her away.

Caleb stepped forward as her hand opened and a syringe fell to the floor. Caleb studied it and then her. Stepping to the door, he motioned the officer in.

"Arrest her for attempted murder. We'll sort out the whys after."

John stepped back to check on Rebecca. "If Ian hadn't been here, she likely would have succeeded." He looked at the syringe Caleb had picked up and put into an evidence bag. "I would be interested to know what she used. We'll have to check the medication cabinet now, so I may know for you before you get it run."

Caleb thanked him, turned to leave, then looked back. "You'll be moving them to a ward?" When John nodded, he continued, "Make it a semi-private and put them in together. It will make it easier to guard them. They're married anyway, so it won't hurt."

Ian laughed at the expression on John's face. "They kept their secret well, didn't they?"

John shook his head. "I suppose you're going to tell me they had good reason to?" At his nod, John muttered, "Of course, they did. They always do."

Abe watched as Shane, Rachel and Timothy walked towards the room Gideon and Rebecca had been moved to. He knew Ian and Murphy were on guard inside and Caleb had two officers outside. He was glad to see one was a female officer. Caleb had mentioned that he had had many come forward and volunteer to help. He felt someone stop beside and looked to see Doug standing there.

“Did you know, Abe, about her stalker?”

Abe shook his head. “She never said a word, not in all those years. I wish she had.”

Doug agreed with him. “I didn’t until Mac said something. Gideon picked up on it right away.”

“Gideon’s good. Given what he went through, he’s learned to read people quickly and well. I wish I could get him on my team.”

Doug laughed. “Caleb says the same but it’s not happening. He’s content where he is. So what’s the plan now?”

Abe shrugged. “Right now, it’s up to Caleb. He has them under police protection.”

“I think I’ll go volunteer.” He turned to leave, and Abe stopped him with a hand on his arm.

“Thanks, Doug. That means a lot.”

“We’re family, Abe. We take care of our own. And I understand Gideon’s family now. I thought that day in the cafe they were suited. God certainly brought them together.”

“He did, and quicker than I would have thought. Gideon is just so right for her.”

“And she’s exactly what he needs.”

****

He stood watching the doorway. There was no way he was getting in there, she was too surrounded. He cursed the fact that the nurse had tried to kill her. That made them even more vigilant. He turned and walked away, steps slow. He would have to find a way to reach her and soon.

****

Caleb studied the white board again and then turned to Ben. "How is the investigation going?"

Ben stared at the white board as well, trying to made sense of what was there. "This guy is good, but I'm beginning to think he has help. The tone of the letters doesn't match the quality of the photos he sending her. I know with cameras today you can get good pictures, but these aren't something an amateur would take, unless they've taken classes or taken lots of photos. Once in a while you can get a good shot but not all the time."

Caleb picked up one of the photos and studied it with his eyes now seeing it through Ben's words. "You're right.   They are too good to go with the notes." He drew a deep breath. "That just expands our hunt."

"I know.   I've already got that started. Where's Eddie at with what he was working on?"

"He's working on the angle of the nurse from last night, trying to find out how she's connected. She's not talking."

"That was strange. But then everything lately seems strange."

Caleb agreed.   He studied the picture in his hand closer. "Ben, did you see that?" He pointed at a section of the photo. "We need to get that enlarged. I think we may have found a clue that will help us move forward."

Ben took the photo and looked at it. "I think you're right, Caleb. I knew there was something off about this photo, but I couldn't put my finger on it. I'll have the lab enlarge it as best they can." He stopped, then continued, "Are you sending them back to the compound?"

"For now. Abe's men are good and they'll just draw in even closer. Ian and Murphy are hurting it happened on their watch." He turned as Frankie entered the room. Activity was happening all around him, but Ben, Frankie and Eddie were the ones he was depending on. "What's up, Frankie?"

"I've been talking to my people on the street. They have heard nothing, which is strange. They always hear something." He shook his head. "How has he covered it up so well for so long?"

"He has help, that how." Eddie spoke from behind him. "I've been running that nurse through the database. She's not who she said she is. She had stolen ID and is not a nurse at all."

Caleb stared at him. "So where is the nurse whose ID she had?"

"I have officers heading to her home. She single, lives alone, has few friends in town. Her home is isolated as well. I don't have a good feeling, Caleb."

Caleb shook his head. "I don't either. This guy, he's not smart enough. Someone has been directing his steps all along. But who? We need to be digging deeper." He looked around. "Has Gideon's boss come up with anything yet?"

Ben nodded. "He said he's on his way in, he has information he wants you to see in person. He also needs to go over it with Rebecca."

"Come find me when he gets here." Caleb walked back to his office, deep in thought. Who was it? It had grown to be more than just a simple stalker, so who was it and why? He sat behind his desk, then leaned back, thinking. He knew it had to be someone who was in Rebecca's life, that she would least suspect. Or someone who knew somebody in her life. He pinched the bridge of his nose. This had just gotten a whole lot bigger. They were trying to whittle it down and it sure wasn't working.

He looked up. Lord, I could sure use your help. What or who are we missing? I know there's something there, something simple. Please direct us to that and help us unravel this before either Rebecca or Gideon get hurt worse than they have.

Chapter 10

Gideon eased his body down on the couch at Rebecca's feet. She had curled up there when they came home and had not moved. Abe was sitting in a chair where he could watch his sister. Gideon knew Caleb was on his way out and that his boss, Sidney Morgan, was in town. What had they discovered, he wondered?

"You know, it took four of them to hold you down last night." Abe watched as Gideon stared at him.

"Four?"

Abe nodded. "Murphy, Caleb, Frankie and the doctor, until they could get a sedative into you and give it time to work. You fought them hard to get to Rebecca."

Gideon swallowed hard as he looked at Rebecca. "I was so afraid that she was dead or that he had gotten to her."

Abe studied the man who had chosen his sister. He didn't think he could have hand picked a better one for her. "What happened last night?"

Gideon shook his head. "I really don't know. We were coming into that curve, someone hit us from behind, and I had no steering. It's like it was sabotaged or something."

Abe looked up as the door opened. "Caleb was looking into that. He's here now. Maybe he has some answers."

Gideon pulled himself to his feet to greet Caleb and then his employer. Once they had their coffee, they settled back in the living room. Gideon refused to move far from his wife.

Rebecca stirred as he sat back down and pulled herself upright. Abe handed her the ginger ale he had brought in for her and she took it with a quiet word of thanks. Gideon pulled her back against him, and then looked at Caleb, Eddie and Sidney. He searched their faces, then his gaze sought Abe's.

"Who wants to start?"

"How about you tell us what happened last night?" Caleb studied his friend's face, catching the quickly covered anxiety there.

"We were hit from behind. He came up very fast, hit us, then stopped. Something went wrong with the steering. I think you'll find it was sabotaged in some way. The next thing, we're in the ditch." Gideon stared at Caleb. "I'm right. The car was gotten to."

Caleb nodded. "Our mechanic went over it. It was. There's no evidence the airbags were tampered with. We just can't explain why they didn't go off?"

Gideon once again looked between the three men. "You're not here for a social visit. What do you have?"

Caleb drew a deep breath. "No, we're not here for a social visit. This has gotten much deeper and darker than just a simple stalker." He looked over at Rebecca. "I'm sorry, Rebecca, it just doesn't seem to be ending, just getting worse."

He reached for one of the folders he had set down and opened it. He passed it over to Gideon.

"Do you recognize this fellow?"

Rebecca studied the picture, then shook her head. "No, I don't. I'm sorry."

Caleb nodded. "That's what we thought. His name is Dustin. We've spoken with him. His only connection is that he would be paid at times to deliver envelopes to you. He had no idea what was in them. We have now put him somewhere he'll be safe.

"Next, the nurse from last night."

Gideon and Rebecca stared at each other, then Gideon spoke, "What nurse?"

"You weren't told, were you? I thought Ian might have mentioned it. We have a nurse try to kill Rebecca last night. Ian stepped in before she got close. She was not a nurse, we have determined, merely someone who decided you needed to die, Rebecca. We are still trying to trace who she is. The nurse whose ID she stole, we're still trying to find her. She was just a recent hire here and hadn't worked any shifts yet." Caleb stopped at the look of horror on Rebecca's face.

"She was that close?" Gideon could hardly get the words out.

Caleb nodded. "She was. Abe is tightening up security here and neither one of you will go anywhere without an escort of some kind. Officers are stepping forward as well, volunteering their own time. You're extended family to them now, Gideon, as well as Rebecca having family on the force. We will do everything we can to protect you, God willing."

Eddie spoke up. "We've been trying to track down your stalker, Rebecca. He's good but he's also not working alone. The tone of the letters are one thing. The photos." He paused. "The photos. Now, they're interesting. They have not all been taken by an amateur. I spoke with a friend from out of town, who knew nothing of what was going on, and showed him a couple. He said they are almost professional in style now. The earlier ones were taken by an amateur. He thinks the ones from about five years

393

ago are when the images started to change. That has expanded who we are looking for."

Rebecca blinked at him. "A professional? No, you said almost a professional. It's possible for an amateur to take really good photos, if they've taken courses or gone on line and studied techniques. Cameras, even inexpensive ones, are very sophisticated now. So you're saying there's more than one?" She shuddered at the thought.

"That's what we're saying. I'm sorry, Rebel, I wish I had better news." He hesitated before continuing. "Whoever it is is getting sloppy. A mistake in one of the photos led us to Dustin. That shouldn't have happened."

Abe spoke up for the first time. "A God moment."

Gideon looked around at the men gathered in the living room. Each would do their best to keep them both alive, but would it be enough? Gideon stared at his employer, narrowing his eyes at the look on his face. This can't be good, he thought. Please, Lord, keep my wife safe and alive. Place that hedge of protection around her.

Sidney hesitated before he spoke, then looking directly at Gideon, handed over two files.

"The first one, Gideon, is the profile of the stalker. Janet picked up that there was more than one and couldn't get past that. This was before we had even figured out there were two. She felt the notes and the later photos were not the work of the same person.

"I'll let you read the report, but this is basically what she says. The initial stalker is a younger male, about 2-3 years older than Rebecca, not well educated. He is likely a loner, not well liked by anyone who comes in contact with him. He will be working a blue collar job, very low paid. He doesn't have a lot of self confidence and was likely bullied as a younger man or child. Janet says he sees Rebecca as someone who can change his life and bring him up to the level she lives at, where he will be respected. She doesn't feel he is a real danger to her, but that Gideon might now be in danger from him as he has stepped into the role he sees for himself with Rebecca, that of husband. She also feels that he is dealing with some kind of an illness but wasn't specific on the kind.

"Now, for the second stalker, that is more interesting." Sidney paused. This was going to be the one that would be so hard to explain, especially when they didn't have the evidence they needed.

"Janet feels the one taking the pictures in the last five years is a female and no related to the original stalker. When did you first start dating Nick?" His kind eyes studied Rebecca as she thought about that and he saw when she understood what he was saying.

"About five years ago or so. We were just friends going out for coffee or a meal or sharing time taking photos and it grew from here." She started to shake her head. "No, you're not saying!"

Sidney nodded his head, disliking what he needed to say. "Janet said something happened about five or six years ago that changed the stalking and brought in the second stalker. She thinks it may be a sister or mother or aunt, some significant female to him who resented Nick's presence in your life. She will have tried all his life to give him exactly what he has always wanted, to make up for who he is. Nick took that away when you two married. Janet strongly feels that the woman was responsible for Nick's accident. You were collateral damage. Tell me about the accident."

Rebecca had begun to shake, fear evident in her face. This was something she had never ever talked about, not even to Abe, not to the police. Gideon's arms tightened around her.

She looked up through the tears in her eyes. "We had been out that day, just taking a day for us. Work was picking up in the studio and we needed to take a break. We had been out hiking. We had found a beautiful hiking trail and would go out there, even just for short walks. There was one area that had had rocks slides near it and we were always so careful." She stopped, overcome with the memories and the emotions. "One minute, we are walking along, talking, laughing. Nick was ahead of me, walking backwards, with his camera up, trying to get a picture for our studio. He wanted one of me so much. There was a rock slide and it took him down. I got caught in the edge of it. I could hear a diabolical laugh as the rocks were covering him." She was shaking her head at the memory. "I couldn't get to him. I couldn't save him." She swallowed, trying to overcome her emotions. "When the dust settled, I heard someone on the trail and called for help. They didn't help. They stood there, but didn't come near us. I could hear a voice saying he got what he deserved. He should have stayed away from me." Her hands to her face, sobs wracking her body. Gideon's arms tightened even more, and his face was buried in her hair.

Chapter 11

Abe stood and walked from the emotion-charged room. He had seen the looks on the men's faces and knew his own must look the same. He stopped as he stepped into the kitchen. His whole team was sitting or standing there, devastation on their faces. Rebecca was loved by each one as a sister. He looked toward the back door and Doug stood there.

"She never said a thing, Abe, when we picked her up." Doug's voice broke.

Abe shook his head. "She didn't, and she's carried this for all these years." He could feel the rage starting to build within him, directed at the unknown. "She wouldn't, not knowing who. She would have thought that if she said something, one of us would have become a target."

Doug nodded, then handed Abe a bottle of water and a warm damp cloth. He didn't say anything, but Abe studied his cousin and then nodded. The line had been drawn and they would do everything they could to protect Rebecca and Gideon.

Abe sat back down and watched his sister, having handed her the bottle of water and cloth. She had drawn on the inner strength he had never known she had and was ready to go forward with the conversation.

"What else did she say?" Rebecca's quiet voice cut through the tension in the room.

Sidney hesitated, studying first her, then Gideon. Gideon, he knew his character and that he would never back down from protecting the woman he loved and adored, even if it meant his life. His eyes went back to Rebecca, and then he nodded.

"Things are escalating again. There are more pictures and more notes in the last year than in other years. Janet feels that time is running out for the male, for whatever reason. Gideon will be a real target now, and they will likely stop at nothing to remove him. The woman, Janet thinks, is well to do, doesn't really need to work given the different times of day the photos are taken. She may well be someone you know on a slight basis. Janet also feels the woman is prominent in some way in town, but has felt the slights, intended or unintended over the years. She has magnified the simplest thing and made it into something huge."

Sidney paused and then turned to Caleb. "I'm not sure there is a lot we can do at present to protect them, other than what we are doing. I know your men and women are digging deep. This woman has hidden well, and likely is hiding in plain sight, thumbing her noses at the incompetent police department she sees. She is feeding the male lies and suspicions to keep him sending letters and she is sending the photos herself. Janet doesn't think the male knows about the photos or there would a mention of them in the notes."

Caleb sat and thought about what he had been told. It was close to what he, Ben, Eddie and Frankie had come up with. "Do you find anything in the photos?"

Sidney nodded. "One of our techs have been working on a program to enhance photos and pick out little details. He's working on the photos now and has said he's found some interesting things. He's still putting together what he found, but he hoped in a couple of days to have a preliminary report for us.

He did say the photos were taken mostly in the downtown area, near Rebecca's studio."

"Near her studio?" Abe stared at Sidney. "She's been that close all these years?"

Sidney nodded. "That's what the evidence is saying. As to why is ramping up, that's something we need to work on."

Eddie spoke up, having just received a text message. "They found the nurse. Her body was found in the woods behind her house. The medical examiner is there now but it looks as if she's been dead for a couple of weeks."

"That's what I don't understand," Gideon spoke up. "How did that imposter know Rebecca would be there last night?"

The other men stared at him and then at each other. "That's a good question." Caleb's mind was racing. "I suspect your accident last night was not related to the stalking and was directed at you for another reason. The nurse likely figured if you got hurt, you would be taken to Emergency."

He stepped away to call the office. When he came back, his face was grimmer than it had been. "We know who the imposter is. It's your foster mother's sister. Her prints were in the system. She has confessed that she wanted to harm you for sending her sister to jail. She couldn't get in to you, so she choose to try and hurt you through Rebecca."

Gideon's eyes slid closed. It was his fault that the accident happened. It was directed at him. He felt Rebecca's hands tighten on his and he opened his eyes to look at her. She was shaking her head.

"Not your fault, Gideon. It's their depravity that did it. I feel sorry for them. They never had the chance or took the chance God offered them."

Discussions wrapping up, Caleb and Eddie left, taking Doug with them. Sidney had stayed at Gideon's request. The two men walked the back yard, talking.

"How are you really doing, Gideon? You've made such changes in your life in such a short time."

"Good changes, Sidney. Rebecca is, I think, the best thing to have happened to me aside from God. It hurts to see her like this. I just wish I could make it all go away."

Sidney listened to the younger man as he poured out his heart. He had been the one Gideon had found just after he was beaten and dumped in another town by his foster father. Sidney had guided Gideon along the way, finding him to have become the best investigator he had ever worked with. But even more, Gideon's faith had stood strong and had strengthened over the years. He would need that now, Sidney thought, and raised his heart in prayer for him.

"So where do we go from here, Sidney?"

"Your friends are working hard, but the stalker has kept well hidden. It's going to be really difficult to find him and her if they are two working together. It's going to take a lot of leg work and a lot of prayer." He hesitated to say what he knew he had to. "It may come to having one of you become the target again, out in the open." He held up his hand. "I know what you're going to say, that it won't work. It may not come to that, but you need to be prepared to appear to lose your bodyguards and be out there."

"I want to do everything I can to avoid that with Rebecca, but you're right. It may come to that. I pray it doesn't. What do you suggest we do now?"

Sidney continued to walk the yard, deep in thought. He looked up to see Rebecca and Abe walking towards them. Gideon reached for her hand and held it tight. He knew things were starting to happen and if they couldn't be found, others might get hurt in collateral damage in the stalker trying to reach them.

****

He stood near the entrance to the compound, out of sight he hoped. He wanted to see her so bad, he hadn't seen her in days. This was not right. She was his and should be with him. Why were they keeping her from him?

She stood back behind him and watched, anger growing with each minute. They would pay for what they were putting him through. And it would be soon.

****

Abe turned to Sidney, even as he continued to scan the area.

"I heard with Gideon asked. Where do we go from here?   I know what I would do but it's not necessarily the right move."

Sidney nodded. He had a pretty good idea of what Abe would do. "Keep up as much protection as you can. These two will rebel and try to escape it. Don't let them. It's a matter of life and death. Make sure someone goes with them everywhere they're off the compound." His eyes searched the area around them. "You have a lot of places someone can hide up there. Your men, I know, search it every day. Bring in dogs if you need to." He looked at Abe. "I'm not telling you anything you don't know or are not doing now.   It may come to it that you'll have to move them.   You can take it to the bank that they know they're here and they will try anything and everything to get to them. Their families need to take

401

special care as well. The way it is escalating, the families may well become a target to get to them."

Gideon felt Rebecca move closer to him. He looked down at her, didn't see fear but saw determination that she was ready once and for all to have this over and go on with her life. He feared that she would do something that would harm her, and he couldn't bear to think of that. His heart raised in prayer, he turned to the two men.

"Caleb and his men are working on this. How can we help?" Gideon asked.

"Right now, let them work. I know you have resources you can tie into, but even if you found something, it wouldn't be allowed in court. We need to be doing the research. If you think of something let either myself or Caleb know. We'll research it. We want as strong a case as we can make."

Rebecca spoke up for the first time. "I am not about to sit around and do nothing. I want this over and over yesterday. They have taken enough from me." She broke free from Gideon's hold and ran for the house.

They watched her, then Gideon took off after her. Abe watched, his heart in his throat. She was getting ready to do something. How could they keep her from that?

Caleb sat down heavily in his chair. He was tired. This case seemed non-ending. They just couldn't find the one key, that one little thing they needed to unravel it. He looked up as Eddie and Ben entered, an envelope in Eddie's hand.

"Don't tell me. Another one?"

Ben nodded. "Joseph found it in the mail and brought it in. They haven't seen it, and I don't want them too."

Caleb's hand froze as he reached for the envelope. "That bad?"

Ben again nodded. "These people are just plain sick. I don't think I've seen anything like this in all my years on the force."

Eddie's face was drawn and white. "I can't understand. How can they get so close and us not know it?"

Caleb opened the envelope and slipped out the note and the photo. His heart grew sick as he read the words and the threats directed at both Gideon and Rebecca. He then turned to the photo, a photo of the accident from the previous night, showing Gideon's stretcher being loaded into the ambulance and the emergency crews working to free Rebecca

"This is from last night. Whoever took it was there."

Ben nodded as he looked up. "They were, and we didn't see them. They must have been just down the road from the crews."

Caleb laid the picture down and studied it, then studied the letter. "Did the lab find anything?"

Eddie shook his head. "They are so careful not to leave any evidence on the note, the photo."

Caleb picked up the envelope and studied it. A mark got his attention, faint but there. "What's this?" He handed the envelope to Eddie.

Eddie studied it. "Now, that's interesting. Looks like a reverse image in ink. I'll have the lab take a look at that." He picked up the envelope, the photo and letter. He was showing the strain and Caleb knew Peg was also very worried about her niece. He made a mental note to have Hannah go see her.

Ben watched Eddie leave, then turned to Caleb. "How do we do it, Caleb? How can we keep them safe against the unknown?"

"Same as we always do, Ben, lots of legwork and a lot of prayer. God is the one in control, and we have a tendency to forget that. He could stop this now but He has chosen not to, why I have no idea." He sat back and studied his friend. "You have an idea of who?"

Ben shook his head. "Not really, just an impression. What Sidney said sounds so familiar, but I can't put a name or a face to either one. I should be able to."

"Me, too, Ben. They sound so familiar." Caleb leaned forward again. "We're putting so much energy into it. You would think we could come up with something, somehow. They can't be that good. If it goes on for too long, Rebecca's going to bolt and Gideon will be with her. Neither one will take being shut up like they are for long."

"I know and that worries me. We can't protect them if they do bolt. Abe's men will stay close. Being there, they're in as much protection, if not more, than we can provide." Ben studied his hands, wanting to say something, but not sure how to continue.

"What's up, Ben? You have something else on your mind?"

"I do. This seems so much like what Frankie and Deirdre went through. I know it's different, but I still can't fathom how people can be so depraved. That last letter. I never want to show it to Rebecca or Gideon. That would be the catalyst to sending them off on their own."

Caleb nodded. "It would, for sure. We'll have to make sure that we intercept any of them. They are getting worse in terms of wording. It makes me think that they are being dictated now, the tone in them has changed so much."

"So, how then do we proceed? I'm for listing every female in town that's a certain age and eliminating them. Did the profiler specify an age for the female?"

Caleb hunted on his desk for her report and opened it. "She suggested in her fifties or older. If it's a sister, it would be younger, but she really felt it was a mother or a mother figure to him. I think you have a good idea there, Ben. Start with those we know work in the downtown area around where Rebecca's studio was. I'll pull Frankie in and have him start working in from the outside of that area. I'm surprised he hasn't picked up anything on the streets."

"He should have. They still trust him. Maybe he will yet. He's put out the word."

Gideon watched as Rebecca wandered the yard. She was lost without her studio and he didn't know how to make it better for her. He wanted to fix it and couldn't. He needed to find something for them to do and he needed to do it soon. He knew she was ready to bolt, and he would be with her when she went.

He turned as Abe came out and handed him a cup of coffee. Abe stared at his sister, then turned his head to watch Gideon.

"She getting ready to run?"

Gideon nodded. "She can't take much more of this, of being cooped up. To tell you the truth, neither can I. We need something to do and somewhere to go."

Abe thought about that, then turned and headed back into the house. "I want to run something by Caleb, seeing as you're still in his protective custody. I'll be back."

Gideon turned to stare after him. What was he up to? He turned and walked down the yard to where Rebecca had taken a seat on the swing. "Room for one more, sweetheart?"

She slid over and when he had sat down and pushed the swing to move, she laid her head on his shoulder. "I need to do something, Gideon. I can't just sit here forever. I know Caleb has them monitoring the mail and I won't get any more of those messages. I'm glad that way, but I can't wait around."

"Abe's gone to talk to Caleb. He's trying to figure something out. We are, after all, in police protective custody. Caleb is just letting us stay here because he knows we should be safe.”

“I know. I’m just being grumpy.” She looked up to see Abe walking towards them.

He dropped to sit on the ground in front of them, leaning back on his hands, legs stretched out with his feet crossed. He waited, a half smile on his face, as he studiously avoided their looks.

“Abe!” Rebecca’s outraged cry broke the silence. “What did you do?”

He smiled and then turned his head to look at her. “I got you free for a couple of days. Some of the guys have to go out on a job, but I have a couple who would love to take a few days and fly off to the sea. They asked if I knew anyone who would like to go with them.”

“Abe, don’t tease. I can’t take it.”

Abe shook his head. “I talked to Caleb. He thinks it’s a good idea to get you away for a while. By that time, there may be a break in the case.”

“They’ve got another letter and photo, don’t they?”

Abe hesitated, then nodded. “Yes, they did, and no, they won’t show it to you. Caleb flat out refuses to. He won’t even tell me what it says, other than it wasn’t pretty.” At her gasp he looked up at her. “I’m sorry, Rebecca. I agreed when he said that. So about this trip, you game for it?”

Abe turned his head a bit more to watch Gideon. Gideon was going through all the scenarios he could think of, then he looked down at his wife. She needed to get away, to have some fun. If it meant leaving here and flying somewhere, then so be it. If it meant their bodyguards went to, then that’s how it would be.

"We're good with that. Who are you sending?"

"Ian and Murphy. They feel bad about what happened and want to make up for it, even though it wasn't their fault. Ian will fly."

Gideon nodded. "So when?"

"I'm thinking tomorrow, but I want to clear it first."

"And where?"

"That's what we're trying to come up with. Finding a spot where you can be isolated but still have amenities. That's hard to do within a few hours from here."

"Talk to Sidney. He has quite a choice of just such properties he can access at a few hours' notice."

Abe stared at him. "Really?"

Gideon nodded. "He's done work for a lot of people who need places to get away for a while or have places that they offer. I'm sure he can find somewhere near here for us. All have really good security. He's very picky about the properties he uses."

Abe rose to his feet. "I'll set up a conference call with Caleb and Sidney and see what we can find." He stared down at the two. "We need to keep you safe, and with the unknown, we don't know where to put you to do that. You're going stir crazy here."

Gideon watched Abe walk away, saying a prayer of thanks for the care he and others were providing. Now, if it worked out and they could get out of the area, maybe Caleb and his men could figure out who was the stalker.

Caleb listened as Sidney offered some properties that he though might work. He had a bad feeling though and was hesitant to agree. "How safe is that last property, Sidney, and what are the access points to it?"

"I think it's the safest I can offer right now. It has an eight foot high stone fence around it, controlled access at the gates; without codes you don't get in. There is a beach but because of the debris in the water 15-20 feet out, you can't get a boat in, and no swimmer comes in that way because of the tides. It might work. I'll text you the information and then you and Abe can let me know."

Abe leaned back in his chair and read over his notes. "You're not happy, Caleb."

"No, I'm not. It's going out there into uncertain territory, where we don't have authority to move in if we need to, that has me worried. I know your guys have contacts but I still would like to see something closer here in our own jurisdiction."

Abe nodded as he looked up. "I agree. I feel like we would be putting them at great risk if we let them go somewhere like there." He paused, then continued, "It's like I don't have the okay from God to move them somewhere else, to some other house. I know that sounds strange but that's how I feel."

"I feel the same." Caleb paused as Eddie and Ben entered after knocking. "What's up?"

"We just got this in."

Caleb took the proffered paper and his face blanched. He handed it to Caleb.

"How did they know we were thinking of letting them go somewhere for a few days?" Caleb's face hardened. "Who is leaking this information?"

Abe took the paper and read it. "This is scary. Your office is clear?"

Caleb nodded. "We search every day. It's just a matter of course because of what all has gone on in the last few years."

"When I spoke with Gideon and Rebecca, we were in the yard." He pulled out his phone. "Matt, do me a favour? Search for bugs in the house and around the yard. Someone knows too much of what we're doing."

Ben nodded at the note. "The only one we don't know well is Sidney. We need to check him out and have his office searched. Who gets to make the call?"

Caleb looked at the three of them, then sighed. "I guess that would be me."

He picked up his phone and dialled through to Sidney, getting his voice mail. "Sidney, it's Caleb Logan. Call me as soon as you can. We have a problem we need to speak with you about, and I would ask that you don't call me from your office. Thanks."

He looked at Ben and Eddie. "Anything new?"

Ben nodded. "I think we've narrowed down the age group for the woman we're looking for. The lab is thinking around age fifty or so, given the timing of the day and the type of photos. It's definitely female."

Eddie continued. "The woman who was hired on as the nurse has finally starting talking, knowing she was facing some pretty stiff penalties. All her correspondence was by mail. She kept it all and I've sent it to the lab. Hopefully they'll find something there."

Frankie tapped at the door and came in. His hesitation was not usual for him.

Caleb studied him. "What do you have, Frankie? I can tell you don't like it."

"No, I don't. I've finally heard from a source on the street. The profiler was spot on. I was told there was a well-dressed, affluent woman going around looking for someone to help her "do away" with someone. No one offered to help, and she moved on. I have an artist with that source, seeing if we can at least get a close picture of the suspect."

"Did your source say male or female?"

Frankie shook his head. "Apparently they were never told. So it could be either. I don't like this. This is getting too bizarre."

Ben nodded. "I know. I just wish I could figure out who."

Caleb's phone rang. It was Sidney.

"I got your voice mail and I am away from my office. What's the concern?"

Caleb drew a deep breath. Sidney was not going to like what he had to say. "Ben and Eddie just brought me a new note, found within the last thirty minutes. Someone knows what we talked about and has threatened them if they leave the compound. I know my office is clear, we search it every day."

Sidney went silent. "So that leaves my office or someone in my office overhearing. I don't like this, Caleb. I thought I could trust everyone here."

"I know. There was only Abe in the office with me and he's not about to do anything to hurt his sister." Caleb thought about the situation. "So what do we do now? We can't use the location we talked about."

"Absolutely not. Let me call you back." His voice trailed off. "I have it. There's a spot I know we can take them to. I'm coming your way and will let you know where it is when I get there. I don't even trust my phone any more."

"Sounds good, Sidney. See you in a while." Caleb hung up and looked at the four men in his office. "Sidney's heading our way. He has a spot but won't say until he gets here. What can we do in the mean while to try and find an alternative place?"

Frankie spoke up. "I know of a place not too far. Very isolated, lots of protection. But I'm not sure that it would work. We can't close off the access like we would need to."

Abe stood and starting pacing. "I'm beginning to think we won't find a place." He stopped and stared at the wall. "How do we find these people? Rebecca has been through enough. We need to stop it."

Eddie studied Abe, then as a thought crossed his mind, he asked, "Why did your mother leave?"

Abe spun and stared at him. "What?"

Eddie repeated himself. "Why did your mother leave? Do you remember?"

Abe continued to stare at him as his mind searched back. "I was 11, I think, Rebecca about 8 or 9. We had been at school, came home, and she had packed up everything of hers and just left. Dad was away with the security team and a client. He had no idea she was leaving."

"Did she leave a note or anything?"

Abe nodded. "She did and it just about broke Dad's heart. I don't think he ever got over it." He swallowed. "He tried to find her but he never could. He said to me not long before he died that he thought

412

she had changed her name. He never felt like she was dead. Rebecca took it hard. She would sit for hours on the front step, waiting for Mom to come home.”

Eddie nodded. “That’s what Peg has said. We’ve talked about it over the years, and your Dad talked to us too. We agreed with him. Peg has said that she didn’t think your Mom was dead, that she had some reason for leaving.” He paused, then looked at Caleb. “I’ve been trying to track her down. I have some leads. I don’t think she ever left this area.”

Caleb looked at him, shocked. “She left her family, but not the area?”

Eddie just stared at him. “That’s what I’m hearing. There was some kind of trust left.”

Abe sank back into his chair. “Are you for real? We were never ever told any of this?” His face whitened. “Do you think she’s involved?”

Eddie shrugged. “We can’t say. That’s what I’m trying to find out.”

Ben spoke up. “I can remember your Mom. We searched for her for so long, I don’t think there was a place we didn’t search. She was just gone.”

****

He stood outside the police department and watched. He knew Abe was in there. He was determined he would follow him and get inside the compound somehow. She was his, not that other man’s. She needed to be with him. That’s what that woman told him. She didn’t care if someone got hurt, just that Rebecca was his.

Sidney met them at the cafe. Here at least, Caleb hoped they could talk without being overheard. He had a quiet word with Mac and the tables around them soon sported "reserved" signs.

Sidney looked around at the men as they waited for their orders. "I've narrowed it down to who it is. Here's the name. I did a security check on her when I hired her, and mine are very, very thorough. Every year, I go back over the security background of every one I have working for me. She has passed every year. I'm looking deeper now that I know she's the leak in my office. I can't take the chance this isn't the first person she's done this with, and for it to be a colleague."

"That always hurts," Ben said, thinking of several over the years. "It's never easy when it's someone we've depended on."

Eddie spoke up. "So where is this place you're thinking of?"

Sidney's eyes searched the cafe, then stopped. "That young fellow by the door, the one around Abe's age. Who is it?"

Frankie took a look. "He seems to be quite interested in our table. I've seen him around but I'm not sure what his name it." He pulled out his phone, and casually snapped a photo, as if he was trying to answer a text. "I'll see what I can find out."

Caleb shot a look over at the table, then at Frankie. "Dig deep, Frankie. I think I know who that is." He looked over at Sidney. "Okay, so where were you thinking?"

Ben listened as Sidney described the place. He shook his head. "That won't work. I know the area very well. There are too many entry points. I was out that way about a week ago. The brush has grown very close to the house. The owners are absentee owners and haven't maintained it at all."

Sidney looked surprised. "That's not they've been telling me." He stopped and his eyes slid closed. "And guess who went out to check it out."

Caleb looked at Sidney. "You have a real problem there. You need to look after it and fast."

Sidney nodded. "I know. I just can't understand. She's always been so thorough, honest and reliable."

They continued to discuss a vacation place for the two but could come to no consensus that would work.

Gideon looked up as Rebecca came and dropped herself on the couch.

"Bored, aren't you?"

She nodded. "And so are you."

"I am but I've had time for studying my Bible that I haven't had in years."

She looked at him. "What are you reading about? I miss the reading together and the study and prayer that Dad used to do with us."

Gideon looked at her, his face softening. "Then, that's what we can do. We'll delve into the Word while we are on an enforced quiet." He looked down at the worn Bible in his hands. "I've just been reading how God protects us, that we wants us to come to Him when we are weary and heavy laden, that He gives us rest. I have read these verses for years, but today they seem to be sinking in."

She leaned her head back on the couch and stared at the ceiling. "Does He really, Gideon? Does He really provide a haven of rest and safety for us?"

"He does, sweetheart, He does." He reached over and pulled her close. "Here, let's search for those verses and then spend time in prayer."

****

She watched as the men left the cafe. What had they been discussing? She couldn't get close enough to hear, that owner had blocked her. She glared at the cafe, thinking of how she would like to deal with him. Maybe she would after she had dealt with Rebecca and Gideon. Then she saw him leaving the cafe. What was he going there? She had told him to stay away and he hadn't. He was going to ruin years of planning. Did she have to deal with him too?

****

Caleb sank into a chair in the conference room. He was tired and just wanted to go home to spend time with his wife and boys. It didn't look like it was going to happen tonight, not that early anyway. He studied the whiteboards, they had increase in number since he was last in here yesterday.

Eddie sat beside him. "I just don't get it, Caleb. Who is it?"

"I think you're on the right track with their mother. I didn't want to say much in front of Abe."

"I agree. She's hard to track though." Eddie sat, deep in thought. "I need to track down the others in the family. If I remember correctly, Peg had a half-brother. I'm not sure where he's at."

Caleb felt chills running down his back when Eddie mentioned that. "Do you know where he was when their mother disappeared?"

416

Eddie had just lifted a cup of coffee to take a drink, and his hand froze. "No, you don't think." He started to shake his head. "Oh, man, that is gonna hurt."

"Nothing about this has been easy. Rebecca has been hurt so many times already. I would hate to see this hurt too."

Eddie stood, too agitated to stay sitting. "I hope it's not what you're thinking." He began pacing the room, avoiding the men and women working. "I'll find out from Peg what his full name is, whether he ever married that she knew of, what his occupation was."

Still shaking his head, Eddie walked through the door, narrowly missing running into Ben.

"What's with Eddie?"

Caleb sighed, staring at the door. "I just asked him if Peg knew where her half-brother was."

Ben sat down and buried his head in his hands. "No, not that. That's all we need."

"I know. It's just getting worse and worse." He looked around. "Any word on a place yet?"

Ben shook his head. "They're still working on it, the last Abe said. I just don't know about that, Caleb. I don't have a good feeling."

"I don't either. If it comes to it, they are still in our custody. I'll just say no."

Gideon looked up as Abe came into the room, saw the look on his face, and waited for him to speak.

"We're trying to find you a spot. We thought we had one but it won't work. It may not happen at all, but we're doing our best."

Gideon glanced down at Rebecca, then with narrowed eyes, looked at Abe. Abe stared back. Gideon knew there was more to it than what he was saying.

"We would like to get away, Abe, but we're content. If it can happen, it will." Rebecca stood and headed for the kitchen. "I'm making supper today, so be prepared to be surprised."

Gideon waited until Rebecca had disappeared, then asked in a low voice, "What's the problem? Something is, I can tell by your face."

Abe looked around to make sure Rebecca wasn't near the door. He could hear her at the stove. "Sidney has found a leak in his office. He's not sure how long it's been there."

Gideon looked stunned, then his eyes narrowed. He spoke a name.

Abe stared at him. "How did you know?"

He shrugged in response. "There's always been something I have never trusted about her." He paused, then continued, "I never said anything to Sidney. I had nothing concrete other than a feeling there was something there." Gideon paused, his eyes staring across the room but not seeing what he was looking at. "Do you have a picture of your mother?"

Abe thought, nodded and then rose to go to the bookshelves. He searched for the right photo album, opened it and brought it back to Gideon.

Gideon stared at the picture Abe had brought to him. He reached for his phone, took a picture and then sent it to Sidney.

"What are you thinking, Gideon?"

"I would rather not say until I'm sure."

Rebecca came back in and dropped down on the couch.

"Did you burn the dinner?" Abe wasn't sure what was going on with her.

"No, I didn't." She got up and almost ran from the room. They heard the back door slam.

Abe stared after her. "I didn't mean anything by that."

"I know you didn't. I'll see what's up." Gideon was up and off the couch and almost to the back door by the time he had finished.

Rachel stood in the middle of the yard, arms tight around her waist. Ian stood near her talking to her. Murphy was at the bottom of the stairs and turned as Gideon stepped down them. A sudden rattling or popping noise startled them. Gideon found himself on the ground with Murphy's hand holding him down. He struggled to get up.

"Stay down," Murphy commanded. His eyes swept the yard. Ian had taken Rebecca down and had her covered with his body, revolver in hand, staring around.

"I need you to stay here. Don't move." Murphy's eyes were still searching the area above the fence. "Gideon, you need to stay here and stay down. Do you understand?"

Gideon nodded. He too was searching the area. Where was the sniper? He knew the sound of bullets only too well. His eyes then went to where his wife was. Ian was up, searching the area, but Rebecca lay still. Gideon's heart sank. Was she okay?

Abe came through the back door, low to the ground. He knew others of the team would be fanning out to search the area outside the fenced yard. He would hear if they found anything. He stopped by Gideon, assessed him and then moved on to his sister. He stayed with her, crouched low, and waited.

His phone pinged with a message and he looked at it, then looked up towards the rocks. He saw nothing at first, then saw the movement of Matt stepping a foot to one side. Abe's head sank to his chest. He thought they were safe here and someone still got to them. He swivelled to stare around, feeling the evil near him. Where was it?

He reached to help Rebecca to her feet, then sent her with Ian to the house. Murphy had already taken Gideon inside. He didn't think either of them were hurt physically, but he didn't know emotionally how Rebecca was. That would have to wait until he had determined if there was still danger.

An hour later, the team gathered on the back deck. Abe searched the area around again, his eyes straining to catch a glimpse of anything out of the ordinary. Caleb stood beside him.

"How did this happen, Abe?"

"That's what I want to know, Caleb. It was too close. The thing is though, we don't know which one of them the sniper was after, if it was only one. It almost seemed as if it was both of them."

Matt spoke up. "There was just no evidence there. A few scuff marks from feet, but nothing we could use as evidence. This is just so strange."

Gideon walked out from the house and stood in front of Abe. "I've had enough. This was too close."

Abe nodded. "It was. I just don't know where we can put you two that you'll be safe."

Gideon stared at him. "I'll find us a place." He turned to walk away, but Caleb's hand on his arm stopped him.

"Don't run, Gideon."

Gideon hesitated, then shrugged off Caleb's hand and walked away. Caleb and Abe stared after him.

"Go with them, Murphy, you and Ian. Don't let them out of your sight."

Murphy and Ian ran for their quarters, knowing that time was of the essence. They knew Gideon was ready to bolt and wouldn't wait for them.

Abe turned as he heard the sound of a vehicle and hit the front door at a run, Caleb on his heels. He made it to the front just in time to see Gideon's car vanish through the gate. He slid to a stop. He was too late. Murphy and Ian would never catch them.

"They ran! I can't believe!" Abe stood on the front steps, hand on his head.

"I knew it was coming, Abe. They were too restricted." Caleb looked around as Murphy and Ian came out of the door behind them. "Too late, fellows. They're gone."

Murphy shook his head. "I knew it. I could see it coming. So, Abe, where do you want us?"

"I think maybe you two should head out anyway. Try and find them and keep them safe."

****

They were on the run. She had scared them enough to make them run. Now, if only she could keep up with them or find them. That would be the hard part.

Gideon watched in the rearview mirror to see if any of them were after them. So far, they were clear. He glanced over at Rebecca. She was quiet and subdued. The shooting had really shaken her. It had him shaken, and he had been shot at before.

"Where are we headed, Gideon?" She turned to look at him, a question in her eyes.

"I'm not sure yet.   Just away from here." Gideon hesitated for a moment at the crossroads, then turned away from town. "I just need to find some place where you'll be safe. Sidney has someone who is leaking information in his office, and I think she is connected in some way to your stalker."

"A leak in Sidney's office?" Fear whitened her face. "How and who?"

Gideon shook his head as he watched the traffic around him.   The traffic was light and he couldn't see anyone who seemed to be following them. "No, I won't say.   It's better if you don't know."

He wound his way through backroads, eyes constantly on the move. It was up to him now to keep them both alive. Caleb, he knew, would be working on identifying the stalkers. Abe would be livid with him for running, and he knew Abe had planned to send men with them. He felt bad about that. In all likelihood he would need their help but in good conscience, he didn't want to put them at risk, not yet, even though that's what they were trained for, even more than he was.

He looked over at Rebecca. She was tired, he knew, and hungry. "How about we stop up ahead at that diner and grab some supper?"

She stirred, then nodded. "That sounds good." She turned her head to watch him. "How long, Gideon, do you think we'll have to be on the run? I know I said I was bored and wanted something to do, but I don't think we can run forever."

Gideon pulled to a stop at the diner, turned off the car, and then shifted in his seat to study her. He reached for her hand. "I don't think we'll be on the run for long. Caleb indicated he was getting close to finding out who it was. I had an idea as well that I sent to him. We'll have to take one day at a time." His gaze went past her to the vehicle pulling in beside them, and he smiled. "And we're not alone. Murphy and Ian just pulled up."

She spun in her seat to stare out the window. "Now, how did they find us and so quickly? We had a head start."

"Murphy's good. He and I talked one day about running and where it might be safe. He stored that away and then instead of trying to follow us, headed here."

Murphy had slid from behind the wheel and was leaning against his truck, arms crossed. Ian stood on the other side, arms leaning on the hood, just watching.

Rebecca turned to Gideon. "Do you think if we took off again, we could get away from them?"

Gideon stared at her, then starting laughing. "I'm game to try if you are, but they have more power under the hood of their vehicle that I do. It would be a game of cat and mouse, with us as the mouse. We might win. We can try."

Her eyes sparkling, she looked between him and the two men outside. "We could, but then again, extra firepower might be nice."

He laughed as he opened his door and then walked around the car. He stopped, leaning against the back door and waited for Murphy to speak.

"You just had to, didn't you?" Murphy shook his head. "Abe couldn't believe that you just ran. Caleb told him of course you would. Everyone else had, so why wouldn't you?"

Gideon shouted with laughter. "Let's go eat, and then I have a place in mind to stay at least for tonight."

Gideon turned to Murphy as they left the diner. "Follow me, if you can keep up. It's a tricky place to find."

Murphy smirked. "I found you here, didn't I?"

"You did, but if you lose me on the way to there, you won't find me. Not many people know it's there."

Gideon kept a watch in his mirrors. Murphy was close but he couldn't see any other traffic. That was good. He pulled off the paved road onto a narrow, treelined road and followed it for a while. He finally parked and then came around to Rebecca's door.

"We have to walk from here, but it's only about 10 minutes in. I know the people who had it quite well, and they have offered it to me many times. They very seldom use it any more. There is no way to connect it with me." He grabbed their bags from the trunk and then reached for her hand. He turned as Murphy parked beside him.

"Isolated or what?" Ian commented.

"It is. Not what you would have chosen I know, but I've been here many times. I know there is more than one way out, if you don't mind walking a bit." Gideon turned and led the way to the cabin, nestled among the trees.

Rebecca could hear the faint sound of a creek and looked around at what she could see in the dark. Gideon moved ahead of them into the cabin and lit some lamps.

"Sorry, it's rustic, no electricity, but it should do for overnight. There's no cell service here either. There are three bedrooms. We'll take this one," Gideon pointed at one. "You two can flip a coin for the others."

"It won't matter. Only one of us will be sleeping at a time." Murphy returned Gideon's stare with one of his own.

Gideon nodded. "About what I figured."

Caleb looked up as Eddie and Ben entered the conference room. "Any word on where they are?"

Eddie shook his head. "Gideon's good. Murphy headed to where he thought they might hear but wasn't sure if he would find them. He did say he would likely lose cell service."

Caleb ran his hand through his hair. "I don't like this. I know they needed some freedom, but this is not good."

Ben studied Caleb. The strain was showing. "Caleb, you need to pack up early tonight. You can't burn the candle at both ends. Hannah and your boys need some of your time and you need to spend time with them. If Murphy and Ian can catch up with them, they should be okay for tonight. No one knows for sure where Gideon was headed."

Caleb started to shake his head, then laid down the papers he was holding, and stood. "You're right. We all need to take a break and pick up fresh in the morning. If I'm leaving, so are you two and Frankie as well."

****

Where was she? Was she okay? Someone tried to kill her today and now he couldn't see her. He couldn't stay here, there was too much traffic coming and going. Who had tried to kill her? She was too beautiful and she was meant to be his. She wasn't supposed to die.

****

Ian came in from the outside. He didn't like this place, the brush was too close to the cabin in spots. Murphy looked up from where he had sitting at the table. He nodded, picked up his flashlight and headed out.   Ian headed for the bedroom he had chosen. He knew they would be on the move again, likely in the morning, and he wanted to catch some sleep. He just prayed that those two didn't make a run for it.

Gideon sat on the bed, back to the headboard and stared out the window at what stars he could see. Rebecca was finally asleep, but she was restless. His thoughts turned to who he thought it was, and his heart lurched. No matter who it was, it would hurt her. His thoughts turned to God.

God, I know You're here. I know You're in charge. It just seems as if you are so far away right now. That's there a curtain blocking us from seeing You work.   Father, please bring us safe into that harbour, that haven of rest You have promised us. Thank You that You are there, protecting, guiding, leading us in every way.

He heard a tap at the door and went out to the kitchen.

426

Murphy stood there, Ian just coming from the other bedroom. "We've got company. I have no idea how they found us, but they did. We need to leave now. First, your phones. Turn them off for now."

Gideon went to rouse Rebecca. He so hated to. She frowned at him, then sight and wearily stepped back into her sneakers. When they came back out to the main room, Murphy had sorted out supplies into a knapsack he had found in the kitchen. They wouldn't be able to carry their bags with them, they would be too bulky. Gideon knew he would get them back at some point.

Moving quietly, but quickly, they headed around the cabin to the back and then into the forest. Gideon took the lead, he knew the area. There would be a road up ahead they would have to cross, but he knew just past there would be another cabin that had phone service.

Ian brought up the rear, looking back every few feet. He could hear commotion at the cottage. Someone was not happy. He prayed they got away before they were found. Gideon brought them to a sudden stop. Someone was up ahead of them. He motioned for them to draw back. Murphy went past him, creeping silently towards the road. He came back, shaking his head, and pointed to a trail off to the side.

"We need to take that. Where does it lead?" His mouth was close to Gideon's ear, his voice barely above a whisper.

"It will take us up and over the ridge. There's another cabin there we should come to. It's quite a walk, though."

"We don't have a choice. There's a vehicle parked and running, right where we were headed. How do they find us?"

"Likely the phones. I have left mine on my desk when I have been away from it for a few minutes. It wouldn't have taken look for her to install that app."

Murphy shook his head. "Who is she working for anyway?"

"That's what I want to know."

****

They had been here. She just missed them. She glared as she stormed through the cabin. How did they know she was coming? No one knew who she was. Even that young man really had no clue. She paced out of the cabin and around it. They hadn't taken their bags. They would have to come back here, won't they? She paused, listening. No, she couldn't hear anything. Finally, she gave up and left. She would be back. She pulled her phone out but there was no service.

428

Chapter 15

Gideon halted just before he came to the new cabin. It had been a long trek, and they were all tired. Dawn was breaking in the distance. He looked around but could see no one. He turned to Murphy.

"Does one of you have a motorcycle license?" Murphy stared at him and he repeated himself.

"Ian does. Why?"

"Because my friend who has that cabin always keeps motorcycles here. He has offered me their use for years. If we can get to them, we can get away. I'll leave them where he can get them back. I think he has a spare phone as well."

"How well do you know this person?" Murphy was buying what Gideon was telling him.

"He's the one of the ones who put me on the path I'm on today. He doesn't know my history, didn't want to know it. He doesn't have any connections in Riverville that I know of."

"If we borrow them, you and Rebecca won't be on the same one. I have to split you two up."

Gideon started shaking his head.

"No, we have to. It's the only way I know of to keep you two safe."

Gideon looked around. "He has an old jeep as well. Looks are deceiving with it. It has a lot of power under the hood." He looked over at Murphy. "Which one?"

"I would say the Jeep. That way, we're together." He turned to Gideon. "You are sure no one knows about this place."

"No. Not that I am aware of. I have never come here before, so I am not sure how anyone would.'

"You wait here with Ian. I'll go over and make sure it's safe. Where do I find the keys?"

Gideon started to shake his head, but at the look on Murphy's face, stopped. He explained where the keys would be. Murphy headed for the cabin and Gideon stepped back to where Rebecca and Ian were standing. Wrapping his arm around his wife, he explained what was going on. Ian's eyes kept scanning the area, not missing much.

Caleb studied his desk once again, buried under paperwork. There were days he really wished he wasn't the police chief, didn't have to deal with all that went with that. Today was one of them. He sighed, then picked up the top file. He might as well get to it while he was waiting for word on Gideon and Rebecca. His hand stopped. Where were they, Lord? I know You have them in Your hands but are they safe? He could only pray that Murphy and Ian had caught up with them.

He looked up a few hours later as Frankie knocked at his door. He motioned him in and then waited.

Frankie looked at Caleb. "Have you heard from them?" When Caleb shook his head, Frankie's gaze went behind him. "I wish I knew they were okay.   I'm getting rumblings from the street. Whoever the stalker is, she is getting more and more anxious. Another source has told me she's back, this time looking for a killer. And it's not just for Gideon. She's after Rebecca now too." Frankie paused, his gaze coming back to Caleb. "That scares me."

Caleb sat for a minute, digesting what Frankie had said. "I have no idea where they are. They ran and I can only hope Murphy and Ian were right about where he was headed. Abe hasn't heard from either one of them, so we're guessing they're together and gone off the grid. Somehow, someone always knew exactly where they were."

"Has Ben or Eddie made any progress on what they were working on?"

"Eddie hasn't said, but I think he's making progress on tracking down Peg's half-brother. That's what he said last night. It's taking time, it's been that many years.

"Ben is still working on the angle of the photos. He's found something that he's trying to track through."

"This is just so bizarre. Why Rebecca anyway?"

"That's what Abe keeps asking, why Rebecca and not him, or not the both of them?"

Ben tapped at his door at that moment and then entered. He sat in silence for a while.

"What's up, Ben? Something is?"

"There is, and I just don't know how to explain it." He stopped, overcome with emotion for a minute. When he looked up, both men saw the anguish in his eyes. "I just don't want to believe what I am seeing, but the facts and pictures don't lie." He opened the envelope he had been carried, one that came from their lab. "They've gone through all the photos, drawn up a time line for us, and then went back over them for whatever information they can dig out. The first few years, there was not a lot there. The last five years." Ben had to stop. He couldn't go on. "I didn't want to show this to you if Eddie was here. It will break his heart." Ben handed over the envelope to Caleb. "I can't stay while you go over this." He got up and walked away.

Frankie and Caleb shared a glance, then Caleb pulled out the photos. His hands stilled as he sorted through them. Frankie had come to stand beside him and look at them while Caleb was. He shook his head.

"This is one sick person. Who would ever of thought of hiding that in the photos?"

"The words are not real clear when you just look at the photos. How was Rebecca expected to see them? These are real death threats." Caleb set the photos down. "We need to find them, and I have no idea where Gideon was headed. No one does. All their phones go right to voice mail, so I am guessing Murphy had them turned off."

Caleb stuffed the photos back into the envelope and then handed it to Frankie. "We're not going to be able to keep this from Eddie, not when he's involved in the investigation. Take them down to the conference room and log them into evidence. Find someone to keep running them to see if they can find anything else that will help."

Caleb stared at his desk and the dwindling pile of paperwork. It would be done today if his secretary just didn't add to it, but he knew she would be. Hannah, he thought, now would be a really good time to give me a name. I could use it.

He stood outside the gate, watching and waiting. He hadn't seen Rebecca in days. Where was she? She was supposed to be with him. That's what that woman kept telling him.

Matt stepped through the gate and stopped beside him and just waited.

"Where is she? Where's my Rebecca?"

432

Matt looked down at the ground, then at the man beside him. "She's not here, Alan. She's gone away."

"She's with him. She's supposed to be with me." The words were slurred.

Matt took a closer look at Alan, and then nodded. Alan was high on some kind of drugs and likely had been for years. He reached out a hand, took his arm, and led him to the SUV that Joseph had driven up. "In you go, Alan. I need to take you somewhere."

"You'll take me to Rebecca?" Alan climbed in the vehicle.

Matt settled into the front seat. They had found one of the stalkers. He glanced back. Alan sat with his eyes closed, almost asleep. No, he was not the one they had to worry about. That stalker was still out there.

Caleb looked up as Eddie tapped as his door, then back at his paperwork. For once, his desk was clear.

Eddie stood, hesitating, not like him at all. "I saw the photos, Caleb. This person is sick." He swallowed hard past the tears. "How could someone do this? Forget that question. After all these years, I get why." He looked up then. "I hear Matt found the one stalker."

Caleb nodded. "He was standing at the gate, out in the open this time. Matt thinks he's been on drugs for years and whoever the second stalker is, she's been stringing him along."

"Why again do we think it's a woman?"

"There are too many pictures taken from a woman's point of view. I think the profiler was right.

It's a woman.   I just pray we find them again in time."

"You and me both."

Murphy pulled up beside them and Ian shoved Gideon and Rebecca in the back seat. Murphy drove as quickly as he could away from the cabin and soon found a highway. "Which way?"

"Left." Gideon studied the area. "It takes us north of town, but we're still in Caleb's jurisdiction. Drive for about 10 miles and you'll find a little Mom and Pop diner. We can grab food from there."

"How do you know all these places?" Ian turned in the front seat to ask.

"I've spent a lot of time around here. And I can remember places for some reason." He glanced around outside, then down at Rebecca. She wasn't saying anything, but he could tell how exhausted she had become. The last few weeks had been brutal on her in many ways. He wanted to lift the burdens from her, but only God could do that. He prayed that she would find that haven of rest with Him.

Ian ran back to the jeep with their food. He just hoped he hadn't raised any suspicions. Murphy headed away, looking for somewhere for them to stop.

"In there, Murphy. There are usually some tables set up that we can use. Not many people outside of the area know about it." Gideon's eyes canvased the area, still not feeling comfortable. He had been living with the feeling of evil for so long, he felt it everywhere.

Murphy pulled up beside a table, with the jeep turned to head back out. He climbed out and looked around as did Ian. When they were satisfied, they pulled the seats forward so Gideon and Rebecca could climb out.   None of them had   much of an appetite, but they knew it might be hours before they ate again.   As she finished, Rebecca leaned on Gideon, her fatigue evident.   Gideon's arm went around her as she surrendered to the sleep she needed.   He gathered her up and tucked her in the jeep, then stood watching as Murphy and Ian talked. He wanted to be in on their plans, but for now he would wait.   If he had to, he would bolt again and take Rebecca with him.   They would find someplace where they could be safe.

Chapter 16

Caleb stood at the window to the interrogation room. Alan was seated there, and Eddie had made sure he had a lawyer. A frown on his face, Caleb tried to puzzle out why Alan had become fixated on Rebecca.

Eddie came in and stood beside him. "Matt said he talked a bit coming in. Alan was bullied during high school and no one did anything. Alan said Rebecca smiled at him one day and gave him her lunch. That's what started it with him."

"Just a friendly look and gesture that turned into an obsession. It still doesn't explain the other stalker. How is she connected?"

"I have people sorting through his background, going back as far as we can, and reaching not just to his family but their friends and acquaintances. He's our key, but I don't think he even understands what he's been used for."

"I don't think we'll get much more from him." Caleb nodded at the window. "I don't think he knows much more than what he's said. Did Matt say if he had seen him hanging around before?"

Eddie shook his head. "They knew someone was but they could never find him. He was always gone. Joseph said he had found some places where someone has stood but he doesn't think it was Alan. He said the tracks were more female."

Caleb shook his head. "So close, yet so far. God has them in His hands. I know Gideon wants this over. When we last talked, he stated that Rebecca needed a rest. He mentioned about how he wanted to find her a haven, that she needed to come find her haven with God." Caleb stopped speaking.

Eddie waited, then turned to him. "What are you thinking?"

"Just a thought. I need to think it through some more and then I think I have a plan to catch the stalker."

"I hope you do. I'm getting tired of seeing Peg worry so much."

****

The fool, she thought, going and getting himself arrested. Just as her plans were coming together. Now what was she to do? It was too late into the game to try and find someone else to take his place. And she still didn't know where they were. All those people around her just stayed where they were. She turned and studied the area around her. Somehow she had to drag her out of hiding. She just had to come up with a plan.

****

Murphy studied the two in the backseat in his mirror. Ian studied the passing landscape. It had grown dark, and he was still driving aimlessly around. Gideon stirred and looked around him.

"There should be a narrow path just ahead on your left. It's hard to see, though. Just wait for a faded saddlery sign. The turn is right there." Gideon watched closely. "It's just up ahead."

Murphy made the turn onto a narrow bumpy track, almost a trail. He could hear the trees and brush rubbing against the jeep.

"How again do you know these places?"

"Friends. We look for out-of-the-way places. It's just how we work. Not many people do that.

When you look to hide someone, where do you go? Motels, safe houses, whatever is close. We always looked for something different.”

“That makes sense. I just hope it works out for us.”

“There’s a turnoff to your right just ahead. There. Take that road.” Gideon looked behind him and couldn’t see any lights. Please, Lord, let us be safe here, at least until we can get rested a bit. I know we still have a long way to go.

Murphy pulled to a stop because a beautiful log cabin. “Wow! You call this an out-of-the-way place?”

Gideon nodded. “It is. It’s hard to find and not many people know about it. If I told you who owned it, you would know why.”

They climbed out of the jeep, and Gideon disappeared around the side of the cabin. Lights flickered on inside, and the front door opened. They entered and stopped. It was as beautiful inside as it was outside, more spacious than it looked.

Gideon watched Rebecca and saw the moment she collapsed in sleep. He caught her up and carried her to a bedroom at the back. Coming back out to the kitchen, he pulled out a chair at the table. Ian had hunted around and found the makings for coffee and had it on.

“Do you know of any way to contact Caleb or Abe?” Murphy kept his eyes on his hands.

“Yeah, there is. There’s a satellite phone here that can’t be traced. Don’t ask how that’s possible.” Gideon stood and disappeared again, returning with the phone. As he handed it to Murphy, he stated, “I only ask that you don’t tell them where we are. If you do, Rebecca and I will disappear again and this time I guarantee you won't find us."

Murphy studied his face as he reached for the phone, then nodded. "For now, we do it your way. If it comes to it, then we take over. Security is what we do for a living."

Gideon nodded, then sank back down into his chair, taking the cup of coffee Ian handed him, feeling the exhaustion beginning to take over.

Abe studied the number that showed on his phone before he answered it. His eyes slid closed as he heard Murphy's voice. "Tell me they're all right."

"They are. We're with them. I won't tell you where we are. Frankly, I'm not certain I even know. Gideon has certainly led us around in circles today."

"As long as they're all right, I don't want to know." Abe paused. "Is there a speaker button on that phone?" He could hear Murphy asking Gideon, and then he could hear Gideon speaking clearly. He put his own phone on speaker.

"Gideon. I know why you ran. I just wish you hadn't."

"Didn't seem like we had much choice, Abe. They found us where we were. They almost killed us."

"I know. We're working on sorting out how that happened. Caleb's with me. He has some news."

Gideon listened as Caleb went over where the investigation stood. He shook his head at the simplicity of the original stalker, then his heart sank as he realized what Caleb was saying about the photos.

"So there really was a hidden message in those photos and we're just finding out now?"

"Keep in mind, Gideon, we didn't know about them until just recently.   Rebecca never said anything. If she had, maybe we could have dealt with it before. That's not the point. The point is that the threats are escalating and we need to find the culprit. At some point, I am going to need to talk with Rebecca again."

Gideon pushed back from the table. He had had enough. He walked away and out the back door. Ian and Murphy exchanged a look.

"Gideon just walked way, Caleb."   Murphy continued to stare at the back door.

"I figured he would. I would too if it was my wife. So tell me what you can about what's going on from where you are."

"There's not a lot to tell. So far, we're safe, sheltered, and have access to a secure satellite phone. We've got transportation, coffee and food. Ian and I plan to rotate shifts again tonight."

"Okay, sounds like you have it under control. Don't suppose you have your original packs with you?"

"Now, that would be telling."   Ian shook his head at Murphy.   "Let's put it this way, Gideon's friends will be owed a lot of postage at some point."

Abe spoke up.   "Do you have any of the equipment with you?"

"No. We had it stashed in the SUV. I don't think they can find it if they're looking for it."

Abe sighed. "That's what I was afraid of."

"We're working blind, Abe, and without the resources that we need. I just don't know how we're going to do it. We're having to go right back to the very basics."

Caleb spoke up. "That's what we're doing here. Just keep them safe. Stay in contact when you can."

As Murphy ended the conversation, Ian headed outdoors. He looked around but didn't see Gideon at first.

"Gideon, where are you?"

Ian heard a sigh from his right and turned that way. In the moonlight, he could vaguely see Gideon standing leaning on a porch support. He went towards him.

"Is it ever going to end, Ian? This isn't what I normally do. I'm normally delving into financial records or in court. I don't think we can run much longer."

Ian studied him in the dim light. He could see the exhaustion and worry that went, as his mother would have said, bone deep. He was getting worried about how much more the two could take.

"I don't know how long it will take." Ian turned to search the darkness around him. "If you were investigating this, where would you start?"

"Financials. It's what I do." Gideon stopped at a sudden thought. "Did Caleb or Abe say if they has searched the accounts for that fellow?"

"No, but I would imagine that they did. What are you thinking?"

"I'm thinking she's starting to get sloppy and careless. She didn't have control over, who was it, Alan?" At Ian's nod, he continued, "That means she is losing control of what she is doing. I would imagine she's already out there looking for someone else to step in. I don't think she'll find someone from our town. Abe's family is too well known and too well liked."

Ian stared, then turned. "Come on, back inside. I want to run something by Murphy."

Gideon listened as Ian and Murphy talked, occasionally adding something. He finally stood and excusing himself, headed for bed. He just needed some sleep. He knew they'd be on the run again at some point. Closing the door behind him, he stood, leaning against. Lord, I don't think we can take much more. It's wearing us out. I look at Rebecca and regret that she's had to go through so much, especially in the last few years. I just don't know how to reach through to her. She's starting to shut down. She needs to find that rest in Your haven, Lord. Protect us. Protect those who are guarding us. Guide Caleb and his people in their investigation. Let it end soon, Lord, just soon.

Ian looked at the closed door. "He's getting ready to run again."

Murphy nodded. "I know. I just hope and pray he takes us with him, but I have a feeling he'll head out on his own." He stood and put his cup in the sink. "I'll take first watch."

Ian nodded and then studied the closed bedroom door again. How did they keep them safe? He shook his head. What idea was it that Gideon had had? And would he share it? Please, Lord, he breathed. Keep us safe. Guide our steps to stay ahead of this woman.

Ian stirred as Murphy nudged him. "What's up?"

"We've got company. I'm not sure who, but I can hear a vehicle coming up from the road."

Ian grabbed his revolver and followed Murphy outside, blending in with the darkness. They watched as the vehicle stopped, and a dark form exited. The man stopped and stared around, then walked towards the cabin. He stopped as he heard Murphy speak behind him.

"Stop right there and identify yourself."

The man turned. "I could say the same for you. You're on private property."

"We're here with a friend. Inside and I want to see your identification."

The man stared at him through the darkness, then turned and walked in, Murphy and Ian on his heels. As he turned, Murphy hesitated for a few seconds. He knew this man but he didn't know his connection to Gideon. Ian headed to get Gideon.

Gideon stood behind the man and spoke. "Hello, Gilles. It's been a while. I knew you wouldn't mind us using your place."

Gilles Youngman turned to stare at Gideon. "What have you been doing with yourself, boy? You look a little rough."

Gideon gave a half smile. "I feel more than a little rough, Gilles. Sorry for the reception. I didn't expect you to be here. We'll be gone in the morning."

Gilles shook his head. "No, that's okay. I told you to consider this your home. But maybe you could introduce me to your friends and they could put their guns away."

Introductions made, the four men sat at the kitchen table. Gideon gave an abbreviated version of why they were there. Gilles studied him as he spoke, his mind work. The multimillionaire manufacturer had always treated Gideon like a son. Now to hear he was on the run, with his wife the victim of a stalker?

"So, how can I help?" The question was simple but heartfelt.

Caleb stood once again in the conference room, studying the activity going on around him. He knew they were missing something, but he just couldn't put his finger on it. It was something so simple he was sure they had overlooked in as not being significant.

"Has Hannah given you a name yet?" Ben spoke from behind him.

Caleb smiled. "No, she hasn't. Not yet. I wish she would and we could wrap this up today."

"I can see you're puzzling something over. What is it?"

"I just have that feeling we've overlooked something small that would break the case wide open."

Ben nodded. "I know. I keep thinking the same thing. Maybe we're just too tired and need fresh eyes looking at the information."

Caleb turned to him. "Who are you thinking?"

"Abe and his men. They're in security. They might see something different than we do. We could swear them in as temporary officers or something and give them access to the material."

Caleb looked at him. "That's a thought but I am sure our good mayor would have something to say about that." Caleb's voice dropped off.

"What did you just think about, Caleb?"

"I have a name I want you to run, someone I had forgotten about." He grabbed a piece of paper and scribbled it down, handing it to Ben. "Find somewhere you're by yourself and run it, looking for everything you can. Bring Abe in on this one. It's not part of the official investigation yet."

Ben took the paper and then searched Caleb's face. He nodded and left, meeting Eddie and Frankie coming in.

"Where do you want us today, Caleb?"

Caleb sighed as he looked around. "We're at a stalemate right now. Ben's running something for me. We need to get back on our other investigations for now. Keep your ears and eyes open, though, for anything that comes back to this." Caleb turned and walked away, feeling like he was abandoning his friends. He knew in his heart he wasn't, but God, he prayed, we need a break. We need to find that scrap of information that will turn the tide.

****

She watched but didn't find them. She searched and they were not in town, not at Abe's compound. Where had they stashed them? She couldn't finish her plan if she couldn't find them. They just disappeared into thin air. She had tried following the police involved, but they didn't lead her anywhere. She couldn't get any help from the people on the street. Word was out and nobody would take her money. What was she to do?

****

Rebecca headed for the coffee pot. She desperately needed a cup to get her moving. She looked around for Gideon, and not seeing him, headed for the back door. She stepped outside and inhaled the fresh scent of the woods, then looked around. She didn't see any of the men and turned to head back inside. She stifled a scream as she came face to face with a man she didn't know and who hadn't been there last night.

446

Gilles studied Rebecca's face and then nodded. Yes, Lord, Gideon has found the one for him.

"I'm a friend of Gideon. Name's Gilles."

She stared at him. "So, if that's the case, where's Gideon?"

Gilles' eyes traveled behind her and he smiled, the creases at his kind eyes deepening. "Standing right behind you. If you take one of your tiny steps back, you'll hit him."

She felt Gideon's hands on her shoulders. Now, she felt safe. "But how did you get to be here? I thought no one used this place much."

Gilles stepped back and motioned her to come back in the house. "I have breakfast about made. We'll sit and talk while we eat. I understand you two have been leading these other two on a real merry chase. I want to help."

Gideon followed Rebecca back into the cabin. She spun as the door closed behind them.

"Where are Murphy and Ian?"

"Doing their rounds. They've already eaten."

She glared at him and plopped herself down into a chair. Gilles set a plate of food before her.

"Thank you. I appreciate this." She still sounded a bit grumpy, Gilles thought, but I would too, if I had to face what she's faced.

Gilles sat and watched as the two ate. Then he spoke.

"Gideon, without going into all the details, talk to me."

Gideon studied his friend, all of a sudden suspicious of why he had come to the cabin. "Why are you here? You never come during this time of year."

Gilles nodded. "No, I don't. I certainly wasn't planning on it yesterday afternoon. But that voice I keep telling you about won't let go. It kept prompting me to come."

Gideon searched his friend's face. "That voice again, eh?"

Gilles laughed. "Yes, that voice. Now, talk to me."

Gideon hesitated, then reached for Rebecca's hand. "It goes back years, Gilles, to someone who started stalking Rebecca. About five years ago, the stalking changed and became more violent. There are now two stalkers. The second stalker is responsible for the death of Rebecca's first husband, Nick." Gilles' eyes turned to Rebecca as Gideon spoke. "There have been both notes and photos. Whoever the second stalker is, they are getting close to her. We ran because we became a target the other day. Murphy and Ian work for Rebecca's brother, and he sent them after us."

Gilles studied his friend. "I know there's a lot more you can't tell me. What can I do to help?"

Gideon turned to watch Rebecca, who looked back at him. "I'm not sure, Gilles. Caleb and his men are working hard to try and figure it out. Abe, Rebecca's brother, is as well. There just seems to be something we can't put our fingers on."

Gilles sat back and thought about what Gideon had been able to tell him, while he studied the coffee in his cup. He loved a mystery but there had to be a thread to unravel and there just didn't seem to be one with this one.

"I would hazard a guess that all family members past and present have been investigated."

"Eddie and Ben, two of the detectives, are working that angle. Eddie's wife, Peg, is Rebecca's aunt, so he has a personal reason to solve this and solve it fast. Caleb mentioned that he's looking at both sides of the family." Gideon didn't say any more but shared a look with Gilles, who nodded. "Caleb is good. His instincts are usually spot on. And he has a secret weapon."

"A secret weapon?"

Gideon nodded. "God speaks to his wife. He tells her who is the culprit and it is always who He says. I just wish He would speak up soon for us."

Gilles laughed. "I'm sure you do." He looked at Rebecca, who had been sitting there quietly listening. "What do you think, Rebecca? What are your feelings about who it is?"

She blinked at him, then gazed as Gideon. "Not one person, other than Gideon at one point, has ever asked me that. They've been too busy trying to protect to even ask how I feel." Her voice was raising in volume as she spoke, her anger and fear becoming evident. "No, they think they know best and ignore this helpless female."

Gilles starting laughing.

Rebecca glared at him. "See, you're doing it too."

Gilles shook his head. "No, I'm not. I want to hear your opinion. Then I plan to go have a talk with Chief Caleb Logan and see how he managed to anger you by overlooking you."

"You know Caleb? Of course, you do." Her hands flew up in the air. "I want my bike. I want to go for a long ride, wind blowing by me, without anything to worry about."

"Bike?"

"She rides a sweet jade motorbike, Gilles. It looks like one of yours."   Gideon bit back the laughter that arose as his wife stared at him and then at Gilles.

"Oh, no. Don't tell me!"

Gilles started laughing in earnest. "We won't tell Mr. Youngman, my dear. It is so refreshing to not be known."

"I'm sorry." Rebecca's voice was very quiet.

"Don't be. Now, talk to me. Tell me what you think and who you would suspect."

With someone finally wanting to hear her side and thoughts, the words poured from Rebecca. Gideon's heart broke as he realized they had all done her a disservice by not talking to her. Gilles listened in silence, making the odd note on his phone. When she was done, she dropped her head on her hands, emotionally spent.

Gilles studied his notes, then his eyes sought Rebecca's. She stared back at him. Then he looked at Gideon.

"I can see that somewhere along the way, the ball was dropped, and it was back when Nick was killed. That investigation was swept under the rug, and I think you'll find money changes hands at some point. Now, to go forward. Rebecca, this is going to hurt you even more. I hired your father's firm years ago, long before you and Abe were teenagers. He was a smart man, knowledgable in his line of work, but too trusting with his personal life at times. Your mother, I met her a few times. She was a wonderful lady, loved her family so much. When I heard she left you, I didn't believe it. I hired someone on my own to find out what happened." Gilles paused, needing a moment to compose himself. "He couldn't find her. What he found were rumours that she had been killed, and that by a relative. He couldn't confirm the rumours, and other than your Aunt Peg, all her relatives seemed to disappear." He again paused, watching the conflicting emotions on her face.

Gideon reached to draw his wife into his arms. "Are you saying one of the relatives is responsible for stalking Rebecca?"

Gilles nodded. "And I would hazard a guess that's where Eddie and Ben, did you say, were heading with this. I wanted so badly to find your mother, Rebecca, just for closure for you. I couldn't. Your father was a very important friend to me. I haven't had much contact with you and Abe over the years and I regret that."

Rebecca nodded, tears in her eyes. "Thank you. I appreciate what you tried to do." She drew a deep breath. "So where do we go from here? And soon I hope."

"There is one other thing, and I am not sure if Peg is aware of it. Your grandfather on your mother's left money in a trust. The other siblings were not in his line, being half-siblings. That was investigated at the time but we couldn't find any connection. The money is still there. There was a time limit on it before it could go to a charity. If memory serves me correctly, then that time is just about up."

Rebecca shoved herself to her feet. "I can't deal with this right now. What I would really like to do is get out on my bike or on a dirt bike and I can't." She turned and walked from the cabin.

Gilles watched her walk away, then got the look on Gideon's face. "It hurts, Gideon, when we can't fix it for them. That's where what we've talked about over the years comes in, how God is the only source for peace, for rest."

Gideon nodded. "I know. I just wish I could fix it. So now, where do you go, Gilles?"

"I'll head off to see Caleb. I haven't seen him in a few years." He paused. "Maybe a reward might help but I doubt it. I would gladly put up the money if I thought it would."

"I know you would, my friend."

****

She was growing more angry by the minute. Where was that woman? They couldn't have hid her that well, could they? They never had in the past. She had been to every spot that woman had ever been and still couldn't find her. Time was growing short and she was getting older every day.

Caleb looked up at the tap at his door, then nodded to his secretary. He rose to greet Gilles.

"It's been a long time, Gilles. How are you?"

"Too long, Caleb. I'm good. And you, Hannah and the boys?"

"We're well." They talked for a while, then Caleb eyed his friend. "You're not here to just catch on our lives. What's up?"

Gilles looked at him, then at the door. "I understand you have some men working on Gideon and Rebecca's case. Can you bring them in or is there somewhere we can go and talk?"

Caleb returned his look, then nodded. "You've seen them."

Gilles said nothing, just sat and waited. Finally, Caleb sighed, "You're not going to tell me, are you?"

Gilles shook his head and then rose when Caleb beckoned him to follow. Ben and Eddie followed them from the department building.

"Does Mac still make those delicious pies?" Gilles asked.

Caleb nodded and they headed that way. Once seated, Gilles began to speak. The eyes of the other three men never left him. From the conversation, plans were made. Ben and Eddie headed off in different directions, determination in every step they took.

Caleb sat back in his chair. "I just wish those two hadn't run. This makes it hard."

Gilles shook his head. "It was inevitable. I'm surprised it didn't happen before it did. I don't think they'll stay where they are for long. This time, Gideon really will take off with Rebecca, and Murphy and Ian won't catch them or find them. That's dangerous."

"I know. I can also see Rebecca coming back here and making herself a target just to end it all."

Gilles laughed. "I can see that very well. If this doesn't end in the next couple of days, she will. And no one will be able to stop her."

Gideon looked over at Rebecca. He was beginning to worry. She was up to something and he didn't know what she was planning. He could only hope she took his with her when she ran, and he was so afraid she was going to run on her own.

Rebecca felt Gideon watching her. How could she tell him what she was planning to do? She knew he would try and keep her from her plans. A hand reached for hers and pulled her to her feet.

"Come on, sweetheart. Let me show you Gilles' bikes. You'll like them."

She allowed herself to be led to the building at the very back of the property. Gideon shoved open a door and switching on a light. She stopped and her eyes roam over the motorbikes Gilles had stored there.

"I think we should leave, Gideon." Her voice was low.

Wrapping his arms around her, chin on her head, he spoke. "I know. I was wondering when you would say that and if you were even going to tell me."

She wrapped her arms around his waist and leaned into him. "I wouldn't go without you. Not without a huge protest. But I think we need to go today. I just have a feeling of evil closing in." She leaned back to look up at him. "We need to end this, Gideon. But how?"

"I know. I don't know how. Gilles will be talking with Caleb today more than likely. He'll have some good ideas."

He felt her nod. His eyes scanned the bikes. Gilles had taught him to ride when he first met him, and he knew Rebecca was a rider.

"Pick out a bike you would use." She looked up at him. "Pick out a bike and get it ready, helmets and all. I'll find some food stuff. I know Gilles has a kitchen out here we can raid."

She stepped back to assess him, then turned to the bikes. He watched as she walked towards one and nodded. You'll regret this, Gilles, she's picked the best. God, he prayed, we need to take the next step. Guide us and protect us.

Rebecca came back towards him. "That one, I think. It's small but it's easy to handle. It's similar to what I ride at home and what I have ridden in races. Are you sure Gilles won't mind?"

Gideon shook his head as he packed water bottles and food into the saddle bags. "No. He wouldn't have made the offer if he hadn't meant it."

She still looked worried. "What if I crash it or something?"

"Then that's what happens. Gilles knows that a possibility and he made the offer knowing that."

Sudden noise caught their attention and they spun to face the door as Murphy and Ian ran in, pulling it shut behind them.

"You were right, Gideon. They found us. I have no idea how." Murphy stood panting, staring at the bikes. "I can see you have one picked out, Rebecca. Which one for us?"

She pointed. "That one. It's almost identical to this one. Can you handle it?"

Murphy nodded. "I've been riding since I was 15. Is there a back door we can get out?"

Ian nodded. "Over there. It's big enough to get the bikes out."

They pushed the bikes out and then quietly closed the door. Ian ran to the end of the building for a quick look and came back. "No sign of them in the clearing yet. Let's go."

Rebecca went ahead, pushing the bike forward. She didn't want to start it until she was away from the clearing. Then they heard noise behind them. The bikes started at first kick, and they were speeding away, Rebecca bent low over the handlebars.

Murphy pulled up beside her after a while and motioned for her to stop. They halted and listened but could hear nothing.

"Did we lose them?" Gideon asked.

"I'm not sure." Ian was off and staring behind them. "We need to split up."

Murphy and Ian exchanged a glance, then looked at the two of them. "We need to split you two up."

Gideon shook his head. "No way. If we do and one gets caught, they can be used for leverage against the other. You guys know that."

At a standstill, the four stared at each other. Rebecca finally turned back to her bike and jumped on, pulling at Gideon. He was barely seated when she took off. Murphy's mouth dropped open at her skill.

"Think you can catch her?" Ian asked mildly.

"Not likely. I just hate to tell Abe we lost them again."

"You can tell him. You're the senior man." Ian spun at the noise behind them. Murphy pulled him back to the bike and they took off, following in Rebecca's track as best they could.

Caleb stopped at the conference room to check on progress. He could sense a renewed hunt and turned to Ben.

"What's up, Ben?"

"Gilles was right. We went back to the investigation years ago and broadened it." He detailed what they had found. Caleb nodded

"Sounds as if we are finally making progress." He looked around. "Frankie and Eddie running down their part?"

Ben nodded. "Frankie called a while ago and was on his way in. He had tracked down someone in another town and had spoken to them. He wanted to update you on what he had."

"Good." Caleb hesitated. "Abe heard from Murphy. They're on the run again."

"Don't tell me. They separated."

Caleb just looked at him. Ben threw the piece of paper he was holding on his desk. "How do we even begin to keep them safe?"

"That's become a real problem. My feeling is that Rebecca will head back here and go on the offensive. She's tired of running. If she doesn't,

Gideon will. And then, I have no idea how we'll manage."

****

She stared around the cabin, searching each room, then stormed out the back door. Where were they? Her source said they were here, and they weren't. They were gone once again. Who had failed her this time? She wanted this over and over yesterday. Her eyes narrowed, she glared around the clearing, then returned to her vehicle. Their vehicle was still here. How did they get away?

****

Abe turned as Murphy and Ian walked in the door, then looked behind them. "Where are they?"

Murphy and Ian exchanged a glance, then Murphy spoke. "We had to split up. We were together, and Rebecca took off on her bike. I had forgotten how good she is."

"So you have no idea where they are?"

Murphy shook his head. "If I had to give a guess, I would say headed this way. Rebecca's had enough and is ready to fight back."

"That's exactly what I was trying to avoid." Abe bite out the words. "She'll go in as a target and then end up dead."

"Not if Gideon has anything to do about it." Ian spoke up. "I just can't figure out how we were found. Gideon was so sure that it was safe, and so was Gilles."

Caleb looked up as Frankie entered. "They ran, didn't they?"

Frankie slumped in his chair. "That's what Abe just called to say. He has no idea where they are right now."

458

"We don't but God does. He is working this for His reasons. It's hard to trust at times, Frankie."

Frankie nodded. "I know. It just so hard to see Peg and Eddie suffering from this as well. Now I understand what Ben and Marg went through."

"Absolutely. It's not easy when it's a family member that is hurting like this." Caleb's eyes met Frankie's. "Tell me what you have."

Frankie's eyes went to the ceiling. "You're not going to like it, I can tell you that already."

"You guys always say that to me, and I never do. So, what do you have?"

Frankie stared at him for a minute. "Gilles was on the right track years ago. Their mother was murdered, she never ever left them."

Caleb sat back, shock in his face. "I often wondered. What else?"

"I don't know if Peg ever knew there was money left to her and Rebecca and Abe's mother. That trust is due to be disbursed in the next month. If Rebecca had died, her share would have gone to a distant cousin. I have tracked down that cousin. She died from cancer five years ago and left a huge debt for the family. They don't want the money, they just want the cousin back."

"So who is it?" He thought a moment, then said, "I want you to list everyone you can think of from town who meets the profiler's notes, no matter how slim. Then start eliminating them. I suspect we are looking for someone who came to town about six or seven years ago, who knows the family from when their mom was alive."

Frankie pulled himself to his feet. He was tired but ready to continue. "I'll get started. I hope we come up with someone soon."

Rebecca hopped from the bike and then turned to face Gideon. "We can't take it any further."

"Just where are we going?"

She pointed. "Down there. I know someone who can help us."

Gideon followed her down the narrow alleyway to an unmarked door. She tapped and then turning the knob, pulled him in behind her. It was a dark and dingy hallway but she didn't seem to notice. She grabbed his hand and led him to the last doorway on their right. She felt around the doorframe and found a key, opening the door and then putting the key back. He looked at her as she shook her head and held a finger to her lips.

Once inside, Gideon was surprised as the cleanliness and neatness he found. He turned to see Rebecca searching through a cupboard and puling out clothing.

"Here, put these on." She thrust clothes at him and then pushed him towards the bedroom. "I have to find some for me."

He returned to find someone who really didn't look like his wife. "What did you do?"

She grinned at him. "Not a whole lot. We just need not to look so much like us. Now we can move around town without worry." She tilted her head and studied him. "No, you need something more. Sit in that chair there."

She disappeared and came back. "Close your eyes." He could feel her hands on his face, and then she said, "Open your eyes and take a look."

He stared at himself. She had put a beard on him! She grinned as he looked up.

"Now you don't look so much like you."

He shook his head. "Now where?"

She shrugged. "Any ideas?"

He thought. "Yes, I do. Come on."

Ben looked up as Eddie sat down beside him and looked over the whiteboard. Information listed was changing and narrowing.

"Any luck?"

Eddie nodded. "Here, read this."

He handed Ben the file he had. Ben shot him a look as he opened it and began to read.

"Really?"

Eddie nodded. "Who would have thought? I still have to verify some things but she is involved in some way. I don't think she's the main one though."

Ben agreed. "There is still someone higher up. Has she brought in someone from outside of town?"

"That would be my guess. It is also my guess that Rebecca and Gideon are back in town somewhere. Rebecca has sources I wish I did." Eddie didn't continue, but Ben caught what he was saying.

"Has Caleb seen this yet?"

Eddie shook his head. "He's not in yet. He said he needed this morning for a personal reason, he'd be in this afternoon."

Frankie slid into a chair beside them and looking around, spoke quietly. "They're back in town. I'm not sure where yet, but they've been seen. Abe knows."

Neither of the other men acknowledged his words. It had come to the point that, once again, they were not sure who they could trust or not trust.

Rebecca led Gideon once again through a maze of alleys and downtown streets. She finally stopped at a rundown building and pushed him inside.

"Why here?" he whispered.

"No one will look for us here for a few hours. You can bet someone knows we're back in town."

"I agree but I still don't see how this building is safe."

She gave a quiet laugh, then pointed towards the rear of the building. "Go that way."

He walked ahead of her, disgruntled at her laugh. This was serious business and she laughed. He stopped when he opened the door, once again surprised at the rooms he found.

"We'll be fine here. The friend where we got this stuff keeps this one as well. He won't mind."

"He?"

She nodded. "A fellow photographer. He likes to live on the edge of society and this is how he does it. Nick and I used to find him here sometimes, beautiful photos spread out." She said a name, and Gideon stared at her. He knew that name. Anyone who knew just a bit about art knew the name.

She turned and crashed down on the couch. Gideon dropped to the floor beside her, leaning back.

"We need to make some plans. We just can't keep running like we are."

"I know, Gideon, but we also need some sleep. We can sleep here for a few hours and not be bothered." She was asleep almost before she had finished speaking.

Gideon stretched out on the floor beside and slept. Neither heard the door open quietly or the man enter. He dropped into a chair across from them and watched for a while, then got up and walked to the back of the apartment.

They came here, just like he thought they would. Now he had a decision to make, one that would affect his life from that moment on. Which way would he take? He reached for his Bible. There he would find his answer.

****

They were in town, she had been told. They had been seen when they entered town, but no one knew where they were now. She had put out a reward on their head, asking for information as to where they were. So far, not one person had taken her up on it.

****

Decision made, he came back and sat in the same chair, watching them as they slept. Gideon stirred first, sitting up and looking for Rebecca first. Finding her still asleep, he looked around, startled when he saw the man sitting in the room. He had not heard him come in. That was not good. The man merely nodded at him.

Rebecca stirred about an hour after Gideon awoke. She touched his shoulder and then looked around as well. She sat up as she saw the man sitting there. They stared at each other, then both nodded.

Rebecca rose from the couch and pulling Gideon up, headed for the back of the apartment, to the back door. Her friend had decided not to sell them out. She was grateful. He had been a good friend of hers and Nick's but this would be the last she saw him. That friendship lay in the past.

Gideon searched the area around them as they walked through it. It was down town, he knew, but not a down town he had ever been in. How did she find it?

She pulled him through another doorway, this time in a small diner. She slid into a booth and he sat across from her.

He shook his head. "I'm not even going to ask."

She grinned. "Blame Frankie. He showed me some of these places one day we were looking for a teenager. He knows some of the most wonderful hidden gems in the city. The food is really good, better than in some of the multi-star restaurants."

She was right. The food was good, or maybe it was just that they were hungry. She kept watch as the door opened and closed. She saw him when he entered and kicked Gideon. He looked at her in surprise, then where she had nodded. How did they get out past him? Gideon's eyes searched the restaurant. There wasn't a lot of choice.

Rebecca motioned to him, and he dropped the money for the meal on the table. She brazenly walked by Frankie, Gideon in tow. Frankie never stirred. She wasn't sure if he had seen them, but chances were he had. If he had, he would be after them shortly. Did they run or did they stay?

Gideon pulled her back into a doorway. "Did he just happen to come in there?"

She shrugged. "He was likely looking for information. That is one of his favourite spots. He has contacts there. We'll know if he saw us shortly."

Minutes passed and no one came after them. They left the doorway and wandered down the street, finally finding a park they could sit in.

"Tell me again, Gideon, where is God in all this?" Rebecca looked pensive, as if she was really trying to understand.

He drew her close, then paused to get his words. "He's here, sweetheart, all around us. He doesn't want us on the run, doesn't want us threatened. But man's depravity and sin causes this to happen. We are hounded and shot at and running and hiding because of evil. I can feel it all around us right now. But God doesn't want us to be forget that He is in control. He allows things to happen but He never lets us out of His hand. He is drawing us into that haven He offers, where we can find peace and rest and comfort. It's just that sometimes the way in is fraught with danger, just like we are facing."

"I can understand that. I just don't get it that we can't find out who it is."

"I am sure Caleb, Ben, Eddie, Frankie, and Abe are working hard to get to that solution."

They sat in silence for a while, then Rebecca shivered. She felt the evil near them, almost touching them. Who was it? She looked around.

Gideon sensed her discomfort and drew her up to walk away from the park. His eyes searched, trying to find an area he felt they would be safe. He really wanted to get her back to her brother, but he didn't know if she would go. And if she did, Abe would never let her out of his sight. He knew what Rebecca wanted to do and he would do the same, make herself a target and end it all. He just feared it would end badly for her.

Frankie tapped at Caleb's door and entered. "I saw them. They've changed appearances but it's them. They're in the down town area."

"Did they see you?"

Frankie smiled. "Yep. Rebecca made it a point to walk right out by me instead of going out the back way."

Caleb shook his head. "Really?" Frankie nodded. "Okay, so we know they're here. How do we get them to come in?"

"I don't think you will. We would need to put out a dragnet and pull them in that way, and I still don't think we would get them."

"Have you spoken with Abe?"

Frankie shook his head. "No, and I'm not about to. He'd head right down there and blow their cover. I have people watching them and I'll get word if something goes down."

"Likely a smart move. We'll give them a day or two, then pick them up on some excuse, if they haven't come in by then."

Abe looked up as Murphy tracked him down in his office. He watched as the man paced the office without saying anything.

Finally, Abe spoke, "What's up, Murphy? You're usually not this restless."

"I know. I just feel that time is running out for them, and I wished I knew where they were. We're heading out in a day or so on that assignment and I wanted them safe before we left."

"I know. So do I, but God is still in control. No matter what happens, I have to remember that."

"I do too, and that's so hard."

"No one ever said the Christian walk of faith is easy. It's difficult. But now that you're here, let's go over our plans. We need to make sure they're solid."

Frankie stood on the other side of the book rack as she looked over the paperbacks in the little rundown grocery store.

"We need you to come in."

She ignored him, reaching for and putting books back as if she had all the time in the world. Gideon sat at the counter behind her, coffee cup in front of him, and watched in the mirror on the wall behind the equipment.

"Caleb is worried about you two. He wants you to come in."

She turned the rack again, looking at new books. "It's not happening," she said. "We're not coming in."

"I was hoping we could do this the easy way. I could always arrest you, you know."

"You won't." She turned and walked towards the back of the store, picking up items from the shelves and then putting them back.

Frankie watched her and sighed. He knew it wasn't going to work, but he had had to try. He watched at Gideon dropped coins on the counter and then sauntered out the front of the building. He would never have recognized him if he hadn't seen him with Rebecca. And speaking of Rebecca, he spun. She was gone. He had left word with the officer watching the back not to apprehend her. He left and wandered around to the back of the building. The officer shook his head. She hadn't come out. That meant she had hidden until he left, and then went after Gideon. Man, she was good, he thought. I could use her on the force.

Ben looked up. "Didn't work, huh? Didn't think it would. It wouldn't have with Deirdre nor Rachel either."

Frankie glared at him. "It was worth a try."

Ben smiled. "Yes it was but now we have to come up with a new plan. Eddie's on his way back from the lab. He says he's got some new enhancements of some of the latest photos, including the one we just got."

Frankie's hands stilled as he was shuffling his paperwork. "Another one?"

Ben nodded. "Yes, and it's even more chilling. It was taken at Gilles' cabin just about the time they ran. She was that close to them."

They looked up as Eddie, then Caleb entered the room. Caleb looked around and then walked to the whiteboard.

"Listen up, people. We have new information, and not one of you will like it, I can tell you that already. What goes up on this board now stays in this room. It doesn't get mentioned anywhere. I am assigning an officer to the door from now on and you will all have to sign in and out." Caleb turned, wiped off some names, and then added one.

"This is a strong person of interest in the case. Our feeling is that she isn't the one running it but she is involved in a very deep way. Find her and we'll find the stalker."

Consternation was rampant through the room as they read the name, then looked first at Caleb and then each other.

Caleb walked back to stand behind the three men.

"Do you have the photos, Eddie?"

Eddie nodded, then handed the package to Caleb. Caleb then handed it to Ben.

"Before you open it, Ben, remember that God is in control of this and He has them in His hands."

Ben shot him a look, then pulled the photos from the envelope. He felt sick as he looked at the new photo of headstones with Rebecca and Gideon's names on them. The date stamp was for that morning.

"What kind of sick individual are we dealing with, anyway?"

"The kind we need to stop now. Frankie, find them. Bring them in even if you have to arrest them. We can't let them wander the streets any more, no matter how well disguised they are." Caleb picked up the envelope and pictures and handed them off to another officer for them to be entered into evidence.

"Things are now escalating and that is a direct death threat. The others were just suggestions."

Frankie headed out to try and find them. He knew it would be difficult, and when he found them, then he had to find a safe place to tuck them away. Caleb was working that angle with Eddie, Ben still working on locating Peg's half-siblings.

Frankie saw them as they crossed the street, once more headed for the diner. He waited as they entered, then followed them across the street and watched through the window. Gideon had chosen the last booth, right near the back door. Frankie motioned for one of the officers with him to head around to the back as he entered the diner. He headed for their booth and slid onto the seat beside Rebecca, making her move over.

"Well, now." Frankie apprised them, noting the fatigue evident.

"Go away. You'll blow our cover."

"Not today. Once we eat, we'll be leaving together. Someone wants to talk with you."

Rebecca glared at him, then snapped open her menu. "If you're paying, I might as well eat."

"Who said I was paying?"

"I did. You're paying for all three meals, or I'll create a scene in here like you've never seen before."

Frankie just shook his head. Gideon stared at her, then dropped his eyes so she wouldn't see the mirth in them.

Frankie directed them out the back as they finished. The unmarked cruiser was waiting and he shoved them inside, climbing in behind them.

"Where are you taking us, Frankie?" Her voice was hard, not like anything he had ever heard from her before.

"That will be wherever Caleb has decided to stick you away from sight. He was working on it when I came to find you, and I haven't heard yet if he's found a place."

"Just take us back to Abe's." Gideon sighed, knowing they had run out of options.

"Can't do that. Abe and the team are away on an assignment and won't be back for a week."

"Great!" They could hear the frustration in Rebecca's voice. "So he leaves town, we're stuck with you, and we have no idea where we're going."

"That about sums it up." Frankie's voice was laced with amusement. "Pull in here, Joe."

Once the cruiser was stopped, and the back door open, Frankie shoved them out the opposite side from him and into the building the car had stopped beside. He went back and spoke with Joe, and the cruiser moved off.

"Why?"

Frankie motioned for them to be quiet. He waited, for what they weren't sure. After about an hour, he led them through the building to the other side, and cautiously opened the door, looking around and up. He beckoned them forward and to a car on the other side of the street. He shoved them into the back seat and climbed behind the wheel.

"Keep down as much as you can. I don't know if this will even work." Frankie's eyes were in constant motion as he pulled away from the curb. He didn't see anyone but that didn't mean someone wasn't there. He headed for Abe's compound, knowing that for the moment it was the safest place for them. He hoped Caleb had come up with a place.

Caleb beckoned for Eddie and Ben to follow him. He headed out of the office and to his car. Once they were away from the department, he turned to them.

"Frankie has them. He's on his way to Abe's right now, even though Abe's away."

"Best place for now." Eddie considered the alternatives. "I can't think of anywhere else to stash them."

"Nor can we. I just don't have a good feeling about it. It's like someone is always one step ahead of us." Caleb took a circuitous route, making sure he wasn't followed, but even then he didn't trust that he wasn't.

Caleb pulled to a stop by the garage at Abe's, then the three men made their way to the house. Frankie was waiting on the front porch.

"Before you see them, Caleb, I think you should know something."

Caleb smiled. "She's getting ready to become a target, or he is."

Frankie nodded. "Both of them are. I can't talk them out of it."

"We won't. Let's go see what they have to say."

The four men walked in but didn't see either Rebecca or Gideon around. Frankie started searching the main floor and Eddie headed upstairs as Ben went out the back door to search the back yard. Caleb searched the basement. The two were nowhere in sight.

"Where did they go?" Frankie looked around. "They were here, they had cleaned up, and were headed to make coffee."

"We're here. Right behind you." The men spun and stared at them.

"Where were you?" Caleb demanded.

"Right where we are now. You walked right by us." Gideon stared at each of the men, standing in an almost-in-plain sight alcove. "And that's scary that you didn't see us, when you're the ones wanting to protect us."

Caleb studied the area where they had been standing. "I agree. It is scary but you knew we would be here."

"You didn't say who you were. We had no way of knowing, not with what we've just been through." Gideon was no longer backing down. He had had more than enough.

"No more games." Caleb pulled out a copy of the last photo he had received and slapped it at Gideon's chest. "Take a look at this. We have run out of time and options. So don't play any more games with me."

Gideon stared at Caleb as he took the photo, then looked down. He heard Rebecca's gasp from beside him. "Interesting, but fake obviously."

"Is that all you can say, Gideon?" Caleb was getting angry and he never got angry.

"Don't start with me, Caleb. I trusted you and Abe and looked where it landed us, targets of a sniper in that back yard." His finger stabbed at the back door. "So, no, we're not playing games." He felt Rebecca's hand clutching his arm. "Tell me, how do you expect to keep us safe? We have been chased, shot at, run around in circles, had to ditch vehicles, and had safe houses compromised. No, we're not playing games." His eyes searched the faces of each of the men standing there. He looked down at Rebecca, seeing the exhaustion and fear now evident in her eyes. He hesitated, then, scooping her up in his arms, walked away from the men.

The four stood, dumbfounded, as he walked away. Eddie took a step to watch where he was headed, then turned. "He's right. We haven't been able to keep them safe. Now we need to come up with a plan."

Gideon was behind him as he finished speaking. "No, no more plans, no more ideas. This is what we're doing. If you don't agree, there's the door. Feel free to walk through it."

They listened at the plan Gideon and Rebecca had come up with, all shaking their heads in disagreement. Gideon stood for a while, watching them debate it, then walked away. It looked as if he and Rebecca would be on their own. He didn't know who he could trust any more.

Ben watched him walk away, then said something to the others that stopped the conversation. The other three stared at him, then at the doorway Gideon had disappeared through.

"Can you repeat what you just said?" Caleb wasn't sure he had hear Ben right.

"He's going to run again and take Rebecca. It's in his eyes. He doesn't trust anyone right now in his head. In his heart, he knows we're working to keep him safe. He's exhausted. He feels like he's been betrayed by people he should be able to trust. He's worried about his wife, and frankly, I would probably be thinking the same if I had been put in that situation." Ben stared around at the three standing there. "You keep forgetting his history, what he went with through his foster father, how he was kept from Rachel, and then lost touch with her for so many years, not knowing if she was even alive. He doesn't want that to happen with Rebecca."

Caleb ran his hands through his hair. "You're right, Ben. I have forgotten that. I was just so focused on who and why, that I lost sight of the past." He looked around, momentarily lost, not knowing quite what he should be doing.

"We're too close," Frankie said, "too close to the situation. We need to step back and assess it as if we didn't know the people. What would we do first and go from there. I'm as guilty as anyone for forgetting that."

Eddie nodded. "I just hope we haven't chased them away already. I haven't heard anything from down the hall for a while."

Caleb spun. "No, you don't think they would have, do you?"

Eddie gave a half-smile. "If it was me, I just might." He turned and walked away, leaving the three staring at him.

Eddie tapped at the bedroom door, but got no answer. He tapped again, and after a minute, opened it. Rebecca and Gideon were gone once again. He walked into the room and looked around, finally seeing a note addressed to him in Rebecca's handwriting.

"Eddie, we've gone. Don't ask where or how. I agree with Gideon. It is time we go on the offensive and force her out into the open. We are coming up with some ideas. You remember our secret mailbox, don't you, that Abe and I used to use when we were kids? Look for something in there in the next 24 hours. Please don't tell Ben or Caleb or Frankie about it. Just you need to know. If Abe is back, send him. Love Rebecca and Gideon."

Eddie re-read the note. Yes, Rebecca, he thought, I do remember your mailbox. Let me know what you come up with, my dear girl. He folded the note thoughtfully and tucked it into his shirt pocket. He then walked to the window overlooking the hills. God, keep them safe. Guide them as they work through this. Give us the wisdom we need to sort it all out.

****

She was searching for them. She knew they were here but where had they gone to? No one wanted to help her. Money just couldn't buy her what she wanted this time, and she didn't understand that. Money always opened doors for her and got her what she wanted. She would have to go back to that compound and search around there again, and she hated the dirt and rocks there. Why did they have to be so difficult?

****

"Where are we going, Gideon?" Rebecca stopped to lean against a rock formation. She took the water bottle he handed her and opened it.

"Have you ever been on a houseboat?"

She stared at him. "A houseboat? You're serious?"

He nodded. "I have one I own that I just moved to the lake here. I don't think too many people know it's mine. I have it registered to a company I created years ago."

She looked at him. "A company, eh?"

He smiled. "A company. At some point, I am planning on leaving Sidney and setting up my own investigative office. The houseboat was to be my residence. It's not real big but it will do for a few days for the two of us."

"Your own company? Doing the same as with Sidney, or something else?"

He shrugged. "I was still working through that when I walked into a certain diner one day and just had to rescue a damsel in distress." A small smile played around his mouth.

"Damsel in distress, eh? Now, I wonder who what was?"

He reached for her hand as he shrugged the backpack onto one shoulder. "Come on, sweetheart, we have about a 15 minute walk and we'll have somewhere to stay for a few days."

477

She stood watching him even as she reached for his hand. "Would you have done it differently, Gideon, if I hadn't been a target?"

He searched her face. "I would have courted you, brought you flowers, taken you out for dinners, walks, just sat and talked. Yes, I would have done it differently. You deserve to be courted and treated like the princess you are. But I would still want you in my life." He stopped, searching for words, the back of his hand brushing down her cheek. "We have may rushed into this marriage, but I plan to make it a lifelong courtship."

She hugged him then. "Thank you. That's so sweet. A lifelong courtship? I can live with that."

Eddie turned as Frankie laid a paper down in front of him. "What's this?"

"I think we have one of them. A security guard I know went back over some of the footage they still had from the drugstore downtown, near where the last photo of Rebecca was taken. He found this photo. I'm running it through to see if I can get a match on anyone."

Eddie took the photo. When he say the face, his hand stilled. "Don't bother searching. I can tell you who she is. I can't tell you the name she's using now, she's used so many over the years."

Frankie looked from the photo back to Eddie. "You know her?"

Eddie nodded. "I do. She's not smart enough to have come up with this on her own. There is still someone out there that we haven't figured out yet." Eddie scribbled some names down on a paper and handed it to Frankie. "Start with these. You may end up finding her with one of them."

Frankie took the piece of paper Eddie was handing him and studied the names. His eyes froze on to one of them. "I know this name. And I may know who she's working with. It's going to take some time, though, to run it down."

"And I don't think we have a lot of time left, Frankie. Rebecca and Gideon are prepared to force the issue and they'll do that in the next couple of days."

"That's what I'm afraid of, Eddie, and I don't think we'll be prepared. Has Doug said anything to you?"

Eddie looked at him. "Doug? No but I wouldn't be surprised if Rebecca's been talking to him at some point. Doug will only help her if she stays within a framework he's decided on. If she won't, then he'll stay back, but be ready to step in if needed. They're like that with one another, always have been. They tease and torment each other, like siblings, but have each other's back."

Frankie studied Eddie. "Do you know where they're at?"

Eddie shook his head. "No, I don't. But I have a way of reaching them. And no, I'm not saying what it is. I won't break Rebecca's trust."

They looked up as Ben entered, then went to the whiteboard. He wiped off some names and then wrote one down. Frankie stared at it, then at the list Eddie had given him. "How did you know?"

Eddie shrugged. "I used to keep track of them, just for peace of mind about Peg. I never fully trusted them."

Frankie handed Ben the photo he was holding. "Here, take this. It's goes with the name."

Eddie started to laugh at the look on Ben's face as Frankie shoved the picture at him. "Frankie's just miffed because you came up with the name when he only had the picture."

Ben laughed as well. "Now we have both. Let's get it out on the street. Things are moving now." He stopped and turned to watch the activity in the room. "I hope the Lord tells Hannah the name soon. I know He's watching over them, but I just wish it was all over."

"So do we, Ben. But this will move it forward."

Frankie had found the woman and brought her in. She had been near the diner where he had found Rebecca and Gideon. A search of her home had turned up a lot of cash, but not much more.

Caleb stood and watched the woman through the mirror, once again wishing he knew who the stalker was and why she was after Rebecca. They weren't going to get a lot from this one, he could tell.

Eddie stood beside him, a sad expression on his face. "Why do they change like that, Caleb? Is sin so worth it?"

"They seem to think it is." Caleb stopped speaking, thinking about what Eddie had asked. "I take it she has really changed?"

"In a way, yes, but she has always been mercenary. Peg saw that as a child."

****

She stood outside the department, buffeted not just by the people moving around her, but by the winds of change blowing her way. She was enraged. Her one contact had been arrested. Now she was on her own. She turned and stomped from the spot she had been standing in so long, ignoring the greetings

480

called to her. Someone was going to pay and pay in a big way, and that person was Rebecca. If she could only find her.

****

Rebecca stood on the deck of the houseboat, feeling the slight sway under her feet. For the first time in days, she felt rested and relaxed. Was this was Gideon had meant when he said God provided a haven, somewhere to rest? Was that what she had to do, find somewhere quiet where she could hear His voice?

Gideon came up beside her and handed her a cup of coffee. Standing shoulder to shoulder, they watched the shore.

"So, what's the plan, Gideon? I know you have one."

He nodded as he took a sip of coffee and hesitated before speaking. "I do, but I'm still not sure if it's right. It would mean putting both of us at risk and I don't want to do that."

"We're already at risk. We need to end this now, Gideon, not next week, not next month. I have been living like this for over 10 years. I've had enough." Her blue eyes were sad but determined.

"I know you have. I just don't want you hurt, you're too precious."

"So the plan is to just walk down town out in the open, go for dinner at the diner, just be ourselves?"

"That's right. I don't know about you, but I'm tired of hiding. I want to be seen out and about with my gorgeous wife." He reached down and kissed her. "So, would you do me the honour having lunch today?"

481

She tucked her hand into his arm. "I would be delighted, kind sir. Do I need to dress up or I am okay as I am?" He caught the uncertainty in her voice, the uncertainty that women give when they're not sure if they're attractive.

"Sweetheart, you're beautiful." He looked around. "Now to find some transportation."

She pointed. "Right there. Doug brought us an extra vehicle he has."

Gideon followed her finger. "And he knew to find us, how?"

"I let Eddie know. When Abe and I were young, we had a secret mailbox down here, near Eddie' boathouse. I reminded him last night. Doug's good with leaving us the car."

"So, my dear, we're off."

****

She stood at her office window and watched as Gideon came around the car to open the door for Rebecca and then, her arm tucked in his, lead her into the diner. How dare they! So brazen! Her hands clenched in anger until the knuckles whitened. She would deal with them today or tomorrow. She didn't have much time left.

Caleb turned from the counter where he was seated, having a cup of coffee and talking with Mac about some issues he was having with vandals, almost choking on the mouthful he had just taken. He couldn't believe they just walked in, so calm and collected, as if nothing was going on. Mac snorted with laughter, and Caleb turned to stare at him.

"Well, now, there's our Rebel. She's back." Mac headed for them, leaving Caleb dumbfounded.

Mac hugged Rebecca and then shook Gideon's hand. After a brief conversation, they headed for a booth at the back of the cafe and he returned to the counter, leaving their order with the kitchen.

"Surprised you, did they, Caleb?"

"Just a little. I knew they were up to something, but I never figured this would be it. He warned me they were done hiding."

"And so they should. It will never stop if they keep hiding and running. God is directing their steps right now. He will protect them."

"And if He doesn't?"

"Then they graduate to heaven from here and are welcomed home." Mac looked past Caleb to the two. "It's not about what we want for them, Caleb, it's about what God wants. There comes a time where we have to step out, trusting God to provide and protect, and then guide us to the haven He prepares for us."

Caleb nodded glumly. "The other three aren't going to be happy."

Mac shook his head. "No, Frankie isn't going to be happy. Ben and Eddie have been around long enough to know that this day would come. It's up to you and your department to provide as much protection as those two will allow you to provide. And I would say, right now, they really don't care how much you provide."

Caleb nodded. "I think you're right." He stood and dug change out of his pocket. "I guess I'll have to go break the news to them."

He stopped as his phone rang. It was Hannah. After talking for a few minutes, he could hear the hesitation in her voice. "You have a name, don't you, favourite girl?"

"I do, Caleb. Each time it gets worse and worse. I just wish God had decided someone else had this job. Am I supposed to consider it a ministry? Because I don't." She sounded very disgruntled.

"Who is it, my love?"

When she said the name, Caleb turned to scan the buildings across the street and focused on one particular set of office windows. He would never have guessed it to be her. He headed for the office. They had a lot of legwork left, and in the meantime, Gideon and Rebecca had set themselves up as targets.

Mac set their food in front of them and then waited, finally sliding onto the seat beside Rebecca. "Are you two sure about this?"

Gideon looked at Rebecca, then at him, and nodded. "Rebecca's lived with this for long enough. It's time to end it."

"And if it doesn't end the way you expect?"

"Then we wake up in heaven, Mac." Rebecca studied him, warming her hands on the mug he had set in front of her. "It's okay either way. God's in control."

Mac nodded. "Your mom and dad would be proud of you. Just don't get hurt. I don't want to have to explain it to Abe." He got up and left.

Rebecca watched him leave. "He's right. I don't want to explain it to Abe either."

Gideon laughed, mirth deep in his eyes. "Then we explain it to Murphy and Ian, and they can explain it to him."

Rebecca started to laugh, tears rolling down her face. "Thank you, honey. I can just see that."

Gideon smiled. It was good to see her laugh. He looked around. He could feel the evil approaching him and he didn't know which way it was coming from.

She had changed from her dress clothes to nondescript dark clothes and tucked her hair up under a cap. Sliding from the back door of her office, she crept down the steps, carefully avoiding contact with anyone. She slipped over the stand leaning against a wall near the vehicle she had seen them exit. She was so close, she could test the victory.

Gideon studied the people around them as they walked back to the car. He could feel the evil even more as they got close to it. He stopped, opened the door for Rebecca, then stopped. He could feel the gun digging into his lower back.

"She gets in the back seat with me. You drive."

Rebecca looked up at him, then slid into the back seat. She couldn't see the face clearly and the woman was trying to alter her voice. There was something she thought she recognized but it danced just outside of her memory.

Gideon climbed behind the steering wheel, watching outside as he did so. He saw Frankie watching them and knew he had seen something. Caleb would have sent him around after he had got back to the office. He felt a bit of relief knowing someone had seen something, but where they were going, he didn't know it they could be followed.

Caleb's phone rang. "As long as they don't ditch Doug's car, we can track them. She has them."

"Already?"

Frankie's voice faded for a moment, then came back clear. "She was waiting for them. She's changed into what we would call her grubby clothes, not what she normally wears."

Gideon watched his mirrors, but couldn't see if he was being followed. He caught Rebecca's eyes, and she gave a small nod. So far, she was fine. His eyes strayed to the woman beside her, but still couldn't get a good look at her. Who was she? Okay, Lord, he thought, it's up to You now to keep us safe and guide them to us. I have no idea where we're going to end up but you do."

"Head for Oak City."

Gideon nodded and then followed the city streets to the highway. Once on the highway, he noticed she kept glancing behind her. So far, he couldn't see anyone but knowing this was Doug's car, they would have hidden a tracker or GPS unit somewhere in it.

"Pull into that gas station, that abandoned one."

Gideon hesitated, then heard a gasp from Rebecca. He glanced back and saw that the woman had the revolver dug into Rebecca's side.

"Around back. And then stop and turn off the car."

When he had done so, she forced Rebecca out and towards a van. Gideon went after them.

"She's not going anywhere without me." He stopped and raised his hands as the revolver turned toward him. "Shoot me, if you think it will stop me but it won't. I'm going with her."

He was motioned forward towards Rebecca. They were forced into another vehicle, Gideon made to take the wheel. His heart sank. There went their only chance of rescue, didn't it? He caught a look in Rebecca's eyes. She was up to something, he knew. He just wished she had shared with him.

"She made them ditch the car." Frankie stared around in frustration. How did they find them now?

Eddie held up his phone. "I've got them."

Frankie spun around to stare at them. "You've got them? How?"

"Don't ask how. Remember that Abe is in security and Rebecca has access to his equipment. I am sure she found something to help track them. She left me word last night on what to do."

"She left you word?" Frankie stood, open mouthed. "You haven't spoken to her since yesterday but she left you word last night?"

Eddie smiled. "I knew where her mailbox was and found the information this morning."

Frankie shook his head. "Okay, you have the information. Now where do we go?"

Eddie held up his phone. "This way. You're driving." Eddie glanced behind him. "Doug will follow but when we get close enough, we'll let him take the lead."

Caleb leaned on his vehicle, listening to the radio chatter. Ben came towards him.

"Have they found them yet?"

Caleb shook his head. "No, they haven't. Eddie's tracking them. That girl is good."

"She had good teachers. She's scary, too."

"Like Deirdre?"

Ben laughed. "Just don't tell Frankie." They were referring to the incident months ago when Frankie and Deirdre were fighting to survive and he called her scary.

Ben turned at a sound. "Abe's back."

"That he is and it looks as if the whole team is with him." Caleb brought Abe up to date on what was happening.

At the name, Abe's face blanched. "It's been her all along?"

Caleb nodded. "For the last five years anyway. We've got the male in custody but he's not the planner."

Gideon pulled the van up to the abandoned decrepit barn and parked, turning off the ignition. His eyes moving quickly, he scanned the area. There was just no way they could get away. *Rebecca, what have you done?* Then his heart turned to God. *God, grant us peace and safety. Protect us. Protect those who follow us.*

Forced from the van, they were marched in to the building. Dust flew up at their footsteps and shimmered in the flickering sunlight coming through the cracks and holes in the building. Eyes constantly on the move, Gideon once again assessed their chances to escape. But somehow, he didn't think that was what Rebecca had in mind. There had been a change in her today, a determination to end it all.

"Over there!" Gideon was pushed towards a rusted piece of machinery, forced to sit, and he felt the click of handcuffs around his right wrist and then to the machine. He looked, but his heart sank. He was handcuffed to metal. There was no way he would be able to escape.

Rebecca stood her ground when motioned to move forward. "No, you're no longer running it. This ends today."

"Of course, it does, my dear. It ends for both of you today." The revolver was raised and pointed at Gieon. "Now move over there or I'll shoot him."

Rebecca stood, not budging. Gideon studied her. She was up to something but what? The woman shoved Rebecca towards the back of the barn. Gideon desperately tried to free himself but to no avail. He could hear words but they were no longer in his sight. He fought to free himself. Hearing footsteps, he turned his head and felt a searing pain along the side of it. Falling into darkness, his last thought was for Rebecca. Please, God, let her live. Let her find that haven You provide.

Rebecca jumped at the sound of the gunshot and spun around. "Gideon!" She moved to run towards him as the woman stepped into her way.

"I don't think so, my dear. He's dead and you will be soon. But first, you need to sign these papers."

"Papers?"

"Yes, these papers."

The woman thrust them at her and instinctively Rebecca grabbed for them, catching the woman's wrist. She threw herself backwards, pulling

the woman with her. The revolver went spinning
from the woman's hand, coming to a stop 20 feet
away. As Rebecca went down, she heard ominous
cracking and felt the rotting wooden floor give way
beneath them.

Chapter 23

"We've got them but they're not moving." Eddie's eyes searched the area ahead of them as Frankie brought his car to a halt.

Climbing out, Eddie saw Doug and his team coming towards him. "They're up ahead, Doug, but I'm not getting movement from them."

Doug nodded, then forged ahead with his team. Spreading out around the building, they moved in on silent feet. Eddie could hear Abe and his team behind him and he knew the paramedics were waiting just down the road.

Doug ran towards them, motioning for the paramedics to move in. "We have them, Eddie, but the building is not in great shape. We'll have to be careful who we send in and how many."

"How are they?" Abe spoke up.

"Gideon's been shot but is alive. Rebecca and the woman went through the floor to the bottom level. The floor around where they went through is not in great shape. We're going to have to be very careful how we go in and how we go down. Until we can get down there, we can't tell how they are."

The paramedics ran for the barn, stopping as they reached it. Dave, the senior paramedic, crept in as carefully as he could, catching his breath as the floor creaked and groaned under his weight. He eased himself down on his stomach and crept forward just enough to look over the edge. He then studied the area around him. It was going to be difficult to reach them, but he was determined to find a way.

They waited for what seemed hours but in reality was not that long. Caleb had arrived, having sent Ben to find Peg and take her to the hospital to wait. He knew Marg would be with her.

The stretcher carrying the unconscious Gideon passed them. They could see the blood on his head, the blood on his wrist where he had struggled to escape. He turned his attention back to the barn.

One of the paramedics had come back for climbing gear. It would be the only way that they would be able to get down to the two women. They had searched around the foundation on the outside but any doorways or windows had been blocked with debris over time and they weren't anxious to bring down any of the building.

Abe had sent Matt in with the paramedics. He was the one on his team, trained as a medic, who would be able to assist the best with repelling down.

One of the ETF men approached Caleb, a strained, dark look on his face. Caleb drew in a deep breath, trying to prepare himself for the worse.

"We'll need the coroner, Caleb. The woman is dead. Dave says Rebecca's alive but he can't really assess her where she's lying. There's not a lot of room. He's thinks she may have a spinal injury. They've got her on a backboard and are getting ready to bring her up. Dave also asked if you could call for a chopper. He feels it better if we fly her in."

Frankie reached for his radio and made the request. The men approached carrying the stretcher. Abe stopped them, staring down at his sister. He nodded and followed them as they headed for the chopper. Not saying a word, he climbed aboard as she was loaded and then the chopper lifted off.

Eddie's eyes never left the building, his heart breaking for Peg's niece. Abe stood beside him, silent, the strain showing on his face.

The families gathered and waited, not knowing how severe the injuries were. As time passed, Abe grew restless and began to pace. Caleb studied him. It was over, finally, for Rebecca but he knew Abe carried a load of guilt for not knowing what was going on and for not stopping it.

The physician came out and spoke for a few minutes with Abe and then went back to the exam room. Abe turned to the room and sought out Eddie and Peg. As he walked towards them, a grim look on his face, Peg's heart lifted in prayer.

Abe squatted down before them and reached for Peg's hand. Rubbing them gently, he spoke, "Gideon's got a wound along his head but he was moving away from the bullet, so it's not severe. They've stitched it up, done the testing they needed to do, and are moving him up to a room."

"Rebecca?" Peg's voice was barely a whisper.

"She's gone for a CT. They're not sure if there's any damage to the spine from the fall. She has swelling around it on some of the imaging. She has some good damage to the right side of the chest, including a punctured lung. They're dealing with that while doing the rest of the testing. She'll be heading to ICU soon. Lots of bruises, cuts, but she's alive."

"Her back," Eddie hesitated to ask.

Abe shook his head. "They don't think it's severe but will have to wait likely for the swelling to go down to be sure. They're amazed she wasn't killed in the fall."

"That was God, Abe." Peg reached out to hug him. He clung to her for a few minutes, then rose and went to find his team. They had all gathered outside, waiting for news.

Caleb stood and studied the whiteboard before he reached to wipe it clean. It was finally over for Rebecca, but they would likely never know the true reason for the last five years.

"It's finally over for her, isn't it, Caleb?" Ben spoke from the doorway.

Caleb nodded. "I think it is. The worst part is knowing she hid it for so many years, so well hidden that Abe didn't even know." He stared past Ben. "We'll need to make sure he has someone he can talk to. He's hurting."

"His team are too. That's what they do for a living, protect the innocent. They all feel like they failed her." He took a deep breath. "Do we have everyone now? There are no more?"

Caleb shook his head. "I hope not. We're still trying to make sense of it all and make sure we have found all her relatives. What makes a person do this, other than greed and depravity?"

"You've said it all there, Caleb. That's what makes them do it."

Frankie followed Abe as he walked through to his sister's cubicle in the ICU. Caleb had asked that he make sure someone was with him. He had elected himself to that position for now and he had made sure someone would be there when he had to leave.

Abe stood by his sister's bed, hands tight around the bed rail. He stared at her, tears clouding his vision. Why, Lord, he asked? Why Rebecca? He reached out a trembling hand and touched the bruises on her cheek, then rested it on her hair. This was his little sister and somehow he had failed to protect her. She hadn't helped, of course, he thought, but he still should have known something was up and done something about it.

Frankie studied his friend and the deep sorrow he was feeling. He finally turned and walked away. They would all need to heal, but Abe would need it more than the others. He stopped on the floor below at Gideon's room. Gideon was asleep now, not unconscious. Frankie knew it would only be a day or so and he would not leave Rebecca's side, no matter what the hospital said. He knew, if it was Deirdre, he wouldn't be anywhere else. He turned and headed back up to the next floor. As he opened the door, he could hear a large commotion.

Pulling his revolver and heading for the noise, he saw Abe restraining a young man, in his early 20's, Frankie thought. Now what?

Abe thrust the young man at Frankie. "Get him out of here. He just tried to kill Rebecca."

Frankie reached for his handcuffs and jerked the young man's arms behind him. "Who are you?" he asked as he snapped the cuffs closed.

When the suspect refused to talk, Frankie shoved him towards the elevator. "We'll head downtown and see if you'll talk."

"I want a lawyer."

"Of course you do. They always do." Frankie looked back at Abe and then past him to where he could see Rebecca's bed. Did they have them all, he wondered, or was there someone else just waiting?

Caleb looked up as Eddie, Ben and Frankie showed up at his door. "Now what?"

"Frankie just brought in another suspect. Abe caught him trying to kill Rebecca."

Caleb's hand stilled. "Her son?"

Ben nodded. "He's not talking but his prints say he is. I hope this is it."

Eddie spoke up. "He's the last, from what the investigation has turned up. We were looking for him and he just dropped into our hands."

"Rebecca's okay?" Caleb keen eyes searched their faces.

"She is. Abe was able to stop him before he got to her."

Four days later, Gideon sat beside Rebecca's bed. She had been moved from ICU to the same floor as he was on. The nurses had gotten used to finding him in her room. Holding her hand, he rubbed his thumb along the back of it and studied her face. The bruises had darkened and were turning yellow and green. The cuts were starting to heal. The doctors were optimistic that there was no spinal damage. The swelling around the spine had started to reduce. She was beginning to rouse from the sedation they had had her under. He was tired, though, and ready to go home. He laid his head against her pillow and drifted off.

Rebecca roused. Blinking against the light, she tried to focus, finally able to bring the twos of everything to one. She looked around. She was in the hospital. She couldn't remember why, though. Her head turned and she saw Gideon beside her. She reached for his hand and then drifted off again. It must be all right, she thought, if he's sleeping.

Chapter 24

Caleb searched the room around him, studying the faces gathered there. It was four weeks since it had ended. Most of the loose ends were tied up. The son was headed to trial soon.

"So why was she after me?" Rebecca's voice cut through the room, catching Caleb's attention.

His eyes turned to her. "Money. Lots and lots of money."

"Money!" She blinked at him, then turned to Abe. "Money? Do you know anything about that, Abe?"

He shook his head. "I can vaguely remember Mom saying something once but she never made an issue of it. Dad didn't either. What's the story, Caleb?"

Before he spoke, Caleb watched Peg. It had really gone hard with her when she realized who it was that had been behind the last few years of the stalking.

"We need to go back to the first stalker. Alan. You don't remember him, do you, Rebecca?" When she shook her head, he continued, "He was one of those bullied and put down at school. You were nice to him and even gave him your lunch one day. That started his fixation on you. It didn't escalate until about five years ago. He never meant you any harm at all. He just wanted to be with you. The woman stalker stumbled onto him one day and realized how she could use him. He would give her the letters he had written and she would forge new ones. That's why where was such a change in the tone of them.

"The gap in the stalking you noticed? Alan had to go every year for three to four weeks for assessment. They never could determine what his actual illness was, so they could never treat it.

"Now to pick up from five years ago. I'm sorry, Peg, to drag up old family hurts. The woman who was after you, Rebecca, was your mother's step sister. She was no relation to your mother or Peg. She knew there was money coming to your mom from a family member. She was jealous and thought the money should have been hers, even though she was not a blood relative. This is where it will really hurt. She tricked your mother into meeting her one day and tried to get her to sign over her share. Your mother refused and she became enraged. I'm sorry, she did kill your mother. We are trying to track down the grave so we can bring her home for you."

Rebecca's eyes filled with tears, and Abe moved over to sit on her chair arm, draping his arm around her.

Caleb continued. "Between Eddie and the others, they have drudged up quite a history of her. When she moved here about six years ago, she changed her name to Susan Howell and set up her office as a victim advocate. She presented such a good front no one ever suspected she was not who she said she was. Because of what she had set herself up as, she had freedom to move around the town. That's how she managed to get your photos. She had some pretty sophisticated cameras."

Peg spoke up. "The thing of it is, there was never a lot of money. It was a trust fund that paid out to charities over the years. We were never to get much of it. The lawyer told me last year, the money was pretty much paid out now. There were just enough left for one more year with the charities."

Gideon spoke. "So, Rebecca went through all this for nothing?" He could feel the anger building inside him and worked to dampen it down.

Caleb nodded. "That's about it. She pretty much worked on her own, not bringing in anyone if she could help it. She wanted it all."

"What happened to the rest of the family?" Abe asked.

"They distanced themselves from her and refused to have much to do with her. They're like Peg here, good hearted. At some point, they would like to meet you and Rebecca, Abe. They remember you from when you were little. It's up to you when and if. I have the contact information when you want it."

Abe nodded, then looked down at his sister. "I'm just glad it's finally over. I wonder if it would have come to all this if Rebecca had something earlier."

Rebecca tilted her head back to look up at him, tears sparkling her blue eyes. "I don't know, Abe. There's a reason it happened and only God knows."

Caleb finished giving the details of the investigation, what he could give before the trial of the son.

"Susan had been tracking you and saw Alan leaving you a note. She convinced him she could help him get to you. He just couldn't understand why it never worked out. He never knew she was using him for her own schemes. When Alan was arrested, he was high on drugs. He had just given up on finding you, Rebecca.

"She had had plastic surgery and we were able to track down her surgeon. She left detailed records in her home.

"Her son….Her son she ignored. She was just so determined to get the money that family fell by the wayside. He resented that and when his mother died, he blamed you, Rebecca, that he would never had a chance to get his mother back. He is the one who ran you off the road. He also nicked the power steering line so it would give. He just didn't expect it to give at the same time as he ran you off the road. She was standing down the road, watching. She had followed him, seen what he did, and just stood there. If you had died, she would have gone after her son and more than likely killed him. She couldn't tolerate anyone getting in her way. That's why she went after Gideon, too. He got in her way. She was also egging on Alan, making him think you only belonged to him and he just had to marry you to get people to like him.

"Our mechanic couldn't find a problem with the airbags, but he did say they were under a recall for not operating as they should.

"The profiler in your office is good, Gideon. She pretty much nailed these two. Somehow, Kay from your office connected with her, and we still are working on that. Sidney suspects she may have connected with Kay during an investigation ad it went from there."

"Why Nick?" Rebecca's question was quiet, barely audible.

Caleb looked at her with compassion. "She thought he would help you get the money and then spend it on your studio. She had to prevent that. You were collateral damage at the time. She needed you alive, she thought, to sign papers, which she had drawn up herself."

They fell silent, digesting what had been said. Gideon watched Rebecca's face and saw the calmness and peace evident there. He knew she had been drawn into that haven God promised. Lord, thank You that You reached her, that You have given her peace. If that was Your planned outcome, thank you.

Rebecca talked quietly with Abe for a while, then rose with some pain still evident in her movements and moved to sit by Peg. Peg hugged her and spoke to her. Eddie sat on her other side and hugged her, then went to Abe and drawing him out to the kitchen.

"You need to let it go, Abe. Holding onto your anger won't work."

Abe stared out the window. "I know that, Eddie. It's going to take some work. I still don't understand how some people operate. I guess I never will."

"Sin does that, Abe, leads them astray, makes them search for things that don't satisfy. Only God can do that. Your sister has found her haven. You need to find yours. Listen to God, He'll lead you there." Eddie walked away, leaving Abe standing in the kitchen. Abe turned and walked back to the livingroom doorway and watched his family and friends. Gideon he studied the longest. He was just so right for Rebecca and she for him. They brought out the best in one another.

Epilogue

Rebecca set her camera down and knelt to study the flowers she was photographing, touching the petals of the roses lightly. She had agreed to produce a book for her publisher friend, but it was to be something totally different from what she had worked on with Nick. She missed him but that chapter was closed. She knew now why Nick had had to die, but it didn't make it easier to have lost him. She would always wonder if the early potential he had shown would have developed and grown.

She turned as she heard footsteps behind her. Gideon stood watching her, his love for her shining from his eyes. He reached a hand out for her and lifted her to her feet. Hand in hand, they wandered through the gardens they had found in a little out of the way place. It had become a favourite place for them to escape.

"Did you get your office all set up?" Rebecca lifted her camera to snap a picture of a butterfly on a bush.

"I did. It's all ready to go. Sidney was understanding, though, that I wanted to branch out on my own and work from here. Gilles has been talking to him. They are looking to set up a foundation for people like Alan, to get them help. He has asked if we would consider sitting on the board."

Rebecca shook her head. "No, I don't think so. It's not where God wants me."

"That's what I told him."

Rebecca turned to him, her mouth dropping open. "You told him what?" She poked him in the chest with her index finger.

Gideon laughed at her, catching the offending hand in his. "I told him you were busy with your own work for God and that had to come first"

Rebecca reached to hug Gideon, and he dropped a kiss on her head. They follow the path until it came to a bridge over a small brook and then stopped and stood there, just enjoying the quiet of the late afternoon, the sunlight filtering through the trees lining the banks. They could hear the whisper of the breeze and the songs of the birds as well as the buzzing of the bees. God was doing a good job today, Gideon thought, finding himself relaxing. It has been a long few months but the trial for the son was finally over. Some questions would never be answered.

"Abe's having a hard time." Rebecca felt her brother's anguish, but could do nothing to help him.

"He is. He's talking though with Greg, and that will help. Murphy says they're heading out again in a couple of days and will likely be gone for two to three weeks."

"That's what Abe said. He's talking more than he used to, but he's not saying as much. Does that even make sense?"

Gideon nodded. "It does."

Rebecca tilted her head to look up at him. "Back when you bought me this ring, you said you had a reason for choosing a pearl and that you would share one day. Can you tell me now?"

Gideon hugged her close and laid his head on hers. "Do you remember that parable about the man finding a pearl of great worth and selling all he had to buy?" He felt her nod. "Sweetheart, to me you are that pearl of great price. I can't sell everything I have to buy you, but I wanted you to have this pearl to remember that's how much I love you, that I would sell everything I had to have you in my life. And that you will always remember that as much as I love and adore you, God loves you so much more and that He did give everything to purchase you. I am so glad you have found your haven of rest within His love and care. I'm just sorry it took what it did to bring you there."

Rebecca couldn't see for tears. All she knew was that her love for her husband was growing by the day, and as he had promised, each day was a courtship in a lifelong promise of days like that.

She leaned back to stare at him and then reached up to kiss him. "To have you say that, after all I have been through by myself and all we have been through together, I just can't explain it. God is working in our lives, my darling, and I pray that He will continue."

She stopped and thought for a while, then looked up at him again. "I have been trying to decide what to do now that I am not a photographer. I would like to take some of the photos Nick and I gathered over the years, sell them and set up a trust and find a place we can develop as a haven for those who need respite, who need to come apart for a while."

Gideon rested his head on his head and closed his eyes. She had come so far and so fast on that road, he had trouble keeping up with her.

"God has laid that on your heart. We'll find the place and set up your trust." He paused. "What would you call it?"

"What else but The Haven of Rest?"

Dear Readers:

Thank you for picking up the story of Gideon and Rebecca and sharing their adventures. Rebecca needed to find her haven of rest and she could only find that with God. How many times have we been buffeted by life and felt like it was just to hard to continue, that life really didn't matter any more?d loves us so much, He desires that we find our own haven of rest with Him. No matter what we face, He is there, each step of the way.

Over the years, I have faced many trials and difficulties, the most difficult being the loss of my parents. But weary, heavy burdened, tired, sore, God has welcomed me to the rest that He promises. "Come unto me, all you who are burdened and heavy laden and I will give you rest." Cling to that promise.

With this book, The Haven of Rest series has ended. I will miss these folks who have people these pages: Frankie and Deirdre, Timothy and Rachel, Gideon and Rebecca. It has been an opportunity to work through thoughts and feelings I have been battling. I look forward to whoever's story is next.

I can hear Abe and his team demanding their stories be told. With eight of them, that will be a large task to undertake.

My prayer for you is that as you have read, you have been challenged to reach out to God and let Him reach out through you.

God bless each one of you.

Ronna